Path *of* a Patriot:

THE DIE IS NOW CAST
1772-1774

BY SELENA JOY LAYDEN

*To Kacey + Adam!
All the best - Happy
Reading!
Selena J Layden*

YCDA
A You Can Do Anything Book

This novel is a work of historical fiction. Some names, places, and events used in this book are those of real people, actual places, and historical events. However, any dialogue presented is purely fictional. Other names, characters, locations, and events either are the product of the author's imagination or are used fictitiously. The author has attempted to accurately depict the historical events from the perspective of the fictional characters.

YCDA
Published by YCDA, LLC, Virginia Beach, VA USA

YCDA, LLC books may be purchased for educational, business, or sales promotional use. For information, please contact Darril Gibson at darril@darrilgibson.com.

Visit us at YesYCDA.com.

Copy editor: Jones Editorial and Proofreading Services
Book cover: Denise Kelly of Tandee Design
YCDA paperback edition published 2013
ISBN: 1-939136-00-8
ISBN-13: 978-1-939136-00-8

Dedication

To Jonathan and the path we've chosen.

Introduction

L ike all children attending public school in the United States, I obviously took many history classes during my school-aged years. In history, we learned about the important people and events of the United States and those of our own state. But growing up in Minnesota, the history in our backyard was perhaps a bit different than what other children in other areas of the United States are exposed to. We learned about the glaciers, some about the Native Americans in the area, the Louisiana Purchase, a bit about the travels of Louis and Clark, and bootlegging in the 1920s. Certainly, these events and people are important to our country and are interesting to learn and I do not wish to diminish their importance. However, the other things I learned about in school, like the American Revolution, the Civil War, and other things, were learned in the abstract. They happened long ago and far away from my little hometown in Minnesota. They didn't have a lot of relevance to my life living just over an hour south of the Canadian border and on the state line between Minnesota and North Dakota. Perhaps because of their intangible feeling, I never felt like I learned a lot about these events. One event happened and then the next event happened, presumably with little connection to each other because we didn't talk much about what happened between. I was always amazed how it felt like nothing happened for fifty or sixty years at a time before the next big event. I often wonder if this is part of the reason many children do not like history because they don't understand how it all connects. Typically, my experiences in history classes were a fast-paced overview of important events, or, what I like to call, war hopping.

I can best describe what I mean by war hopping as learning a little bit about a war that was important to the United States, like the American Revolution for example. You learn some important dates, an important person or two, and then, as soon as it starts to get a little bit interesting, it is time to stop learning about that war and jump a few decades to the next one, like the War of 1812. A little geography gets thrown in there and by the time the class gets to the Civil War, the school year is almost over and your teacher quickly sums up the twentieth century figuring, since you lived during this time, you should know a thing or two about it. Of course they seemingly forgot that I and my classmates weren't born until almost the end of the century and the events after the industrial revolution have actually had a significant impact on our present lives. When the next year comes, you get to start this process all over again. I feel the need to digress here for a moment. Please note, I am not pointing the finger. Being an educator myself, I understand the many constraints placed upon teachers and why breaking this cycle is nearly impossible. But, from my perspective as a student, what I know about American History, or history in general, comes more from my own investigations than my time spent in history class.

I should mention, if you couldn't tell already, I have always had an interest in history. My father was, what I like to call, an avid armchair historian. Those who knew him teased him about having the Smithsonian in his basement and his love of learning and history was passed on to me. My father also served for twenty years in the Air Force and I was taught to have pride in my country and those who sacrificed their lives and comforts for what we have today. I did a lot of reading about history and was fortunate enough to travel to various parts of the country as a child. I visited museums and historical sites and I enjoyed learning about all the historical events and people I wasn't necessarily being told much about in school, if at all.

When I started school at the College of William and Mary in Williamsburg, Virginia, I was more than intrigued by my surroundings. The places I'd heard and read about while growing up were suddenly at my doorstep. I was able to really see these places that were the cornerstone of the foundation of America. William and Mary was founded in 1693 and has a rich history of its own. The Wren Building, located on campus, was designed by Christopher Wren and is the oldest academic building still in use in America today. The College boasts attendance by three U.S. Presidents: Thomas Jefferson, James Monroe, and John Tyler. William and Mary also lays claim to numerous presidential cabinet members, ambassadors, Supreme Court judges, senators, congressmen, and other historical people. The College appreciates and embraces its history and students have a lot of exposure to American history without even leaving campus.

Yet, when you step off the campus, you cross the street and step directly into Colonial Williamsburg, a living museum where the buildings are maintained to look like they did in the mid-18th century and people are dressed in period clothing. Just down the road is Jamestown where John Smith and the English first landed and formed the colony of Virginia. Just a little further down the road is Yorktown where the Americans defeated the British during the final major battle of the American Revolution. The area is called the Historic Triangle. The history in the area surrounds and envelopes you. Honestly, you would have to make great effort to avoid it. When you go to the grocery store, it is not unusual to run into a man in a tri-corner hat or a woman with a Colonial Era dress and bonnet.

While in college, I enjoyed learning about the area, the Colonial Era, and the American Revolution. As I was learning about this time period of our country's history, I realized I had come to know a lot about the battles and the politics of the era. However, I began to wonder what was going on in England during the war and the events leading up to it. In my reading, I was learning a lot about the men who contributed to the eventual independence of America but I started wondering what it was like to be a woman during this era. I wondered how difficult it must have been for them. Having a dad in the Air Force, my family was very lucky in that he wasn't reassigned often so we didn't move around much. But he had to leave my mom and me a fair amount for his assignments. I imagined that, not dissimilar to our current times, women during the American Revolution had a lot of worries as they cared for their families and their homes that weren't only left behind, but many of which were under threat or, worse, were caught in the middle of the battles and skirmishes of the war. I started to wonder why I hadn't read much about these stories.

All of these thoughts brought me to want to write about the American Revolution from a different perspective. I wanted to show what it was like to grow up as a woman during the American Revolution. I also wanted to explore the idea that perhaps the fight for independence wasn't maybe as clear cut as we are now often led to believe. Those who fought for our independence took a great risk, not only because they were committing treason, but also because they were leaving behind their comforts and safety in exchange for the unknown. *Path of a Patriot: The Die is Now Cast*, the first in the series, features Emma, a young girl born in England but comes to America at a difficult time in our history. She and her family struggle with the events that are leading up to the American Revolution. Though Emma feels a strong affinity to her beliefs and her homeland in England, she grows even more worried about keeping her family together during the uncertain times unfolding around her.

Table of Contents

Chapter 1
Merry Olde England

Emma stared out at the front porch and saw the rain. Her mind was filled with the dreariness of the past few months; her heart was heavy and her eyes filled with tears. It was a cold and gray day outside the day the letter came. The rolling countryside was already saturated with rain. It was the fifth straight day of rain and the skies showed no chance of letting up anytime soon. Emma, a young girl of about sixteen, sat in the drawing room of her aunt and uncle's home staring out the window at the rain. Emma's mood mirrored the weather she watched. She had been waiting for word from her parents who had been living in the American Colonies for almost a year now. Rumors were going around about the state of affairs in the Colonies, and Emma was beginning to ponder the relative safety of her parents.

The day had been a poor one from the start. Edward Findley had stopped by earlier that day. Emma may have enjoyed Edward's company but it was nothing more than a close friendship. Unfortunately, it was common knowledge that this was much to Edward's distaste. A few years older than Emma, he

1

had been trying to gain her affections since she had been a child. Luckily – for Emma at least – her father, James Huntington, a wealthy English Lord, had only consented to the marriage on the condition that Emma fully agreed.

James had told her, "I don't care who you marry Emma, as long as you're happy."

Emma let out a small sigh as she continued to watch the rainfall. There were now sheets of rain descending from the heavens.

"Emma, Emma, it's come," called Benjamin, Emma's elder brother, as he entered the drawing room.

Benjamin had just turned eighteen. He was a tall boy with a medium build. He looked so much like their father with his light brown hair, but he too had his mother's bright blue eyes.

"What's come, Benjamin?"

"It is a letter from Father."

Emma smiled, her mood changing almost instantly.

"Read it aloud Benjamin," she said joining him on the sofa.

"Dear Benjamin, Emma, and William," he began quickly after tearing open the envelope. "I must apologize for the delay in my correspondence. It has been quite busy here in the Colonies and your mother and I have had much business to attend to. Since that schooner ran aground in Massachusetts in June, there has been much chaos from both the English citizens and the Colonists. The British are quite upset about the whole affair."

"I should say so; quite uncivilized behavior from the Colonists, setting the boat on fire and such."

"Emma, please. 'But enough about the news from the Colonies. I hope that you are all doing well and that you are being treated kindly. Things are going well for your mother and I, but times are becoming much harder. I am afraid that times are changing right before our eyes. I tell you this because I fear the worst consequences are nearing. People are having very radical ideas right now. I want you all to be safe and you should also know that our letters might become even sparser."

"Why?" asked Emma urgently.

"He answers if you allow me to continue," Benjamin said teasingly to his sister. "'The mail system here is going to be difficult to traverse, at best. I am afraid that other ships may not make the journey so readily what with the schooner being attacked by the Colonists. I must confess the other reason that our correspondence will lessen. This is because I am being called away for my services. I cannot divulge exactly what that entails right now for fear of this letter being seen by the wrong eyes, but I am going to be leaving Virginia for a few weeks. It is probably best if you do not reply to this letter but await my next correspondence. I love you all and want you take care of each other. Your mother sends you all her love. Sincerely, Father.'"

There was a pause in conversation from both Benjamin and Emma.

"Where do you think that Father is going?" asked Emma.

"I don't know. I bet he's going to Massachusetts to help the English capture those responsible for the schooner incident."

"Perhaps. What do you think of the Colonists, Benjamin?"

"I'm not really sure. I mean, many of them are from England, but from what I have heard it is almost as if they've completely lost their roots; their sense of pride of country when they get to the Colonies. They see themselves as English but they have different ideas of how things should be."

"Why? How?"

"I'm not sure Emma. I just hear stories."

"Like what Benjamin?"

"Emma, Benjamin," came a voice from the hallway. Their cousin Miranda was calling them. Miranda was eight and she was the nosiest and most malevolent child that either Benjamin or Emma had ever met. "Mother wants to see you both in the parlor." With this, she disappeared. Benjamin gave a little cough that was very scornful.

"Benjamin, do try and keep your temper," chided Emma.

"I do try but that woman is abhorrent. She only allows us to stay because of the money that Mother and Father send to her."

"Benjamin, that is a little harsh."

"Emma, when I think of what would happen if the situation were reversed. Mother and Father would never accept one dime to take in our cousins, and there are five of them versus the three of us."

"I agree, but we are very expensive to keep, I'm sure, and besides, she loves William."

"That is because William is still young and impressionable. She can change what William thinks."

"Benjamin, again, I think you are being too judgmental."

"Emma, do you really not agree with me? Look me straight in the eye and tell me that you feel she has our best interests at heart. If you can do that, I will drop the subject completely."

There was a moment of silence. Emma opened her mouth to say something but then changed her mind and turned away from her brother to go and see her aunt.

"You see, you do agree."

"All right," said Emma hastily. She stopped in the middle of the hallway and dropped her voice to a low and urgent whisper. "I do agree with you, but we are living under her roof right now and there is nothing we can do about it."

"We'll see about that." Emma gave Benjamin a very quizzical look and wanted to ask him what he meant by his statement but didn't have a chance; Benjamin walked away from her at that moment and went toward the parlor.

They bowed ceremoniously to their Aunt Sylvia. She nodded her head but did not return any other courtesy. Sylvia Bradbury was an older sister to Benjamin and Emma's mother. Emma had inherited her blonde hair and blue eyes that were prominent on her mother's side as well as her petite figure. Though Sylvia shared blonde hair and blue eyes, her face was rigid and hardened. She had no look of warmth about her, unlike her sisters. Sylvia was so petite she often looked sickly and Benjamin, to Emma's hidden amusement, often commented on his aunt's unusually long neck. Yet, the biggest difference between these two sisters was that Sylvia lacked Elizabeth's natural grace and eloquence. Unfortunately, life had caused both Sylvia's demeanor and her looks to harden.

The eldest of the three sisters, Sylvia had married late in life. She was very bitter about the whole situation. She did not seem to love her husband, Charles; she loved his money and his reputation, and even his station in life but not the man himself. Charles was a favorite in the court. His family had been close friends of the royal family and consequently, Charles was made a Lord under his Majesty King George III who took the throne in October of 1760. Thus, with her husband's money and the attention she received from her newfound title, along with rarely seeing the man, Sylvia got along quite well. Sylvia and Charles had five children and the four eldest were sent away each year to a boarding school so that neither Sylvia nor Charles had to deal with them for the majority of the year. Richard, their youngest, would soon be sent away to school as well.

Elizabeth had one other sister as well, Margaret. She too was older than Elizabeth, but not by much. Benjamin and Emma had seen her only when they were very little. She and her husband had set off to live in the colony of Maryland; around the time Benjamin was born in 1755. Eighteen years later they knew that she now had six children, but they had not met all of them. They had not seen them in many years, since the last time Margaret and her husband, Peter, had visited England with their two oldest children.

Benjamin and Emma took a seat in the parlor with their aunt and she had tea served. No one spoke for a few moments. Benjamin never spoke much during tea, or really anytime that his Aunt Sylvia was around. Emma had merely learned to not speak until her aunt spoke to her. Finally, their aunt broke the silence.

"Now, my dears, I am sure that it has occurred to you that summer holiday will be over shortly and we need to determine exactly where everyone will be living."

Emma's face dropped. Though her father had been in the Colonies for years after fighting in the Seven Years' War, it had been late November when their mother and father had permanently left for the Colonies and thus, it was impossible to be sent to a school. They'd had tutors all year, but it seemed only too obvious now that their aunt was talking about it; they would be sent to a boarding school like their cousins when term restarted.

"What do you mean, 'exactly where everyone will be living'?" asked Benjamin with a note of force in his voice.

"Precisely," Sylvia began coldly, "as I said, dear Benjamin. You certainly didn't expect to have such an easy year this year as last? No. That will not be the case. Now I think that William will do well going to a nice boys' school and Emma, you are going to join Viola at her school for the finest young ladies. My biggest problem is you, Benjamin. However, I was thinking that maybe you could go off to Oxford."

"Oxford? Aunt Sylvia, I so sincerely regret to tell you that I will not be attending Oxford this fall." Emma knew that Benjamin had no trace of regret in his voice; however, she was never sure if her aunt noticed this lack of respect that Benjamin often splayed whilst in her company.

"Well Cambridge then?" she suggested slightly annoyed. Before Benjamin could answer, Emma put a hand on his arm.

Benjamin took the sign and merely shrugged his shoulders to his aunt. "Now that that's settled, you may both take your leave then. I will send the necessary letters tomorrow."

Benjamin and Emma stood. Emma looped her arm through her brother's and they left graciously. Benjamin opened his mouth immediately but Emma put a finger to her lips and continued to guide her brother upstairs and into a sitting room.

"Benjamin, before you even speak, listen to me. You really can't expect her to do any different for us than her own children, can you?"

"I expect her to do what our parents would do and nothing less." With that, Benjamin left Emma alone in the sitting room with nothing but a sigh and her thoughts for company.

The rest of the day was more miserable than it had started. Emma disliked arguing with her brothers very much and especially now that their parents weren't with them. They ate dinner that night in silence among the Bradburys. Not that anyone really noticed; neither Benjamin nor Emma ever spoke much during dinner, as there were always so many guests of her aunt and uncle's whom they did not know. Not to mention that their comments were rarely welcome.

Emma laid down that night to finally fall into a troubled sleep. She dreamt about the next few months and could not shake the feeling of impending doom that had come down upon her. She knew that she was being silly. School couldn't possibly be that horrible. She awoke many times during the long night, but none were as prominent as the one around six that morning.

"Emma, wake up. I have to talk to you."

"Benjamin!" she exclaimed, slightly alarmed. "What's wrong?"

"I have a brilliant plan Emma."

"What are you talking about?"

"You don't really want to go to that girls' school, do you?"

"No, not really," replied Emma falling back into her pillow, now a bit groggy that the shock of her awakening was starting to wear off, remembering how much she liked her bed and how early it really was.

"And you don't want William to have to go off to school either, eh?"

"No, I suppose not, but I don't think that we have much of a choice in the matter Benjamin," said Emma with a big yawn.

"But we do Emma. Don't you see? It is so simple."

"No, it is early in the morning, enlighten me a little," said Emma quite annoyed at Benjamin for waking her as she had just finally fallen into a slightly better sleep.

"Emma, I've been thinking about it all night, and I don't see any other option. I've been planning for a while, but this put me over the edge. We don't want to go to school, so we leave."

"What?" she said, sitting up and now paying much closer attention.

"Right, we just leave. My friend Thomas is going to come and get us at midnight tonight and we will take off."

"Where would we go?" Emma asked believing this to be a joke now.

"To Virginia, of course."

"To Virginia? But why?"

"To be with Mother and Father. The only reason we couldn't go in the first place was because we had to finish our tutoring year and they wanted to get settled before they sent for us. Well, it's been ten months, they ought to be settled by now, don't you think?"

"Probably, but Benjamin, how would we get to Virginia?" Emma asked. She was humoring him as she chuckled at his ridiculousness.

"On a ship."

"Well obviously so, but how would we pay for that Benjamin?

What ship would take us?" She was starting to wonder if he was serious.

"There is a ship called the *Expedition* going to America tomorrow night, leaving at one o'clock. I have three boarding passes for that ship. It doesn't take us straight to Virginia, but we will land in Boston and then take a carriage to Williamsburg."

"But how did you afford this?" asked Emma now sitting up and realizing just how serious Benjamin was about the matter.

"With the funds that Father sent in his letter for our continued care."

"Benjamin, that money doesn't belong to you; it belongs to Aunt Sylvia and Uncle Charles." Emma's apprehension was now growing to a paramount level.

"But Emma, don't you see that if we leave, they won't need to continue caring for us; we'd be gone." Emma didn't know what to think. She liked the idea of leaving her aunt and uncle's home for good, but it seemed wrong to just leave in the middle of the night. She wondered what her mother would say.

"Don't you think that they will be angry?"

"Probably at first, but I think in the long run they will be glad to have us gone."

"And you think that they are just going to let us walk out that door?"

"I don't think that they are going to have a choice in the matter as I don't think we are going to tell them Emma."

"What about William? He couldn't keep this quiet."

"I thought of that as well. We aren't going to be able to tell William until we are on the ship."

"I think he'll figure it out when we are sneaking out of the house, Benjamin."

"I will make up some story. Perhaps we can tell him we are going on an adventure and we can't tell anyone. That wouldn't even be lying. He would be really excited about it too."

Emma had run out of ideas. She had no other arguments to pursue.

"What do you think?"

"I just think it's not the right thing to do."

Benjamin looked at his sister. He knew he could talk her into anything.

"Do you really believe that it's not the right thing to do? I mean, I know there are better circumstances under which this could happen, but sometimes the ends justify the means."

After a slight hesitation, Emma nodded. "All right. I shall be ready to leave by midnight tonight," conceded Emma.

"Good, and pack everything you can. Also, I need you to pack up William's things without him seeing you do it, or anyone else for that matter."

"I won't be able to do that until it is almost time to leave then, Benjamin."

"Don't worry, we'll figure out something." Benjamin noticed his sister's face. "Emma, it will be all right. I promise you it will all work out."

Emma sighed and nodded again. "Who knows, maybe it will be the best thing we ever do for ourselves."

"That's the spirit. Now, I am going to go down to breakfast; I am famished."

"Has it stopped raining yet?"

"No, not yet. Why do you ask?"

"I wanted to go for one last ride."

"Emma, I will have Thomas come and collect your horse. He will take good care of her for you." Emma gave Benjamin a sad smile, and he left her.

Emma got up and dressed. She began pulling out her trunks and packing. Then reality started to hit her. Where were they going to stay? They surely couldn't make it to Virginia in just one day. Emma didn't know how far it was, but she was sure it was a few hundred miles from Williamsburg to Boston from what her parents had said. But she was going to be able to see her mother and father again; something she hadn't done in nearly ten months. This thought filled her with so much joy that she all but forgot how difficult the task at hand would be. She took out a quill, some ink, and two pieces of parchment and began to write two letters.

Within a few minutes, she had completed both letters. She put them in envelopes and addressed each one. The first was addressed:

Mr. & Mrs. Peter Seager
14 Waxbury Lane
Gaithersburg, Maryland

This letter was for her Aunt Margaret. The other letter was for her father's brother and family and was addressed:

Mr. & Mrs. Alexandre Huntington
8 King Street
Boston, Massachusetts

Emma sealed both envelopes, finished packing, and put her trunks under her bed for safe keeping. She brought the letters downstairs and gave them to one of the house servants to be sent out in the day's post. She wasn't sure about what her Aunt Margaret's reaction would be to her letter but she knew that her Uncle Alexandre would be thrilled.

Benjamin and Emma had met Alexandre and his family many times. Alexandre had come to England and stayed with Emma's family more than once, though it had been a few years since the last time they had seen each other. In fact, it had been about four years since Alexandre had come to England and perhaps eleven or twelve since Emma had seen her cousins from that side of the family.

Emma went and joined the breakfasting members of the household.

"You look as though you have recovered nicely from our chat yesterday, Emma," said Aunt Sylvia scathingly. Emma's good mood could not even be brought down by her aunt. She merely smiled and gave a sweet reply.

"I have Aunt Sylvia. Thank you for asking." Sylvia was so taken back by this, she did not respond to Emma.

However, not everyone was as silent as Sylvia and poor William, being only five, couldn't help himself; he had to ask.

"What was Emma upset about?"

"I wasn't dear; eat your breakfast and then Benjamin will take you upstairs and play a game with you for a while," replied Emma quickly.

"Well, you might as well know now my dear William; I am going to be sending you all off to school this year. You are going to go to a school for boys beginning at the start of September."

Poor William's face crumbled. He did not cry, but it was obvious from his facial expressions that it was taking everything in his being to not burst out in tears. Emma shot her aunt a look full of contempt. She took William by the hand and brought him out of the kitchen. Unfortunately, Benjamin's temper could not be quelled so easily. As Emma reached the stairs, she could hear Benjamin raising his voice to their aunt.

Emma looked down at her younger brother and could see the tears begin to flow from his eyes and down his cheeks. She quickened her steps. It would not help the situation to have her aunt know how much pain she had inflicted upon the child.

Emma knew they would never make to William's room so she ducked in her own room and pulled William in with her. She quickly shut the door and not a moment too soon. William now began wailing. Emma went and sat down on the window seat taking William with her. He climbed up and sat with her in her lap.

"William, I promise it will all be all right."

"No it won't. I don't want to go to some stupid old school. I want to stay here with you and Benjamin. I want Mum and Papa." Emma could tell it would be difficult to pacify him and she knew that having a scene today would only cause more difficulties for them that night.

"William, Benjamin and I have it all figured out, but you'll have to trust me, all right?"

William stopped crying and looked at his sister with great wonder and curiosity in his eyes.

"So I don't have to go?" the child asked with a slight quiver of excitement in his voice.

"William, can you keep a secret?" William nodded. "All right, I promise you will not have to go to that school."

"But how do you know?"

"You have to trust me and you can't tell anyone that I said that."

"What about Benjamin?"

"You can tell Benjamin but not when anyone else is around. Besides dear, he already knows."

"How?"

"No more questions right now, but I need you to go into your bedroom and wait until Benjamin comes and gets you. Can you do that for me?"

William nodded and climbed down from the window seat. He had finished crying, and Emma could tell his little mind was now working out all sorts of possibilities of what could happen.

A few minutes later there was a knock on her door.

"Come in," she called.

"Hello. Is he all right?" asked Benjamin.

"He's fine. I promised him he wouldn't have to go to school there."

"What did you say to him?" Benjamin asked closing the door behind him quickly.

"It doesn't matter. I told him to wait in his room until you retrieved him; however, in a little bit I want you to go and get him and take him somewhere so I can begin packing some of his things."

"Are you all packed up then?"

"Yes, nearly. The trunks are under my bed. What did Aunt Sylvia say to you?"

"When I yelled at her you mean? She said that I had no right to say what I was saying and that if it weren't for my mother and father, she would throw me out on the street." Benjamin smiled as he finished imitating his aunt with her high pitched tone, but Emma gasped.

"Benjamin, do not begin a war with her now," said Emma reproachfully. "We need everything to run smoothly. I don't want her thinking she needs to watch you any more closely. Now, are you packed?"

"Yes, I have one small bag left but all of my trunks are with Thomas."

"How on earth did you accomplish that?"

"He came last night to fetch them and bring me the ship passes, and I figured the less we need to drag out tonight, the better."

"You're probably right. You do amaze me sometimes though; you know that, don't you?"

"Yes, I am quite aware of it. I know you look up to me." Benjamin laughed and left Emma to go and get William. Emma gave him a look of exasperation then smiled slightly at the thought of her brother's impudence.

Emma finished packing a few more items from her armoire and then went into William's room. Benjamin had taken him down to the drawing room to play a game with him. Emma pulled out one of his trunks, which still held quite a few of his possessions.

"I wonder if he remembers half of this stuff is in here..." Emma pulled out an old stuffed bear and hugged him tenderly remembering times when she was still with her parents in the countryside of Sussex.

They had owned a beautiful home on expansive grounds. The estate had belonged to their father's family for generations. Currently, the estate was kept up by the servants, but remained empty for the most part with the occasional guest of the family. Presently, Mr. Benjamin Franklin, who was a long time friend of the Huntington family, was staying at the house. In fact, he had been staying at the house off and on as his business allowed him to for the past few years. Though it had been quite some time since Emma had last seen him.

After his successful efforts during the Seven Years' War, Emma's father had been called upon by King George III to go to the Colonies as a representative. Her father, James, had risen to do his duty for his King without question. Unfortunately, this had meant that Benjamin, Emma, and William had to leave their estate as well to live with their Aunt Sylvia and Uncle Charles.

Emma sighed and put the toy bear back into the trunk. She began to remove William's clothes from the clothes press and place them into the trunk. In about a half hour, she had completed packing all of William's clothes and many of his toys.

"Well, I think that is about all I dare to pack for now." Emma looked outside. Still raining. "It must be about time for lunch."

Emma placed William's trunk back where she had found it and headed down to the parlor to find her brothers. On the way she ran into her cousin Viola. Emma was usually tolerant of everyone, but from past experiences with Viola, Emma had little patience for her cousin.

Viola was twelve and she was the most spoiled child that Emma had ever met. She whined constantly and had outright fits if she didn't get her way. Because of this, her parents gave her pretty much everything she asked for and gave her to a servant to tend to her the rest of the time.

There were two of Emma's cousins who didn't bother her much, Michael and Eleanor. In Emma's mind they were actually quite normal given their family. Michael was the eldest, fifteen, and had somehow managed to escape the unpleasantness that seemed to plague the rest of the Bradbury family. He was polite all right, but mostly Michael kept to himself. He preferred staying out of the house as much as possible. He enjoyed leaving for school in the fall and often stayed during holidays. Michael had been gone most of the summer holiday as well, traveling to Italy to study. His prolonged absences were, of course, encouraged by his parents as they had no desire to see him; much in the same fashion as he had no desire to see them.

Eleanor was six. She was not as spoiled as her two older sisters. She asked for little and, like Michael, she found solace in keeping to herself. Now that she could read, she threw herself into books and was actually quite an advanced reader for her age. In fact, Emma, being an avid reader herself, often loved to listen to Eleanor discuss recent books she had read.

"Where do you think you're going Emma?" asked Viola stepping in front of Emma to stop her.

"Downstairs," replied Emma indifferently. She went to walk past Viola.

"So I heard that you are going to come to my school."

Emma was ready for Viola's snide comments; she never missed an opportunity to make one to Emma. Emma sighed a little.

"That's what I heard as well."

"Well you should get one thing straight: it is my school, and I don't want you going around telling people that you are related to me."

"I don't think that you will have to worry about that much Viola."

"Oh and why is that?"

Emma thought of some pretty rude comments to return to Viola's question, but she reminded herself that they would be leaving that night and didn't want any other hazards standing in their way. Thus, Emma contented herself with saying little to Viola and leaving the whole thing a mystery.

"You'll have to wait and see."

"See what?" asked Viola but Emma had squeezed past her now and continued on her walk down the stairs leaving Viola puzzled at the top of the staircase and calling after her.

Emma walked into the drawing room to find her brothers sitting in an armchair. William was listening to Benjamin read to him. Emma sat down in an armchair opposite of them and listened to the end of the story. When Benjamin finished, William jumped down to put the book on the shelf.

"Emma, you missed a good story. Benjamin is the bestest reader there is," said William.

Emma smiled at her younger brother and reflected for a moment on his childlike simplicity.

"Best dear, not bestest," she corrected mildly. William smiled at her. "Why don't you go and see if lunch is ready dearest?" William agreed and left the drawing room.

"All ready?" asked Benjamin.

"Mostly. What can be done is done."

"Good. Are you ready?"

"Mostly. It seems like a drastic measure but I suppose that it is needed."

"I know Emma, but as you say, it is needed. There is nothing else we can do."

"I just feel badly about it."

"There really is no need. They will be glad, and so will we. If it makes everyone happy then what harm can there be?"

Emma wasn't sure, but she nodded and when William returned to inform them that lunch was indeed ready; they headed off together to the dining room.

The rest of the day passed without incident and for this, Emma was glad. William went to bed around seven thirty. "Let him get some sleep; he'll be better off that way," Benjamin had said to Emma after dinner. Emma agreed it was for the best.

The hours between seven thirty and eleven thirty passed extremely slowly for both Emma and Benjamin. Both had tried to pass the time in various ways. Emma had tried to read, but found she was rereading the same sentence again and again while looking up at the clock every few minutes. Then she tried sewing, but she lost count so many times that she was spending more time correcting her mistakes than making any progress.

Finally, about ten thirty, Emma and Benjamin headed upstairs to their rooms. Benjamin told Emma he would come and get her at eleven thirty and to be ready with her trunks. Emma nodded, but said nothing. She could feel a knot that felt as though a heavy weight were sitting squarely on her chest and her stomach was beginning to feel a little queasy.

Emma entered her room and shut the door. Her things were packed. She had an hour to waste until Benjamin returned. Emma listened for a moment. The house was silent. It was not unusual for Emma and Benjamin to be the last to retire at night. Their Uncle Charles was in London for the week, and their Aunt Sylvia always went to bed early. All of their cousins were younger than them and, except for Michael, their aunt made sure they were all in bed by nine o'clock every night.

Emma decided she could change into her traveling clothes now, so she put them on and pinned her hair up. She heard the grandfather clock in the hall chime eleven. *Only another half hour*, she thought. She sat down on her bed and looked outside. The rain had finally stopped now but the wind was still howling. Emma was glad the rain was done, and she supposed the wind would provide good cover for them.

After what seemed like an eternity, there was a small tap on her door. She quickly opened it and found Benjamin standing in front of her. He came in and shut the door.

"Good, you are ready. You just have those two trunks there?" he asked.

"Yes, is that too much?"

"It should be all right. I am going to bring one of them down. Thomas should be down there waiting in a few moments. When I return, he will bring the second trunk down. You and I will go and get William. I will bring him down and get him settled in the carriage; you finish packing his things and come down."

"Benjamin, we are going to have so much luggage."

"Don't worry about it, you have two trunks, William and I have one a piece, the one we are sharing, plus we each have a small bag."

"Yes, but that is five trunks in all."

"But it won't be a problem, I promise you. When you come down, I want you to go and sit in the carriage with William and keep him quiet. I am hoping he will stay asleep."

"He may; he is an awfully heavy sleeper." They heard a horse in the street.

"All right, that might be Thomas down there now. I am going to bring this down. I shall be right back."

"Be careful Benjamin." Benjamin nodded and left Emma's room with one of her trunks.

Emma waited quietly but she heard a noise in the hallway.

Emma held her breath. She decided she'd best see who was out there. She went into the hallway and almost ran over Viola.

"What are you doing?" Viola asked.

"Why aren't you in bed?" Emma asked basically pulling Viola into her room so they wouldn't wake anyone else.

"I heard you. You are going to be in trouble."

Emma had to think quickly. "Why do you care?" she asked.

"What?" Viola responded with some surprise. She had expected Emma to fight her.

"Why do you care if we leave?"

"I don't," Viola said. "I mean, I guess I don't care what you do."

"Think about it for a moment. You hate having us here. According to you, we make your life miserable, right?"

"Right," she replied thinking through this.

"And just think how much better life will be when we've left and you have your house back to the way it was before. Oh, and you won't have to deal with me being at school with you. You'll never have to admit we're related."

Viola smiled at that. "Good," she snorted.

"So maybe it's in your best interest for us to leave too," Emma carefully suggested.

"Yes, maybe it is best for everyone," Viola said.

"And you can certainly be the one to tell your mother tomorrow. I won't even be here to stop you."

Viola considered for a minute. Apparently, it was tempting.

"But I feel like I should do something about this," she said giving her last protest. "Mother might be angry."

"I think you need to think about you right now. What's best for you, Viola?"

"For you to leave," she said quickly.

"Then I think you have your answer."

Viola stood, looked at Emma, and a slow smile spread across

her face. Emma could only imagine the evil thoughts going through her cousin's head but she didn't have time to waste. She led Viola to the door.

"Remember, if we can't get out of here tonight, you're stuck with us for a very long time."

"Oh, I won't be saying a word," Viola said. "But I'm not going to wish a safe trip for you. It would serve you right to drown or something."

"Goodbye Viola," Emma said gladly.

Viola left and Emma took a deep breath. It seemed this crisis had been averted, but she didn't trust Viola. She needed to hurry.

A few moments later, Benjamin returned with Thomas beside him. Thomas smiled at Emma and held out his hand. She gave him her hand and he politely kissed it.

"It is good to see you Emma."

"It is good of you to do this for us Thomas, thank you. We owe you a lot."

"Do not think of it. This one needs to go down?"

"Yes," replied Benjamin. "Emma, let's go and get William." Emma wondered if she should tell Benjamin what had just transpired. She decided against it worrying that Benjamin would want to confront Viola. Right now, Emma just wanted to hurry and get out of the house.

Benjamin left Emma's room and Emma laid a letter on her bed. It was addressed to her aunt and uncle. She too left the room and shut the door. They quietly went down the hall to William's room. Because of his age, William's room was off of the governess's room just like Richard's and Eleanor's rooms. This meant that they had to be doubly quiet.

They entered his room silently. Emma held a lantern in front of them. Upon entering, she went over to his bed with Benjamin. Benjamin picked up the child and Emma placed a blanket around him. William stirred a little but did not wake. Emma threw the remaining things into his trunk and packed his small bag with clothes for when he woke – he was still in his nightshirt. She then headed downstairs after Benjamin, while placing a hat over her bonnet.

In the entry hall, she grabbed William's and Benjamin's cloaks as well as her own and went out to the carriage. Benjamin had just placed William inside and was heading back inside the house for the last trunk. Thomas helped Emma into the carriage. Benjamin returned shortly and the driver fastened the last trunk on the back of the carriage. Benjamin and Thomas entered the carriage, and Thomas told the driver to go.

As they pulled away from the house, Emma breathed a small sigh of relief. They had made it. They were going to be all right now.

"It's all right now. You shouldn't have any difficulty making that ship," said Thomas.

"Thank you Thomas. You have been a better friend than I could ever have imagined or asked for," said Benjamin.

"Yes, thank you Thomas; we owe you more than we can ever repay you, I'm sure."

"Thank me when you get to Boston safely. For now, just hold your breath that nothing goes wrong."

The rest of the ride was taken in silence. All the riders had many things on their minds. Emma was still worried. Thomas was right, there was still much that could go wrong.

However, luck was on their side and nothing did go wrong, thankfully. They made it to the dock. Their trunks were unloaded and placed on board for them. Emma and Benjamin bid Thomas goodbye and thanked him again. Benjamin carried William onto the ship, and they found their quarters.

The ship was near empty of passengers but fairly full with cargo. Emma supposed this only made sense as they were leaving at such a late time.

They got William settled in his bed. He woke up momentarily but fell asleep almost immediately again. Benjamin crawled into bed with him, and Emma took the other bed. They were on their way. The ship set sail at precisely one o'clock, but all three of them were already fast asleep secure in the knowledge that they were finally safe.

Chapter 2
The Town Meeting

The voyage on the ship took just over a month. It had been a long journey, but not incredibly difficult in the grand scheme of things. They'd had fair weather conditions and a strong wind from the east to push them. With much teasing from Benjamin, and much queasiness on her part, Emma finally found her sea legs after a week or so. From then on, the journey was much smoother for everyone.

William had been delighted by the whole story. Of course, after a fortnight, the story that William told and the actual story were quite different. According to William's version of things, they had been kidnapped by pirates, saved by Thomas and then the only way they could escape the pirates for good was to take refuge as stowaways on this ship. Of course, Benjamin didn't help the situation at all. In fact, he added to the story every time William retold it. The sailors had taken a liking to the three children, and William often followed them around recounting his version of events and learning about being a sailor.

Benjamin too was learning to sail. He found the whole thing invigorating, not to mention he enjoyed being on deck with the salty air and the sea spray. He was good enough to tell the other men the truth about the events that William had conveyed, but all three of them were careful not to relay too much information on who they were for fear of what would happen to them once they reached Boston. It was funny to Emma, but no matter how many miles they put between them, she was still sure that her aunt and uncle would find them and make them return to England.

Emma spent much of her time below deck so as not to get in anyone's way, but also because she was still getting used to the attention she received from the sailors. They were not vulgar around her, but she was the only female on the ship and with her fair hair and complexion, as well as her mesmerizing blue eyes, the sailors often tried to catch glimpses of her and get her attention as much as possible.

The captain of the ship, Captain Donshill, turned out to be a good friend of Thomas's family and thus was extremely nice to Benjamin, Emma, and William. He dined with them every evening and was always good to keep them up on their current status. Captain Donshill also spoke to them about the current affairs in the Colonies.

"So, yer goin' to Boston? Is that yer final destination then?" asked the Captain one evening after dinner.

"No, we are traveling southward from there," Benjamin replied.

"Well, when yer in Boston, if you get a chance, go on up to Beacon Hill and take a look at them houses. I can't imagine livin' in one of them houses. They are so big."

"Really?" asked Emma politely.

"Yes, as a matta fact, the man that owns this ship, Mr. John Hancock, he lives up there."

After the long voyage at sea and the constant feeling Emma had that they would never arrive, they finally docked in Boston in late October. The ship landed in the harbor and Benjamin,

Emma, and William bid farewell to everyone on the ship. Their trunks were carried down for them and placed on the pier.

"Now what Benjamin?" asked William. Emma was amazed by her younger brother. His enthusiasm for the expedition was still not dampened in the least, even after the long month aboard the small ship.

Emma watched her brother for a moment.

"You two stay right here, I am going to see if I can arrange some transportation."

"But Benjamin," Emma began but it was too late; he had already taken off.

Emma stood by the trunks. William sat down upon one. Emma listened to her brother talk about adventures and other things with enough attention, but her focus had turned to the crowd around them.

The main thing that Emma noticed was how people spoke. They certainly didn't sound like proper Englishmen. Then she heard someone mention the name Huntington. She turned and looked in the direction of the speaker.

"Alexandre Huntington. It has been so long since I last saw you. Tell me, what are you doing down at the pier today?"

"I'm down here to hopefully see my niece and nephews, Gregory. They are supposed to be arriving from England any day now."

Emma felt her heart jump. It was their uncle. She grabbed William's hand and started walking toward him. Alexandre noticed her walking toward him and a smile came across his face. He bid adieu to the man he was speaking with and headed toward Emma and William.

Emma gave her uncle a great hug. Alexandre looked down at William and smiled. He bent down and greeted the child with warm sincerity. William, having never met Alexandre, was affable but shy. He hid behind Emma's skirt as much as he could.

Alexandre was kind though and did not press the boy to come out.

The three of them walked back to their trunks.

"Where is Benjamin?" Alexandre asked.

"Good question. I tried to catch him, but he took off to arrange something," replied Emma.

"Well, he will be back then. Tell me, how was the journey?"

"It was long. However, I cannot complain much. We had perfect weather and the sailors were very friendly."

"Good. My God, Emma, I cannot believe how much you have grown. You are practically a woman now." Emma could feel her face flush.

"How is your family? Are they well? I haven't heard from you in a while," Emma said trying to divert attention from her.

"Well, there is much going on here, I am afraid. However, the family is well. Marianne and Edmund are back in school now, and they seem to be enjoying that. Jonathan just turned five this month so he has just started school as well; though he has not taken to it yet. I think it will take some adjustment. Oh, and then there is Sebastian. He is just like any other boy nowadays. He is anxious to join the militia so he can join the fight."

Emma laughed a little thinking that her uncle was making a joke. However, from the look he gave her, she realized she was mistaken.

"But Uncle Alexandre, you can't be serious. Fight for the militia? For the rebels? But that is treasonous."

"Ah Emma, things are different here as you will soon see. However, I will not impress my opinions upon you. You shall find out in good time. I had assumed your parents were keeping you better informed, but I see now that I was mistaken."

Emma went to reply, but at that moment Benjamin returned.

"Uncle Alexandre? It is so good to see you. But, how did you know we were coming?"

"Did your sister not tell you?" Alexandre got a grin on his face now, fully realizing the situation. Emma didn't quite make eye contact with her brother. Benjamin looked nonplussed.

"Tell me what?"

"I wrote to him to inform him we were coming. I knew that we would need a place to stay once we arrived."

"And I am glad she did. We are delighted to have you all. It has been so long since we've seen you. Now we can show you our home just as you have graciously shared your home so many times before."

Alexandre had settled the argument. Benjamin had apparently not found transportation and his uncle was, therefore, a welcome sight.

Alexandre called his carriage around and saw that Emma and William were comfortably settled inside. Then he and Benjamin helped the driver load the trunks and stepped inside as well.

It was a fair day. The weather, though chilly, was sunny and bright. Emma was certainly glad to be back on the dry land and the sight of her uncle had rejuvenated her spirit a bit; though she could not deny that her legs still felt as though they were swaying as upon the ship.

The ride to her uncle's home was a jovial one. They spoke of days gone by and of their family. They were only in the carriage for a short time when they reached a residential street. They drove down the street and came upon a quaint little cul-de-sac.

"Up there you can see Beacon Hill. Very nice houses up that way," said Alexandre.

"The Captain on the ship told us about Beacon Hill," Emma replied, looking up at the houses and trying to guess which one might belong to a ship owner.

"And this is our cul-de-sac," said Alexandre.

There, in the middle of the cul-de-sac was a white house with green shutters. The carriage stopped outside this house, and

Alexandre got out first followed by Benjamin. William jumped down next, and Alexandre waited to hold his hand out to Emma to help her down. "Isabelle is out of town for a few days visiting her sister I'm afraid, but there is plenty of room, and plenty to do in Boston. I daresay we will not miss her much," said Alexandre lightheartedly as he escorted Emma inside, followed by William and Benjamin.

Once inside, they were greeted by Alexandre's children. Jonathon, being five as well, made William a bit braver. Within moments, the two of them were off playing together, leaving the others to talk.

"I thought William might like the room next to Jonathon's, although it isn't exactly close to the two of you," said Alexandre.

"That's fine, he will probably be happier this way," replied Benjamin.

"Uncle Alexandre," began Emma, "I thought you said your children were in school now."

"I did say that. There is a very good school here in Boston and so they are able to come home every day after their lessons. Why don't we have some tea? I think that Sebastian should be home now. I will go and fetch him. If you two just want to go and freshen up and then join us in the sitting room, your rooms are the last two on the right side." Emma and Benjamin nodded and headed upstairs.

"I can't believe you wrote to him Emma."

"Why not?"

"Because I thought we were going to keep it a secret."

"Well I knew the letters wouldn't reach them until we were safely away from England anyway Benjamin. There is something else you should know, however."

"Oh, what's that?"

"Well, I wrote two more letters."

"To whom?"

"One to our Aunt Margaret, and another to Aunt Sylvia and Uncle Charles."

"And what did you say Emma?" asked Benjamin trying to keep his voice even and calm.

"I wrote and told Margaret that we were coming to the Colonies and would be perhaps dropping in on them. I told Aunt Sylvia and Uncle Charles that we had left and that they needn't worry about us, nothing more."

Emma saw that her brother was not happy with her but as they were safe and staying with relatives because of her, he couldn't say too much. They went into their respective rooms.

Emma was glad to see a normal bed. Her trunks had been brought up for her. She pulled out an afternoon tea dress of dark green and changed clothes. Afterwards, she went out into the hallway and found her way down to the sitting room where her uncle, cousin Sebastian, and brother were waiting for her.

When she entered, they all stood and Sebastian pulled out her chair for her. She sat down and the three men sat as well. Being the only female, Emma felt it her responsibility to poor the tea. She began listening to the conversation that she had entered upon. The men were discussing the current events.

"As I was saying, it was just not right to acquit those men. How can we expect the English to abide by the same laws as we do if they are given differential treatment?" asked Sebastian.

"I disagree with you son. Those men received a fair trial. It shows that we can be quite civilized and reasonable. It's the same as before though. I swear if it weren't for Sam Adams, we would still have Preston's troops here in Boston," concluded Alexandre.

Emma was very curious about the happenings in the Colonies, especially as she was worried about her father and his connections with it all.

"Excuse me gentlemen, may I ask a question?"

"By all means Emma."

"I am not quite as current with events as you seem to be; could you please explain your statements?" Sebastian gave Emma a look of appraisal but said nothing and turned to his tea. Alexandre looked at his niece and patiently began to explain.

"You see, Emma, back in March of 1770 some British troops were in Boston. A group of people started bothering them, throwing snow and such. One of the snowballs hit a British soldier and his musket went off resulting in the British opening fire on the crowd."

"Well, if this mob was harassing the King's soldiers, I should think they were justified in protecting themselves."

"Murder is rarely justified Emma. There were women and children in that crowd. They had no right to open fire. They killed five men and injured six more. A great man and Bostonian by the name of Samuel Adams insisted that the governor, Thomas Hutchinson, remove these troops immediately. He did so and the troops occupied neighboring islands in the harbor. Mr. Preston and eight of his men were tried for murder and found guilty, but on a much lesser charge.

"Then, I am sure you have heard about our most recent news; a schooner off the coast of Rhode Island in Narragansett Bay ran ashore. Some of the Colonists from Providence went out, sent the crew to shore, and burned the ship."

"Yes, I had heard this. What a dreadful thing for the Colonists to do."

"Yes, well, in September the King offered a 500 pound reward for these people and then announced that their trial would be in England."

"I don't see what is so horrible about that. Besides, King George was right to offer the reward. The Colonists should not have done something so violent."

"What is so horrible about that is that those people won't get a fair trial. Also the King has now made it quite clear that the English are above the Colonies' laws," replied Sebastian.

"I am afraid that I don't follow you."

"If an English man is caught and tried in England the law is likely to be more relaxed for him than if a Colonist is caught and tried in England. Also, it undermines our whole judicial system in the Colonies," retorted Sebastian. "He might as well tell us we can't worship in our churches or grow our own food any longer."

"But if they are getting a trial, I see no difference." Sebastian opened his mouth and started to make another remark, but must have decided against it because shut his mouth again. Emma was smart enough to take the hint though, and didn't push her opinions. Benjamin was the first to break the silence.

"So what else is going on with the Colonies?"

"Well, you have actually come at a very exciting time. Sam Adams has called a town meeting, and we will be going. You are more than welcome to come and watch if you would like," replied Alexandre.

"What has he called the meeting for?" asked Benjamin.

However, before anyone could answer, William and Jonathon came bounding into the room.

"Emma, Emma you have to come and see this!"

"William, it is not polite to interrupt adults' conversation," reprimanded Emma.

"Ah, that's all right Emma. What did you find William?" asked Alexandre.

"Emma, they have this really neat tunnel upstairs."

"They have what?"

"Oh, that. It's nothing important Emma; this house just has a secret room upstairs. It was here when we purchased the house," said Alexandre.

"Emma, come and see it!" exclaimed William.

Emma smiled at her younger brother. "Gentlemen, excuse me please," said Emma standing. The men stood to see her out of the room. Emma went upstairs with William and Jonathon. As she reached the stairs she could hear Benjamin asking Alexandre and Sebastian more about the town meeting.

She reached the top of the stairs and climbed through the tunnel with the boys to find a huge room waiting on the other side. The room contained a large table and eight or nine chairs. Emma looked around and saw that the room had no windows and no other exit.

"Isn't it great Emma?" asked William.

"Yes," she said distracted, "it's very interesting. I wonder what they use this for."

"Father has meetings here sometimes," said Jonathon.

"What sort of meetings, Jonathon?"

"I don't know; a bunch of men come over and they talk. I don't know what they talk about because I am not allowed to come to the meetings. They say that I'm too young."

"Who comes to these meetings?"

"Mr. Adams comes, but I haven't ever met the other men. Sebastian goes to them now too."

"I see," said Emma starting to get a pretty clear picture of what was happening.

"But last week a new man came."

"Oh?"

"Mm-hmm. It was Mr. Adams cousin, John Adams. He is a lawyer here in town. Father says he is a really smart man."

"I see. Well, I think we should go back down to the others boys," said Emma. She was really disturbed by this revelation but didn't say anything further to the boys.

"All right," said the boys together.

The rest of the day was pretty uneventful. Emma was still mulling over the information that Jonathon had given her.

She was having difficulty understanding how her own uncle could associate with such lowly people. She was having an even more difficult time understanding how her cousin could be so opinionated, especially since his opinions went completely against her own beliefs.

Emma lay in bed that night and continued to think about what she had been told during the day. She hadn't had a chance to speak with Benjamin again. She began to wonder what he thought about everything. Surely he didn't agree with their atrocious ideas either.

The night went on and so did the next day and then the next. Emma found herself so busy over the next week with meeting her uncle's friends and acquaintances that she hardly had time for much else.

"This certainly seems to be a central point," Benjamin had said at one point. Emma agreed. However, she had little chance to speak with her brother privately during the week.

Finally, November came, as well as the town meeting that everyone seemed so insistent upon attending. Emma, being a woman, was not invited to attend the meeting. This was not against her wishes by any means though. Yet Benjamin decided to go for curiosity's sake. Emma had told him flat out that even if she had been invited, she wouldn't go.

Emma had been invited over to the Melcher's home for the evening to keep Mrs. Melcher and her two daughters company during the meeting. Emma was glad for the distraction, but during the course of the evening, she soon wished she were anywhere but with the Melcher family. It was true; they were very nice people, but they insisted upon talking about the Colonies and seemed to not be concerned that what they were saying was nothing short of treason in Emma's mindset. They seemed to agree with her uncle and cousin that the Colonists were right in their vigilante violence.

Emma struggled. She wanted to be polite, she was a guest in their home after all, but she found she just wanted to run away from all of it. She didn't want to talk about the Colonies or the events that were going on. She just wanted to get to her parents and escape all of this craziness.

After an exhausting evening with the Melcher family, Emma finally arrived at her uncle's home shortly after the three men had returned. However, they weren't alone. Her uncle had company and Emma, having spent all night trying to be polite, was tired of it. She wanted only to go to bed, but she knew that it was ungracious to do and thus stuck her head into the parlor.

As soon as she was seen, the men stood to welcome her. She recognized a few of them.

"Emma, come in, come in. I want you to meet some people," beckoned her uncle.

Emma entered the room compliantly and noticed her brother, Benjamin, was deeply engrossed in a conversation with her cousin, Sebastian.

"Emma, this is Mr. Melcher. I know that you had the pleasure of spending this evening with his wife and daughters at his home."

"Yes, Mr. Melcher, it is very nice to meet you. Thank you so much for your hospitality this evening."

The man bowed to Emma but because of his height, nearly six feet tall Emma thought, he barely seemed to have moved. His bushy hair made Emma feel as though he were only twenty or so though she knew having daughters of about her age he must be quite a bit older.

"It was certainly my pleasure to be able to be so accommodating. My wife always enjoys having the company, you know."

"And this is Captain Tillig. He served in the British Navy a few years ago," Alexandre continued.

"Oh, Captain Tillig, it is so nice to meet you." Emma was glad to finally meet someone who would surely agree with her.

"I am sure it is nice to see someone who has your same roots still in them, eh?" asked the Captain.

"It certainly is Captain Tillig. At least you haven't picked up this American accent yet." The men around Emma all began laughing. Emma laughed politely though she was quite serious about the matter.

"And finally Emma, this is Mr. Adams."

"Miss Huntington, it is a pleasure. I have heard much about you from your family. They speak very highly of you."

"And I have heard much about you from my family as well," Emma replied noticing the man's tatty red suit. It looked as though he had slept in his clothes for the past three or four nights.

"I hope it isn't too bad, you know I do have quite a reputation at times." The men around Emma began to laugh again. The joke escaped Emma.

"That is what I hear Mr. Adams."

The men around Emma had begun to disperse a bit now leaving Emma to speak with Samuel Adams alone.

"Seriously, I hope you enjoy your stay in Boston and that whatever your opinion of me is, you will not hold it against our fair city." Mr. Adams had a playful grin upon his face almost as if he knew what Emma was thinking.

Emma now felt a little ashamed. She was staying in her uncle's home, and it wasn't right for her to insult her uncle's guests.

"Mr. Adams, do forgive me, I think we have gotten off on the wrong foot. Boston is a lovely city for what I have seen of it."

"Have you been to the inner harbor yet? Oh but how thick of me, you came here by ship of course."

"Yes, it is quite impressive down there however. It all seems so efficient."

"It is. It is a new age and that is why the decisions made tonight were made."

"I beg your pardon, but whatever do you mean, Mr. Adams?"

"Have you not heard, Miss Huntington? We have decided to discuss three new proclamations that would make the Colonies, or at least Massachusetts, self-governing."

"What? But that is-," Emma began.

"Miss Huntington, you are young and I am sure, being in England, you have been unaware of our current predicament. Therefore, I will ask you to please not make rash judgments when you do not understand the roots or basis of these ideas."

Emma was at a loss for words. Sam Adams was standing in front of her speaking of treason to her but telling her that she didn't understand. These people were mad; there was no other explanation for it. Emma thought things were crazy around her but she could now see that these crazy people were the impetus behind the recent events. What took Emma by the most surprise was that it wasn't as though he was angry or even that he disagreed with her entirely; it was a mere statement put to her to ask her to become more informed before offering her opinion. Emma couldn't even take offense to the comment, which inevitably made her more irritable with the situation.

"I'm sorry Miss Huntington, but if you will excuse me it is time for me to be going." Emma nodded her head. Mr. Adams kissed her hand gently and told her he was sure they would meet again soon. They said goodbye and Mr. Adams left.

Emma made a beeline for Benjamin. He was still talking with Sebastian and others had now joined their conversation as well. Emma hadn't even heard a word of what the men were talking about, but she came up and gave Benjamin a look to tell him she wanted to speak with him. Benjamin politely excused himself from the group and the two of them headed out into the gardens in the back of the house.

"What is it Emma?"

"Benjamin, have you been listening to what these people are saying?"

"Yes, I have."

"About the American Colonies being self-governing and such?"

"Yes. I was at the meeting remember?"

"Benjamin, you surely don't agree with them, do you? I mean, it is completely ridiculous. In fact, it is treasonous."

"From your point of view, but if you really listen to what they are saying, it isn't as it seems. I didn't realize what all England was doing to the Colonies Emma. For example, in many Colonies, but starting with Virginia, they are boycotting English goods."

"But why? I mean, don't they need those things?"

"They may, but they are doing without because the English are taxing everything so highly. The Colonists feel that it is not right and therefore are arguing against taxation without representation."

"They want representation in Parliament?"

"They do, and I believe the deserve it. After all, many of them are from England originally; why did they have representation in England but no longer now that they have moved to the Colonies?"

"But Benjamin, to just say that they are not going to be under English rule any longer? I mean, what if Wales just decided one day that they were going to be their own country?"

"Emma, first of all, they aren't saying they won't be under English rule, they just want to govern themselves. Also, this taxation without representation is a big deal. In 1768, Mr. Sam Adams wrote a circular letter that opposed this. It called for all of the Colonists to unite in their actions and oppose the British government. However, just for writing this, many assemblies have been disbanded; when Virginia started boycotting British goods, the Governor of Virginia got rid of their House of Burgesses."

"Then the Governor obviously thought that he was in the right, Benjamin."

"But Emma, to just disband the House of Burgesses of Virginia? It didn't matter much though; they met the next day in a pub in Williamsburg." Benjamin laughed at this.

"Benjamin, it is not so funny."

"Emma, I am merely amused at their boldness."

"So they disobeyed a direct order from their Governor?"

"Emma, sometimes you have to question authority."

"Not when that authority is right Benjamin."

"But who's to say that old King George is right?"

Emma was about to tell her brother exactly what she thought about that but William came out to get them at that moment.

"We'll be there in just a moment dear," said Emma gently. "Benjamin, I am not going to argue about this with you. However, my next question is how much longer you want to stay in Boston? I received a letter from our Aunt Margaret today saying that she would be delighted to have us stay with her while we break our journey in Maryland."

"As much as I like Boston I agree we should start to head down to Williamsburg. I think maybe we should leave day after tomorrow."

"Agreed. Uncle Alexandre has gotten us a carriage to use for the journey."

"All right, I will inform him of our plans tonight."

"Thank you. I will go and begin packing."

Emma turned from Benjamin still in shock about what he had said to her. However, she felt it best not to argue with him at the moment. He would forget all about these silly matters as soon as they left Boston. After all, it was natural to get caught up in things when you were right in the middle, and Boston certainly seemed to be the middle of things right now.

The night passed slowly. Dinner was almost painful for Emma. Many of the men had stayed for dinner and would not stop talking about the meeting and the plans for Massachusetts. Emma began to feel quite nauseous about the whole thing. One man in particular had caught Emma's attention. His name was Jeffrey Ainsworth. He was sitting directly across from Emma at dinner and was quite intrigued by her.

"Tell me, Miss Huntington, how do you like our fair city?"

"Boston is quite different than I had guessed," said Emma truthfully.

"In what way?"

"There are many things that are different than I had imagined."

"I'm assuming you've been to cities before," said another man who was sitting on Emma's left.

"Yes, I have. My family and I used to go into London all the time," replied Emma with a bit of hostility in her voice.

"London is quite different than Boston," said Mr. Ainsworth.

"Have you been to London?" Emma asked with a bit of intrigue.

"Yes, I have. My grandfather lives near Surrey."

"My family lived near Sussex," Emma replied. "But the main thing that surprised me was the bustle of Boston."

"Surely there is bustle in London," said the man next to her.

"There is, but I was surprised to see so much of it here in the Colonies," Emma replied flatly.

"I take it that you don't approve of what we have been discussing all evening," said Mr. Ainsworth.

"Mr. Ainsworth, I cannot deny that the course of the current discussion is not much to my liking."

"I kind of figured that," said Mr. Ainsworth laughing a little. Emma wasn't sure how to take his statement.

After dinner was over, Emma insisted that William go upstairs. She felt it was not right for him to hear the radical ideas of these fanatical men. As for Benjamin, he was an adult and he could make his own choices. Besides, Emma wasn't going to stop him.

Emma decided to disappear after dinner as well. She went

into her room and lay down on her bed. She had difficulty falling asleep that night. She kept having dreams that King George himself had heard what had been said in Alexandre's home that night and British soldiers were storming the house.

The next day passed by very slowly as well. However, Emma was able to keep herself busy. Her Aunt Isabelle had returned late during the night and so Emma was quite engaged by her. While she was not in her aunt's company, Emma saw to it that things were being packed and everything was getting ready. Her aunt kept asking if they would consider staying just a little longer but Emma and Benjamin kept insisting they really needed to press onward. Finally, after dinner that night, Isabelle conceded defeat.

Emma had another troubled night for sleep. Her dreams were more vivid than the night before. She awoke early; the sun had just started to come up over the horizon. Emma stood and dressed quickly. The weather outside was quite cold. November had definitely brought cold air with it, and it was difficult for Emma to get used to.

She went downstairs to find Benjamin already sitting up with Sebastian, Marianne, and Alexandre. As she entered, the men stood to greet her. She took a seat next to Sebastian and across from Benjamin. She bid everyone a good morning and joined in eating breakfast. A few minutes later, Isabelle entered with Edmund.

"So, are you two all ready to take off then?" asked Isabelle trying to make polite conversation.

"I think so. Everything is packed, and I sent a letter to our Aunt Margaret and Uncle Peter yesterday morning letting them know we are coming," said Benjamin.

"I still just cannot believe how big you two have gotten. It seems like only a very short time ago you were Edmund's age," said Isabelle.

"Well, I must say, it has been extremely good to have you all here. Remember, you are always most welcome to stay with us if you are in Boston again," said Alexandre.

"Yes, and you will have to come and visit soon. What with everything going on, Boston promises to be a great site of activity," added Sebastian.

"We will definitely have to come and visit again, won't we Emma?"

"Yes, but you have been much too kind to us. We certainly thank you for that," replied Emma courteously. After all, the whole stay had not been horrible. Emma had been able to meet her two other cousins and was able to catch up with this part of her family.

The rest of breakfast followed in much the same manner and soon, with William awake and breakfasted, the three Huntington children were on their way southward.

Chapter 3
Introduction of the Widow Dillingham

The journey was long and extremely uncomfortable. There was snow during much of the trip and the snow had made the condition of the roads very poor. Because of this, they didn't reach Maryland until quite a few days later. Emma had never been so glad to get out of a carriage in her life.

Benjamin and Emma had said very little to each other during the trip. Both of them still remembered their argument from the other day; though neither brought it up, neither had forgotten it either. Emma remembered her father and his stubbornness. Both she and Benjamin had inherited this trait from him; this was both a good and bad trait, which caused them to hit heads on more than one occasion.

The journey from Boston to Maryland lasted not quite two weeks. They stopped briefly from time to time to eat. They mainly slept in the carriage, as they wanted to press on. Alexandre was well connected and for this, Emma was grateful. He had connections all along the coastline and the travelers were able to simply obtain new horses each time they stopped and required it. This meant that they didn't have to stop for as long and they could continue their journey, thus reaching their destination more quickly.

Finally, on a cold day in early December, the three travelers gratefully reached Maryland. Emma was especially glad to reach a brief stopping point. She was growing increasingly fatigued from the long carriage ride not to mention that she and Benjamin were still not on the best of terms. They often lost their tempers with each other during the long hours spent in such a small proximity. They tried to contain their irritation with each other so that William did not catch on, but this was becoming ever more difficult. It would do them all good to expand their distance from each other for a while.

Benjamin got out first, and then helped Emma out. William hopped down right after Emma. No sooner had they gotten out of the carriage than a man and woman came running out of the house to greet them accompanied by two children, and two or three people that looked like servants. The house was a little ways out of the city and reminded Emma of their own estate in England, though it was much smaller.

The man and woman – their Uncle Peter and Aunt Margaret – were both in their forties. Margaret looked a lot like Emma's mother. She had the same facial features and small body type as Elizabeth did. However, it seemed that Margaret had lost the girlish figure that she once had. Peter, on the other hand, reminded Emma of William's overstuffed toy bear. He was a large man and fairly broad, though not portly.

Peter came out and shook Benjamin's hand and gave Emma a quick hug. He then picked up William and put him on his shoulders. Their Aunt Margaret was almost as affectionate. She gave both Emma and Benjamin hugs and then took Emma by the arm and began talking very quickly to her about how glad they were to see them. Emma and her aunt were joined by a younger girl, perhaps ten or eleven years old. Emma was introduced to the child and found she was her cousin and that her name was Bianca. A boy, that resembled his father immensely, was dragging Benjamin into the house. He looked to be about fourteen or fifteen years old. Emma soon found his name was Christopher.

They were brought immediately into the house and given warm tea and a place by the fireside.

"You must be frozen to the core," said Margaret. "You just sit there and warm up now. Oh, so you have met Christopher and Bianca. This is Joseph; he's just turned nine. The other two, Maria and Nell are already asleep. They wanted to stay up to wait for you but we had no idea how late you'd be."

"That's all right. It was a rough trip; we didn't know how late we would be either," replied Benjamin.

They all sat and talked by the fire for another hour or so and finally, half falling asleep herself, Emma announced that William needed to go to bed. Margaret quite agreed and sent them straight upstairs with Christopher and Bianca to show them where they were all sleeping. Benjamin did not follow Emma's lead however. In fact, he stayed behind engrossed in conversation with their Uncle Peter.

Christopher took William into a room at the end of the hall and Bianca showed Emma her room three doors down. Bianca was enthralled with Emma. Bianca looked just like her mother, but she had chestnut brown hair and eyes that matched. She had the same small figure that Emma had. Emma knew that in a few more years, after the awkwardness of being ten years old had passed, Bianca would be quite a striking girl.

Bianca sat on her bed and talked to Emma while Emma unpacked. She was impressed with all of Emma's dresses and commented on each one. Flattered as Emma was by this attention, she was completely exhausted and could barely keep her eyes open. She was quite glad when her aunt called Bianca downstairs. Emma bid her cousin goodnight and shut the door behind her. Emma undressed, practically fell into bed, and was asleep almost instantly.

Emma awoke the next morning feeling as though she had just fallen asleep because she had slept so heavily. The morning was bright outside and Emma was looking forward to seeing some of the countryside. There had not been much snow once they had reached Maryland. Emma got out of bed and dressed. She looked around her bedroom, noticing it for the first time. The walls were a pretty country blue. She had a four-poster bed and her bedspread was crisp and white with little blue flowers embroidered on it. The house reminded Emma of her home in England; however, the house was much smaller and filled with much more activity.

In fact, at that very moment Emma heard a crash downstairs. She stuck her head out of her room and followed the sound down to the kitchen.

"Oh Emma, I am so sorry that we woke you," said Margaret apologetically. Emma had to laugh at the situation before her. Two young girls had obviously gotten into the flour because it was now covering not only the two girls, but also Margaret, Bianca, and every wall and piece of furniture in the dining room.

"It's no problem, I was awake anyway. Is everything all right?" she asked, suppressing a giggle.

"Oh, it's nothing out of the ordinary. Now girls, out of the dining room and get upstairs and cleaned up." Margaret was exasperated, but she seemed to be able to see the humor in the situation as well. "And don't get it anywhere else girls!" she yelled as they headed out of the room and up the stairs.

"Do you want some help Aunt Margaret?"

"That's very nice of you Emma dear, but no, don't worry about it. I can get it cleaned up and I can have Mary and Prudence help me, or Helena if she would ever come in this morning."

"How is Helena?"

"Oh, she's well. She's just outside doing some morning chores. But she is as good as ever. She's engaged now you know."

"Oh?" asked Emma politely. She did not really want to hear about how her cousin was now going to live the perfect life and that she, Emma, only had so much time before her chances were over.

"He's a very nice boy and I am glad for her, but it seems so early to me."

"It does?"

"Well, she is only sixteen. I mean, there is plenty of time still."

"There is?" asked Emma, quite surprised by her aunt's attitude.

"Of course there is. Oh don't tell me that you are jumping into anything?"

"What? Oh no. I mean, no, there's no one right now."

Margaret had begun to clean up the dining room and Emma was helping her.

"Oh. It's not a bad thing dear. It will happen if it is the right time for you."

"You surprise me Aunt Margaret."

"Why? Because I think it is silly to get married for the sake of convenience? Emma dear, I was twenty-two when I got married, and I am so happy that I waited. Peter is wonderful and we have a very beautiful family. I live in a house that I love and basically, I just really enjoy my life. If I had married at sixteen, I wouldn't be where I am. I didn't even know Peter at that time and I would probably be living in either Georgia or Scotland right now."

"That's interesting; awfully different lives. But it is really wonderful that you are happy. It's just… well… there is an awful lot of pressure-"

"There is someone isn't there?"

"Sort of. I mean, there is this man; his name is Edward Findley."

"Do you like this man?"

"You see, he comes from a good family and my parents approve of him very much. He is quite a decent man and could provide...so much for me-"

"But you don't like him?"

"Oh, I do like him. Very much indeed. He is actually one of my dearest friends. The problem is that I don't love him."

"I see. There is nothing wrong with that Emma. It is very natural for you to have male friends. I mean, you really haven't had many females in your life while you were growing up. Girls, you had best be almost clean, I am coming up there in just a moment," Margaret yelled the last bit up to her daughters.

"Well that's not entirely true."

"I mean you have only had brothers, and I know you look up to Benjamin quite a lot." Emma flushed. She remembered her argument with him from before they had arrived and she felt silly now. "Emma, perhaps you should speak with Benjamin. I'm not sure what is going on, but you two don't seem quite right."

"What do you mean?" asked Emma a bit more defensively than she meant to sound.

"Just that your mother has always said how close you both are to each other and you have barely spoken to each other since you arrived."

"I've been tired. I'm sure that Benjamin has as well."

"Well, it is none of my business Emma, just think about what I said. Now, why don't you go and see the grounds a bit while I just finish cleaning up?"

Emma nodded.

"Girls, that's enough. I want you down here in one minute," called Margaret after hearing the girls giggling upstairs.

Emma took her cloak and decided to take her aunt's advice. She went outside to look at the grounds. They weren't very impressive at the moment as the trees were bare and there was a small amount of snow on the ground. However, Emma could imagine that in the spring and summer months the trees and flowers were absolutely lovely.

Emma continued to walk on for a bit and suddenly she spotted her brother Benjamin a little ahead of her. She quickened her pace so as to catch up to her brother. She overtook him quickly as he wasn't walking very fast.

"Benjamin," Emma began tentatively.

"What is it?" he snapped at her.

"I just wanted to ask you, well, actually I wanted to apologize."

"For what?"

"Well, I just think it is rather silly that we are at odds with each other for something that doesn't really affect us," she said with a little laugh.

"Emma, you don't seem to understand. This does affect us, a lot in fact," Benjamin replied with no sound of humor in his voice.

"Benjamin, I don't understand. Of course it doesn't affect us. We are British subjects and shall remain so no matter what happens with the Colonies. As long as that is so, then we have nothing to worry about."

"Emma, these people have been wronged by our King. They have suffered at his hand; they will not sit by and allow it to happen again. And, I must say I don't blame them."

"But Benjamin, this has nothing to do with us. We did not do anything to the Colonists nor do we have any business with them."

"Emma, their business is going to become the business of the world."

"What are you talking about?"

"You don't really believe that good old King George is going to let Massachusetts succeed from Britain without a bit of resistance?"

"Of course I don't. However, I don't believe that Massachusetts is any match for England."

"Unfortunately I have to agree with you. However, that is the problem those men we met are working on; them and quite a few more."

There was silence between them now. Emma wasn't sure what to say to her brother. There was now something between them that had never been there before, though Emma couldn't quite place her finger on it. She had never seriously disagreed with Benjamin before but it was something more than that, much more to Emma. For some reason his words really her heart. She felt betrayed and angry with him.

"Emma, look, I can't tell you what to believe but please, just think about what I have said today; promise me that."

"Benjamin-" Emma began.

"Just think about it; that's all I ask." Emma couldn't argue with him; she was afraid of what she would say. She merely nodded and Benjamin smiled. Emma was glad to see this, even if she still thought her brother was wrong.

They continued to walk outside until Emma could no longer stand the cold air. They headed back up to the house and just before they reached the door, something hit Benjamin on the back of the head.

"Ouch, what in the-?"

However, he didn't finish his sentence because as the pair turned to see the source of the intrusive object, something hit Emma on her arm. They then saw what had thrown the foreign objects – William, Maria, and Nell were having a snowball fight behind the house.

Emma laughed at the children but Benjamin's reaction was

a little unpredictable. He went over to the three children; he looked like he was going to hit the roof. Emma went to grab for his arm to stop him but she didn't react quite quickly enough.

He stomped over to the three children with a look of utter fury on his face. William, Maria, and Nell looked terrified. Suddenly he bent down and scooped up a handful of snow and threw the first snowball at William. Benjamin smiled broadly now. A grin spread over William's face too that now matched the look on Benjamin's face. William took off running but not before picking up a handful of snow and lobbing it back at his brother. The girls both squealed with delight and started running. Emma also headed over and joined in the snowball fight. A little while later, their cousins Christopher and Bianca came out and joined in as well.

The seven of them had a wonderful time tossing snowballs at each other for the afternoon. After about an hour, Emma found herself tired, wet, and very cold. Finally, about four thirty, Joseph came outside to tell everyone that dinner would be ready in a little more than an hour.

"Emma, don't go!" protested William and Nell.

"No, I have to. I am soaked through and freezing. I'll see you at dinner. You had all best come in soon as well," replied Emma as she went into the house.

As she entered the house, she removed her cloak and shoes, not wanting to drip all over the floor. As she started upstairs, Emma saw her cousin Helena and her Aunt Margaret.

"Have a good time dear?" asked Margaret.

"Oh, yes. It was quite fun," replied Emma panting a little and very flushed in her face. Margaret smiled but Helena gave her a strange look that Emma wasn't sure how to interpret; if she had to guess, it was a look of distaste. She did not hang around to determine this though. "I'm just going to head upstairs and change before dinner."

"Of course, we'll see you in a bit," replied Margaret.

Emma smiled and continued up the stairs. As she reached the top, she heard her cousin say something.

"But Mother, you see. This is what I am talking about. It is such a poor example for Maria and Nell, but especially for Bianca."

"Dear, I think you are overreacting," replied Margaret not seeming to take much heed of her daughter's worried state.

"Ever since they arrived, all I have heard about is Emma this and Emma likes that and she speaks so exquisitely and so on."

"Helena dear, she just arrived yesterday and, if I do say so myself, I think that you are jealous of her."

"I am not. I just don't believe that she is setting a good example going outside and acting like she is six years old."

"Helena, she is a well-bred and gracious young lady and just because she is not doing exactly what you think is proper, does not make her any less of an eloquent young lady," reprimanded Margaret. "She is well educated and intelligent and she is extremely kind. You cannot blame her for-"

But exactly what her aunt was going to say, Emma didn't know for she heard the others enter the house at that moment that Helena and her mother stopped talking very suddenly.

Emma hurried into her room wishing she hadn't been so wet, as she had left a mark on the floor. She knew it would dry; she didn't want anyone to know she had been standing at the top of the staircase.

So she doesn't think that I am a proper young lady? Well, I will show her exactly how a proper young lady acts, Emma thought to herself.

Emma got undressed and dried off. She was soaked through to her corset. Emma then changed her clothes into her most eloquent dinner dress. The dress was a royal blue that matched her eyes. The bodice was fitted and had lace strung through the stomacher and around her collarbone. The skirt was full and had a stylish bustle on the back. This was Emma's favorite dress. Emma had worn it to dinner with the King himself not even a year before.

Just before her parents left the previous year, they had been invited to the King's dinner and ball. Benjamin and Emma had been included in the invitation. She danced with many of the men of court and had the time of her life.

Emma sighed. She missed her home in England tremendously. Of course, Emma didn't much miss her Aunt and Uncle Bradbury's home, but the Colonies were uncharted land in Emma's mind. Their practices were foreign to her and they spoke with an accent that Emma found quite common and lowly. Even the wealthiest man in these Colonies could not compare with the men of court in England.

Emma began to put up her hair and happened to catch sight of herself in the mirror. "What am I doing? These people have opened their home to me and I am trying to show them up. This is silly." Emma sighed again and took off her dress, put it away, and pulled out a more conservative and plain dress for dinner.

Emma put on a dark wine colored dress that had a plain bodice and high waist. The skirt was still full, but not as much. Emma put her hair up so that it sat low, on the nape of her neck in a small twist. She took one more look in the mirror and felt better about her decision to change clothes.

Emma set off to dinner downstairs. As soon as she entered the hallway, she ran into Benjamin.

"Hello," said Emma surprised by Benjamin's presence.

"You look nice Emma," said Benjamin with a grin.

"Thank you," replied Emma wondering if Benjamin knew what she had just been thinking about.

"Wasn't that fun?"

"It was. It has been so long since we've had that much fun," said Emma with yet another sigh.

"Yes, it has," he said offering Emma his arm more out of habit than anything, but Emma was glad of it, for it meant he was no longer upset with her. "So, how much longer do you think we should stay here?"

"Well, I'm not sure Benjamin; I wouldn't mind getting off soon."

"Uncle Peter has asked us to stay through the winter at least."

"The entire winter?"

"He figures the weather might cause us some trouble if we head off much earlier."

"Is the snow that bad south of us?"

"He says it's deep in northern Virginia and even the mail has been having trouble getting through. I guess they had a pretty big storm last week."

"I didn't expect to stay quite so long here."

"No, nor did I, but I think it is as good of a place as any Emma. I mean, I don't think we should stay the entire winter but I don't think it would hurt to stay through Christmas at least."

"Christmas is still an awful long ways away."

"Not really, it is the beginning of December now; it's really only less than a month. Besides, my main reason for wanting to stay is William."

"What about William?"

"Well, he likes it here. I think it is a good place for him. He's happy here."

"He is happy here," said Emma in agreement. "And I suppose it isn't that long until Christmas, and it will be nice to spend Christmas with family."

"I think so too. That's why I have already sent a letter to Mother and Father explaining our decision."

"You already sent them a letter, before you even asked me?"

"Well, I had to send them a reply Emma."

"A reply to what Benjamin?" asked Emma becoming quite angry.

"Their letter. There was one waiting for us when we arrived."

"Why didn't you tell me?"

"I don't know. I just forgot Emma. It is in my room; you may read it after dinner tonight. To paraphrase, they are not happy we didn't tell them about our decision, but they are glad we are safe and have found our family in Massachusetts and Maryland. They think that we should stay here until the weather is better as well. Mother suggests March."

"March?"

"Yes, but I think she is being overcautious. You know Mother. Father thinks we should stay until after the holidays and the New Year."

"But, how did they-"

"Find out about everything? Father said that Uncle Alexandre wrote to him upon receiving our, rather, your letter." Emma blushed but knew that Benjamin wasn't angry at all with her. After all, things had certainly worked out for the best because of those letters. However, Emma wasn't so sure about staying quite so long; she had been looking forward to seeing their mother and father for Christmas.

However, Emma didn't have any more time to reply to Benjamin because they had entered the dining room. Their Uncle Peter was sitting at the head of the table speaking to their cousin Christopher about something, but Emma couldn't quite hear what it was. Bianca, Maria, and Nell were also sitting in their respective places at the table.

Benjamin pulled out Emma's chair for her and then took his own seat on the other side of the table. Emma began looking around the rest of the table.

At the head of the table was her uncle and on his left was an empty chair that Emma knew belonged to her aunt. Next to Margaret's chair were two empty chairs followed by Christopher. Emma was seated next to her cousin with William on her left and Maria at the end. The other side of the table had its own missing people. There were two empty chairs on her uncle's right side followed by Benjamin. Benjamin was surrounded on either side by empty chairs. Then came Joseph, Bianca, and little Nell.

Emma was curious to whom all the empty chairs belonged to. She didn't have to wait long however, as four people entered the room almost immediately. Peter stood and welcomed his guests. The men at the table followed suit. Benjamin practically jumped out of his own seat. This forced Emma to suppress a small giggle.

"Richard, Gregory, welcome, welcome. Please, have a seat," said Peter. Emma surveyed the men. Gregory was short and sort of stumpy, Emma thought. He had a thick neck that gave the illusion he actually had no neck at all. His hair was gray and he had a thick mustache to match. Richard, on the other hand, looked an awful lot like her uncle. He was on the tall side though not an impressive height by any means.

"Peter, it is nice to see you again. This is my wife Ruth, and my daughter Felicity," said the man called Gregory. Emma now took the women into account. Ruth was fair skinned and had faded red hair. She had a medium build but there was a shadow of a young girl in her that was still somewhat visible. However, what stuck out most to Emma, were her green eyes. They were very bright. Emma turned her attention to the younger of the two. She was the image of her mother. She, however, had bright red hair that was tied neatly upon her head. She had the same green eyes that reminded Emma of bright, glowing emeralds.

"Pleasure ladies. Please, have a seat. May I make a few introductions of my own?" The four newcomers took their seats and listened attentively to each introduction. "This is my oldest boy, Christopher and my youngest boy, Joseph," he said motioning to each one in turn. These are my three youngest girls, Bianca, Maria, and Nell."

The guests nodded to each child as they were introduced. Maria and Nell were squirming with the excitement of being addressed. Bianca was trying to look highly sophisticated and important. She kept looking at Emma out of the corner of her eye to emulate her behavior.

"These two are my nephews, Benjamin and William Huntington and this is my niece, Emma. Children, this is Mr. Lee and this is Mr. and Mrs. Dillingham and their daughter."

"It is a pleasure to meet you all," said Richard.

"Yes, thank you for having us for dinner tonight Peter," said Gregory.

"Oh Gregory, it was my pleasure. Margaret has been asking me to invite you for ages. I'm glad that you could come."

"Where is Margaret this evening?"

"She and my eldest daughter, Helena, are attending to dinner. Ah, here they are now. Margaret, you remember Richard and Gregory?"

"Of course; gentlemen," she said nodding her head to the two men.

"Margaret, it is lovely to see you again. This is my wife, Ruth."

"Ruth, of course; I met you at the Atherton's last spring."

"It is nice to see you again Margaret," said Ruth.

"And this is my daughter, Felicity," Gregory continued.

"It is lovely to meet you dear," replied Margaret.

With that, introductions were completed and dinner was underway. The table groaned under the weight of the food placed upon it. Emma had to marvel at the trouble that Margaret had gone to for her guests. She had been in the kitchen all day supervising the servants and making sure that everything was going to plan.

Dinner was going well enough. The conversations were interesting but polite, and Emma was actually beginning to enjoy herself. She became engrossed in a conversation with Christopher; all the while keeping an eye on William.

Finally, dinner was drawing to a close and no matter how well it had gone nothing had prepared Emma for what came next. Well, that wasn't quite true. When she looked back on it, she knew she should have seen it coming.

"I know Peter but the correspondence and communication between the Colonies has been strained and scattered at best, especially when it comes to complaints about the English. If we don't stand together, we will never get anywhere and you know as well as I do that would be a travesty and the gravest mistake," said Richard as he pounded his fist on the table.

"Richard, I agree but what is there to do? I mean, that little meeting in Boston has caused us enough trouble," replied Peter.

"Quite so Peter, but it was an important step in the progression of our cause," said Gregory. "After all, Sam Adams has been such an active supporter of everything."

"Yes, he has. He was really upset by those men being sent to England for trial," Margaret.

"And that is quite understandable. That was just an outright insult to the Colonies," said Ruth becoming quite incensed.

"I quite agree," said Peter, "but even Sam has said we need to lay low and let things settle a bit before we act again."

"Well, settling and waiting might be good for some, but I think it is time to act," said Richard.

"I know how you feel about this Richard; you have already expressed your views on this. However, I agree with Sam Adams on this one. He feels we need to organize ourselves a bit before our next move. Besides, Mr. Washington quite agrees," said Gregory as if this Mr. Washington's opinion settled the matter.

The strange thing was that this did seem to stop the conversation, or at least the argument.

Emma was quite amazed by all of this. The conversation itself was enough to enrage Emma, but the quite sudden and abrupt halt to the conversation took her by surprise and even curbed her anger. The table was silent now. Apparently, the conversation had grasped everyone's attention and the sudden stop had left everyone speechless.

"Well, I think it is time to send my young ones off to bed," said Margaret hurriedly. There was a murmur of agreement along the table. Margaret stood up and now that the idea was sinking in, Maria and Nell began to complain. "That's enough girls. Time for bed; say goodnight." The girls echoed goodnight to everyone. "Bianca, Joseph, you too."

Bianca's face dropped. Emma knew how she felt. It was hard being ten. You were expected to be an adult but you were still often treated like a child. However, Emma knew that Bianca would soon wish she had the readymade excuse of being a child and needing to leave. Emma felt that she was often trapped in situations.

Finally, all the children were leaving the room and Emma stood to bring William upstairs as well.

"You surely aren't retiring for the evening Emma dear?" asked Ruth. Emma desired nothing better than to say yes but she knew she couldn't get away with leaving so early in the evening.

"No, I just need to bring William up to bed. I shall return soon."

"Do I have to go to bed?" asked William as he rubbed his eyes and yawned.

"Yes, you are tired."

"No I-I-I'm not," he said yawning.

Emma laughed at her brother. "Yes you are. Come along now."

As Emma reached the staircase, she could hear her uncle inviting the men for brandy and cigars.

Emma and William reached William's room and went inside. Emma took one of the candles from the hallway and lit the lantern by William's bedside. She pulled out his nightshirt, as he got undressed. Emma waited for him to get ready. In the meantime, she pulled back his blankets for him. William climbed into bed and Emma tucked him in. Emma leaned down and kissed him goodnight and went to blow out the lantern.

"Wait," said William suddenly.

"What dear?"

"Emma, could you sit down for a moment?"

Emma gave her brother a nonplussed look but sat down on the side of the bed. "What is it dearest?"

"Are you mad at Benjamin?"

"What? No. Not at all. Why do you ask?" said Emma trying to figure out how much William could know.

"Because you seemed mad at him before." Emma couldn't lie to William. She had always been taught that no matter how terrible the truth was, it was better to be honest. She had also always told William this and how could she expect him to be honest if he saw her in such a dishonest light.

"William, I was a little angry with Benjamin before."

"But not now?"

"I am not angry at Benjamin. I do not agree with him completely though."

"So you are arguing?"

"No, we are disagreeing."

"What's the difference?" he asked. Emma had to marvel at the simplicity that youth brought to situations.

"It means that, well, that we…basically it means we we're arguing without verbalizing it."

"I don't understand."

"Honestly, neither do I dear."

"But what don't you agree about?"

"William, you might be too young to understand this but-"

"I'm not too young," William protested.

"But, sometimes people believe certain things are right and other things are wrong…"

"Like you shouldn't steal?"

"Right, just like stealing. Stealing is wrong. So is breaking things that belong to other people, right?"

"Right," William replied happily. It was apparent he was enjoying being able to understand and keep up with Emma on such an adult topic, as Emma had explained it.

"Well, a couple of months ago, some men from the Colonies broke a ship from England."

"Why?"

"Well…I don't know for sure actually."

"Well if they didn't have a reason, then it was definitely wrong and they shouldn't have done it, but maybe they had a really good reason." Emma stared at her brother. He had a point. Then again, they really couldn't have had a reason to destroy a British schooner. "Anyway, why are you and Benjamin fighting about that? Neither one of you had anything to do with that, did you?"

"Of course not. We are just disagreeing about whether the Colonists should have done that."

"But why?"

"William, I don't know how much you know about this but people in the Colonies don't think that they should have to listen to King George anymore."

"How come?"

"That is something that I really don't understand."

"But there must be a reason?"

"I'm sure there is, but whatever it is they don't think they should have to listen to the King anymore and they are doing things that aren't right because of it."

"I don't really understand Emma."

Emma sighed. Her brain was beginning to hurt. "Neither do I dear, but it is time for you to go to sleep, and I need to get back downstairs. I have been away much too long, I will be missed."

"All right, goodnight Emma," he said as he rolled over and closed his eyes.

"Goodnight my love," replied Emma.

"Oh, and Emma?"

"Yes?"

"I really like it here. Everyone is so nice."

Emma smiled. "I'm glad dear. I like it here too. Goodnight."

"Goodnight."

Emma leaned over and blew out the candle and left the room. She was fairly perplexed about the conversation she had just had with her younger brother. However, she didn't have much time to think about it as she knew she was surely being missed.

By the time Emma returned to everyone else, the women were sitting in the parlor having an after dinner drink.

"Emma, would you like a night cap?" asked Margaret.

"No thank you. I'm fine."

"What took you so long? I was starting to think you had run away," said Ruth.

"Oh no. William just wanted to speak with me. It is rather difficult for him to be so far from Mother and Father for so long now."

"Oh, of course. I couldn't imagine being so far away from my own children, especially for so long…" and Ruth was off discussing this new topic.

Emma nodded in the appropriate places but really wasn't listening intently.

After a few minutes, Emma was able to sneak away for a moment. However, she was caught by Felicity before she reached the doorway.

"I'm sorry to bother you, but may I beg a moment of your time Miss Huntington?"

"Oh, of course Miss Dillingham," said Emma feeling a bit incensed but trying to feign patience.

"Please, call me Felicity."

"All right. You may call me Emma."

"Emma, thank you. How are you liking Maryland so far?"

"It's all right. We just barely arrived so I haven't seen much of Maryland I am afraid. Are you from here?"

"What? Oh no. I am from North Carolina."

"Oh…. Forgive me, but what are you doing in Maryland?"

"My father attended a meeting in Boston. From what your aunt tells us, we were almost directly behind you."

"Most certainly. But are you continuing your trip?"

"Eventually. My father is going to be headed to Pennsylvania but he wanted to bring my mother and me to Maryland to stay with his mother… my grandmother."

"So you are going to be around for a while then?"

"Yes, it certainly seems so."

"Where is your father headed to in Pennsylvania?"

"Philadelphia."

"I see."

"So, you have two brothers then?"

"Yes, only two. Benjamin and William."

"That's lovely."

"Do you have any siblings?"

"No, I am an only child," Felicity replied.

"I see."

"So, your parents are in Williamsburg then?"

"Yes, they have been there together for about a year now."

"Do they like it?"

"I believe so."

"Wait a moment, are your parents James and Elizabeth Huntington?"

"Yes."

"I've met them. Yes, I have actually stayed with them while my parents and I were in Williamsburg last summer."

"You did?"

"Yes. They are lovely people. My father speaks very highly of your family. I am glad to finally meet you then."

"You flatter me."

"No, not at all I'm sure." There was a pause in the conversation. "So, how old is your eldest brother?" Felicity asked as her cheeks flushed.

"He just turned eighteen last June," replied Emma without much notice. Emma heard the clock in the hallway and was glad to hear it ring ten o'clock. "I think that I am going to retire for the evening. I am extremely tired. I do hope you will forgive me."

"Of course. Thank you for the conversation. I am sure I will be seeing you during the rest of your stay here."

"I look forward to it," Emma replied. She then bid her goodnights to the others and headed upstairs toward her room.

Before entering her room, she snuck into William's room to check on him. She was glad to see that he was completely asleep. She bent down and gave him a small kiss on his forehead and then went to her own room.

Emma got undressed silently and almost fell into bed. She was asleep almost immediately. It was merely too bad she didn't stay asleep that night...

Emma awoke with a start. She had been having a strange dream but she couldn't remember much of it now. It had something to do with Benjamin and another man that Emma didn't know. She felt very tired still but her mind was completely awake and racing. Emma rolled over and briefly wondered what time it was. It seemed very late. Emma tried to go back to sleep but she had a difficult time turning her brain off.

After a while, Emma determined that her struggle to return to sleep was useless for now and thus decided to get up and get some water. She went over to her bedside table but found that the pitcher was empty. She was a bit put out by this but still wanted something to drink, and so Emma pulled on a robe over her nightdress and put on her bed slippers. She took the candle from her bedside table and lit it from one of the lanterns in the hallway.

Emma found her way down the hall and reached the staircase. From the staircase Emma heard voices downstairs. She didn't want to interrupt anything so she made her way down the stairs and tried to stick to the shadows near the wall. Emma continued to head toward the parlor where an extra pitcher was always kept and got a glass of water. On her way back, Emma again tried to stay inconspicuous but after catching a bit of the conversation ensuing inside, she stopped suddenly outside the study.

"I just don't know. That verges on treason Richard."

"And nothing else we've done has verged on treason?" asked another man and everyone gave a hearty laugh.

"Peter, the time has come. We can no longer standby idly whilst the British troops traipse about over the Colonies, while we are taxed into poverty by the King, and yet we have no representation in Parliament," said a man that Emma did not know.

"John, I understand your feelings but we stand no chance right now. Ben Franklin himself says that until the Colonies stand together we stand no chance," said yet another man whom Emma did not know.

"Ben Franklin is not the be-all end-all in American policy," replied the man named John.

Emma felt badly listening to a conversation that she was surely not meant to hear but she was held to her hiding spot by a fervent curiosity.

"What actually upsets me the most is this taxation on tea. It is utterly ridiculous that the Colonies are subjected to such unfair levies, but we are not able to collect one shilling from the British on our goods, not to mention the huge debt that England still owes to us from the French and Indian War," said yet another man Emma did not know.

"Well gentlemen," said Peter after a pause in the conversation, "I think that we have accomplished much tonight and the hour is growing quite late. I move to disband for tonight and reconvene next week."

"I think that is a good idea Peter. Tempers are running high and the candles are running low."

"All right. Well, goodnight then," said Mr. Lee.

Emma froze. She was in the middle of the hallway and the men would be coming face to face with her in seconds. Emma didn't have time to run upstairs and she would be spotted for her eavesdropping. Emma turned quickly and headed back toward the parlor.

After Emma had only gone a few feet, the first of the men entered the hall. The others followed him and Emma was surprised to see so many people. After a quick count, Emma found that there were nearly ten men, most of whom she did not know.

The men were still very busy with discussions, though their topics had shifted to business and such other things. Peter was bringing up the rear of the group and walking with the men to the door. The other men were almost to the front entryway, but Peter turned and looked behind him. Emma could have sworn that he saw her, but he said nothing to her and did not acknowledge her at all. He put his arm around one of the other men and walked him to the front door.

Emma could hear the men leaving but she did not wait around. She left her hiding place and went back to the stairs. She then hurried up them and went straight to her room shutting the door behind her. Emma felt as though someone had taken her air away from her. She absentmindedly drank the water that was still in her hand and stared at the floor. If her mind was racing before she had gone downstairs, it was nothing compared to how fast she was thinking now.

Suddenly there was a knock at the door. Emma almost dropped the water glass she was holding. She set the glass down and went over to the door.

"Emma, it's Peter. May I come in?"

Emma looked down at herself. She was still wearing her robe and bed slippers. She went to her door and opened it.

"Uncle Peter, yes, please come in."

Her uncle took a deep breath. "I am not a man to stand on pretense, and so I shall not prevaricate."

"All right," said Emma taken aback by her uncle's behavior. He was usually an agreeable and tolerant man, so it was odd for him to be so candid and forthright; especially with Emma, considering they had just recently become well acquainted even though they were family.

"May I sit down?"

"Please," said Emma gesturing to the chair under her desk. She then sat down on the bed taking off her bed slippers before she sat down.

"How much did you hear?" he asked in an extremely serious tone.

"I'm sorry?"

"How much of the conversation in the study did you hear?"

"Uncle Peter, I am really sorry. I was thirsty and wanted a glass of water. I was coming back from the parlor as your guests were coming out. I didn't want to be an inconvenience and I am certainly underdressed to see strangers, so I decided to wait in the hallway until everyone left," said Emma quite quickly.

"Emma, I am not upset with you dear, I merely need to know how much you overheard."

"Not too much really. I merely heard Mr. Lee lamenting about levies."

"Is that all?"

Emma nodded even though it wasn't the complete truth. She had heard a bit more and though she didn't exactly know why, she didn't feel as though she wanted to admit that to her uncle at the moment.

"All right. I need to ask you a favor now."

"What is it?"

"I need you to not tell anyone about what you saw or heard tonight: not a word to anyone."

"But why?"

"Because a lot of people could get into a lot of trouble if the wrong people found out that we met tonight."

"Like who?"

"That's really not any of your business," snapped Peter with his temper raising.

"I'm sorry. I didn't mean to intrude. Of course I will promise. You have my word," Emma replied with surprise at her uncle's temper.

"Thank you. Emma, you may be seeing a few things in the next few months that you will not understand, but I ask that you trust both your aunt and myself and I will continue to ask that you remain silent about all of it."

"I am afraid I don't understand."

"Emma, there are many things that are going on in the world that you may or may not be aware of. However, as long as you are my guest, I will ask that you keep your vow of confidence."

"Uncle Peter, although I may not agree with your philosophy, you have my word that I will not breathe even a hint of what is happening here."

"That is all I can ask of you. Thank you."

"May I ask you a few questions though?"

"You may ask; though I will not promise to answer."

"Of course. Who were all of those men?"

"They are all men who are not in agreement with the crown."

"I don't understand why you feel the crown is such a horrible institution."

"Because no man should be subservient to another merely because of his bloodlines."

"But then you and the others must certainly disagree with the practice of slavery?"

"That is, unfortunately, a difficult question to answer. I myself disagree with the practice of slavery."

"And the other men?"

"Each has his own ideas."

"But surely that must unnerve you?"

"Emma, you will learn that when you need to band together for a specific common goal, often your politics on other issues must fall by the wayside for some time. You have to set priorities."

"I am not sure that I entirely agree with that."

"You are young still, Emma. I am afraid that you still have much to learn about compromise."

Somehow Emma felt that it was her uncle that had much to learn but for the moment, remembering that she was his guest, she held her tongue.

"Are those men all from Maryland?"

"No, not all of them."

"That one man, John I think his name is, he sounds very impatient."

"Mr. Adams is also young and impertinent, however he is now passionate and dedicated and probably just what we need."

"Is he a relation of Mr. Samuel Adams?"

"Yes, they are cousins. Do you know Sam Adams?"

"I met him in Boston at my Uncle Alexandre's home."

"Of course. If there isn't anything else, I think that I need to turn in for the night, and I am sure you must be tired as well."

Emma smiled but said nothing.

"Well, goodnight then."

"Goodnight Uncle Peter."

Peter left his niece's room and pulled the door shut behind him. Emma stood again and pulled off her robe. She then pulled back her covers for the second time that night and got into bed. It took Emma quite some time before she fell asleep. Her mind was reeling with ideas, but once asleep, she did not reawake until morning.

Morning broke early. Emma opened her eyes and yawned. The sun was shining in her window but because of the winter, the rays were much weaker than Emma thought they usually were. Emma stood and dressed silently. She put on a tea dress that was pale slate blue in color. She then headed downstairs for breakfast.

"Good morning Emma," called her aunt.

"Good morning Aunt Margaret."

"Why don't you sit down and have some breakfast? We had a little bit of snow come through last night so the ground is covered, but I am heading into town today if you would like to accompany me."

"I would very much if it is not too much of an inconvenience."

"Of course it isn't dear. Helena will be coming with us. She'll never admit it but she wants to go and see Frederick."

"Who?" asked Emma before she realized how rude this sounded.

Margaret seemed to take no notice though. "Frederick Alamonté, her fiancé. He is quite a lovely boy but they so rarely are able to spend much time with each other. Anyway, she is going to spend the afternoon with him whilst we are shopping."

"All right."

"Also, I want to stop in on Mrs. Dillingham today. I promised her last night that we would." With this, Mary brought in a plate for Emma. Margaret, who had obviously already eaten, sat down with her niece. Emma wondered how much her aunt knew about the preceding night's events. "Well, I must say that Miss Felicity was quite taken with you and your brothers last night."

"Really?" asked Emma with little enthusiasm. She figured that Felicity was a lovely person but she had not been enthralled with her in the least.

"Quite so. In fact, her mother is being called away with her father and I think it is ridiculous to have her stay in that big house of her relation's with no company."

"Didn't she say her aunt or somebody was there?"

"No dear. It is her aunt's home but they are away, already in Pennsylvania."

"What is in Pennsylvania that is drawing everyone there?"

"A lot of discussion. At any rate, I have invited Felicity to stay with us as well while her parents are gone."

"Oh, that was nice of you."

"I thought that you could use some company."

"That was kind of you Aunt Margaret but I am quite well on my own."

"Mm-hmm." Her aunt then picked up Emma's finished plate and told Emma to grab her cloak. "It is chilly outside so make sure that you dress warmly."

Within a few minutes, Emma, Margaret, and Helena were all set and on their way into town.

The carriage ride was nice. Emma thought that the countryside was lovely and enjoyed the light snow that had fallen and softly blanketed the ground. Margaret and Helena were talking about Frederick and many others whom Emma did not know. Thus, Emma did not speak much on the way into town but listened politely and watched the passing scenery.

After about twenty minutes or so, they reached the town limits and a little further on, the carriage came to a halt in front of a small home. The house was brick and had black trim. Helena was greeted by a servant and escorted out of the carriage.

"We will be back to collect you around four o'clock Helena," said Margaret as the carriage door was closed.

"All right Mother," replied Helena, who obviously felt that four o'clock was much too early to leave her fiancée's home.

The driver started off again. In only a few more minutes, the carriage came to a stop and Margaret made to get out of the carriage. Emma followed suit and the driver helped both women down.

"Thank you Albert. We shall be finished in approximately two hours."

"Very good mum," replied the driver.

Margaret and Emma headed down the very busy street. Both sides of the street were lined with stands that sold just about anything and everything that Emma could imagine. Some had different foods including freshly baked breads and rolls, nuts, fruit – although the fruit did not look too good; it was, after all, November – and more. Other stands carried jewelry, paper, quills, and much more. Also, most stands had stores behind them so if you didn't find what you wanted, you could certainly go inside and look there as well.

"I don't like to take the carriage down here. First of all, it is much too crowded with people so you hardly move, and I do so enjoy wandering about."

"Of course," replied Emma still enthralled with the set up of the street. "That is completely understandable."

The women continued down the street. Margaret stopped every so often to pick up this and that and made a few purchases here and there. The women then stepped into a shop that carried ink, quills, paper, and the like. Emma always loved these sorts of stores. They reminded her so much of books and she loved the different ink colors and types of quills. Emma decided that she could purchase a new quill and bottle of ink as well as a bit of parchment for letter writing.

In the back of this store, the man had a small supply of books that were for sale. Emma shuffled through the books for a bit and found one that she would have absolutely loved to have. However, books were expensive and she knew it would be frivolous to buy something so extravagant right now.

"What is that Emma?"

"Oh, it is only a book I was looking at," replied Emma with a bit of melancholy in her voice and a small sigh.

"Do you read much?" asked Margaret as they exited the shop.

"I used to read all the time. I love reading, but there has been a lack of books for me to put my hands on of late. Also, Aunt Sylvia and Uncle Charles don't particularly enjoy reading and don't have many books in their home." Her aunt smiled at this but said nothing. "I was thinking of getting my Christmas presents today, but I do not know what to get for your children."

"Emma, you needn't get anything for my children, nor for your Uncle and I."

"Now that we have been civil, let's be honest, what do they like?"

Margaret laughed but finally the two decided to shop together for presents for the upcoming holiday.

Emma had a wonderful day. She enjoyed walking around and looking at all of the splendid items to purchase. The cold air was exhilarating to her as well and the company of her aunt was magnificent. Margaret and Emma ate lunch at a little café on the same street as the little shops. Emma had never eaten at a place like this before. The day reminded her of one that she would have spent with her mother.

As they were eating lunch, a man came to the table where the women were sitting.

"Excuse me," said the man.

"Well, Jeffrey Ainsworth, is that you?" asked Margaret.

"One and the same."

"What are you doing down here?" Margaret asked as she stood and hugged the young man whom Emma had met briefly in Boston.

"I was up in Boston but I am now heading southward to take care of some business."

"Where are my manners, Jeffrey Ainsworth, this is my niece, Emma Huntington."

"Yes, we had the pleasure of meeting in Boston," said Mr. Ainsworth.

"It is nice to see you again Mr. Ainsworth," replied Emma.

"I must admit that I am surprised to see you here," said Jeffrey Ainsworth.

"Well, we are heading to Virginia and it was logical to stop and stay with my aunt and uncle," Emma stated.

Jeffrey Ainsworth smiled. "Well, how long are you going to be in town?" asked Margaret.

"Just a couple of days."

"Do you have dinner plans tonight?"

"I do as a matter of fact. My brother is in town as well, but just for tonight, so we are going to have dinner together."

"And tomorrow?"

"I must admit that I am pretty busy and much engaged the entire time I am here."

"That is too bad; I would so love to have you out to the house."

"I tell you what, I can't promise but if I have a free moment, I will come out to your house and see everyone."

"All right, I suppose that will have to suffice then." Margaret and Mr. Ainsworth laughed together.

"Well, I must be going. Mrs. Seager, Miss Huntington, it was a pleasure to see you both."

Both women bid the young man so long and finished lunch.

Finally, the two women gathered up their purchases and headed back to the carriage. Albert loaded the packages into the carriage and Margaret and Emma entered still chatting away about the afternoon as well as about Mr. Jeffrey Ainsworth.

"Albert, we will be going over to the Widow Dillingham's home. It is on Fourth and Pine," said Margaret as she settled herself in.

"Of course, ma'am," replied the driver.

"Emma dear, I am so excited for you to meet the Widow Dillingham. Gregory's mother is a delightful woman. She is quite old I must say though. She is probably the oldest person I have ever met, oh not that that makes any difference, it is just a nuance you see," said Margaret babbling onward.

It was strange to Emma. Emma was not one to spend her afternoons gossiping away about Mrs. So-and-so's dress or Mr. So-and-so's affairs and so she often found daily conversation babble to be pointless and tedious, but her aunt was so animated when she spoke that it not only held Emma's attention but Emma found herself actually enjoying it at times.

"I am looking forward to meeting her."

"Oh, and Felicity will be there as well. Her mother has been called away and has decided to continue with Gregory on to Philadelphia. Felicity's grandmother will also be leaving soon to go to London. She returns to London about every five years or so and stays for quite a long stretch. Strange if you ask me, once on that ship was enough and I have been on the frigate more than once – which is much too much for me."

"It is such a long trip. If the Widow Dillingham is as old as you say, is the journey not dangerous for her?"

"I'm sure it is, but she is a stubborn lady and is not going to be deterred easily. Anyway, I have decided to ask Felicity to come and stay with us after her grandmother leaves. That house is much too large to be in all alone, especially for such a young girl."

Emma had already heard her aunt say this, but she was enjoying the conversation so much, she didn't mind.

"How old is Felicity exactly?"

"I believe that she is seventeen."

"I see. You think highly of her family, do you not?"

"Gregory is one of Peter's dearest friends. He has been to our home many a time and I have grown to respect him and esteem him very highly. I have only just met Ruth myself but Peter has always spoken very highly of her from the times he has stayed in North Carolina with them."

"They seem like a lovely family."

"They do, don't they?" With Margaret's final words, the carriage came to a halt in front of a lovely and large manor that rested right in the middle of town. Emma had a feeling that it had been one of the first homes built in the town, especially considering its location.

The house was brick, which seemed to be the style of the area. It had at least three floors from what Emma could tell from the outside and then one final floor that sat only over half of the house. Emma assumed the top floor was the servant's quarters. The shutters were a very pretty blue and the front door matched the shutters. Outside, there was a small wrought iron fence that

surrounded the front yard leaving a trail to the front door for
visitors. The fence was completely for decoration though, as it
was not more than three feet high and could easily be jumped
over if someone had wanted to.

Margaret and Emma were greeted by a doorman and stepped
out of the carriage. Emma followed her aunt up the front walk
and they were let into the house. Upon entering, Emma saw the
front hall. The staircases surrounded the main entry hall leaving
the ceiling open so that Emma could look all the way up to the
top of the house. The staircases were marble as well as the floor
in the entry hall.

Margaret pointed toward a powder room and gestured for
Emma to use it if need be. However, Emma was sure that she
looked all right since the carriage ride had not been too long. Her
aunt smiled at her as she continued to look around.

A well-dressed servant, as far as servants were concerned,
came to them and asked them to follow her to the parlor. Emma
followed her aunt and they headed toward the parlor. All the
while, Emma was marveling at the artwork she saw scattered
upon the walls. The house was breathtaking.

Margaret and Emma were announced and entered the parlor
to find Felicity sitting with an older woman whom Emma
presumed to be the Widow Dillingham. Margaret went directly
to the older woman and bade hello to her. She then introduced
Emma and the two of them were offered a seat. Margaret and
Emma sat down after saying hello to Felicity as well.

Emma looked around the parlor. The room was a deep wine
color. The furniture fabric was all based in cream colors and
the wood furniture and hardwood floor were a dark mahogany.
There was also beautiful artwork in this room as well including
a portrait of what Emma assumed was the older woman as her
younger self.

The portrait was striking. The woman in the portrait had dark chestnut colored hair and bright green eyes; the same eyes, in fact, that had been passed on to Felicity. The woman's skin was extremely fair but this only accentuated her other features. The woman in the portrait was beautiful.

"That was me, you know dear," said the old woman in Emma's native accent. Emma then turned her attention back upon the woman sitting in front of her.

"It is a very beautiful portrait," said Emma sincerely. The woman sitting in front of her still had a shade of the beauty she had once maintained in her earlier life. She was quite fair skinned, in fact, both in the portrait and now in front of her; it was possible that only Emma herself rivaled the woman's fair skin. Her hair had turned from deep brown to silvery white but her eyes still gleamed in green, though they had faded from time.

"Thank you. I must say that you are quite lovely yourself my dear." The old woman spoke clearly and eloquently.

Emma flushed immediately which seemed to satisfy the old woman.

Tea was brought in shortly afterwards and served by Felicity at her grandmother's command. Conversation was light but interesting enough. Felicity did not speak much at all. Emma would have wagered that she did not speak more than five words during the entirety of the afternoon. This struck Emma oddly though she did not know why.

"I am told that you have just arrived from England."

"Yes," replied Emma. "We arrived in Boston a little over a month ago, at the end of October."

"Ah Boston. Is it still such a fanatical town?"

"It is busy."

"I do not wish you to think me forward, but at my age that is not a major concern, so I must ask why you left England in the first place."

"My brothers and I left England to rejoin our parents. They are living in Williamsburg right now."

"Her parents are Elizabeth and James Huntington," said Margaret.

"Your sister, Elizabeth?"

"Yes, my youngest sister. Do you remember meeting them?"

"I may be old Margaret, but I am not senile." The old woman seemed quite put out and Emma did not like the turn of the conversation; yet she also felt as though she wanted to laugh at the abruptness of this comment. "I met your parents soon after they first arrived here in the Colonies," the old woman finished turning back towards Emma.

"Did you?" asked Emma, for lack of anything better to say.

"Yes. They are lovely people. I am glad to finally have a chance to meet their daughter whom they speak so much about. You are even lovelier than they said you are dear."

Emma blushed yet again but did not speak.

"I have a good sense of people so you needn't think that a high compliment. Rather it is merely truth. I also don't just mean lovely in your attractiveness. You seem a good soul," she concluded.

"Thank you, but you flatter me extremely far beyond what I am worthy of," replied Emma still blushing furiously.

"Nonsense. I do not speak in flattery. I speak in truth and truth alone. You can do that when you are an old, rich woman, like me."

Emma did not know whether to laugh or not at this statement.

"I was wondering, Felicity," said Margaret, mercifully changing the subject for Emma, "if you might come and stay a turn with us once your grandmother has left for England?"

Felicity brightened a little and looked toward her grandmother but still said nothing.

"I think that is a fine idea. Then you won't be alone here in my house and wandering about aimlessly," stated the Widow Dillingham quite matter-of-factly. Felicity smiled but not too much so as to seem overeager.

"Well good, now that is settled," replied Margaret.

Emma was watching the whole situation unfold before her. She had the strangest feeling that Felicity's happiness at staying with Margaret and Peter did not have much to do with their family, but rather more so with Emma's immediate family.

After a while longer, tea was cleared away and Margaret disappeared with Felicity to do some things for her grandmother. Emma stayed with the elder Mrs. Dillingham in the parlor.

"So, how do you like the Colonies so far?"

"They are all right, though they are certainly not home."

"Ha ha, that is quite so, quite so. The Colonies are a far cry from England. Tell me, what of your brothers?"

"What would you like to know about them?"

"Whatever you wish to share my dear," replied the woman coyly. Emma knew this was some sort of a test that she was being subjected to.

"I have two brothers," she began confidently.

"I see."

"My elder brother is Benjamin. He is just turned eighteen a few months ago. He looks much like a younger version of my father."

"His education?"

Emma found this a strange question.

"Benjamin, as well as myself, was educated by private tutors from five years onward. Benjamin ended his education at the age of seventeen soon after we went to live with my other aunt and her husband."

"Why did you move in with them?"

"We moved in with them after our parents came to the Colonies. We both continued our education until the summer holiday. Benjamin only turned eighteen this summer."

"And your other brother?"

"My younger brother, William, is five years of age. He only began his education less than a year ago, but whilst we are traveling I am trying to continue it so he does not fall too far behind."

"That is very good of you."

"It is nothing but prudence as I simply do not wish for him to fall behind because we are not in the midst of our parents. Thankfully, he is very bright. He will, of course, return to formal education as soon as we reach Williamsburg."

"Of course," said the old woman. It was almost as if she were considering every word that Emma said very carefully and analyzing it, then saving it for a later date.

"From what I have been told by not only your parents but others as well, all three of you are quite intelligent."

Emma blushed but said nothing.

"You have no other siblings then?"

"No, only the two brothers."

"Interesting."

"So, when do you set off for England?"

"In about a week. I wish to ask you a favor Emma," said the old woman.

"Of course, please," said Emma uncertainly.

"May I continue correspondence with you whilst I am away and call upon you when I return?"

Emma was fairly taken aback by this request. It was very bold but more so odd to Emma. What could this woman possibly want with her? However, she had nothing against the woman and felt that it would be wrong to refuse.

"Of course you may. It would be my honor if you would."

"Thank you. Now, I am going to ask you to take your leave of me. I need to rest." Emma curtsied her way out of the room and found both her aunt and Felicity just returning down the stairs.

"Your grandmother said she was tired."

"It is time for us to leave anyway Emma. We need to go and retrieve Helena. Thank you for the visit Felicity. We will see you tonight then?"

"Yes, thank you for stopping and also again for your kind offer," replied Felicity almost glowing.

"It will be our pleasure. Good day."

"And to you. Emma, I shall see you tonight." Emma nodded but did not know what tonight held for her.

"Goodbye Felicity," Emma said.

"Goodbye."

Emma and her aunt stepped back out onto the street. Margaret gave Emma a strange look of satisfaction and the two women entered the waiting carriage.

"We'll be heading back over to the Alamonté house, Albert," Margaret told the driver.

"Yes mum," he replied and the carriage set off.

"I'm sure that Helena will not be so happy for our return but I swear the two see each other far more often than either of them believes. Ah, but to be young," said Margaret.

"Aunt Margaret, when is the wedding to be?"

"They have set a date of January eighth."

"That is coming up awfully soon."

"It is. However, I think Helena has almost everything ready and decided upon now. They are getting married in our church, of course and Helena has her dress – I only have a few more alterations to do to it."

"I'm sure that Helena will make a lovely bride," said Emma,

now remembering, for some strange reason, what Helena had said about her after the snowball fight.

"I think it will be lovely. However, that reminds me, one of Peter's nieces was supposed to be a bridesmaid but she has set off to England because her grandmother is not well-"

"Uncle Peter's mother?"

"No, no. Her mother's mother. Anyhow, we were wondering if you would possibly like to step in and stand with her?"

"Me?"

"It would mean so much to all of us if you did." Margaret was gleaming with anticipation. So much so, in fact, that Emma knew she would not be able to say no to her aunt though she was certain that it had been Margaret's idea and not Helena's. Of course, Emma had to wonder how Helena felt about the whole thing.

"Of course I will. I would be honored to do so."

"Wonderful! Now, what are the chances that your brother, Benjamin would be in the wedding as well?"

"It is difficult to say; you will have to ask him," said Emma matter-of-factly. Margaret's face fell a bit. "I mean, I am sure that he would, but you will merely have to mention it to him," added Emma hastily. This seemed to be enough for Margaret at least because she resumed her discussion of the wedding plans.

Emma listened to her aunt placidly but said little else during the ride. Eventually, they reached Frederick's house. Helena came out shortly afterwards and they set off back towards home.

Helena was quiet but satisfied. Margaret announced that Emma had agreed to participate in Helena's wedding and that they would ask Benjamin upon arriving home. Helena seemed content with the news. Emma assumed that she had already been informed that her mother would be asking her cousins, Emma and Benjamin. The remainder of the ride was spent with Margaret discussing everything from the colors to the food that would be included in the wedding. When the carriage finally arrived home, Margaret was busy trying to make sure that dinner was almost ready, as they would be having guests; Felicity Dillingham was among those who would be arriving shortly.

Chapter 4
Holidays in the Colonies

Emma went up to her room to change for dinner. She was tired but pleasantly so. The day had been a long one, but Emma had enjoyed herself immensely.

One thing still troubled her as she put her purchases away that evening: why was the Widow Dillingham so anxious to keep correspondence with her? It wasn't as if the elder Mrs. Dillingham had no relations. In fact, Felicity was just about Emma's age, only a year older, so it wasn't even a last grasp at youth that the old woman craved.

"Emma!" shouted a small boy as he ran into her room.

"Well hello William, how are you?"

"I missed you. Did you bring me anything fun?"

"Actually, I did bring you something sort of fun."

"What is it? What is it Emma?" William exclaimed as he jumped with excitement onto Emma's bed.

Emma pulled out a small yo-yo and handed it to her brother.

"A yo-yo! Thanks Emma. It's great!" With that, William gave his sister a quick hug and ran out of the room to go and show his young cousins his new toy.

Emma smiled at her brother's happiness but shook her head at his enthusiasm. It had been so long ago since Emma had been that way. Emma let out a small sigh.

"Here you are. Aunt Margaret said you were back," said Benjamin from the doorway leaning on the frame.

"Here I am. How are you?"

"I am well. Did you have fun in town today?"

"I did. I picked up a few gifts for Christmas and saw Jeffrey Ainsworth. Do you remember him from Boston?"

"Sort of," Benjamin replied.

"I also met with Felicity and her grandmother."

"You saw Felicity?" asked Benjamin quickly standing straight.

"I did. She is coming over for dinner tonight," said Emma giving her brother a strange look as she tended to picking out a dress for dinner.

"She is? Alone?"

"I assume so. I mean, Aunt Margaret and Uncle Peter are having other guests as well, but Felicity's mother and father have left for Philadelphia now, and her grandmother is leaving for England in a week."

"So she is going to be all alone in town?"

"No, actually, Aunt Margaret asked her to come and stay with us while her grandmother is gone."

"Well, at least she won't be alone then."

"Why do you care, Benjamin?" asked Emma finally settling on a dress and staring Benjamin directly in the eye.

"No reason really. I just know how I would feel if you were left all alone in a strange city."

Emma didn't really believe this was the whole truth but she had no time to quiz her brother because Bianca entered to announce the arrival of some of the guests, and that dinner would be ready shortly.

"Let me change," said Emma pushing Benjamin out. Benjamin exited the room.

A few moments later, Emma entered the hall to find that Benjamin and Bianca had waited for her.

Emma, as well as Benjamin, had taken a liking to Bianca, and realized her excitement at having her older cousins in the house. Benjamin offered her his arm and Bianca took it as ladylike as she could – especially as she was quite a bit shorter than Benjamin – and the two of them headed downstairs followed by an amused Emma.

When they reached the base of the staircase, Emma and Benjamin were swept in completely different directions by the guests. Emma saw that Benjamin somehow had the fortune of running into Felicity while she was swept into a group of men having a conversation about plantations.

Emma lost track of her two brothers quickly. The house was extremely full. There were many people whom Emma did not recognize though she was starting to become more familiar with some of the numerous faces that were lining the walls of her aunt and uncle's small home.

Finally, dinner was announced and Emma, being escorted by a young man named Andrew Welsing, along with the other guests, entered the dining room. The table had been extended as far as it could go. Emma noticed that the children were eating in a different room. This included Bianca, much to her young cousin's dismay. Emma wished longingly that she could join the children in the other room.

Andrew Welsing pulled out Emma's chair for her and took his own seat that happened to be right next to Emma. Emma didn't mind sitting by Andrew, he was an amiable young man. His mother had come from England just before Andrew had been born, though his father was from the Colonies. Andrew was the eleventh of twelve boys in his family. He had no sisters. His parents had both come from wealthy families. His mother's father had been very close to the governor of New York and had held a lesser office while maintaining a large estate when they first arrived in the Colonies. Emma had been told all of this within ten minutes of meeting Andrew. Emma always found this type of display a little bit of a nuisance, but it was something that she was used to dealing with.

On Emma's other side, however, was a man whom Emma had not heretofore met. He was fairly attractive, but much older than Emma. He was wearing a wig that was the custom of the era. He seemed to be a refined man, almost aristocratic.

After dinner had begun and everyone had become engrossed in the meal and the conversation, the man leaned over to Emma and began to speak to her.

"So, I am told that you are James Huntington's daughter."

"Yes, I'm Emma Huntington," replied Emma a bit surprised by the man's curtness in his tone and manner.

"It is a pleasure to meet you Miss Huntington. I am Brent Carrington."

"It is nice to meet you Mr. Carrington."

"My wife, I am sure you have not met her yet, is over there," he said nodding his head in the direction of a middle-age woman with chestnut colored hair and eyes that matched. She still retained some of her youthful beauty, but it was obvious that her good looks were fading with her age.

Emma smiled and the woman smiled back at her.

"Mrs. Carrington and I had the privilege of meeting your parents when they were in New York about six months ago. I have not met a nicer, nor nobler, and decent pair of people as your parents."

Emma's eyes dropped, but she thanked Mr. Carrington for his

kind words.

"There is no need for thanks. My words are not compliments they are merely the truth and there is no need to thank people for the truth. Anyway, we were told about your arrival by your dear aunt and uncle and ever since we have been anxious to meet you and your two brothers."

"You certainly flatter me sir, but I am afraid we are going to disappoint."

"Nonsense Miss Huntington. You are too modest, much like your parents. However, I would be much honored to meet your brothers after dinner."

"It would be my pleasure to introduce you to them."

"Grand," replied Mr. Carrington. His attention was then directed elsewhere by some of the others at the table. Andrew Welsing caught Emma's attention again.

"Fine man, Mr. Carrington."

"Do you know him Mr. Welsing?"

"Everyone knows Mr. Carrington. He is probably one of the wealthiest men in the Colonies."

Emma knew that this piece of information was meant to impress her but it had hardly accomplished its intention. Andrew must have caught on as well however, because he continued as though he hadn't even drawn breath.

"He and his family are some of the most respected people in the Colonies as well. They come from good stock, some of the first to arrive here."

"Where are they from?"

"They are from England, same as you and I."

"No, I mean in the Colonies."

"Oh, they live in New York in a town called Cobleskill. They ride down to Maryland quite often though."

"People surely don't merely ride down to Maryland every day, do they?"

"Heavens no. Most are coming back from the meeting in Boston."

"I see," said Emma, her voice turning uncharacteristically cold.

"However, Mr. and Mrs. Carrington are returning from visiting her sister who is ill in North Carolina. Mr. Carrington has a brother here in town and so they decided to break their journey here. Quite coincidental you might say."

"Quite so," replied Emma now more sweetly upon hearing this new information.

Dinner continued in much the same fashion. There was no mention of the Colonies and England. The men discussed business such as their plantations, though Emma noticed there were a few merchants present as well. One of the local printers was in attendance as well as a bookseller. The women conversed about clothing and above all, other people. Emma despised the way that women gossiped continually about other women, discussing their hair and clothing and especially other people's personal affairs. She seldom listened to such discussions and even more rarely participated.

After dinner, Mr. Carrington and his wife approached Emma almost immediately.

"Miss Huntington, this is my wife, Cordelia Carrington."

"Mrs. Carrington, it is a pleasure to meet you."

"The pleasure is most definitely mine. I have wanted to meet you since I first met your parents. They are such wonderful people and speak so highly of all three of their children."

"As I told your husband, you flatter my family with praise surely beyond what we deserve."

"Nonsense dear. Your family is among the finest I've ever met."

At that moment Benjamin came over to see his sister with William at his side. Emma smiled when she saw them.

"Emma, I am going to bring William up to bed."

"All right but first, Benjamin this is Mr. and Mrs. Carrington. They know our parents and have wanted to meet us. These are my brothers, Benjamin and William."

"Mr. and Mrs. Carrington," said Benjamin politely nodding to them.

"Mr. Huntington, William, I am so glad to meet you both," said Mrs. Carrington. Mr. Carrington held out his hand to Benjamin and nodded ceremoniously to him. Mrs. Carrington began to fuss over William.

"Well, I need to get this one up to bed so I do beg your forgiveness for my absence," said Benjamin.

"Of course," replied Mr. Carrington.

"Goodnight William," said Mrs. Carrington. "It was very nice to meet you. Oh it has been a long time since we have had one that young in our household."

"You have children then?" asked Emma, feeling that this couldn't be too offensive of a subject.

"Yes, we have four boys."

"Four boys? No girls then?"

"No, but I long for the day when my boys are married and I can fawn over their wives and children," said Mrs. Carrington laughing.

"So your boys are not married then?"

"No. My eldest is engaged however," replied Mrs. Carrington.

"Dear, I am sorry to interrupt, but I think that Mr. Moyer requires my aid. Miss Huntington, if I do not see you again tonight, I am very glad I had the pleasure of meeting you and I am certain we will be seeing each other again soon."

"Of course dear, go on," said Mrs. Carrington as she playfully pushed her husband away. With that, Mr. Carrington went off and left the two women alone to continue conversing. "As I was saying, my eldest, Kenton, is engaged to be married to a nice girl from a good Massachusetts family by the name of Throckmorton."

"Throckmorton?"

"Yes, have you met any of them?"

"No, not that I am aware of, however I have met so many new people in this past month or so I have been in the Colonies that it is entirely possible."

Mrs. Carrington laughed.

"Yes Miss Huntington, I daresay it is possible. I know what you mean though. I dislike large parties for that very reason. Then I feel so badly when someone comes up to me in the street and says hello and I cannot even remember their name."

"I understand completely. However, I promise you I won't come up to you in the street and expect you to remember me."

Mrs. Carrington laughed again.

"Miss Huntington, I have been looking forward to meeting you for so long, I do not believe I could forget you."

Emma blushed a little; however, Mrs. Carrington pretended to not notice and continued with her family history.

"My next eldest son is Philip. Philip just turned twenty-one but he decided at an early age he wanted to learn a trade. Thus, he became an apprentice at the age of thirteen and now is employed at one of the major papers in Philadelphia."

"The one run by Mr. Franklin?"

"Yes, do you know Mr. Franklin?" asked Mrs. Carrington.

"I do, he is a great friend of our family. He has stayed in our home during his journeys to England."

"He is such a wonderful man."

"He most assuredly is."

"Anyway, my next son is nineteen. He is the spitting image of his father in most ways. He is strong-willed and stubborn but he is decent and has high morals. He is attending college at William and Mary in Williamsburg. Why, I am sure that you will meet

Cole when you reach Williamsburg. Your parents are so good to have him to dinner at least three or four times a week."

"I am sure it is their pleasure," smiled Emma.

"Well, I am glad that your parents are such wonderful people. Cole is very lucky to have met them. We are very lucky that they have taken him in so readily. Finally, my youngest, Toby, he is, well he must be about your age. He is sixteen. Toby is going to enter the service of God."

"You must be very proud of having such a successful family, Mrs. Carrington."

"To be sure I am. I thank God every day for my family's luck and success. Now, tell me about your travels, I am sure that you are glad to be stopped for now."

"It is nice to rest here but I must admit I would much rather be headed to Williamsburg. Our parents feel we should stay here until the spring however."

"Very sensible. I completely agree. In fact, Cole is staying in Williamsburg for Christmas as well. The weather along that road has been unpredictable at best."

Emma and Mrs. Carrington continued talking for quite some time. Emma was reminded of her mother as she conversed with Mrs. Carrington. She also enjoyed speaking with the woman as it meant she didn't have to speak with some of the other guests about any particular subject she didn't want to.

The night had been a pleasant one. When Emma finally reached her bedroom the hour was quite late. It was probably near one thirty in the morning. Emma was tired but content, and thus she easily fell into a relaxed and peaceful sleep.

***

The next few days passed in a blur for Emma. There were many people coming and going from her aunt and uncle's home but few stayed long, and Emma didn't formally meet most of them. She tried to make herself useful getting ready for the Christmas holiday. She often found herself in the kitchen helping with the baking or with the younger children trying to entertain them and, for all intent and purpose, keep them out of the way.

After another week, Felicity did indeed come to stay with the Seager family. She took the room next to Emma's and was a frequent visitor at odd hours. Emma was beginning to like Felicity, however, and as her aunt had predicted, enjoyed the distractions. One morning about four days before Christmas while sitting in the parlor with her aunt and sewing a sampler, Emma decided to ask her aunt a question that had been in her mind for a while.

"Aunt Margaret," she began.

"Yes dear," her aunt answered while mending a pair of Joseph's pants.

"I have a question to ask you, and I am afraid you will find me impertinent for asking it."

"I am sure not. If it will ease your mind, you may ask me your question no matter the nature. If I do not wish to tell you the answer I simply shall not answer it."

"All right, I suppose that's fair. Do you know about Uncle Peter's late night gatherings?"

Margaret stopped sewing instantly and looked at her young niece.

"Yes. I did not realize, however, that you were aware of them."

Emma blushed immediately. "I accidentally walked by one of them during the first week we were staying here."

"Does Peter know?"

"Yes. He and I spoke about it."

"Emma, I do not know what he said to you, but I am going to ask you to not tell anyone about it, not even your cousins."

"Do they not know?"

"Helena knows and Christopher knows, but I feel the others are much too young."

"I already gave Uncle Peter my word so you needn't worry about anyone finding out," replied Emma quickly.

"Thank you dear."

"Why do all of those men come here?"

Margaret sighed and then took a deep breath before speaking. "Emma, I am not going to pretend that you are a child, but I am afraid that I cannot confide that information in you. It would be too dangerous for you to know right now."

Emma did not answer her aunt. She didn't know why she had even brought up the subject; she was merely curious and felt this was an opportune time to ask.

"Now, are you all ready for Christmas?" asked Margaret trying to change the subject gently.

"I believe so. I know that William is getting anxious for it to be here."

"Good. We will be having dinner Christmas Eve with the Carrington's, and then going to church that night. Christmas day we will spend at the house and we will have an early dinner. Is that all right with you?"

"That will be fine. It sounds much like how we spend Christmas at our home."

"I surmised as much."

Later that day, Emma decided to go out for a brief stroll as she had been inside for about three days. She grabbed her cloak and muff and went out into the chilly air. Her cheeks flushed immediately and she could see her breath in the air. It was certainly winter now; though Emma was not used to such cold winters. The winters in England were usually very wet but not typically so cold.

Emma headed for the garden path and followed it for about five minutes when she came upon a scene that she was not meant to see. Benjamin was seated on a bench with his back to her. Sitting next to him was none other than Felicity. They were holding hands and had just finished a soft kiss. Felicity was flush, but Emma was not sure whether it was from the cold air or from the possibility of her corset laces loosening slightly within the past minute.

Emma did not wish to embarrass the two however, as it was a compromising position to be in. Thus, she turned and slipped back up toward the house. All would have gone well and they would never have known her presence had it not been for the ice on the path. Emma slipped with an almighty whoosh and fell to the ground. Both Benjamin and Felicity stood quickly and turned to see Emma lying flat on her back staring at the sky and seeing stars that weren't really there.

"Emma, oh my goodness," cried Benjamin as he ran over to her. Felicity was directly behind him. They reached her within seconds. Emma was all right but she had had the wind knocked out of her and she had twisted her ankle.

"Emma, are you all right?" asked Felicity with concern.

"I think so but I don't think I can walk," replied Emma now trying to stand and finding it impossible to put weight upon her right foot.

"It's all right. Put your arm around me, I've got you," said Benjamin picking her up and then proceeding into the house.

"My goodness, what's happened?" asked Margaret immediately clearing a space for Emma on the sofa and guiding Benjamin to set her down.

"It is nothing of much concern, merely a sprained ankle Aunt Margaret," said Benjamin with little sympathy in his voice.

"Bianca, go and fetch some ice and a warm cup of tea. Emma, are you all right?"

"I will be fine. I just slipped on some ice while I was out

walking. I must have turned too quickly," replied Emma as she glared at Benjamin.

"That ice is treacherous. I will have Peter take care of it when he returns home. For the time being, I want you to stay here and rest with your ankle up."

"I am really fine," replied Emma.

"Do not argue with me," said Margaret with such authority in her voice that Emma could not even begin to argue.

Bianca returned with some ice and the tea. Margaret waved Benjamin and Felicity out of the room and forced the tea upon Emma.

"Drink this," she said. Bianca carefully removed Emma's shoe and stocking. Margaret placed the ice inside a tea towel and then upon Emma's ankle. Margaret told Bianca to leave as well and then began fussing over the pillows, trying to make Emma more comfortable.

"I really am all right. It will just take a day or two to heal."

"And for a day or two, you will not move from this sofa. What were you doing outside anyway?"

"I just wanted to go for a walk, I was in need of some fresh air," replied Emma.

"Well, you are just lucky that Benjamin and Felicity were out there as well," said Margaret. Emma wanted to tell her that had they not been out there, she wouldn't have turned so quickly and would not have fallen; however, she felt that her brother would be mortified if she told their aunt about such business that involved him.

The day continued much in the same manner. The family came into the parlor to visit Emma and they even decided to move dinner as well so that Emma would not have to eat alone.

The table was set up and Emma sat with her foot propped up on an adjacent chair. On Emma's other side was Christopher and across from her was Benjamin, seated next to Felicity.

Dinner conversation was not particularly interesting. It mainly revolved around the weather. Eventually, Maria brought up Christmas. The children were becoming ever more excited and with Christmas a mere four days away, Emma couldn't blame them in the least. In fact, Emma was finding herself becoming more excited for the holiday as well.

That night, Benjamin helped Emma get up to her bedroom. Her ankle was no longer swollen, but her aunt was still making a huge fuss over the whole affair.

Emma went to pull out a nightdress and Benjamin turned to leave. Before he exited her room, however, he spoke quite suddenly and quite gravely to her.

"I know what you saw Emma and-"

"I saw nothing Benjamin," interrupted Emma.

"And I thank you for your discretion," he said as a smile slowly spread over his face. Emma blushed a little.

"It is nothing for you to worry about, but I have to ask you how serious this is?"

"It is a long story Emma."

"Do you really like her?"

"I do. She is intelligent and passionate and very beautiful."

"She is attractive, but I do not know her all that well."

"That is a shame."

Benjamin looked very embarrassed about the whole thing and Emma knew it would be best to drop the subject for now. He would confide in her when he was ready.

Benjamin left his sister to finish getting ready for bed. Emma had a troubled sleep that night and awoke early the next morning. She stood and dressed for the day. Her ankle did not give under her weight, but it was still a little sore.

After she was ready for the day, Emma went downstairs. The day was not particularly exciting; she helped her aunt bake and was able to get all of her presents wrapped.

Benjamin and Felicity were in the drawing room reading. Helena had gone to visit with Frederick for the day. Christopher and Joseph were off with their father. Margaret was flustered with the preparations for having the extra people for the holidays.

After Margaret had inspected every inch of Emma's ankle and determined it really was all right, Emma decided to go outside and watch William play with Maria and Nell. Bianca soon joined her and sat down directly next to her.

The child was still enthralled with her older cousin and often followed her whenever possible. Emma didn't mind. Bianca was rarely a bother and Emma enjoyed her younger cousin. Bianca reminded Emma of herself when she was younger. She was such a contrast to her other cousin of about the same age, Viola. Emma smiled to herself as she briefly wondered what happened had when Viola told Charles and Sylvia she knew that Emma and her brothers had left and didn't alert anyone. Even though she was sure Sylvia was glad to be rid of them, she knew Viola probably had gotten into trouble. It was unfortunate that Emma had to trick her cousin, but it was a necessary evil. Emma sighed as she thought about it.

"Emma," Bianca began sensing Emma's melancholy mood.

"Yes dear," Emma replied.

"I'm so glad that you are going to be staying for Christmas."

Emma smiled. "I am too. It will be nice to be with family again."

"Weren't you with family last Christmas?"

"I was with my aunt and uncle in England."

Emma remembered Christmas the year before. It had been a horrid event. Her parents had just left about a month before and that was still difficult for them to get used to. However, Sylvia and Charles weren't even around on Christmas Eve. They had attended some party with their friends from court leaving all the children home to amuse themselves. The next day was not much better. Sylvia and Charles were home, but Sylvia was in a poor mood from being tipsy the night before and Charles had avoided her and the rest of the family as much as he could.

"So you were with family," said Bianca.

"I was, but you have to remember my parents had just left us, it was difficult to not spend Christmas with them," was the only answer that Emma could give her cousin. After all, Sylvia and Charles were her aunt and uncle as well and it wasn't up to Emma to tell Bianca how to feel about them.

"I think it would be really hard to be away from my mother and father for Christmas."

"It is, but you make do with what you have," said Emma smiling.

"Why did you choose to come to the Colonies, Emma?"

"That is a long story."

"We have time."

Emma smiled at her young cousin. It seemed children always had time when someone didn't want to explain something to them.

"Well, my brothers and I missed our parents and we wanted to be with them. It just seemed the right thing to do."

"Father says that we all have paths to follow in life. Do you think that's true?"

"I suppose we do. I think that our choices govern our path though."

"I think so too."

After a while, Emma made the four children go into the house. Their noses were pink and their hands were now like ice. She had them go and change their clothes and then sit by the fire to warm up. Margaret soon came in with some hot chocolate for the children.

Later that evening, Peter and the boys returned home with

some decorations for the holiday. Emma loved the decorations and could smell the cold air outside. She now knew it was Christmas.

That night, Emma again had difficulty sleeping though she wasn't sure why. She did not rise quite as early, but it was not because of being asleep. The next night was the same. Emma finally got up on the day before Christmas Eve and went downstairs. She had breakfast with Joseph and Christopher.

After breakfast, Emma went into the parlor to read for a while. The weather was taking a turn for the worse outside. The snow was falling gently as Emma entered the parlor, but as Emma read, it began falling harder until she had difficulty seeing out of the window.

Her younger cousins and William were growing restless and with everyone in the parlor for the day, Margaret was becoming almost unnerved. Emma could tell it was affecting Benjamin as well. He had difficulty dealing with the whining of the children, not to mention their restlessness also made him more restless.

"Emma, why don't we go into the music room and you can play for everyone?" asked Benjamin.

Emma did not particularly like to play for anyone, but her cousins were beginning to make even her nerves unravel a bit and when Margaret jumped at the idea, Emma felt she really couldn't say much to the contrary.

"All right," replied Emma and they all followed Peter into the next room where the harpsichord was located.

Emma sat down and began to play some Christmas music. Everyone sang along and the afternoon passed quite nicely from that point onward.

After dinner, Peter and Margaret gathered everyone in the parlor and took the Christmas decorations out. Margaret allowed the children to put some of the decorations out as well. Everyone was getting into the spirit and the annoyances from the morning melted away.

Emma noticed how much Benjamin was near Felicity. Emma thought about the red haired girl that seemed so smitten with her brother. It all seemed very sudden to Emma. They had just met less than a month ago, and though they spent much time together, Emma had difficulty understanding how they could be so enamored with each other so quickly. She also wondered what her parents would say about it not to mention what would happen once it was time for them to head south.

The family finished decorating and lit the evening candles. Emma sat on the sofa next to her aunt and William lay upon her lap. It really was beautiful. Emma began to think about her parents and supposed that if she couldn't be with them, her aunt and uncle's home wasn't such a bad place to be.

Emma kissed her younger brother gently on the top of his head. At least he would have a real family Christmas this year.

Eventually, Emma told William he needed to go to bed. Bianca said she would take him upstairs and Emma agreed to come in and say goodnight before she went to bed. Joseph, Maria, and Nell followed Bianca and William. This left Margaret and Peter, Helena, Emma, Christopher, Benjamin and Felicity in the parlor together.

"So, Helena, are you growing excited for the wedding? It is only a short sixteen days away," said Felicity.

"I suppose I am. It just doesn't seem that close to now. By the way, Emma, the seamstress is coming the day after Christmas to take your measurements for your dress. I gave her approximations so I am sure she has begun to put the dress together but she'll need to have you put it on."

"Of course. What time is she coming?"

"She will be here midmorning. I would say around ten o'clock."

"All right."

"Felicity, she also has your gown done. She will be bringing it by when she comes for Emma."

Felicity blushed. Emma did not know that Felicity was in the wedding party as well. For some reason this surprised Emma.

"Well, I did not get much sleep last night, so I think that I am going to go to bed," said Benjamin. "Goodnight everyone."

"I think that I too am going to head to bed," said Margaret. Peter followed his wife and they both said goodnight but not before Margaret told Christopher he probably needed to go upstairs as well.

Helena stayed with Emma and Felicity for a while longer but not much. After she went to bed, Emma was about to say goodnight to Felicity as well but Felicity stopped her.

"I was wondering if we could chat for a moment?" asked Felicity.

"I suppose so. What do you wish to talk about?"

"I want to talk to you about your brother."

"Oh?" asked Emma.

"Well, I know that you saw…" she began, but quickly blushed and couldn't finish her sentence.

"Felicity, please, er, don't worry about…anything. I can assure you of my discretion."

"Well, er, thank you Emma. I appreciate that."

"Please, don't mention it. It is nothing to concern yourself with."

With that Felicity smiled at Emma and left the room, her face still red with embarrassment. Emma didn't follow her immediately; she figured that Felicity would want to get to her room before Emma got upstairs.

Emma sat down on the sofa. Her thoughts began to wander. She was glad that Benjamin had found Felicity. They seemed very happy when they were with each other. They had only known each other a short time, but they fit together so well that it seemed as though they had known each other forever. Emma's thoughts continued to wander until they reached Edward.

It had been months since she had seen him. In fact, Emma had seen him the day that they had left England. When she had left him last, he had just asked her to marry him again. Emma wondered where Edward was now. She knew that she didn't have feelings for Edward as anything more than a friendship, but was that enough? Would, as Edward had assured her many times, feelings develop as they began a life together?

Emma, lost in thought, began to pace and finally headed up to her room.

Emma paced a little more upon entering her room and then remembered she was supposed to say goodnight to William before she went to sleep. Emma doubted whether he was still awake, but she liked to see the peace that he exuded when he slept.

Emma opened her door again and went down the hall. The house was quiet. Emma assumed most of the house was asleep by now. She entered William's room and went over to his bed. She sat down in the chair in the corner and closed her eyes. Emma listened to the rhythmic inhaling and exhaling of William's breathing.

Emma startled awake. She had no idea what time it was but it was still pitch black outside so she knew it was still nighttime. Emma rubbed her eyes and stood. The candle she had brought in had melted quite a bit and had gone out. Emma made her way over to William's bed and kissed the child gently on the forehead. She then pulled up the covers and made her way out into the hallway again.

Emma relit her candle from a lantern that was always lit in the hallway. She then saw the clock also located in the hallway. *Two fifteen,* she thought. Emma made her way into her own bedroom and pulled on a nightdress. While she dressed, Emma caught two separate glimpses of light outside her window. She went over to the window and tried to find the origin of both flickers.

One of the sources was by the garden and was rather weak. Emma assumed that it came from a small kerosene lamp. She couldn't make out who was holding the lamp but there were two people connected with that light source.

The other light source was actually more than one kerosene lamp, but they were very close. Emma, again, could not make out who was holding the lamps but she could see that there was a small group and judging from their statures, the group most likely consisted of men.

She stepped back from the window and thought. Should she go and wake someone? Should she ignore it? Who could be out at such a late hour? Were the two light sources connected with each other?

Emma decided she needed to see who the owners of the light were. She put on a robe and headed downstairs with her own kerosene lamp. She made sure to keep the lamplight small and weak so as not to draw attention to herself. When she reached the back door, she pulled on her royal blue cloak and headed outside into the night's cold air.

Emma followed the small path that led to eastern most part of the grounds. There she saw the larger of the lights and found out that it was indeed as she had suspected for it was not one large light but several small lights. Emma brought her own light down as low as she could without it going out. She then ducked behind a nearby tree and listened.

"I just don't know Peter. The British already feel as though Sam is trouble. Not to mention Mr. Hancock. Did you see the paper?" asked one man.

"No, what did it say?" asked another.

"To quote they said Sam Adams is 'the most dangerous man in Massachusetts'," replied the first man.

"Nathanael, I really don't think that Sam is in any danger," said Peter.

"Mr. Greene, I must agree with Peter. However, I think it will be good for him to lie low for a little while. After his meeting in Boston, the British have been watching him quite closely."

"Yet another injustice," snorted a man that had not yet spoken.

"Gentlemen, the hour is late and we have accomplished much. I feel we should disband for the Christmas holiday. We can meet again after the New Year."

"Agreed. Gentlemen, thank you for coming tonight. I know that it is difficult to make the journey safely. Please mind your paths on the way home," said Peter.

Emma knew that she was well concealed and would not be spotted, but she took out the remaining weak light of her lamp and she remained in her place until the group of men disbanded. To Emma's surprise, however, her Uncle Peter did not pass her hiding spot but rather turned and went in the opposite direction. Emma was tempted to follow him but she already felt a little bad about her eavesdropping and so, after all the men had left the area, she headed back up to the house with no light in her lamp and quite forgetting about the other light she had previously seen from her bedroom.

Emma put her cloak back while internally hoping that no one had seen her enter or exit the house. She then snuck back upstairs to her room and shut the door. She placed the kerosene lamp on her bedside table and took off her robe. She gave one last sidelong glance out of her window and no longer saw any of the lights.

Emma crawled into bed. The hour was late but her mind was reeling. Emma lay awake with her mind spinning so quickly that she could barely make sense of it all. Finally, exhausted from her midnight stroll and the thoughts in her mind, she fell asleep again.

The next morning, Emma was awoken by the commotion of mass chaos. She got up and dressed quickly. Emma put on a plain wine colored dress; the color flattered her features. Emma placed her hair up in a low bun at the nape of her neck. She knew the day was going to be busy to begin with but from the sound of it, the day was going to be filled with much fussing and clamor.

Emma went downstairs to face the commotion. What she saw made her laugh out loud. Helena was chasing Maria. Maria was running from room to room with something in her hand, but Emma couldn't quite see what it was. Joseph was yelling at both Helena and Maria for making too much noise while he was trying to read his lessons to which Helena snapped back that it was Christmas, and he was only trying to read his lessons because he wanted to impress his new tutor because he fancied her. Bianca was screaming at Helena for being so improper and standing in the middle of the floor with tears in her eyes. William was laughing at all of them and Nell was sitting in the corner crying over the whole affair. Margaret was nowhere to be seen though, and so Emma went down to see if she could help calm the situation.

Emma stopped at the foot of the steps and cut off Maria grabbing the child and stopping her in her tracks. She forced Maria to give Helena back the object she was carrying which Emma could now see was a letter from Frederick. Helena gave her sister one last ferocious look and left the house grabbing her cloak on her way out. Emma assumed she was going to go and fetch her mother.

Emma made Maria go upstairs and change her dress as she had gotten ink all over it, which Emma assumed had come from Joseph. Maria laughed at the ink on her dress but complied with her cousin's direction. Emma told Joseph to go into the drawing room to work on his lessons. Joseph wasn't happy about being told to move but did not openly protest, and he collected his things quietly. William had stopped laughing out loud and Bianca was a bit calmer. Emma asked them to help her clean up. They both did so without any objection. Emma then went over and picked up Nell and sat down in one of the armchairs. She calmed the child down and had her help William and Bianca clean up.

By the time Helena and her mother returned, the rooms were almost clean, Maria had returned with a new dress and was helping clean as well, and all the children were again calmed.

"Emma, may I speak with you?" asked Margaret.

"Of course Aunt Margaret." Emma followed her aunt out of the parlor and into the dining room.

"Emma, thank you for handling that. Sometimes my children get a bit unruly."

"It is not a big deal Aunt Margaret. William gets the same way. Children will be children. I am glad that I could help."

"It is much appreciated," said Margaret as she sat down. "Prudence, will you fetch me a cup of tea and one for Miss Emma as well please." The servant nodded and left to go into the kitchen.

Emma took her aunt's lead and sat down in a chair across from her.

"Emma, it has been so good to have you and your brothers here. I have enjoyed the company very much."

"We enjoy being here. I still am very appreciative of all you are doing for us."

"Please don't mention it again."

"I am serious though. William has become so comfortable here and for that especially, I am sincerely grateful. I am sure that my parents are as well."

Prudence reentered with the tea and Margaret began to serve.

"I received a letter yesterday."

"Oh, from whom?"

"It was from your father."

"My father? What did he have to say?"

"Well, he was writing to thank us, of course, for caring for all of you which has been my absolute pleasure."

"Anything else?" asked Emma sensing that this was not some idle chat they were having.

"Well, your mother is not feeling well."

"What's wrong with her?" asked Emma feeling a sense of urgency.

"It is nothing serious right now, but I wanted to tell you. I felt as though you should know."

"Is she all right?"

"Your father says that she is doing well. She just came down with something, but the doctor says she should be back on her feet very soon. They told me to tell you how much they love you children and that they miss you."

Emma sat nonplussed for a moment. It couldn't be that serious or her father would have said it was serious.

At that moment the doorbell rang.

"I wonder who that could be," said Margaret. "Oh, I bet it is the seamstress. I almost forgot she changed the appointment to this morning."

"This morning? I thought she wasn't coming until after Christmas."

"She wasn't, but she said she had to come out this way anyway today and didn't want to waste the trip."

Margaret stood and left Emma alone with her thoughts for the moment.

Emma hoped her mother was all right and she worried about her. However, Emma wondered if her father was with her now. He had told them he was going to be away from the plantation for a few weeks, but had he returned yet or not?

It happened that the visitor was indeed the seamstress.

Margaret called to Felicity and Emma. Felicity's dress needed a few minor alterations so Emma consented to allow her to go first.

While Felicity climbed up on the stool so that the seamstress could fix the hem length, Emma decided she didn't really want to sit and watch. She excused herself and said she would be in the parlor reading until she was needed.

As Emma entered the parlor, she ran right into her brother, Benjamin.

"Oh, excuse me Emma."

"I'm sorry Benjamin. What are you doing?"

"Oh, er, nothing. I was just, er, looking at the decorations."

"They're beautiful, aren't they?"

"Yes."

"Benjamin, have you spoken to Margaret lately?"

"Not about anything in particular. Why?"

"Well, she received a letter from Father."

"Oh?"

Benjamin sat down and Emma followed suit. Benjamin had a concerned look on his face.

"Father said that Mother was ill."

"Ill? Is she all right?"

"Apparently it isn't too bad. I suppose Father just wanted to inform us."

"I suppose." Benjamin was obviously thinking what Emma was but neither voiced their concerns. "Well, I have some things to attend to and then Peter wanted to see me."

"All right."

But before Benjamin left, Peter entered the parlor.

"Well Merry Christmas to you both," said Peter.

"Merry Christmas," both Emma and Benjamin replied.

"How is everyone today?"

"Well," said Benjamin.

"You aren't too tired then?" asked Peter with a smile on his face.

Both Emma and Benjamin blushed but Emma was quite surprised to see that Peter's gaze was focused on Benjamin.

"What do you mean?" Benjamin asked as casually as possible.

"Ah, we all have our late night activities. You needn't worry about yours," Peter replied. Suddenly it dawned on Emma that the second light had come from Benjamin and Emma had only one guess who had been with him in the garden. "And how are you today Emma?"

"I am well."

"Good, Prudence said you fell asleep in William's room last night. She caught you in the chair in there as she headed to bed herself."

"Yes, but I woke up a bit later and went into my own room."

"That's good. I find sleeping in chairs gives you a pain in the neck. Well, Benjamin, are you busy?"

"Not at all, I was just coming to find you actually."

"Good, Emma will you excuse us?"

"Of course," Emma replied with minor relief that she had not been caught for her own midnight stroll.

Benjamin left the parlor with Peter and Emma picked up the nearest thing with words, which happened to be a pamphlet entitled *The Sommersett Case and the Slave Trade* by Benjamin Franklin. It had been printed at the end of June. Emma knew Mr. Franklin by more than reputation, so she began to read the pamphlet with great gusto.

After a while, Felicity came in to tell Emma that it was her turn. Emma put the pamphlet down and went in to be fitted for her dress for Helena's wedding.

Before Emma knew it, it was dinnertime. The Carringtons arrived, as scheduled, and Margaret served quite the feast. They had pheasant for their main course amid so many side dishes that the table literally groaned under the weight of the food.

Mrs. Carrington had happened to take a seat next to Emma's and Emma was glad for it. Emma didn't exactly know why but she felt extremely comfortable with Mrs. Carrington.

"Emma dear, tell me, how are finding Maryland?"

"I cannot complain too much. I love the countryside. It is quite beautiful but…" Emma stated but unintentionally allowed her sentence to drift off.

"You must miss England though?" asked Mrs. Carrington, though not as much in a question as an end to Emma's statement.

"I do. I miss our home. We had a lovely home with beautiful grounds."

"I'm sure you did. Your parents have spoken of their previous home and it sounds just charming."

"It really is."

At that point, dinner was winding down. Dessert had been served, Indian pudding, and the ladies were rising to change for church.

Emma went up to her room and pulled out a velvet dress in forest green with a white lace stomacher. Emma placed her blonde hair into a loose twist that allowed a few strategic strands to fall across her neck and graze her face.

Emma went to make sure that William was also getting ready, but as she entered into William's room Bianca came in and found her.

"Emma, I was wondering… Would you mind helping me?"

"What do you need help with Bianca?"

"I can't get my hair to go the way I want and Helena won't help me." The child looked like she was on the verge of tears.

"Oh dear," began Emma with a small laugh, "come here, I'll help you."

Emma brought Bianca over to the chair in William's bedroom and sat her down. Within a few minutes, Bianca was happy and William was dressed and the three headed down to get ready to leave for church.

The next morning was Christmas Day. William woke Emma up quite early, but she made him wait until the rest of the house was awake – which wasn't too long considering Maria and Nell were possibly even more anxious than William.

When all the presents were opened and everyone was starting to feel as though they could crawl back into bed, Margaret handed Emma, Benjamin, and William one final present.

Emma turned the envelope over in her hand while seeing that her brothers had each received their own letters. She looked on the back of the envelope and saw her father's seal.

William and Benjamin had already begun opening their letters. The rest of the family was dispersing to have breakfast. Emma tore open the letter breaking the royal blue seal and taking out the crisp parchment.

> *To My Dearest Daughter,*
>
> *I am so thankful that God is bringing you ever closer to your mother and I; to your new home. Though I have already expressed my displeasure at your sudden and secret departure from the care of your Aunt and Uncle Bradbury, I am very proud of what you have endured. I am also extremely grateful to your Aunt and Uncle Huntington and your Aunt and Uncle Seager for taking you in and taking care of you and your brothers.*
>
> *I am, however, sorry that your mother and I can't join you for Christmas. Presently, business is calling me away from Williamsburg yet again. I shall be leaving within the week. Again, I want you to stay in Maryland until the spring. I feel that I should tell you, things are becoming ever*

more unstable. I want you to be very cautious and mindful of your brothers – both of them.

For now, I shall content myself with your safety and wait until my family can finally return to each other and be together. I love you very much. Your mother also sends her love and best Christmas wishes. Please tell your Aunt and Uncle that they continue to be in our prayers and we wish them the best of luck. Until I see you again…

All My Love,
Father

By the time Emma had finished reading her letter, the rest of the family had left for the dining room. The three Huntington children were all that remained in the parlor.

"Benjamin, Father says that he loves and misses me and that he is excited to see us again. He says he has a big surprise waiting for me when we get to Williamsburg," said William very excitedly. "Hey, maybe Father named Williamsburg after me?!" William was completely serious, but the childish innocence of this last statement made both Benjamin and Emma laugh.

"William, why don't you go in and have some breakfast? Emma and I will be there in a few minutes."

"All right."

After William left, Emma caught her brother's eye.

"What is it Benjamin?"

"Did Father mention anything about leaving Williamsburg in your letter?"

"Yes, but just that he was leaving sometime this week."

"But where is he going, especially when Mother's sick?"

"I don't know. I think that the whole thing is strange."

"Emma, Benjamin," called Christopher as he neared the room. "Mother wants to know if you want breakfast now."

"We'll be right there Christopher," said Benjamin.

Christopher left the parlor and went back into the dining room. Emma was rereading her letter. She was looking for something that she missed. There had to be something. Where was the heartfelt Christmas message? Where was the actual message? Her father really hadn't said anything of importance after all. Really all he had said, in fact, was that they missed her, but that they didn't want to see her right now. For some reason, this letter bothered Emma immensely. Now she could feel tears start to swell in her eyes but she didn't want to cry. She wouldn't cry in front of Benjamin.

When Emma looked up to see her brother's facial expression, there was none. In fact, Benjamin had already risen from his seat and was leaving the room.

"Benjamin-" Emma began.

"Come when you are ready," was all that he said to her. He hadn't even turned to face her.

What a Christmas this was turning out to be. She had slept little. She hadn't received anything from her mother and father but a feeling of concern that was consuming her. Now she was alone in the parlor fighting back tears of which she did not know the source.

Emma rose and followed Benjamin. She placed her letter in her pocket and joined her family in the kitchen.

The rest of Christmas passed without incident. In fact, other than the visits of the Carringtons, Emma found little to amuse herself with during the next while. She was kept increasingly busy by the upcoming wedding. Between the dress fittings, helping with the arrangements, calming her aunt, and taking care of letters from different guests, Emma was kept quite busy.

The New Year too passed with a haze of excitement and bustle and with the wedding now only a week away, the entire household was beginning to feel the pressure as well as Helena's often unstable temper. Thankfully, Emma did not see Helena much as she spent most of her time at Frederick's house in town.

Mrs. Carrington came over every couple of days to help out and stayed for tea. Emma enjoyed her company immensely and was growing quite fond of the woman. Her husband was often busily employed by Peter, but on the occasions where Emma was able to speak with him, she found him rather amusing in his manners and speech. He had a great wit about him that Emma found absolutely delightful. Emma had finally met Kenton, the Carrington's eldest son. She had to admit that their son was every bit as charming and eloquent as his father.

However, amongst all the commotion and visitors that persisted, Emma continued to remember the nebulous letter from her father. Without any further communication, Emma grew more and more concerned, though she would not admit it, not even to Benjamin.

Benjamin had also grown very busy. He spent much of his time in the company of Felicity. She was happy for them both. She had begun to like Felicity as she was getting to know her better. They spent many nights awake and talking about all sorts of issues.

Finally, the day of Helena's wedding had arrived. She and Margaret had planned a large wedding in their family's church. Emma had never met so many members of her family all in one spot as well as the numerous friends of her aunt and uncle.

Emma was dressed in her flowing, pale blue bridesmaid's gown and was waiting to be lined up for the ceremonial march into the sanctuary of the church. Her escort was her brother Benjamin. She was glad that he had been paired with her.

The ceremony was a long one, but in the end, Helena was happy and had the brand new last name of Alamonté.

Emma gave Helena her greatest congratulations, but was soon pulled in all directions to meet this person and that. She finally fell into a nice conversation circle with a group of ladies. Mrs.

Carrington came up behind her and soon stole her attention away, however.

"Emma dear, I would like you to meet my second eldest son, Philip and my youngest, Toby."

With a great smile, Emma gave a small bow of her head in a ceremonious and polite manner. Each man replied eloquently.

"I am pleased to meet you."

"As we are you. Mother has not stopped talking about you from the moment that she met you. It is nice to finally put a face to a name," said Philip. Emma blushed immediately which both men seemed to think appropriate.

Emma soon found that she liked the other two Carrington boys as well as Kenton and Mr. and Mrs. Carrington.

"Now all you have left is to meet my other younger brother, Cole," said Philip.

"You must forgive his absence however; I am afraid that the weather has been hard on the roads from here to Virginia. Many are having difficulty getting through," added Toby.

Emma marveled in each man. They were each very different in their own way but they all had the same telltale signs that made you see almost instantly that they were brothers. They all took after their father's looks. All three were on the tall side and were well proportioned. Though they all had dark hair like their mother's and green eyes from their father.

Their personalities could not be more different from each other, however. Kenton was righteous and felt that appearances were extremely important. However, Emma could tell that he had his heart in the right place and was an extremely well bred gentleman. Philip was a little skinnier than his brothers. He was much more outspoken, though Emma assumed this came from working for a paper. He was genial without being abrasive. Toby was going to be a minister. Emma felt that there was really no better way to explain him. He was much more reserved and quiet; which Emma found odd considering he was the youngest of the Carrington children.

"The roads to the north must not be in such bad shape though, Mr. Carrington. I mean, you did come from Philadelphia, did you not?" asked Emma.

"You have a good memory Miss Huntington," replied Philip. "Yes, I did come in from Philadelphia. I only arrived yesterday. However, with Mr. Franklin gone, I must be heading back before the end of the week."

"You work for Mr. Franklin then?" asked Emma already knowing the answer.

"Yes, do you know him?"

"Rather well. He has stayed with my family on many an occasion whilst in England."

"It is too bad that your family is not there to accommodate him this time then."

"He's in England now?"

"Yes, he left months ago."

"I didn't realize."

The remainder of the reception was spent amidst fairly unintelligent discussion and a flurry of introductions. Emma was able to introduce the Carrington brothers to her own two brothers, and Benjamin and Philip had hit it off pretty well.

As the final guest left the Seager home, Emma almost collapsed into her bed. It was a very late hour and she slept better than she had in weeks.

After the wedding, Helena and Frederick went off to their holiday. Frederick's parents and extended family were from Austria originally and Frederick had always wanted to visit the homeland of his ancestors so their holiday was spent in Austria.

The rest of January passed without any events of real interest for Emma or her family. Felicity and Benjamin were growing ever closer. Felicity's parents had written to inform Felicity that they were not going to be back any time soon. Their business had engaged them much longer than they had originally guessed. They gave her the choice to stay in Maryland or join them in Philadelphia. Emma was not surprised that she chose to stay in Maryland. Felicity's grandmother had kept her word and wrote to Emma often. She received about a letter a week from her and tried to reply about as often. Felicity, however, had only received a couple of letters from her grandmother and both were extremely short. Emma continued to wonder at the old woman's interest in her.

Chapter 5
Setting Sights Southward

At the end of January, Emma turned seventeen. Her birthday was fairly uneventful, but fun. She had enjoyed it enough but was actually quite glad that it had passed.

William was growing bigger every day. Emma could hardly believe that he needed new clothes again by the time February came along, as he had gotten new ones for Christmas.

With February came a couple more birthdays. Bianca turned eleven and Nell finally turned five. Both girls had extravagant parties and Emma again was able to see the Carringtons as well as many other guests including Captain Tillig whom Emma had not seen for quite a while. There was a strange excitement in the air during both parties. Emma had noticed it each time, but figured it must have had to do with the girls' birthdays.

By the end of February, Emma was growing impatient to leave her aunt and uncle's home and continue the journey southward. However, she seemed a bit alone in her impatience. Benjamin had grown fond of Felicity and did not want to leave her, and William was growing very used to his life in Maryland.

But time does not stop for anything and February passed allowing March to blow in like the lion it often is. The weather was terrible with gale force winds and much rain. Emma's impatience was growing much worse until she could barely stand it much longer. Finally, on the ninth of March, the rain stopped and the sun came out. It looked as though the roads were finally going to dry out a bit, and they would be able to take off.

However, the roads could take quite a while to dry out and by the time they might have finally dried, the rain began again. Emma's patience was extremely thin now, and she was showing outward signs of her keenness on leaving which involved her needing to quell her temper.

Near the end of March, the Seager household received some news from Virginia. There was a letter that arrived for Peter around the twenty-fifth or so.

"What is it Peter?" asked Margaret as she watched her husband's face change during dinner one night.

"It is a letter from Mr. Lee."

"What does he have to say?"

"There have been some developments," was Peter's reply. His tone had a strange finality to it that stopped the table's conversation. A few moments later, Margaret changed the focus of conversation, though Emma was no longer listening to her aunt, but rather intently watching her uncle.

She was trying to recall where she had heard that name. It finally came to her. She had heard of Mr. Lee during the night she overheard her uncle's meeting when she snuck downstairs during the early hours of the morning.

After dinner, Margaret made sure that the smaller children were taken care of quite quickly. They were cleaned up and sent up to their rooms. Benjamin and Felicity had settled in the parlor to read together for a while. Margaret was obviously trying to talk to her husband but the servants in the kitchen sidetracked her and her children upstairs kept calling to her.

Christopher sat down in the dining room and worked on

some of his schoolwork. His teachers had given so much to him lately that he was often working on it late into the evening.

Emma was really left with nothing to do and so she went into the study only to find her uncle rereading the letter he had received during dinner.

"I'm sorry Uncle Peter, I didn't mean to bother you," she said blushing.

"Emma, come in. You are no bother," Peter told her smiling warmly.

Emma sat down across from her uncle at his desk. She shifted a bit uncomfortably. She had not intended to find her uncle, but rather to catch up on some letters that she had been neglecting for a while.

"I'm sure you are curious about my letter from Mr. Lee."

"Not particularly," Emma lied.

"Well, I will tell you there are some new developments in our cause Emma."

"And whose cause would that be?"

"It should be the cause of all, but it will be the cause of the Colonies."

"And what are these developments, Uncle?" Emma asked stiffly.

"Well, my niece, I shall tell you. The Virginia House of Burgesses has appointed an eleven member committee."

"And for what purpose have they been appointed?"

"They will be a committee of correspondence to communicate with the other Colonies regarding common complaints against the British."

"What are these complaints?"

"There are many Emma, but there are many of these members that you have met."

"Oh?"

"Three of these members are Thomas Jefferson, Patrick Henry, and my friend, Richard Henry Lee."

"Do I know any of the other members?"

"I think you might, but I am hesitant to tell you."

"Who are the other members?"

"No, I do not believe it is my place to tell you Emma. You will find out in good time."

"I'm afraid that I don't understand Uncle Peter."

"You will my child, you will." There was something strange in her uncle's tone that made Emma want to ask more but she knew that he was done speaking with her about the matter.

"If you will excuse me then, Uncle Peter, I am quite worn out. I think I am going to head to bed."

"Emma, the roads should be good enough for you to travel on in only a couple more days."

"Thank you Uncle Peter," she said as she stood up. "This month has certainly been good for little but bad weather."

"Well, you know what they say Emma; March comes in like a lion but goes out like a lamb."

Emma gave a small but polite laugh and left the room. On her way toward the stairs, Emma passed by the parlor. Benjamin happened to catch her eye. He followed her up to her room.

"Emma, are you all right? You look very pale," said Benjamin as he closed the door to her bedroom.

"I'm fine. I just had a strange conversation with Uncle Peter."

"Oh? What about?"

"Well, he was telling me about his letter from dinner. Mr. Lee has sent him correspondence indicating that a chain of correspondence has been set up in Virginia."

"To what end?"

"It has been set up by the House of Burgesses to make common complaints about the British. Can you imagine?"

"Imagine what?"

"Can you imagine making complaints against the British?"

"Emma, do you really want to hear my answer?" asked Benjamin with some amusement at his sister.

"Anyway, Peter told me some of the members' names."

"And?"

"Well, he told me three of the people and said that I knew more, but then he wouldn't tell me who they were; saying that I would find out soon enough and that he wasn't the one who should tell me."

"And?"

"And what? Isn't that enough?"

"I suppose so, but what does it matter Emma?" Benjamin was sitting at her writing desk but looking at her quite intently.

Emma was pacing her room and she could feel that her cheeks were quite flushed from anger.

"Emma look, settle down. I know that you are upset but you need to calm down. I was just speaking with Felicity-"

"Benjamin, the other thing that Peter told me was that we would be able to leave within a couple more days."

"That is what I wanted to talk to you about."

"What about?"

"Well, I was speaking with Felicity and her parents are still not going to be around for quite a while. Her parents live in North Carolina and she will have to make her way back there eventually so, I was thinking that she could just accompany us."

"What?"

"I have asked Felicity to join us as we head to Williamsburg and then to stay with us until her parents come back down south."

"And?"

"And both she and her parents think it is a wonderful idea so she is going to come with us. I just wanted you to know."

"You didn't think you should tell me this before?"

"Do you really mind?"

"Well, no," said Emma truthfully. "I mean, I like Felicity, I just don't-"

"You just don't like not being told things, and you are already mad about Peter not telling you something."

"Benjamin, that's not fair."

"It might not be but at least it is honest."

"What is that supposed to mean?"

"Nothing. I think we will leave on the twenty-eighth."

"That's three days from now."

"It will take three days to get everything ready and together. Besides, I think we also need to figure out where we are going to stay once we get into Virginia. Williamsburg is fairly far south in Virginia."

"I have already spoken to Mrs. Carrington about this. They have some very good friends north of a town called Fredericksburg and they are offering us lodging there for as long as we will need it."

"It is settled then. Will you please send out the necessary letters tomorrow morning?"

"Yes. It will all be taken care of."

"Thank you. I will tell William in the morning. I am sure he is sound asleep now."

"I'm sure he is," was Emma's only reply.

"Well, at least we're leaving, that should make you happy."

"I am happy to continue on towards home and toward our mother and father."

"Well, I am going to go back downstairs and tell Margaret and Peter as well as Felicity our plans."

"Fine. I am going to bed."

"Goodnight then," said Benjamin with a smile.

"Goodnight," replied Emma. She could feel her face was still flush with anger. Emma hated being angry at her brother or at any of her family. The biggest problem with it all was that Emma really couldn't pinpoint why she was so mad. It was true that Peter had annoyed her with his insinuations, but he really hadn't done anything to make her angry. She really was happy that Felicity was coming along. She hadn't spent much time with Felicity lately, but she always enjoyed her company and didn't think that anything would be different once they had left Maryland. But it still stood that something was bothering Emma. Something was bothering her a lot.

Emma lay down on her bed and stared at the ceiling. She was back in her insomniac phase lately and often spent many a night lying awake and staring at the ceiling. Emma had chronically suffered from this annoying ailment since she was a child but it came and went in phases. She would be fine for months and sleep normal hours and then, quite suddenly, she would have difficulty falling asleep and lay awake for hours upon hours until utter exhaustion took over allowing her to sleep. However, she was almost always up with the sun, able to fall asleep or not.

Finally, Emma did drift off to sleep.

Her night was filled with fitful dreams, none of which she could remember once she awoke. She slept little and was up early. She breakfasted before the rest of the household was awake.

Emma went into the family study and sat down to begin writing a letter. The letter came to her slowly. It was almost as if her mind was full of fog. She assumed it was from the lack of sleep she had received.

After writing the letters she needed to, some of the house began to stir a bit. Emma decided she wanted to go and see Mrs. Carrington once more before she departed. She asked Margaret if she could borrow the carriage and around ten o' clock, Emma set off to go to the Carringtons' home.

Mrs. Carrington was delighted to receive her and Emma was escorted into the large parlor. The parlor had clean white walls that were decorated in long squares. The furniture in the room was all done in navy blue. Emma felt the room was very inviting and she was glad she had decided to come.

"What brings you out our way today, Miss Huntington?"

"Well Mrs. Carrington, I am afraid that I have some news."

"Oh, and what is that dear?"

"Well with the weather finally cooperating a bit, my brothers and I are going to be heading to Virginia in just a couple more days."

"Oh, that's too bad. I mean, I am very happy for you of course, Miss Huntington. I know how long you have wanted to get going again, but I must confess that I will be losing one of my most favorite new friends and conversationalists."

"You aren't losing me Mrs. Carrington. You are always welcome to visit us in Virginia, I know I can speak for my parents on that matter, and we can always keep correspondence if you like."

"I would like that very much dear. I must tell you that these past few months of getting to know you have been wonderful. You have been just like a daughter to me and I appreciate you keeping an old woman company."

"Of all the things you are Mrs. Carrington, old is not among the adjectives that I would use."

The women laughed a bit.

"But it will be good for you to see your mother again. I know that you have missed her so."

"I most certainly have. It has been so long since I have last seen her."

"Is she doing better now?"

"As far as I know she is. I haven't received any word from them lately. My father isn't actually in Virginia right now."

"Oh? Where is he, then?" asked Mrs. Carrington trying to make light conversation.

"I'm not entirely sure to be honest. I just know that he isn't in Williamsburg."

"Well, I am sure that he is engaged in some important business."

"I'm sure that he is."

"From what Cole tells me in his letters, the weather there is very nice. You should have no trouble once you reach Virginia."

"I should hope not. I am ready to be settled in one spot."

Mrs. Carrington laughed a little. "I'm sure that you are. I know that I would certainly be tired of traveling by now if I were you. By the way, how is your cousin, the new Mrs. Alamonté?"

"Aunt Margaret just received word from her the other day. She is well. She is enjoying Austria but is anxious to return to America. They had a pretty bad trip on the ship. A lot of people were sick, I guess, but they both made it with little trouble."

"Well that is good indeed."

"How are your children now Mrs. Carrington? I haven't heard about them lately."

"Well, Kenton is getting married next month so we have been very busy planning for that. I swear the time passes so quickly. It seems just yesterday he was learning how to walk and now, he is going to walk down the aisle."

"But you like the girl he is marrying, do you not?"

"Oh I do, not as much as I like you, of course," Emma blushed, "but she is a fine upstanding girl from a decent family. I don't like that Kenton will be living in Massachusetts however. All of my children are going so far from me."

"But Toby is not very far, is he? And Cole will certainly return to Maryland after he is done with his education?"

"Toby is not too far. He is in Delaware, only about a day's ride from here, but he wants to move farther north, to New Hampshire or Connecticut perhaps. We will eventually be returning to New

York. Of course, goodness only knows what Cole will do. He is almost finished with his education, but I know he likes Virginia an awful lot. I can see him wanting to stay down there and then what do I do? It isn't as if I can move and be closer to all of my children. In fact, New York is about as good of a compromise as any to be honest."

"Well how are the others doing?"

"Philip returned to Philadelphia. He is as busy as ever, especially with Mr. Franklin in England now. But, he likes it. He is getting a chance to write a lot which has always been his passion."

"Well that is good. But, may I ask, what is Mr. Franklin doing in England?"

"He is trying to settle some things with the English on behalf of the Colonies. To be completely candid, he is trying to avoid going to war with the British."

"Well, that is certainly a good thing, especially with the hotheads that have been stirring up trouble here in the Colonies."

"I must agree; if the differences can be settled without going to war, that is certainly what we need to strive for. Anyway, Toby is back at his seminary and is enjoying it very much. He is almost done with his time there and will soon be able to have parishioners of his very own."

"Well that is certainly impressive."

"And Cole is doing very well from his letters. He is almost done with school and is looking into having a plantation from what I can tell. He is very ambitious."

"I can tell. And how is your husband, Mr. Carrington?"

"Oh, he is the same as always, Miss Huntington. He still has a crick in his back, but his head is as clear as ever and he has been involved in advising for the Colonies. Now, enough about my family, tell me about your own."

"Well, Margaret and Peter are well. Bianca and Nell are coming off their birthday highs so they are well too. Christopher has been busy with his schoolwork. Joseph and Maria are the same as always. William is getting so big, I swear Mother and Father aren't even going to recognize him."

"And how is Benjamin? I must tell you that both Kenton and Philip were quite impressed with him, which is saying something. Kenton and Philip differ so much in their beliefs of what is important that sometimes getting them to agree on anything can be difficult at best."

"Well, that is kind of them and I will be sure and tell Benjamin. He is doing well. He is anxious to be getting on as well."

"And how is Miss Dillingham?"

"Felicity? She is well. She is actually going to be coming with us."

"She is?" Mrs. Carrington asked taking a sip from her teacup and smiling coyly over the rim.

"Well, Felicity is from North Carolina and her parents are stuck in Philadelphia right now, and so they want her to head toward home as well and Williamsburg is a lot closer than Maryland."

"It certainly is. Is there any other reason she is accompanying you?"

"None that I am aware of, Mrs. Carrington."

Mrs. Carrington had a strange smile on her face and Emma knew that she was implying there was something between Felicity and Benjamin; though Emma assumed this as well, she had no concrete evidence of the match and thus felt it was not her place to speak openly about it.

After the two women had enjoyed a lovely afternoon together, Emma said her goodbyes and got ready to leave.

"Miss Huntington, just a moment; I want to give you

something that I would appreciate if you would give it to my son."

"All right," said Emma.

"But you must make me a promise," said Mrs. Carrington.

"What's that?"

"That you won't open it and that you won't give it to him until you have been in Williamsburg for at least six months."

"That might be almost a year from now Mrs. Carrington."

"I know. I want to put this note inside as well."

She went over to her secretary and pulled out a piece of parchment, a quill, and some ink. She scratched something onto the parchment and rolled it up. She then placed her seal of wax upon it to close it and put the small piece of parchment into the tiny box. She closed the box and gave the entire thing to Emma.

"Do you promise me?"

"Of course I do."

"Thank you. I will see you soon my dear. Take care of yourself and your brothers. Be careful. I know you will like the Moyer family."

"I'm sure they will be wonderful," replied Emma. The Moyer family was the family that Mrs. Carrington had arranged for Emma and her brothers to stay with in Virginia. "Thank you so much for everything you have done for me Mrs. Carrington. I shall write to you once we reach the Moyers' plantation."

"Please do. I will expect the letter now."

"Of course. Goodbye Mrs. Carrington."

"Until we see each other again Miss Huntington," replied Mrs. Carrington.

Emma left the house and crawled back into the carriage with Albert's help. She instructed Albert to head back to her aunt and uncle's house and after they had been driving for about ten minutes, she fell asleep.

Emma was surprised when they reached the Seager home. She blinked the sleep from her eyes and was ready to get out of the carriage when Albert opened it for her.

Emma stepped down and headed inside. She had much to do with little time to accomplish everything.

"Emma, how are things going?" asked Margaret right before dinnertime.

Emma was in her bedroom packing her trunks. She was carefully folding her dresses and placing them inside the opened trunks.

"I'm fine. I feel as though I have much to do. It seems like we have been here for so long."

"It has been an absolute joy to have you and your brothers here," said Margaret as she sat upon Emma's bed and began folding Emma's stockings.

"It has been a wonderful experience to stay with you Aunt Margaret. I have enjoyed it very much, and thank you for your hospitality."

"I do have a question for you though dear."

"What's that?" Emma asked not stopping her packing.

"Do you think ill of your uncle and my family and friends?"

Emma stopped suddenly as she was taken aback by the suddenness and forwardness of this question. She did, however, catch her aunt's meaning, but was uncertain how to respond. Emma sat down at the desk and faced her aunt, though she did not directly look at her.

"I do not feel ill toward you or your children in any way Aunt Margaret nor do I feel enmity towards Uncle Peter. I have met many of your friends and enjoy the company of many, though I do not share the sentiments of some."

"My question is this Emma: do you harbor animosity towards our beliefs?"

Emma took a deep breath. "Though I do not condone all of

your affairs and beliefs, I do not feel that you are a bad person in any way."

"But you do condemn some of our beliefs." It was not a question but a mere statement. Emma did not think that her aunt even had meant to say it. She wasn't really sure what to say. No, Emma did not agree with her aunt and uncle and their political beliefs, and she didn't feel that she could honestly lie to her aunt about it. Emma's silence was enough of an answer for Margaret.

"Emma, I know that it must all seem wrong, even surreal to you. You came from a place where we would be hanged for our thoughts and actions and if we did what we were doing in England, perhaps they would be right to do so, but this isn't England. You must remember that. Things are very different here and we are being denied the things that you took for granted in England."

"But Aunt Margaret, I cannot sit by and idly listen to the treasonous statements that have been spit from the mouths of your most honored guests, from the mouth of your husband. I know what has been going on here. I know about the secret meetings and the affairs that Uncle Peter is part of and I have given you my word that I will never tell a soul about them, but I do not do this because I think what you stand for is right. I do this simply because we are family and because I do not want your children to grow up without a father."

"Emma, that is not what I want either but I cannot allow the man I love to live a lie and I do not want my children to grow up to be at the mercy of Parliament and a King who cares nothing for their wellbeing. I don't want my children to be thought of as less than the commoners of England simply because they live on different soil."

"The Colonists are not thought of poorly simply because they are Colonists. The animosity that is growing between England

and America is due to the upheaval from the Colonies."

"I am afraid that you are wrong Emma. My children will not be able to lead the life that they want as long as we are under British rule. King George and Parliament are taxing us from every direction and we have no say in any of it."

Emma knew that she had no right to argue with her aunt. There was an awkward silence between the two women.

"I can only say that you know where I stand Aunt Margaret."

"And I must say that you will be standing there alone and the bottom will fall out if you don't think about what you are standing for."

There was another pause. This one was longer.

"I am sorry if I have caused any hard feelings for you," said Emma remembering the hospitality that her aunt had shown to her family.

"There are no hard feelings Emma. You and your family are welcome here any time and I would like it ever so much if you would write to me, at least once you get to Williamsburg."

Emma agreed with little discussion and her aunt left her to finish packing. Emma began to think. She had always thought that with age came wisdom. She held the belief wisdom was something that just came to you. Yet, from her recent experiences with all of her extended family, Emma was no longer sure this was the case. Perhaps wisdom came from another source. She pondered this for a while. She would pack William's things in the morning.

The next couple of days passed by in a flurry of packing and visits from people to say goodbye, wish them a safe and swift journey, and varying offers of aid. They thanked everyone profusely for their kindnesses and on a cool spring morning, they entered the carriage to leave Maryland. Emma wondered if she would ever see Maryland again.

Chapter 6
The Hunting Party

The trip was not a bad one though it took a while. It was slow going for quite some time because, even though the roads were finally dry, they were still in poor condition from all of the rain that had fallen. Twice they broke a wheel in large holes on the road and the horses couldn't go for too long because the poor traveling conditions were hard on them, not to mention their passengers.

Emma was amazed at William's good behavior and patience. Benjamin and Felicity were trying to make the best of it all and because they were together, they weren't having that difficult of a time. In fact, Emma was probably in the worst spirits of everyone. She never slept well while traveling, and she had begun to suffer from lack of sleep long before they had set out. She also had a strange sense of impending doom that had fallen over her. She just felt as though she needed to be home and would often wake up in cold sweats with an ominous feeling.

Finally, after days and days of travel, the carriage reached the plantation outside of Fredericksburg.

Upon arriving, the four travelers were escorted from the

carriage and into two bedrooms that they would be sharing. Benjamin and William would take one and Felicity and Emma would take the other. Felicity and Emma were lucky enough to not have to share a bed, as there were two single beds in the room.

The four were told that the master of the house and his wife were not in, but they had been expecting them and they should make themselves as comfortable as possible. Worn out from a long journey in the carriage, all four decided to take a nap before dinner.

Emma, to no surprise, could not fall asleep. After about an hour of trying to fall asleep, she got up and went down to the parlor. She was surprised to see Benjamin already there.

"Couldn't sleep again?" he asked her.

Emma shook her head.

"Want to go for a walk?"

"All right."

"It's nice out; you shouldn't need your cloak, just a light shawl perhaps."

Emma nodded and went to get a shawl and a hat. When she came back downstairs, Benjamin was waiting for her and they set off onto the grounds of the plantation.

"The doorman told me that there were some paths we could follow that would be a nice walk," said Benjamin.

Both brother and sister were silent for a while. Both seemed to have a lot on their minds. However, Benjamin was the one to finally break the silence.

"Emma, I must admit that I am a bit worried about you."

"About me? Why ever for?"

"Well, you haven't been sleeping well for quite some time. You are looking quite thin lately, and the color in your face hasn't been what it should be."

"I'm fine Benjamin. I am merely homesick and tired of traveling."

"This is not the fatigue of traveling nor is it the weariness endured from homesickness; there is something else that has been plaguing you."

"It is nothing Benjamin."

"It is something or you would not look so ill. Is it something that I have done?"

"No, it is nothing that you have done, nor that William or Felicity has done."

"Then what Emma? If you cannot tell me, than whom can you tell? We used to talk about everything. Do you remember that?"

"I do remember but your time has been much preoccupied by another of late."

"Is that what this is about?"

"No, it is nothing to do with that. I am happy for you, honestly I am."

The two were passing by massive cotton fields that were just being planted for the season. Emma looked out over the fields to see hundreds of dark-skinned men and women scattered across the fields all busy with the planting. *Slaves*, she thought to herself. Emma had never been on a plantation before, at least not one in the Colonies and certainly not one that utilized slave labor.

"Then what is this melancholy that has taken you over?"

"I cannot say Benjamin."

"Because you are not at liberty to say or because you do not know?"

"A bit of both. I had an argument with Aunt Margaret a couple of days before we left Maryland. The subject of this argument is what I am not at liberty to speak about. I gave my word that I would tell no one."

"Then you know that I will not ask you to betray your word."

"The argument is troublesome to me, but that is not where my worries begin."

"Where, pray tell, do these worries begin?"

"That, I do not know. I mean to say, they began a few months ago, but I do not know what I can attribute their cause to."

"Is there anything else? Anything that you are at liberty to discuss?" Benjamin asked with mild amusement in his eyes but forced seriousness upon his face.

"Actually yes, but you will think me silly."

"I promise not to laugh," said Benjamin with an encouraging smile. Emma had not seen her brother smile at her in months and suddenly, this hit her. She could feel the welling of tears in her eyes but she refused to cry. She looked away from her brother and back out toward the fields. The Virginia landscape was pretty.

"I have a strange feeling. I cannot put a name on this feeling; I feel as though we are needed at home though I cannot say why."

"Do you have any idea?"

"None. I only know that I want to be home and that there is something wrong there."

"But surely if something was wrong, we would have received a letter from Mother or Father."

"I suppose you are right but there is something else."

"What is it Emma?"

"Where did Father go?"

"When?"

"Over the Christmas season. He wrote in my letter that he was leaving Williamsburg. Where was he going? And did Mother go with him? From my letter, it did not sound as if she did."

"I do not know where he went, but I do know that it was important Emma."

"Why do you say that?"

"I do not know what your letter contained for I have a feeling that mine was different but like you, I too have secrets I am not able to divulge."

"Is he all right Benjamin? And Mother?" Emma had a strange sense of urgency that filled her.

"As far as I know, they are both fine. As far as their current health and status, I know as much as you. What I know has more to do with Aunt Margaret and Uncle Peter."

"And you are not able to tell me?"

"No."

"Then I too respect that, Benjamin."

"We should head back towards the house, it must be almost time for dinner and our hosts will wonder where we have gotten to."

Emma nodded and they turned back toward the house.

"Emma, some things are going to be very different in Williamsburg than they were in England."

"I assumed so. I mean, after all, we are thousands of miles from England. It would surprise me more if things were exactly the same."

"I am glad to hear you say that because I worry about you."

"Benjamin, I am really fine." There was a long pause in the conversation as both Benjamin and Emma took in their surroundings. "Benjamin, have you noticed all of the slaves that are here?"

"Yes, this is a large plantation and apparently they use slaves to do everything here."

"I feel that is almost barbaric."

"You shouldn't prejudge."

"Do you think that slavery is all right?"

"Of course I don't, but obviously our hosts do and we mustn't judge them for it."

"Of course," replied Emma.

"Emma do you remember our home in England?"

"Quite well actually."

"Could you imagine growing cotton there?"

"I don't think that it would grow as well in England."

"I'm sure it wouldn't but it would be strange to see the fields so full with crops rather than the horses Father kept."

"Didn't Father say that he had crops now as well?"

"He did. I guess it is another cash crop. I think he said it was tobacco."

"Mmm," replied Emma. The two continued on their way and reminisced about their childhoods in England before their parents went to the Colonies.

By the time Benjamin and Emma reached the house again, they were laughing.

As Emma and Benjamin entered the plantation's house, a severe looking man who seemed to be in charge of the household met them.

"Mr. and Mrs. Moyer are requesting that you are ready for dinner within a half hour, and they like their guests to be well dressed for dinner," stated the servant.

"Thank you. Please inform them we will be at their disposal," said Benjamin gracefully.

Benjamin and Emma went up to their appointed rooms and readied for dinner. Felicity was still sleeping so Emma woke her to make sure she was ready as well. Then Emma pulled out a lovely burgundy dress. It was complete with lace stomacher and matching lace at the end of her sleeves that happened to only reach to just past her elbow before the lace took over extending another few inches on top and hanging about eight inches underneath. She then looped her hair eloquently on the back of her head leaving only a few small curls to frame her face.

Felicity's dress was much in the same fashion but was a bright blue color and she did not have lace at the end of her arms. Emma helped her with her hair, putting it in a fashionable knot at the nape of her neck.

There was a knock at the door and Benjamin and William entered both looking very proper. Benjamin took Emma's arm and Felicity and William followed the two. Emma was surprised he did not take Felicity's arm, but it was probably more fitting that he accompanied his sister since Felicity was merely a family friend.

As they reached the dining room, Mr. and Mrs. Moyer greeted them.

"It is lovely to have you in our home. I do hope that you have made yourselves comfortable in the rooms we have provided," said Mrs. Moyer. "Please, do sit down."

Benjamin pulled out a chair for Felicity because Mr. Moyer was pulling out Emma's chair for her.

"We are so very pleased to meet you all," said Mr. Moyer.

"The pleasure is ours Mr. Moyer," said Emma.

"Yes, we are deeply indebted to you both for your hospitality," replied Benjamin.

"Oh, think nothing of it. Mr. and Mrs. Carrington spoke so very highly of you that we could not possibly think of not having you stay with us. I also had the pleasure of your aunt and uncle's company during my own stay in Maryland. I did not have the pleasure to meet you all I am afraid. Besides, the journey from Maryland to here is long enough. I surely can't imagine you continuing on all the way to Williamsburg without a stopover for a few days at least," said Mr. Moyer.

"How was the journey Miss Huntington?"

"It was very long and the roads are in quite poor shape but we had good horses at our disposal, and God was definitely by our side," said Emma.

"Well, thank goodness for that," replied Mrs. Moyer.

"Mr. Huntington, from what Mr. Carrington says you have had quite a long journey – all the way from England. Whatever has brought you to Virginia?"

"Well Mr. Moyer, my mother and father have moved to Williamsburg, and my brother, sister, and I are going to join them there. Miss Dillingham is going to be staying with us for a while as her parents are in Philadelphia right now but will soon be returning to North Carolina, where they normally reside."

"I see. Now Mr. Huntington, you must tell me, being from England and all, you surely must be a good shot."

"A good shot Mr. Moyer?" asked Benjamin a bit nonplussed.

"Well surely you can handle a gun quite well." Benjamin now understood.

"I have nothing to be ashamed of if that is what you are implying Mr. Moyer."

"Aha! Good, good. I suppose you come from a long line of good marksmen."

"My family is certainly accomplished. My father taught both Emma and I everything he knows about it."

"Both of you?" Mr. Moyer asked looking and surveying Emma.

"Emma is actually quite good."

"Benjamin is certainly the hunter though," Emma added.

"That's true; Emma doesn't hunt."

Mr. Moyer laughed.

"Then tomorrow you must accompany me Mr. Huntington. Some of the county boys and I are going hunting, and I would be grateful for your company."

Benjamin considered for a moment. Emma wondered what he was thinking about.

"All right Mr. Moyer, I am glad to accept."

"Good, that will give the womenfolk here a chance to do those womenfolk things that I can't stand to be part of."

"May I come too?" asked William suddenly.

"I don't think so William," said Emma tenderly. "I think you should stay here with us."

"But I don't like doing that womenfolk stuff either," said William with consternation.

Mr. Moyer nearly upset his dinner from his laughter. The rest of the table enjoyed a small chuckle, though Emma herself was trying hard not to laugh at Mr. Moyer. William, in his naivety, could not understand what was so funny.

"Oh, your brother amuses me very much," said Mr. Moyer as he slowed his laughter and wiped a small tear from his eye. "If it is all right with you Miss Huntington, he is more than welcome to come with, and I will personally assure you he will be safe and sound."

Emma flushed. She really did not like the idea of William going but the invitation was sincere and William was begging her to go.

"I suppose it is all right, if you are sure Mr. Moyer, that he will not be any trouble."

"I am absolutely positive. Besides, it isn't good for him to be surrounded by women all day. Makes a man soft you know."

Benjamin was smiling as he ate his meal but said nothing. Felicity was engulfed in conversation with Mrs. Moyer about the Moyer family. Emma looked at William's face and smiled.

"Then it is all right with me," replied Emma with a final note of surrender.

"Yippee!" shouted William. "Now I won't have to go and be all soft."

Mr. Moyer began laughing again. Emma was glad he found the situation funny because she certainly did not find William's comments amusing. However, even Benjamin let go of a little laugh this time.

Dinner was good but it had been a long time since Emma had sat through such a formal dinner. Her aunt was a wonderful cook and the few servants that they had were extremely good as well, but Margaret was often up and down helping the servants and conversation was as varied as could be not to mention the hubbub from all of the children at the table. Emma realized she had begun to miss her cousins in Maryland.

After dinner Emma insisted that William go to bed, especially since he would be up early the next day to go hunting. Mrs. Moyer and Felicity had taken off somewhere together and so Emma was left with Benjamin and Mr. Moyer.

"Why don't we go out onto the veranda and take in the night air. It really is quite a beautiful landscape at night out here," said Mr. Moyer.

Emma grabbed her shawl again. The night really was lovely and the landscape was very nice, but the April air had not brought the warm nights along with its warm days.

"Well, I'm sure that you have both been fairly deprived of news recently," said Mr. Moyer.

"Actually we have sir," said Benjamin. "How is Virginia fairing in everything?"

"About as well as the other Colonies, I'm afraid. It seems that some sort of entanglement is inevitable at this point though I am glad that we are still talking to Parliament. However, Virginia has always had a mind of her own and some of the men are taking matters into their own hands."

"What do you mean Mr. Moyer?" asked Benjamin.

"Well, I don't know if you heard or not but they have started a correspondence committee and they are urging other Colonies to do the same. It looks as though they might have some followers but it is hard to tell yet."

"Well open lines of communication surely cannot be a bad thing."

"It is not. But, you know, I was speaking to one of my neighbors the other day; well surely you must know whom I mean, Mr. Washington is even known in England after everything he's done."

"Mr. Washington, yes, he fought in the Seven Years' War. Do you remember Emma?"

"Not really. I mean, I have certainly heard the name, but I was quite young whilst that war was being fought and you know how it is when you are so far from what is happening, it sort of slips by you."

Mr. Moyer smiled slightly at this comment as if to say, "Women!" in an exasperated tone. Emma tried to ignore the patronization.

"Yes, I do remember his name Mr. Moyer, please continue," said Benjamin.

"I thought you might. Your father was under his command in the French and Indian War. Anyway, he was telling me that he was talking to Mr. Jefferson, and apparently big things are happening up north."

"What sort of big things?"

"Well coming from the north, I am sure that you have heard about the *Gaspee*."

"The little schooner?" asked Emma remembering the commotion over it while they were in Boston.

"Yes, that's it. Well, that didn't go over too well, and now the British are pestering ordinary citizens and accusing them of things that just aren't so."

"For example?" asked Emma bitterly.

"Emma," chided Benjamin.

Emma realized her discourtesy and her face flushed.

"I apologize for my sister's insolence Mr. Moyer. She is not of the same opinion as many of the men in this country," said Benjamin.

"It is of no matter. Women so rarely understand these things anyway."

Emma was offended by this comment but knew better than to outright insult her host especially after her minor outburst.

"Besides, I think it is time that we head in. The air is only going to grow cooler, and I know that Mrs. Moyer will be looking for me before too long."

Benjamin took Emma's arm but gave her a reproachful look. Emma hung her head. She had meant to be suspicious of Mr. Moyer's comments but she had not meant to be rude, and she felt badly for doing so.

"Well, I think that we are going to retire for the evening Mr. Moyer but thank you for a lovely evening and an enlightening conversation. I shall see you bright and early tomorrow morning," said Benjamin guiding his sister.

"Yes, thank you ever so much for all of your hospitality Mr. Moyer," said Emma not wanting to make eye contact with her host.

"Think nothing of it and yes, I will see you bright and early Mr. Huntington," said Mr. Moyer with the same energy and liveliness that he had shown at dinner.

Benjamin and Emma headed upstairs and their host walked toward the north side of the house on the main floor.

When they reached Emma's room, he pulled her inside and closed the door behind him.

"Emma, what was that about?"

"I'm sorry Benjamin. I forgot myself."

"I noticed. Mind you do not forget yourself again. That was extremely rude. If you do not agree with a person, that is fine, but when you are a guest in their home, and especially when you do not even know them, please feel free to keep your stupid mouth shut."

Emma felt the tears in her eyes welling up. It was extremely unusual for Benjamin, let alone anyone, to reprimand her, especially for something like etiquette.

"For the rest of our stay I forbid you to discuss politics in any form or fashion. You are not to speak about your opinions on any related matter."

Emma nodded. She knew she had done wrong and she was not even going to argue with her brother. She could not even raise her head to look at him. Benjamin noticed his tone and her reaction and he sat down beside her. He put his arm around her and Emma could feel her tears falling gently against her cheek.

"I'm sorry. I did not mean to become angry. You know that you were wrong, and that is enough."

"No, you are right Benjamin. I shall heed your requests."

"It will be all right Emma. Do not cry. We shall be home soon and you will be able to see Mother and Father again."

Emma nodded; her tears were subsiding.

"You are merely tired. I know that you haven't slept well in weeks. What you need is simply a good night's sleep."

"I'm sorry Benjamin."

"It will be all right. Don't worry Emma; we will be setting out in a few short days from here."

"Benjamin, may I ask you something?"

"Of course," he said gently.

"Who is this Mr. Washington?"

"Well, as much as I remember, he was a great war hero from the Seven Years' War. I believe the Colonists call it the French and Indian War."

"What did he do?"

"He was in charge of an American Army regiment and he led them victoriously against the French when they were trying to profit from the English lands."

"I barely remember this."

"Well Emma, I was only seven at the time it ended which makes you only five; it really isn't surprising you don't remember much. What I know about it is mostly from my studies and a little from what Father has told me."

"So he is a good man?"

"I hear that he is a gentleman and people speak highly of him."

"And Mr. Jefferson?"

"He is one of the men who have set up the correspondence committee."

"So he is against the throne as well then," Emma stated.

"I'm not sure. Emma, this matter isn't as black-and-white as you might imagine. Just because people have complaints against the throne doesn't make them traitors, and just because people aren't complaining about England doesn't make them England's allies. People are on a continuum and though you have met some of the radicals, not everyone is like that."

"I just don't understand why the throne is so bad? Why England is considered so bad here?"

"England isn't so bad. I love and miss England terribly, but I can sympathize with the problems that the Colonists are experiencing. It must be very frustrating to deal with all that they are dealing with."

"But why are they so angry Benjamin?"

"Because they are being wronged and their pleas are not being heard. This Mr. Jefferson, for example, I have been told he has written literally thousands of letters to King George and yet nothing changes for him or his compatriots."

"Why does King George not listen?"

"I don't know the answer to that Emma. To be honest, I think that is the question of the hour. But, for now, why don't you get into bed and try to get some sleep? I have a feeling that Mrs. Moyer is going to keep you quite busy in my absence."

Emma smiled, "I have the strangest feeling that you are correct Benjamin. Oh, and Benjamin…"

"Yes?"

"Thank you."

"For what?"

"For being such a great big brother."

Benjamin smiled and pulled the door shut behind him. Emma undressed and got into bed. She was joined a few minutes later by Felicity who was talking wildly about Mrs. Moyer and all of the plans that lay in store for the two girls. Emma drifted off to sleep long before Felicity had finished talking.

The next morning, Emma awoke early. She got up and dressed and headed downstairs not really expecting anyone to be awake. Upon entering the dining room, however, Emma was surprised to find Mr. Moyer eating with Benjamin and William and some other men whom Emma had yet to meet. Mrs. Moyer was running around like a chicken with her head cut off trying to arrange everything for the men to leave.

"Do sit down and have some breakfast with us Miss Huntington," said Mr. Moyer.

"I trust that you slept well dear," said Mrs. Moyer.

"Very well, thank you," replied Emma.

"Gentlemen, this is Miss Huntington," said Mr. Moyer to the rest of the table "Miss Huntington, I would like you to meet Mr. Ainsworth, Mr. Rablin, Colonel Fones, and Mr. Balcom. I, of course, don't expect you to remember all of their names," said Mr. Moyer in a jovial manner and as an aside, he added, "I hardly remember them all myself." The joke was obviously humorous to the entire table and Emma laughed politely as she nodded at the men and took a seat next to William.

Almost before Emma could blink, one of the house servants had placed a plate in front of her.

"Mr. Ainsworth, it is a pleasure to see you again," said Emma politely.

"And you. It is kind of you to remember me," Mr. Ainsworth replied.

"We are still waiting for a couple more to join us this morning," stated Mr. Moyer.

"Ah and Andrew and George should really be here soon, the day is wasting away," said the handsome and young Mr. Ainsworth.

"Calm down Jeffrey," said Mr. Rablin to Mr. Ainsworth. Mr. Rablin was certainly not as young as Mr. Ainsworth but he was still good looking, and had probably been even more so in his youth. "They'll be here. It isn't as if this is the only day we will be out after all."

"Precisely how long will you be out?" asked Emma.

"As long as it takes to get our catches Miss Huntington," said Mr. Balcom, who was about as old as Mr. Moyer.

"Ah, here is Andrew now," said Mr. Moyer.

Much to Emma's surprise, she turned to greet the new guest only to see Andrew Welsing.

"Gentlemen, Miss Huntington, this is Mr. Andrew Welsing," said Mr. Moyer.

Andrew hadn't even entered the room yet as he began talking to Mr. Moyer.

"Cornelius, it is so good to see you again," said the young Mr. Welsing. As he entered the dining room he spotted the Huntington children.

"Come and have some breakfast; we are still waiting for George," said Mr. Moyer.

"Miss Huntington, Mr. Huntington, William, it is under odd circumstances that we meet again.

"Mr. Welsing, it is most certainly a pleasure to see you again," said Emma eloquently.

"I am sure the pleasure is more mine than yours," replied the young man with a coy smile.

"What brings you to Virginia?" asked Benjamin.

"I might ask you the same thing, but I am here for the grand hunting. I come every year. Beatrice and Cornelius are my aunt and uncle. I usually spend summers here."

"Well, we are still on our way to Williamsburg. We are merely breaking our journey for the moment," said Emma. She was still amazed at the coincidence of seeing both Jeffrey Ainsworth and Andrew Welsing again. It had been a while since she had seen the men in Maryland; she had certainly not expected to ever see them again in all honesty.

"I think I heard a horse outside which only means that George must be here," said Mr. Ainsworth.

Sure enough, within a few moments, another man entered. Emma guessed he must be about forty years old. He had a kind face but a broad stature. You could tell by looking at him that this George was an impressive and important man.

"George, you finally made it," said Mr. Moyer.

"Yes Cornelius, I am here. I had a few things to attend to this morning before I left, and Martha was in need of some assistance with the plantation affairs."

"I want you all to meet Mr. George Washington. Mr. Washington lives over on the next plantation; Mount Vernon he calls it. George, you know most everyone but I want you to meet the Huntington children. This is Mr. Benjamin Huntington, Miss Emma Huntington, and William Huntington."

"I am pleased to meet you all. I know your father quite well. He stays at our plantation when he is called to business up north."

Benjamin and Emma both gave courteous nods to the newcomer whom they had previously heard about. William, on the other hand, just couldn't contain his question.

"You know my father?" asked William.

Emma took hold of William's hand under the table and squeezed it gently to silence him while Benjamin gave him a reproachful look. William turned his gaze downward but Mr. Washington gave the child a big smile.

"Yes, I know him quite well. He is a good man. I am just

pleased that I have the pleasure of finally meeting his children that I have heard so much about."

Emma blushed at the man's kind words.

"Well, have some breakfast then George," said Mr. Moyer.

"I thank you but I have already breakfasted this morning."

"Well then, let's get ready and be off. The daylight is burning at our heels," said Colonel Fones.

The men came to a general consensus and began readying themselves. Emma went outside with them to make sure that William was taken care of and to grab a quick, final word with Benjamin before he mounted his horse.

"Make sure you take care of him Benjamin. Do not let him out of your sight. Promise me?"

"I promise he shall ride with me." One of the servants handed the boy up to his older brother and when they were finally in place, William blew his sister a kiss.

"Miss Huntington, may I beg a moment of your time?"

"Of course Mr. Welsing," replied Emma kindly.

"I just wanted to say that it was really nice seeing you again. I have thought of you often since we met at your aunt and uncle's home. I am glad that fate has granted us this chance meeting."

Emma blushed from his words.

"You are very kind Mr. Welsing. I do wish you luck in your hunting endeavors."

"Thank you Miss Huntington," replied Andrew as he too mounted his horse.

Mrs. Moyer and Emma stood and watched the men go out of sight down the road. Emma knew they wouldn't be back for a few days but all the same, she hoped they made their catch soon.

"Well then," began Mrs. Moyer once the men were out of sight. "Why don't we head back into the house and have a nice chat whilst we wait for your friend, Miss Dillingham, to awaken?"

"Of course," replied Emma still watching the now vacant road.

Mrs. Moyer took Emma's arm and they walked into the house. Mrs. Moyer led Emma into the drawing room and sat down in an overstuffed armchair. Emma followed suit.

They talked about their families for a while. Emma learned that the Moyer's had ten children, two of which had died as babies, leaving them with eight. They had seven boys and three girls. With the two that had passed away, they were left with five boys and three girls. All of the Moyer children were now grown with families of their own, but they all lived relatively near the Moyer plantation.

Emma was almost completely talked out by the time Felicity came into the drawing room. The three women talked some more and around noon they had lunch served out on the veranda.

"I just love eating out here but Mr. Moyer will rarely consent to it. He has such terrible sneezing fits from the dust."

"But he enjoys hunting?" asked Emma with some amusement.

"I know it is a strange thing, but I cannot really argue with him."

After lunch, the three women went back into the house. Mrs. Moyer stated she needed to rest for a while, but sent the girls outside for a walk. Emma was actually glad to go for a walk and to be away from the constant chatter of Mrs. Moyer.

"Isn't Mrs. Moyer just wonderful?" asked Felicity.

"She is very nice but I cannot honestly say that I have much of an opinion of her yet Felicity."

"I think she is wonderful."

"Did I tell you who I saw this morning?" asked Emma trying to change the subject.

"Who?"

"Mr. Welsing, from Maryland. Did you meet him?"

"I'm afraid I don't remember that name though I honestly might have met him. I feel as though I met so many people while in Maryland, but I know I don't remember all of their names now."

"I feel the same way but all in all it was good to see a familiar face. I also met yet another man who knows my father."

"You did? Who is that?"

"A Mr. Washington."

"Mr. George Washington, from Virginia?"

"Yes, I was told he lives in a plantation not far from here, Mount Vernon I think he calls it."

"Yes, Mount Vernon. He is a very well known man Emma," said Felicity with a lot of excitement and awe in her voice.

"Benjamin told me that he fought in the Seven Years' War and helped defeat the French."

"I assume that you are talking about the French and Indian War and yes, he did. He was instrumental in the defeat of the French. In fact, I don't know if England would have won the war if it weren't for the efforts of George Washington."

"Well, anyway, I guess my father has been staying at Mount Vernon on some of his trips northward. I wonder what business my father has in the north."

"Well, Mount Vernon would be a good stopping point. After all, it is about a day's ride from here to Williamsburg."

"Yes it makes sense but what is my father doing north of Virginia?"

"I don't know that I can say, Emma," replied Felicity.

"Well, I didn't really expect you to know Felicity; I was more talking out loud." Felicity nodded but said nothing.

The girls walked a while longer and continued talking about all the men Emma had met. The conversation shifted a bit back to Benjamin, Felicity's favorite subject, and eventually, they returned to the house just in time to freshen up for tea.

As the girls sat and drank tea with Mrs. Moyer, Emma noticed it began to rain a bit outside.

"I do hope this doesn't last long. It shall certainly spoil the hunting trip," said Emma.

"Oh, don't worry much. I swear those men would continue hunting into the dead of winter if they could. A little rain surely won't stop them," replied Mrs. Moyer.

After tea, the ladies spent some time working on samplers in the parlor. Eventually, Mrs. Moyer said that her hands grew tired and she began to read aloud. Emma was actually glad for this because it meant she didn't have to answer any more questions for a while, as Mrs. Moyer's tongue was kept busy with the words on the pages before her.

During this time, Emma continued to watch the weather out of the corner of her eye and noticed that the rain not only had not let up but was in fact coming down much harder. She knew that the men were perfectly safe, but she worried that Benjamin and William would catch cold and that might delay their travels.

After an eloquent dinner, Emma decided she was going to go to bed. She took out *The Sommersett Case and the Slave Trade* by Benjamin Franklin that Margaret had given to her and continued to read it until she fell asleep. Felicity was still not upstairs yet when Emma fell asleep.

Emma awoke with a jolt very early the next morning. In fact, it was still extremely dark outside. She couldn't remember what had woken her but she stood and looked out the window. The rain was coming down very hard now. Her heart fell a little because she knew that even if her brothers were miraculously lucky enough to not catch cold, the roads would be in no shape for driving on for a few days.

Emma looked over and found that Felicity was in bed and fast asleep. Emma pulled on her robe and decided to go downstairs for a while.

Emma entered the study. She was completely awake now and figured she might as well do something productive so she took out some parchment and a quill and sat down to write a few letters by candlelight.

It was difficult to see in the candlelight, but Emma kept the parchment close enough to the flame. The first letter that Emma wrote was to her Aunt Margaret. Emma wrote about her brothers going hunting and about meeting up with Mr. Welsing and Mr. Ainsworth again. She inquired after all of the Seager children as well. When she finished the letter she placed it in an envelope and addressed it. She then began another. This one was to Mrs. Dillingham in England.

Emma addressed the letter and stopped. She hadn't written to the elderly lady in quite some time; not, in fact, since a while before she had left Maryland. She began by telling her of their progress toward Williamsburg. She then wrote that she was staying with the Moyer family but did not write anything about her feelings toward them. Emma's letter was extremely short and she felt as though she should add more. Emma decided to write about the Colonies and the latest from Virginia and its correspondence committee. She stayed to the facts and put in no opinion or emotion, simply explanation. Emma ended her letter with a little note about Felicity remaining with them and about Felicity's status. She signed the letter and sealed it in an envelope.

The Widow Dillingham's letters to Emma had been very eloquent and friendly. She told Emma about her travels and the people in England. She filled Emma in about the newest things going on in England. Her letters, though friendly, were not extremely personal and Emma was glad for it. She liked the woman but for some reason did not have an exceeding amount of trust for her.

Emma took out a third piece of parchment and was about to begin another letter when she heard a loud ruckus outside. She stood and brought the candle over to the window. There was a man on horseback that had just ridden up and a few other men followed him. Immediately Emma knew it was the men who had been hunting. She ran to the front door only to meet Mrs. Moyer already waiting with the door open. The wind was howling and there was so much rain coming in the house that the bottoms of Emma's robe and nightdress were drenched. There was a big crack of thunder and a large bolt of lightning and in the light of the storm, Emma saw what was wrong.

The first man entered the house; it was Mr. Moyer. Mr. Balcom and Mr. Washington followed him and they were carrying a third man, Jeffery Ainsworth. Emma could see that Mr. Ainsworth was bleeding profusely but could not see the cause of the blood. Mrs. Moyer led the men into a small bedroom on the main floor and had them lay him out. She told one of the servants to call for the doctor immediately.

Emma was swept to and fro with the men but suddenly panic struck her and she searched for her brothers. She did not see either of them nor the other men.

"Where are the others?" she asked Mr. Balcom, but she received no reply. The men were concerned with the bleeding man in front of them. Emma was near hysterics now but was trying to remain as calm as she could.

Suddenly she heard her name being called but the voice wasn't saying Emma; it was calling for Miss Huntington.

"Miss Huntington, Jeffery would be much obliged if he could see you," said Mr. Moyer.

"Me? He barely knows me," said Emma as she fought back her panic-stricken tears and entered the small bedroom. The others cleared a path and Emma knelt by the bed.

"Miss Huntington, I'm sorry," began Jeffrey.

"For what Mr. Ainsworth?"

"Please, call me Jeffery."

"All right, Jeffrey. What are you sorry for?" Emma had but one thing on her mind: her two brothers.

"I tried to stop him but I was too late." Emma's panic was high but she was regaining her composure.

"Tried to stop who Jeffrey?"

"I tried to stop William but I was too late," Jeffrey said in tired breaths.

"Where is William?"

"I don't know. He ran off. I tried to stop him but... I was just too late."

"Jeffrey, what are you trying to tell me?"

"I wrote this letter to you. I don't think I was ever meaning to give it to you. Promise me that you won't read it until I'm gone."

"Jeffrey, you aren't going anywhere. You'll be all right," but Emma's mind was now on her brothers, not the man who was dying in the bed in front of her.

"Promise me."

"Of course I promise," said Emma. "Just hold on Jeffrey, the doctor will be here soon and you'll be fine, you'll see."

"I'm so sorry Emma..." and with that, Jeffrey's hand fell to his side and his breathing subsided. Emma felt herself take a sharp intake of breath but remembered nothing after that.

Emma awoke a while later on a chaise in the parlor with Felicity at her side holding her hand.

"What happened? Where am I?" Emma began.

"Shh. You fainted but you are all right. You are in the parlor of the Moyer house." Suddenly Emma had a rushing feeling fall upon her and stop suddenly right in the middle of her throat. She remembered everything, the entire conversation.

"Mr. Ainsworth?"

"He's gone Emma," said Felicity gently.

Emma jumped up from the sofa, which startled Felicity.

"Where are Benjamin and William?" demanded Emma.

Mr. Washington entered the room at this point.

"Where are they? I want to know right now." demanded Emma.

"Miss Huntington," began Mr. Washington, "may I have a word alone with you?"

"Yes," said Emma. Felicity took her cue and left the room. "Do you know where my brothers are?"

"I do. They are safe and sound."

"Where are they and what has happened?"

"Please sit down. I will explain everything."

Emma was surprisingly calmed by Mr. Washington's voice and she sat down again upon the sofa.

"Your brothers will be arriving at Mount Vernon even as we speak. William probably has a broken arm but he is all right. We ran into some nasty business while we were out. We had headed westward to hunt, but the rain drove us even farther than we had intended. Unfortunately, we were driven right into the path of some Indians."

"Is everyone all right?"

"No. Your brothers are all right though. Our group was separated and Colonel Fones is with your brothers. I am positive they headed north to Mount Vernon. We were driven a bit farther south, to here. An arrow caught Mr. Ainsworth in the chest.

"What Mr. Ainsworth was going on about was that he did indeed try to save your brother William. That is when the arrow caught him. William was directly in the line of fire and Mr. Ainsworth jumped from his horse to protect your brother. In the act of doing so, William fell down the hill, which actually worked out for the better. Mr. Welsing was at the bottom of the hill and grabbed William and they, including your older brother and Colonel Fones, headed northward whilst Mr. Moyer, Mr. Ainsworth, Mr. Balcom, and myself headed southward. Mr. Ainsworth, unfortunately, did not survive his attack."

"Was anyone else hurt?"

"I would reckon that quite a few of those Indians aren't in too good of shape right now. Your brother, Mr. Huntington, is quite a good shot."

"I know he is. He learned from my father," Emma said with distraction.

"I might have guessed as much," said Mr. Washington with a strange pleasure about the whole thing in his voice. "I do thank you for making Mr. Ainsworth's last few moments more comfortable."

"I don't know how much I did but if it was anything that helped, I am glad that I could be of service."

"It was far more help than you will ever know. Now, if you will excuse me, I need to see about heading back to Mount Vernon myself. My wife will be worried and I want to make sure my guests are well for their trips home."

"Mr. Washington," Emma began, "thank you very much for taking care of my brothers and for telling me what has happened."

"Thank you for your kindness."

With that, Mr. Washington took his leave. Emma stood again and went into the main hall. Mrs. Moyer was busy running around, as usual. Mr. Moyer and Mr. Balcom were having a low conversation in the corner but looked up and smiled at Emma as she entered the hall. Felicity was waiting for her.

"Are you all right Emma?" she asked.

"I'm fine." Emma was still extremely worried but did not feel it was appropriate to voice her concern at the moment. Just then, Mr. Moyer came over to her.

"Thank you for your compassion this morning Miss Huntington. I know that it was a comfort to Jeffrey in his last moments on Earth. I have just sent word to his mother. His father is no longer alive. I am sure that his mother will be arriving soon. Mrs. Moyer will see after her so you needn't worry your precious head over that," he was leading her to the stairs.

Emma was glad that everyone was so calm. Their calmness was calming her. She was just about to go upstairs when she heard yet another horse enter the path to the house.

The rider dismounted and the horse whinnied. Emma could not make out who the person was but when the door opened, Emma saw that it was none other than Benjamin and she ran to him.

"I'm so glad that you are safe, Benjamin," exclaimed Emma. She now had tears spilling down her face and she could barely catch her breath. She latched onto her brother and was not going to let go of him for anything.

"I'm safe. I'm fine," he said as he patted his sister reassuringly.

"What news have you Benjamin?" asked Mr. Moyer.

"Colonel Fones is no longer with us," said Benjamin gravely. "He did not make it out of the woods."

There was silence in the room. No one spoke and no one looked at each other. Benjamin was the one to break the silence.

"And what of Mr. Ainsworth?"

"He has passed away as well," answered Mr. Balcom.

There was more silence. Emma could not believe what she was hearing. How could this have happened? Why did she have to witness it all?

Several days later, with William finally back at the Moyer plantation, indeed having a broken arm, and with the funerals over and life starting to drift back into normalcy, Emma found herself still asking the exact same questions.

"How can this have happened?" she asked Benjamin as they strolled by the fields.

"It is one of those funny things in life Emma. I certainly mourn for Mr. Ainsworth and Colonel Fones, but I thank God that it was not William."

"Or you Benjamin."

"I also thank God it was not more of us," he continued.

"Benjamin, you might think this ill-mannered but I feel as though I must get it off of my chest."

"What is it Emma?"

"Seeing Mr. Ainsworth die…"

"I'm sure it was horrible."

"He was in so much pain and then, he simply ceased to live. It was horrible but it was almost indescribable Benjamin."

"I'm sure that it was and I do not think you ill-mannered for bringing it up. I am glad that you are not openly discussing it, but all things considered, that was a pretty horrible sight for you. Of course it should bother you."

"Have you ever seen someone die Benjamin?"

"No. I have been fortunate enough to have thus far escaped that experience."

"It is just hard to believe that someone is there and then they are gone; in only a single breath, someone can fade from the Earth and cease to be."

"That was God's intention. Be glad he did not have to suffer any more pain than he did."

"He was so young Benjamin. He couldn't have been much older than you."

"He was twenty, barely older than I."

"It just doesn't make sense."

"It is God's will Emma. It doesn't have to make sense. God has a plan and this is all part of it. Know that Mr. Ainsworth is not alone and from what I have been told, he carried a lovely memory of his dying moments with him forever," said Benjamin.

Emma smiled. It sounded so much better when Benjamin discussed it with her.

Later that day, Emma was back in her room and packing to take off for Williamsburg. They would be leaving the next morning. She lifted her robe and a letter fell out. Emma had all but forgotten the letter that Mr. Ainsworth had given to her. She held the letter in her delicate fingers and ran her smooth hand over the outside of the envelope. It was still sealed. She stared at the letter for quite some time but could not bring herself to read it now either. She put it inside her trunk and went back to packing. The letter would have to wait.

***

Emma had not been bothered much since the death of Mr. Ainsworth. The others were curious about her connection with him. Benjamin had told her that Mrs. Moyer had asked him if there was some sort of understanding between Emma and Mr. Ainsworth. Emma was mortified, but Benjamin informed her that he had cleared it all up. The idle gossip of women was something that Emma simply could not bear and this was yet another example of why Emma detested the favorite activities of her gender.

Emma was in the drawing room doing a little bit of reading – she was now almost finished with the pamphlet that Benjamin Franklin had written for the second time – when a servant entered to announce company.

"Miss Huntington, Mr. Washington is here to see you."

"Please show him in," replied Emma with some surprise. She stood to graciously accept her guest.

"Miss Huntington, I beg you forgive me for my intrusion," said Mr. Washington.

"Not at all Mr. Washington, it is my pleasure to see you again. Please, sit down."

Both sat but Emma could tell that the visit would be short.

"I hear that you are taking your leave of us," he began.

"We are. We will be continuing on to Williamsburg tomorrow morning. We have been a burden here long enough."

"Nonsense, you are certainly no burden in our little corner of the world."

Emma was confused by the extreme generosity that had been shown to her and her brothers by so many. She often pondered it while she lay awake at night.

"I must say that I have been very grateful to meet you and your brothers. I enjoy your mother and father's company an immense amount. I am merely glad to have met the entire family."

"Well, I am glad to have met you Mr. Washington. You have certainly made us to be more at ease during our stay here."

"I don't know what I have done but if so, I am glad to be at service. I do, however, have an ulterior motive for my visit today I am afraid."

"What is that?"

"First of all, I was wondering if you might give your father a letter for me?"

"Of course, it is no trouble at all. I have some other mail for him as well from some of our relatives."

"Well, this is a very special letter that I am afraid must remain confidential. It is truly for his eyes only Miss Huntington."

"Then I shall carry it on my person and will deliver it to him myself immediately upon our arrival."

"But I am sorry to be the one to tell you that your father will not be there upon your arrival."

"Oh? Do you know where he will be?"

"I do, but I am not at liberty to say."

"On whose request?"

"On the request of your father. But I do entrust you with this letter and ask that you care for it and its contents until your father arrives home."

"Do you know when that will be?"

"That, I can honestly say, I do not know for sure. If I were to guess, I would say that it shouldn't be much longer; he has been away for quite some time now."

"Mr. Washington, I have a favor to ask of you."

"Of course," he replied.

"Have you heard of my mother as of late?"

"No, not that I recall. My wife is better about keeping in touch with her but she has not mentioned anything lately."

"Thank you. I was just wondering. I must confess that I have not heard from her lately either."

"Before I take my leave, I do have one more thing, if you permit me."

"Yes?"

"I just wanted to say that I am very glad that we had the chance to meet and if there is ever anything that I can do to be of any aid to you or your family, please do not hesitate to call upon me."

"I certainly thank you for this, Mr. Washington."

"I was wondering if your brother is about?"

"Benjamin?"

"Yes."

"He is probably out riding with Mr. Moyer. I know that Mr. Moyer wanted one last run with Benjamin. They should return shortly though if you would care to wait."

"I will head out to the stables and catch them there." He stood and Emma stood as well. "Until we meet again Miss Huntington." He nodded his head politely, Emma returned the gesture, and he left the room.

Emma looked at the letter in her hands. It was a plain letter in a plain envelope that was simply addressed, Mr. James Huntington.

"How odd," said Emma under her breath. She took out her book and began reading but within a few minutes, she was interrupted again.

"Miss Huntington, I am sorry to bother you but there is a Mr. Andrew Welsing here to see you," said one of the servants.

"Thank you, you may show him in," replied Emma. She had not really seen anyone since the funerals a couple of days before; thus she was quite surprised to have two visitors within only minutes of each other.

Emma still had the envelope in her hand but she did not have pockets so she stuck the letter inside her book to mark her place and set the book on the table beside her as Mr. Welsing entered the room.

"Mr. Welsing, how good to see you again," said Emma.

"Miss Huntington, it is very good to see you. You look well," said Andrew.

"I am well enough. And you?"

"Good, good."

"Would you care to sit down?"

"Thank you," he replied and they both sat. Emma could tell this was going to be a longer visit so she settled in and made herself a bit more comfortable. "I heard that you were leaving tomorrow and I wanted to come and say goodbye to you. I was not able to see you before you left Maryland; I didn't want to pass up the chance again."

"That was kind of you Mr. Welsing," said Emma.

"Well, I just don't know when I will be down by Williamsburg again."

Emma found this comment odd but did not want to appear rude. "Do you visit Williamsburg often?"

"Every so often I suppose. I have an aunt that lives down there."

"Forgive me Mr. Welsing, but I am confused. Are you not from Maryland?"

"No, I am originally from Connecticut via England."

"I'm sorry. I don't quite catch your meaning."

"I was born in England, but we returned to Connecticut soon afterwards. My father was born and raised there. My mother came from England and they settled in Connecticut. However, both of my parents were killed during the French and Indian War…"

"I'm so sorry," said Emma with heartfelt sympathy.

"Thank you. But with them gone, I was sort of tossed around you might say. I spent some time in New Hampshire with my aunt and uncle, in New York with my grandfather, in Georgia with one of my distant cousins, in England with my great-grandmother, and in Virginia with my grandfather's sister, not to mention spending many of my summers here with the Moyers."

"Goodness, that is a lot of moving around I should say."

"It was, but it gave me a keen sense of direction." Emma laughed politely. "Seriously though, it did give me a good sense of all of the different kinds of people."

"And your conclusions are?"

"That there are no conclusions. It really doesn't matter where someone is from – it matters only what they believe."

"Those are some wise words."

"Don't go and give me too much credit now." Emma laughed again. This time she actually found the joke to be funny. She still had mixed feelings on the man who sat before her but he was good company at least.

"Where did you stay in England?"

"I was actually in Wales."

"Oh, I see. Did you like it there?"

"It was all right. A bit odd I must say."

"Why do you say that?"

"The people there are just different and it rains all the time. It puts you in a right sour mood sometimes."

"The people or the weather?" asked Emma.

"I guess it could be both…or either, though I meant the weather. I need sunshine. I don't do well with only rain for days upon days."

"I don't suppose many people do. What does your grandfather do in New York?"

"He owns a large estate right now but he used to be the governor's right hand man."

"Really? Did he enjoy that?"

"I guess. I really don't remember much of it. I was pretty young."

"Didn't you tell me once that you had eleven brothers?"

"I don't know if I told you or not, but indeed I do have eleven brothers."

"Where did they all go during your being shipped around?"

"I was ten when my parents died. I have one younger brother and he and I were together during all of the moving around. As for my older brothers, most of them were out of the house at school or working on apprenticeships by then. My three brothers that are just older than I were given to other relatives along the way but mostly resided in New York with one of our aunts."

"How old is your youngest brother?"

"He will turn eighteen in a couple of months." There was silence. Emma was usually fairly adept at keeping the conversation going but her mind was beginning to wander to the things that needed to be done before bedtime, and it would be almost dinnertime soon. "Miss Huntington, I have wanted to say something to you but have lacked the courage for some time now to convey my message."

"Yes Mr. Welsing?" asked Emma completely clueless as to what the young man wanted to ask of her.

"Well, I was thinking…" But what Mr. Welsing was thinking,

Emma did not discover. At that moment, William bounded into the room. His arm was still in bandages and a sling but he had adapted quite well to the injury.

"Emma, I can't find my yo-yo."

"William, don't be so rude. You just interrupted Mr. Welsing."

"Sorry. Hello Mr. Welsing."

"Well hello William," replied Andrew cordially. "I'm sorry about that. Now what did you want to ask me?"

"It doesn't matter. We can talk about it another time. William, are you ready to get to Williamsburg then?"

"I sure am. Do you think that they might have named Williamsburg after me?"

Andrew laughed. "You know, they just may have done that. They knew you would be coming and wanted to give you a welcoming present."

"See Emma, Mr. Welsing thinks that they named it after me."

"William, you know very well that they did not name Williamsburg after you."

"How do you know?"

"Because they named Williamsburg many, many years before you were even born. They named Williamsburg after King William."

"Fine. But do you know where my yo-yo is?"

"I think it is packed dear and don't go taking it out because I have everything packed just the way it needs to be and I don't want you losing anything."

"But I need my yo-yo."

"You don't need it right now. You can have it back when we get to Williamsburg tomorrow."

"Well, I think that I need to be going," said Mr. Welsing.

"Well it was very good of you to drop by Mr. Welsing. I am hopeful that I shall see you again. Please do stop in if you are ever to return to Williamsburg; we would be glad to have you visit us."

"Thank you Miss Huntington. I just might take you up on that offer. Well, have a safe journey; I shall be thinking about you. William, it was good to see you."

"It was nice to see you too," replied William with a big smile on his face. Andrew shook the young boy's good hand and then turned to face Emma.

"Miss Huntington, a pleasure, as always."

"Mr. Welsing," replied Emma cordially. With that, Andrew left the drawing room and Emma turned her attention back onto William. The child was still going on about his yo-yo but Emma decided it was time for him to go and get ready for dinner. She too needed to get ready and so she picked up her book and headed upstairs to her room.

Emma's mind focused on her conversations from the afternoon. Both were almost cryptic in their very nature, but Emma could not pinpoint why. Whatever the reasons, they were not odd for the same reason, Emma was sure of that. She wondered what Mr. Welsing had wanted to ask of her.

Emma also remembered the letter that Mr. Washington had given to her. It was not so unusual that she was asked to deliver a confidential letter to her father. She had done so many times in England when her father served in the House of Lords. Why should the Colonies be any different? However, she began to think about what Mr. Washington had said about her father being away. Where was he? Why wouldn't he be there when they arrived? But alas, Emma had no answers to these questions, nor the other many questions that were passing through her mind of late.

Dinner was a fairly subdued affair Emma felt. All things considered, Emma expected that there would have been many guests and that dinner would have been quite the ordeal but it really wasn't bad. Emma was grateful for the stillness but confused. It was almost as if it were the calm before the storm.

After dinner, Emma played cards with Mrs. Moyer, Felicity, and William. William wasn't the best at cards but he was learning, and Mrs. Moyer enjoyed fawning over the boy. Benjamin sat off a little with Mr. Moyer discussing things that Emma couldn't quite hear.

Emma had learned that the Moyers had quite an extended family. They had both been born and raised in Virginia and had lived on their plantation since they had been married. The plantation had once belonged to Mr. Moyer's father but with his death, the plantation was passed down to the oldest son and so, Mr. and Mrs. Moyer came to own it.

After about an hour, Emma made William go to bed. He protested a little but not too much. Emma could tell he was also excited to finally reach the town they would soon call home; the town he still insisted was named after him.

A little while later, Emma too headed to bed. Felicity came up only about a half hour afterwards and told Emma that Benjamin had also gone to bed.

Morning came early. Emma was up and had breakfasted by the time the sun was breaking the horizon. Benjamin and Felicity were up as well. Felicity said she would care for William, so Emma saw to the luggage while Benjamin and Mr. Moyer went over the final travel plans.

By the time the sun had broken away from the horizon, all four travelers were packed into the carriage and were saying their last farewells and thanks to the Moyers. The carriage pulled away and they were off.

All four travelers were in good spirits. William was having a bit of trouble with his arm, as the carriage jounced over the rolling landscape but nothing that was too tremendous.

The carriage was making good time. The roads had actually

cleared quite well after the rains. Emma had expected another day like their travels from Maryland but was quite happily surprised to be wrong in her assumptions.

By early evening, the carriage was very near to pulling into Williamsburg, and all three siblings were very excited to be close to their new home. However, before they reached the bustling town, their carriage was stopped by six men in eloquent red coats.

Chapter 7
Arrival in Williamsburg

"Please excuse the inconvenience but we need everyone to step out of the carriage whilst we search its contents," said a young man to the travelers in their native accent.

"Excuse me good sir," began Benjamin, quite even-tempered Emma felt, "but what is the meaning of this?"

"We have orders to search each carriage that is traveling southward to Williamsburg and yours fits that description. Now, please step out of the carriage or you shall be forced from it." Another young man in uniform opened the carriage door.

Benjamin stepped down first and then aided Felicity, William, and finally Emma out of the carriage. Emma could feel her face burning. What on Earth was the meaning of such an intrusion? Not only were the men looking in the carriage, but in their luggage as well.

"Sir, if you will be good enough to step over here with me, I have a few questions for you," stated yet another man in red uniform. Felicity too was pulled away leaving Emma and William with the remaining men. All together, there were six men in uniform, two of which were on horseback.

Emma strained to listen to what they asked Benjamin, but she was unable to pick up any of the conversation.

"Sir," Emma began speaking to one of the soldiers, "I was wondering if it is common practice to stop English citizens in their travels?"

"It is not common practice, no miss. However, we have our orders."

"And what pray tell are you looking for?" Emma asked with indignation towards the British soldiers.

"I am afraid that I cannot tell you that."

"And then I must ask if you know who my father is," Emma said.

"I do actually, but even the name of Lord Huntington is not enough to override my orders Miss Huntington," the soldier stated quite bluntly.

"Emma, how long is this going to take? I'm tired and I want to see Mother and Father," said William with the smallest amount of whining in his voice. Emma could tell that the child was indeed tired, and she was sure his arm was hurting him a fair bit.

"I don't know dear. Hopefully it won't take too long." Emma said this last part to the soldier searching her trunk.

A few minutes later Benjamin and the officer he was speaking with returned to Emma and William; Benjamin had a strange look on his face as if he were trying to convey something unspoken to Emma. Yet Emma did not understand the message.

"Emma, these men require my presence for the time being-" Benjamin began but Emma cut him off.

"What? For what possible reason?"

"I'm not sure but they are going to see to it that you and Felicity and William arrive at our home safely. I shall be along as soon as possible."

Emma had a questioning look on her face but Benjamin's face told her to not press the issue. Something was happening that she did not understand and now was not the time to make waves. Emma took over from there before William had time to draw a breath, let alone protest.

"We will see you at home then, Benjamin. If you gentlemen are finished; William, get in the carriage," said Emma briskly pushing her younger brother towards the door of the carriage.

"I shall see you soon Emma."

"Mr. Huntington, this way please," said the officer on the horse.

"Miss Huntington," said another of the men, "may I help you?" he asked as he aided her back into the carriage. Felicity joined them within a few minutes and the carriage set off now complete with armed guard, but minus one traveler.

William began to ask a question but Emma silenced her brother. She and Felicity merely stared at each other and then out of the windows only to return staring at each other all the while, saying nothing.

They arrived at a large brick home that sat adjacent to other homes that formed a horseshoe shape around a very large courtyard. At the far end of the courtyard sat an even larger brick home that seemed to belong to someone very important.

"That's the Governor's mansion," said Felicity when she saw Emma's eyes wandering.

"I see," was the only reply Emma could give.

The carriage doors were opened and Emma, Felicity, and William were helped out of the carriage. Four servants came outside to help the travelers. They, of course, did not recognize Emma or William but did, thankfully, recognize Felicity. Much to Emma's relief, it was Felicity's turn to take charge, and she fulfilled her duty perfectly.

"Francis, take our things inside and set up our rooms. Mr. Benjamin Huntington will be along shortly, so be sure to set his things neatly in his room as well."

"Yes Miss Dillingham. We been waitin' fo' yo' arrival," she replied.

"We were unfortunately delayed by the rain up north. Please take William inside and see to his arm. The journey has not been kind to it. Then make sure he gets ready for bed. It has been a long day for all of us."

"Ah course," was Francis's reply. The three other servants saw to the luggage, and Francis led William inside leaving Felicity and Emma with the uniformed men.

"Thank you, kind sirs, for seeing us home. We greatly appreciate the favor," said Felicity to the lead officer upon horseback.

The men nodded and Emma felt a small surge of threat pass through her. She felt extremely uncomfortable and wanted to run into the house, but she planted her feet and followed Felicity's lead.

As the men in red coats left the drive, Emma slowly turned to face Felicity. Felicity gave her a small sidelong look but then returned her attention to the leaving soldiers. When they were out of sight, Felicity turned and took Emma's arm.

"Let's get inside," was all she said to Emma.

Once inside, Felicity still maintained command. The servant named Francis returned.

"Francis, this is Miss Emma Huntington. I am sure that their rooms are ready for them."

"Yes Miss Dillingham. We knew you was comin' and so we has everythin' ready fo' you. Mr. William is in bed now. He was plum tuckered out and he jus' fell asleep righ' there in front o' me."

"Very good. Please prepare a pot of tea for Miss Huntington and myself and have it served in the drawing room."

"Yes Miss Dillingham," said Francis.

"Then please inform Mrs. Huntington that we have arrived if you haven't already done so."

The servant hesitated. Felicity repeated her request but again, the servant did not move.

"What is the matter with you? Are you unable to attend to my requests?"

"As a matter o' fact Miss, yes. I shouldn't be the one to tell ya'll but I guess ya'll need to know…"

"What are you talking about?" asked Emma. Panic had now gripped her but she still remained in control of herself. "Where is my mother?"

"Well, Mrs. Huntington, she went and got sick…" she explained.

"Yes, Father wrote and told me that."

"Well, the doctor couldn't do nothin' fo' her and she jus' got sicker an' sicker." There was a hesitation. Emma felt a large lump form in her throat. "Finally, the doctor tol' us there weren't nothin' mo' he could do and not quite a month ago, Mrs. Huntington passed away, God rest her."

Emma's throat now felt as though it was totally closed off. She found it extremely difficult to breath. She heard voices around her but she could not tell what they were saying to her. At one point she found herself sitting on a sofa with someone sitting next to her, holding her hand but she didn't know who it was. The tears began to slowly flow from her eyes and splatter onto her cheeks. She gasped for breath. She felt someone put their arm around her and embrace her but still, she did not have her senses about her.

After about ten minutes, Emma suddenly began to see again. Her tears had subsided and her breath returned to her. Exhausted and confused, Emma no longer had the strength to cry.

"Are you all right Emma?" asked a familiar voice; it belonged to Felicity. "I'm so sorry, I had no idea."

Emma looked around and saw Francis cowering in the corner watching the situation.

"Francis, is it?" asked Emma kindly.

"Yes Miss Huntington."

"You did not tell my younger brother this, did you?"

"No miss. I didn't tell nothin' to nobody – 'cept ya'll," she stated emphatically.

"Good. I need to be the one to tell him."

"Emma, have some tea," said Felicity calmly and tenderly.

Emma accepted the cup but did not drink from it. Her mind was reeling. So much had happened in such a short time that she didn't know where to begin. She turned back to Francis.

"Are you the head servant here?"

"Yes Miss Huntington. I is the head house servant here in town."

"In town?"

"Yes'm. Gracie is the main house servant out at the plantation and Oliver sees to all the grounds both here and at the plantation."

"Will you please inform the other servants of our arrival? Also, do you know where my father is at?"

"Las' I heard Miss Huntington, he was goin' to Philadelphia but he don't tell ol' Francis much o' his business. He's been gone since Christmastime."

"Does he know about my mother then?"

"Oh yes. He was right broken hearted about Mrs. Huntington passin' away. I had the minister write him a letter to tell him – see, I cain't read or write so Reverend Quillet did the writin' fo' me."

"But he didn't return for the funeral?"

"Ol' Francis don't want to stick her foot in her mouth now so alls I's goin' to say is that he was very upset about Mrs. Huntington, and he knows all about it now."

"Fine. Anyway, please inform the servants of our arrival."

"I can do that right away Miss Huntington."

"Good. Also, where is my mother?"

"Yo' parents has a family lot they begun out at the plantation."

"Thank you Francis. You may leave now."

Emma turned toward Felicity who in turn looked at Emma with more sympathy than Emma wanted to see. Emma resolved that she would not cry about her mother until everything else was taken care of. There would be time for grief later.

"Felicity, what was that all about? Why were we stopped like that and who were those men?"

"Those men are part of the British Army. I'm not entirely sure why we were stopped to be honest. What worries me more is why they took Benjamin."

"Why did they take him and to where?"

"I know neither answer. I can only hope he is all right."

"Is this a normal occurrence here?"

"It can be quite common at times; though I don't know if I would say normal."

"For what possible purpose is this allowed?"

"The British are suspicious of all traffic in and out of Virginia just as they are around Massachusetts and Pennsylvania because that is where most of the turmoil is happening. This particular occurrence.... It is difficult to say, but I did see them open all of the mail we carried which leads me to believe they were trying to intercept a message of some sort and believed we might be carrying it."

Emma thought about this. Her mind was so full at the moment it seemed to take her eons to think about it but suddenly the thought came to her like a bolt of lightning. The letter Mr. Washington had given her. She had taken it out of her book and placed it in the stomacher of her dress so she would live up to her promise of carrying the letter on her person. She did not share this information with Felicity. If what Felicity was saying was true, then that letter must be more important than Emma could ever have believed. She made a vow to protect that letter at all costs until she hand delivered it to her father immediately upon his return.

"How long do you think it will take until Benjamin is able to get here?" asked Emma.

"It is always difficult to tell. I think we should wait up for him though."

Emma nodded but placed her tea down on the table and stood up.

"Where are you going?"

"I know that William is not asleep yet, and I have some news that he needs to know about," replied Emma. Felicity nodded.

"I'll wait here. I shall fetch you if Benjamin gets here before you return."

With a heavy heart, Emma left the drawing room and headed upstairs. The house was large and difficult to navigate in the dark, especially since she had never seen it in the light. She poked her head into a couple of rooms to see what was in them. She found the room she assumed to be hers as her trunks were laid out but now empty. Emma assumed Francis or one of the other servants had unpacked for her. She entered the room.

There was a large four-poster bed in the center of the room. The walls were light blue and the floor was mahogany colored. The trim on the walls was a cream color. The wood of the armoire matched the wood of the floor. Emma opened the armoire to find all of her clothes neatly placed away. There was a desk in the corner, just like the one she had had in her room in England. One trunk was left untouched. Inside the trunk lay Emma's personal effects. She closed the trunk; she would put the things away later.

Emma went back out into the hallway. Finally she stumbled upon William's room. She opened the door quietly, but William called to her immediately.

"Emma, will you tuck me in? I'm scared." Emma went over to her brother but sat down in a rocking chair beside the bed.

"William, come over here and sit with me," said Emma gently. He did and Emma proceeded to tell her young brother, as gently as possible, about the death of his mother whom he had not seen in over a year, and now, he would never see again.

"So Mother is in Heaven?"

"Yes she is. She is in Heaven with the angels now and she is looking down on us and taking care of us just as if she were here."

"But she's not here."

"No, not physically, but you know what?"

"What?"

"If you look really hard, you can find her."

"Where?"

"Right here," said Emma as she pointed at William's heart. "Right here where she's always been, and where she will always be."

The young child cried and Emma rocked with him. Not a single tear fell from her face as she comforted her younger brother. She remained resigned to keep her word to herself.

Finally, William fell asleep and Emma tucked him in. She gave him a kiss on the forehead and left the room. Tired from the day of traveling, exhausted from the ordeal with the men in the red coats, and the news of her mother, Emma returned to the drawing room to find Felicity had fallen asleep on the sofa.

Emma did not want to wake her, as she was sure Felicity must be exhausted as well. She sat down in one of the armchairs and stared at her surroundings. They were familiar but not. It was an odd sort of feeling for Emma. She could sense her parents in the house, but without their physical presence, it seemed cold and uninviting.

A few hours later, with the first bit of gray light coming up over the horizon, the moment right before dawn, Emma awoke from her troubled sleep and stood from the armchair she had inhabited all night. As she stretched her stiffness away, she looked out the window and just happened to see her older brother come around the corner and head for the house.

Emma did not bother to wake Felicity but simply ran to the front door to greet her brother. She opened the door for him and he entered quickly shutting it behind him.

"You are still up," he stated.

"I fell asleep in the chair waiting for you. Are you all right? Is everything all right? What happened, Benjamin?"

"I am fine. I was taken to a place and asked questions about our journey. I told them we were coming to meet our parents here in Williamsburg. We left England last October. From there we spent a bit of time in Boston where we first landed and stayed with our aunt and uncle. We then headed to Maryland and stayed with our mother's sister and her husband for the remainder of the winter.

"After we left Maryland, we broke our journey in northern Virginia and were stuck by the weather. We are arriving in Williamsburg to meet up with our parents just today. They seemed to think we might be carrying some sort of letter."

"Then what Felicity thought was true? Benjamin, Mr. Washington came to see me before we left."

"I know; I saw him as well. He gave you a letter addressed to our father that you promised you would keep on your person."

"How did you know that?"

"He told me. Did you give it to them?"

"No, they do not know about it."

"Good. Let's keep it that way. Whatever is in that letter needs to stay a secret until Father reads it."

"I agree. That is why I still have it with me."

"Good, keep it there."

"Anything else happen?"

"No, they merely asked me these questions repeatedly. Finally they seemed to think that I didn't know what they wanted to know and they brought me back here."

"I am so glad that you are safe."

"And you three?"

"Quite safe. William is in bed sleeping. Felicity fell asleep a few hours ago and is still in the drawing room on the sofa and I am here."

"Where are Mother and Father?"

Emma's heart sank. She now had another person to tell about the unfortunate circumstances she had found upon entering the house of her parents.

"Well, Father is supposedly in Philadelphia and has been there since Christmas."

"And Mother?"

Emma took a deep breath and recounted what she knew about the death of her mother. She watched Benjamin's face change as she spoke, but she continued to speak, and quickly. She knew if she stopped, it would not come out. When she finished, Benjamin looked as if he had the wind knocked out of him. When he finally spoke, it was in monotone and without much thought.

"I need to get some sleep."

"Your trunks are upstairs already."

"Thanks Emma. Goodnight." Emma opened her mouth to reply but it seemed that Benjamin wouldn't even hear her if she did, so she did not respond; she merely watched him head up the stairs.

Emma's head was pounding. Without much sleep and with the lead weight that now resided over her heart, she too went up to her room to lie down for a couple more hours. Much to her dismay, she did not fall asleep again.

When Emma got up for the day, she changed her clothes – she

hadn't even gotten into her nightdress – and headed downstairs. She had quite a bit of business to tend to and she wanted to ask some more questions of the servants; not to mention she wanted to take a look around town and head out to the plantation for a while.

Emma was the first to rise that day. She had breakfast served to her, but she did not eat much. From the lack of sleep her stomach was quite queasy. Emma stared out the window from the breakfast room and thought about her mother and father. She felt the same lump well up in her throat but she pushed it back down and tried desperately to push her thoughts from her mind.

It was already late April now. Emma thought of the immense amount of time that had passed since they had left England. It had now been approximately seven months since they had boarded the ship that brought them to their waiting fates.

When Emma felt that she could not possibly eat any more, she called to have the table cleared, and asked the servants for some company to go into town. Emma was told that Curtis would be the best candidate as he often saw to much of Mr. Huntington's business in the town anyway.

Emma realized for the first time that no one in the Colonies called her father Lord Huntington other than the soldier she had met the night before. This was odd for Emma as it wasn't exactly courteous to not call a Lord by his title. She would have to remember to ask her father about this when she saw him.

Emma wrote a note to be given to either Felicity or Benjamin when they awoke and also gave instructions to tell William she would be back around noon, and if he wanted to go to the plantation with her, he should be ready to go after lunch.

Curtis offered to bring around the carriage but Emma didn't want to go too far and so she decided they should walk. Emma grabbed a light shawl, a bonnet, and her hat. The temperature was very mild and Emma could tell that summer would be on its way soon enough.

They didn't have to walk very far. In fact, the middle of town was less than a two minute walk from the house. Curtis pointed out all of the interesting sites as they passed each one. Emma took all of this in trying to learn her way around.

Emma and Curtis stopped at a few of the shops. Emma would go in while Curtis waited outside. Emma's favorite was the bookseller. Emma entered and saw a wondrous sight. There were books everywhere. The walls were filled with them as well as the many tables that were set up along the store. The store also sold parchment and ink as well as quills, inkbottles, and wax. Emma was extremely tempted to make a purchase but she restrained herself. She then headed into the dry goods store. A man in his middle thirties came out to assist her.

"May I help you, Miss…"

"Huntington. Emma Huntington."

The shopkeeper's face lit up and he wore a great big smile.

"Surely you aren't the daughter of Mr. James Huntington?"

"Yes, I am one in the same."

"It is my supreme honor and pleasure to meet you Miss Huntington. Your father is a great friend of all in this town. I am Mr. Withers, Mr. Paul Withers."

"It is a pleasure to meet you Mr. Withers."

"I am also so sorry about your mother." Emma swallowed hard.

"Thank you Mr. Withers. Her death was extremely difficult to bear."

"I'm certain it was, for it was difficult for the people in the town." He must have noticed Emma's distress about the subject because he continued to another subject quickly. "Now, what can I do for you today?"

"Not too much actually. I was trying to become acquainted with the town's layout but I do need some tea."

"Tea?"

"Yes. You do sell tea, do you not?"

"Yes we do. Let me just get some down for you. We keep it on the upper shelves so the kids don't play with it. You certainly don't want sticky fingers on the tea bricks."

"No, you certainly don't."

Mr. Withers got the tea for Emma and she paid the man.

"So when do you expect your father to be home again? He has been gone for quite a long time now."

"Actually Mr. Withers, my brothers and I just arrived last night. I am not entirely sure when to expect him."

"Well, I wouldn't think it would be too much longer. Too much happening around here for him to be away up north for too long you know."

Emma wanted to say that she didn't know and ask exactly what was happening around here and whether or not it had anything to do with their welcoming committee from the previous evening, but she fought her curiosity as she had just met Mr. Withers. Emma's father had always told her to be cautious of the questions you ask of strangers.

"Well thank you Mr. Withers. I am sure that I shall be seeing you again."

"I'm sure you will. Oh, and tell your father to come and visit when he returns. We've missed him around here."

"I will do that. Good day to you Mr. Withers."

"And you Miss Huntington."

Emma left the shop and found Curtis still waiting for her outside. He took her small package from her so she wouldn't have to carry it.

They continued to walk around for some time. Emma was enthralled with the bustling town. There were people everywhere, which actually delighted her. She had spent so much time in the country that she had forgotten what the town life was like. Curtis showed Emma the Governor's mansion, the church, and the rest of Merchant's Square, which is what they called the middle of town where all of the shops were located.

"Curtis, do you have any clue as to where my father might be right now?"

"Well, Miss Huntington, I don't right know fo' sho' but I do know he was headin' fo' Philadelphia when he left in December. From there, he was really not too clear on his plans but he'll be back soon enough. Don't you worry yo' pretty head about that one."

"Hmm," was Emma's only reply.

After her tour of the town, Emma and Curtis returned to her parents' home on Duke of Gloucester Street. She entered the house only to find it extremely quiet. Curtis said he would take the tea to the kitchen for her. She thanked him and soon ran into Francis.

"Francis," she began.

"Yes Miss Huntington?"

"First of all, call me Emma."

"Yes Miss Emma."

"Where is everyone?"

"Well, Mr. Benjamin is still upstairs, he ain't come down yet. Miss Dillingham is in the parlor awaitin' fo' ya, and I sent Mr. William outside to play. That po' chile is needin' sometime in the out of doors."

"I'm sure he is. Did he say if he wanted to go to the plantation with me?"

"He did Miss Emma. He says he wants to go wid ya. He's already eaten and everythin' so he is all ready."

"Good. Could you bring him in and tell him we will be going soon. Also, can you have the carriage brought around for us?"

"Yes Miss Emma."

Emma went into the parlor and found Felicity. She was half reading and half watching the world outside from the comfort of an overstuffed armchair.

"Felicity?"

"Emma, I'm glad your back. You had a visitor this morning."

"A visitor? But who even knows that I'm here let alone who would be visiting me?" asked Emma.

"I'm not sure but he left his card for you."

"He?"

"Yes. I didn't see him, but Francis told me it was a young man. The card is in the tray by the front door."

"Thank you. I will look at it later. Where is Benjamin?"

"He hasn't come out of his room yet. I'm not sure if he is still sleeping or not. I tried to knock on his door this morning to see if he wanted to have some breakfast but he did not answer me."

"He might be still asleep. He didn't get in until almost sunrise this morning."

"It was that late?"

"Yes. He said they kept battering him with questions about our journey, but they escorted him home this morning. He was all right though. Anyway, I also told him about our mother; that may be keeping him isolated as well."

"Perhaps."

"Well, William and I are going to head out to the plantation. Would you care to join us?" asked Emma.

"No thank you. I think that I shall stay in town. I have some business of my own to attend to, and I would like to see Benjamin at some point today."

"All right. Well, will you inform Benjamin of our whereabouts when he emerges?"

"I shall certainly do that. Have a good time. I think you

will like the plantation your parents keep. It is quite lovely and probably one of the largest in all the southern Colonies."

"I shall see you later this evening, Felicity."

"Goodbye Emma."

Emma left the parlor and found William waiting for her in the hallway all ready to go. Emma replaced her bonnet on her head as well as her hat. She smiled at her younger brother and he gave her an affectionate smile back.

Both Emma and William got into the carriage and they set off. Emma watched the countryside pass by her as she spoke with William. Emma was amazed at his resiliency to the news he had been bombarded with the evening before. He occasionally made reference to his mother but did not weep as he had upon hearing the news. However, the conversation was steered away from the grave events that had taken place.

"Did you enjoy the town this morning?" asked William. "Tell me all about it?"

"Williamsburg is a nice town. They have lovely shops and the landscape is quite beautiful. There are so many people that are bustling about, but it was a nice change of pace this morning."

"Emma, why are we going to the plantation?"

"I want to see it first of all. We haven't ever seen where Mother and Father spend their time. Also, I want to see what is taking place in Father's absence."

"What do you mean?"

"I want to make sure that the plantation is still being productive just because Father isn't here to oversee it."

"Oh."

"Did you ever find your yo-yo dear?"

"Yes, it was in my trunks, just like you said."

"Good. By the way, how is your arm feeling?"

"It is all right. It hurt a bit after yesterday but it felt better this morning. I cannot wait to have the sling and bandages off though."

"I'm sure you are anxious but we want to make sure that it is healed first."

"I know," said William as he heaved a sigh of resignation.

"Perhaps we will see if the local doctor can take a look at it to see how much longer you need to keep it that way."

After a few more minutes, Emma and William were at the gates of the Huntington plantation. The plantation had been bestowed with the name Beacon Hall. Emma read the name of the plantation sign as they entered. The gates to the plantation were wrought iron but they were covered in charming and neatly kept ivy that had climbed all the way to the top of the spokes of each post and all the way along each piece of fence.

The gates opened for the carriage and they headed up the drive toward the house. The house was exquisite. It was similar to their home in England. Emma let out a small gasp of breath as she first laid eyes on the building.

The carriage came to a halt and the footmen helped Emma down. She was greeted by a woman whom she guessed to be Gracie and a man whom she guessed to be Oliver. William was at her side. After they were away from the carriage, it set off to the stables to allow the horses to breath and be watered.

"Miss Huntington, we is so glad to meet ya'll," said the woman kindly.

"You must be Gracie?" asked Emma.

"Yes'm and this here is Oliver. We is in charge o' all o' the servants out here at Beacon Hall."

"It is nice to meet you," said Emma.

"We are pleased as punch to be meetin' ya'll. You must be Mr. William?"

"Yes, I'm William," said the child glad to be recognized.

"What happened to your arm chile?"

"I broke it."

"It is a long story," added Emma.

"Well, Miss Huntington…"

"Please, call me Emma."

"Miss Emma, if you wants to see the grounds, I'd be happy to take you out," said Oliver.

"That would be lovely. In fact, let's do that first so the dark doesn't creep in on us whilst we are out."

"Do you want the carriage back?"

"No, we can just take horses out if they are handy," said Emma knowing perfectly well they would be if she knew her father.

"We gots two o' them all ready fo' you."

"Good. William, why don't you go inside with Gracie and see the house? Oliver and I will be back shortly and we'll have some tea."

"All right Emma," replied William with a little disappointment in his voice. Emma knew he wanted to go with her but riding a horse wasn't exactly what his broken arm needed.

The horses were brought around and Emma mounted – sidesaddle of course – and the two were off. Emma followed Oliver and asked questions here and there. They reached the fields fairly quickly and Emma saw the tobacco plant that her father had spoken about for so long.

"I've never actually seen a tobacco plant before," said Emma.

"Well Virginia is one o' the best places to grow it. We got the right climate fo' it. It and cotton is what folks grow 'round here."

"That's what I am told. How is the production coming along?"

"Well, the tobacco jus' got planted last month, but we been havin' warm weather and so the plants is jus' poppin' up like you wouldn't believe."

"Do you oversee this all?"

"Mos' o' it. Your father is usually quite involved in it all but wid him gone, I's done mos' o' the overseein'. Miss Emma, I needs to bring somethin' up to ya but I don't want you to think I'm bein' bad."

"What is it Oliver?"

"Well, the servants ain't been paid recently. I mean, we understand wid yo' father gone and yo' mother, well her passin' on an' all, but we gots to get paid soon."

"You mean… you mean that you aren't slaves?" Emma regretted the question almost as soon as she spoke it. Oliver had the look of an ashamed man, but there was a sense of pride in his look as well.

"No Miss Emma, we is paid servants."

"I'm so sorry for my comment. I merely assumed that you were… Well I am glad that you are paid servants and I shall be glad to pay you all your wages. I must say that I certainly don't agree with slavery; I was appalled when I found out, or thought I found out, that my father was keeping slaves."

"No Miss Emma. Your father is one o' the on'y ones who pays his servants. We is all free men. Well, mos' o' us anyway. Some o' the people here is indentured servants, but they will be free too someday. 'Specially workin' for yo' father."

"I have to tell you Oliver, I have been reading this pamphlet by Mr. Benjamin Franklin about slavery and the travesty of the practices in the south especially. I could loan it to you sometime if you would like to read it," said Emma.

"That's kind o' you Miss Emma, but I don't know how to read."

"You don't know how?"

"No, mos' of us don't."

"Well then you shall learn. Reading is very important and you shall learn if I have to teach you myself."

"Really Miss Emma?" asked Oliver with much enthusiasm in his voice. Emma nodded and Oliver smiled at her. This smile was one of warm gratitude and appreciation.

"We can get the wages when we return to the house."

They rode on a little further and Emma saw some other smaller homes.

"Whom do these belong to?"

"These is the servants' houses. Well, mos' o' the servants. Some o' them travel a little ways but mos' everyone lives here."

"I see."

"Well, that's 'bout it Miss Emma. Was there anythin' else you were wantin' to see?"

Emma hesitated. "Actually yes, I would like you to show me where my mother is buried."

Oliver nodded but said nothing. He turned his horse a bit and Emma followed. They reached the site of the grave, and Oliver helped Emma down from her horse. He remained with the horses, however, so Emma could have a few moments alone.

Emma walked over to the grave marker and read it softly to herself.

"Elizabeth Corinne Blaine Huntington. Born November 25th, 1735. Died March 2nd, 1773." Emma knelt down by her mother's grave. She had never thought she would have to look at a tombstone that bore the name of her mother; certainly at least not until she was much older.

Emma stared at the angel engraving that had been placed on the marker and she bowed her head and began to pray.

After about a half hour, Emma stood again and went back over to where Oliver was waiting.

"We can head back up to the house now."

When they got to the house, William came running out to meet them.

"Emma, Emma guess what!"

"What William?" she asked as she was helped down from the horse.

"My room, it looks just like my room in England."

"Really?" asked Emma.

"Yes and it even has my bed from home."

"I'm sure it is just a bed that looks like yours, William," said Emma but he had not heard her. He was ushering her inside to show her more. "Thank you Oliver, for your help. If you come inside and wait for a moment, I can get you what we discussed."

"And look Emma, it is the same furniture that we had in our parlor in England."

Emma stopped dead in the hallway. She could see into the parlor and she could also see that her younger brother was right. In fact, the whole house was decorated in much the same manner as their home in England, not to mention that the structure was extremely similar as well. The rooms were located in the same place, and they were all the same size with few minor differences that made the house a little better than their home in England. It was strange and because of the similarity, Emma knew where everything was located.

Emma went to the study and found the safe behind the portrait, the same portrait of Emma's mother Elizabeth that hung in the study in their home in England. She opened the safe with no difficulty and took out what was needed to fulfill the wages of the servants. This was all according to a note she had found upon her father's desk stating this sort of information. Emma was sure it had been left for her mother in her father's absence. She brought the money back out to Oliver and he said he would disperse it accordingly.

"I see you is right at home Miss Emma," said Gracie as Emma entered the drawing room and asked her to serve tea.

"This house has an uncanny similarity to our former home in England," replied Emma.

"That was Mr. James's plan. Miss Elizabeth always missed that ol' house in England so much that when they built this plantation house, Mr. James built it to look like that house and they shipped in mos' o' the furniture. Much of it came from your ol' house even."

"That is so interesting," said Emma distractedly as she was still enthralled with the décor.

William sat down with Emma and tea was served. After tea, Emma decided that they needed to get back to town. Gracie assured them that everything was being taken care of. Emma told her that they would be out now and again to stay. Gracie said she was glad to hear it and Emma and William climbed back into the carriage and set out yet again for Williamsburg.

By the time they got home, it was getting dark. Emma made sure William had a bit of dinner and then sent him off to bed. She did not eat much; she still found she had no appetite. Felicity found her shortly after William headed upstairs and asked her for a moment.

"What is it, Felicity?"

"Benjamin still has not emerged from his room. I am very worried about him."

"I'm sure he is fine Felicity. I would not bother him any more tonight. If he does not emerge by tomorrow evening, I shall speak with him. I will make sure that Francis brings up a tray for him."

"I have already had her do so. He has not touched it."

"He shall eat when he is hungry is about all I can tell you." Emma knew that Felicity meant well, but she also knew that Benjamin dealt with difficult news by isolating himself from everyone. She also realized how little she had eaten and did not worry much about the news of his fasting for the day.

"If you feel that is for the best, Emma," said Felicity.

"I really do Felicity. This really is what Benjamin does. He always has. This is how he deals with difficult news not to mention that he is probably exhausted. Honestly, he probably spent most of the day sleeping."

"I'm sure you are right. Well, I too am quite tired; I think that I shall turn in for the night."

"All right. I shall see you tomorrow Felicity."

"Goodnight Emma." With that, Felicity headed upstairs to the guest room that had been made up for her.

Emma sat down on the sofa and put her feet up. It had been yet another long day. She heaved a small sigh. What a nightmare the past few weeks had been for her. However, it could only get better from here. Suddenly Emma remembered that she had had a visitor earlier that day. She stood and went out to the hallway to find that they actually had quite a few cards left for them during the course of the day. However, one of the cards had a note attached to it. Emma picked up this one and read the card.

"Mr. Edward Findley. Edward? In Williamsburg?" Emma thought this strange but felt her heart lift a little at the sight of a familiar name. She took off the attached note and began to read it.

Dearest Emma,

I am glad to finally hear of your safe arrival in Williamsburg. I am sure that your journey has been quite long and tedious but you are finally at home. First and foremost, I send out my deepest sympathy about your mother. Your mother was one of the finest ladies that this world has ever known and she shall be sorely missed by all who knew her. My deepest condolences to you and your family on your immense loss.

On a happier note, I am glad that I will finally be able to see you again. The Bradbury's were quite concerned about you and your brothers after your hasty departure. I wish to keep this note brief, but please allow me to take the courtesy to call on you for a visit tomorrow afternoon around two o' clock. I hope that this is satisfactory to you. If not, please

send word with one of your servants and I shall rearrange my schedule for you. Until we see each other again, I shall remain...
  Sincerely yours,
  Edward G. Findley

Emma closed the letter and closed her hand around it. It would be very good to see Edward again. Her eyes were heavy with want of sleep and so Emma decided to head to bed herself.

Emma had somehow managed to sleep in a little, much to her surprise. When she did awaken, the sun was quite high in the sky, at least comparatively to what she was used to. She stood and stretched a bit. It actually felt good to get up for a change. She looked out the window to see a lovely, sunny day. She was sure it would be warm out. She dressed in a lovely light blue dress that was quite becoming with her fair hair and blue eyes.

She headed downstairs to have breakfast; she was actually fairly hungry, as she really hadn't eaten well in quite a few days. After breakfast, Emma decided to go out into the yard and take in the morning air.

When she entered the yard, she found Felicity and William outside playing catch with a ball. She went over to say good morning to them.

"Emma, good morning, I trust you must have slept last night," said Felicity.

"I did thank you. It felt really nice."

"Are you not sleeping well again, Emma?" asked William.

"I slept well last night, but I have always found it difficult to sleep when we travel."

"But you are better now?"

"I believe so. Where is Benjamin this fine morning? He should be out here enjoying the warm sun."

"He still has not come out from his room," said Felicity.

"Ah, perhaps he still is sleeping as well," replied Emma appearing as if she was not concerned with her older brother's continued isolation. On the contrary, Emma was beginning to worry quite a bit about her brother. She knew he had not eaten all day yesterday, though she couldn't badger him much for that as she had done the same. However, she worried about him and hoped that he would soon emerge feeling a bit better.

"Emma, do you want to play with us?" asked William.

"Not right now dearest. In fact, why don't you go inside and ask Curtis to come outside and play with you so I can steal Felicity away for a while? How would that be?"

"All right. Thanks for playing with me Felicity," said William as he ran towards the house.

"My pleasure dear," replied Felicity.

"Would you care to walk with me?" asked Emma.

"Of course, what is troubling you?"

"Actually, I wanted to speak with you about something on a bit of a different note."

"Whatever you wish to speak about is all right with me."

"How often have you been in Williamsburg?"

"Fairly so. When I was younger my grandparents lived here, right near your father's plantation actually. After my grandfather died and my grandmother moved up to Maryland, my father inherited their home. My grandmother still maintains the deed to the house, but neither she nor my parents use it much, only when we are traveling through and even then we do not always stay there. However, when I was young I spent almost every summer here."

"So you would venture to say you know Williamsburg quite well then?"

"I know the layout of the town if that is what you are asking but as to the people, well, there are some families I know and some that I do not. I honestly have not spent much time here since my grandfather died and that was almost six years ago now. Emma, forgive my curiosity but is there a reason to this line of questioning?"

Emma did not want to completely divulge her reasons to Felicity yet so she replied, "Not particularly, just trying to make conversation. I merely was in want of companionship. I hope you do not mind."

"Not at all. I am sorry to have asked."

"There is no need to be sorry."

"What did you do in the summers in England?"

"Well, we mainly stayed at home. We often had many visitors during the summer months and so many stayed with us that we were hardly in want of company."

"It must have been an exciting place for you to grow up."

"It was a lovely place to grow up actually. I do so miss it at times."

"Do you regret your decision to come here?"

"I do not regret the decision to come to Virginia…" said Emma though she did not finish her sentence.

"You have other regrets though?"

"Who among us is not without some regret, if they live long enough?" asked Emma with a sad sort of laugh.

"It is a shame that you feel that way Emma."

"Can you honestly tell me that you live with no regrets?"

"I cannot honestly say that I have never had one regret, but time mends all. Besides, from all mistakes come change and it is all within God's plan."

"That may be, but it does not always lessen the blow."

There was a short span of silence that hung between the girls. Felicity finally broke the silence.

"Emma, my father is a good friend of a man who teaches at

the college. I was wondering if you would care to go and visit with me. I am supposed to see him around eleven and have lunch with him and his wife."

"I don't know…"

"I would consider it a great favor. They are very nice people you see, but I have nothing in common with them; though luncheons with them are hardly ever boring, I do not ever fancy spending vast amounts of time with them."

"I suppose I could go with you, but I need to be back here no later than one thirty."

"That should be no problem and it will give us a readymade excuse to leave," said Felicity. "I just need to go and freshen up and then we can be off. We can honestly just walk if you like. The college is not far from here. You can see it at the end of Duke of Gloucester Street."

"That's the college?"

"Yes, it really is a lovely place. I just love the architecture of the buildings."

The girls headed back to the house. Emma stopped by where William had conned not only Curtis, but also a couple more of the servants, into playing with him. Felicity continued ahead. As Emma came near, all of the servants stopped dead in their tracks. Emma had to laugh at the abruptness in their cease of action.

"It is all right. I told William to find someone else to occupy him this morning. William, I merely wanted to tell you that Felicity and I are going to meet with a friend of Mr. Dillingham for lunch. I want you to be good while I am gone and do not cause any trouble. Curtis, will you look after him whilst we are out?"

"Yes'm. I'd be honored to do that," replied Curtis.

"Thank you. William, please behave."

"I will. See you later."

"Oh, one other thing William, Edward will be stopping by later this afternoon."

"Edward? Why's he coming here?"

"To visit, I suppose," replied Emma.

"But I don't want to see him. He isn't very nice Emma, and he doesn't really like me. He's just nice to me because he likes seeing you."

Emma blushed over the last part of William's comment.

"William, that isn't very nice. You don't have to stay, you merely have to say hello to him, and you'd best be polite or no dessert tonight after dinner. You know Mother and Father taught you better than to be rude to guests."

"I know. I will be nice. Just don't make me stay too long."

"Goodbye William. Have fun with Curtis and the others. I shall see you later."

"Bye Emma."

Emma walked into the house. She didn't really want to change clothes and so she went up to ask Felicity if what she was wearing was nice enough. Felicity told her it was more than nice enough. Emma was glad of it. They walked down the stairs together and headed toward the college.

When they arrived at the Hamblin's house they were greeted warmly. The Hamblin's lived on Jamestown Road, which was right across the street from the college.

Emma and Felicity were announced into the parlor and met by both Mr. and Mrs. Hamblin.

"Felicity, it is so good to see you," said Mrs. Hamblin.

"You have gotten so big. You were but a wee little one the last time we saw you," added Mr. Hamblin.

"Mr. and Mrs. Hamblin, it is good to see you as well. This is my dear friend, Miss Emma Huntington."

"Miss Huntington, it is a pleasure. You must be related to Mr. James Huntington," said Mr. Hamblin.

"I am. He is my father."

"Your father? He never mentioned having children. For that matter, he never mentioned being married," said Mr. Hamblin.

"I suppose he must have been though," said Mrs. Hamblin. "Now that I come to think of it, I am sure he did. I heard her name more than once whilst shopping in town."

Emma found this all very strange. Perhaps her father was not as well known as she had thought. At any rate, she found it very odd that the Hamblin's knew her father, but did not know he was married or had children. Everyone whom Emma had met that knew her father knew about her as well; often more than she wished they knew about her.

"Well, lunch is being served out on the patio. Why don't we go out there? I am famished," said Mrs. Hamblin and the other three followed.

The lunch conversation was sparse. It mainly revolved around the college and Williamsburg. Mr. Hamblin told Emma and Felicity he would take them over to the college after lunch and show them around. The girls agreed that would be nice.

Other than the brief interludes of silence, Mrs. Hamblin spoke about not having any children and her annoying sister-in-law that was staying with them; though she was not around today to have lunch with them.

After lunch, Emma gladly stood and was ready to go over to the college. Emma now knew what Felicity meant about the Hamblin's. They were nice enough people and lunch wasn't exactly boring, but there was something not quite right about them, though Emma couldn't place her finger on it.

Mr. Hamblin escorted Emma and Felicity over to the college and showed them the buildings. Emma's favorite was the Wren Building, which had a lovely courtyard behind it and very nicely kept grounds in front. Mr. Hamblin then took the girls inside to see a classroom that wasn't in use at the time.

As they entered the great hall, Mr. Hamblin and Felicity went into the classroom but Emma stayed in the hallway and was looking at the artwork. Emma then saw someone out of the corner of her eye, but she saw him a moment too late. By the time she had turned enough to see him fully he had run right into her and completely knocked her off her feet.

"I am so sorry, I was running late and I wasn't watching where I was going. Please it is my fault entirely," said the young man. "Please allow me to help you up, Miss..."

"Huntington," replied Emma as she took the young man's hand and gently rubbed her hip where she had fallen.

"Huntington, Emma Huntington?"

"Yes, how do you know who I am?"

"I know you parents quite well."

Just then, another young man yelled at him from outside to hurry.

"I'm so sorry, I must be going. Please forgive me my rudeness. Perhaps we shall see each other again soon," he said as he ran out of the building and closed the heavy doors behind him.

Emma stood there dumbfounded with her stomach in knots. She had been completely knocked off her feet and onto the ground. She'd met someone who was obviously well acquainted with her parents, well enough to guess her identity at least, but he did not mention his name. What struck Emma the most about the young man however, were his striking green eyes. Emma had seen herself in those eyes, even in the brief moment of their interaction. They reminded Emma of the bright green from the rolling hills of Britain.

"Emma, are you all right?" asked Felicity upon her reentrance into the hallway.

"I'm fine, did you see that young man?" asked Emma.

"No, I'm sorry, I did not. Did you know him?"

"No, I don't believe so, but he knew me. He knocked me onto my feet."

"That was awfully rude."

"He didn't do it on purpose Felicity. He just didn't see me. He apologized."

"Well I should hope so. You're all right though?"

"Fine, fine."

"Well, that bell we heard just a few moments ago from the tower meant one o'clock; we should be getting back to your house."

"You're right. We need to be going. Mr. Hamblin, it was nice to meet you."

"And you Miss Huntington. I hope we shall meet again sometime," he replied.

"I'm sure I shall see you around Mr. Hamblin, and please thank your wife again for the lovely lunch."

"I will do that. Felicity," he said as he nodded to her.

"It was nice to see you again Mr. Hamblin. Thank you for the tour," she replied but not very warmly.

"Until we meet again ladies," said Mr. Hamblin and he left the Wren Building and walked across the lawn toward Jamestown Road again, undoubtedly heading home as well.

The girls went out the front doors of the building and headed down Duke of Gloucester Street toward the Huntington residence. By the time they reached the front door, Emma was sure Edward would be there any moment. He was always extremely punctual.

Felicity waited with Emma. Emma knew it was because she wanted to meet the man that had repeatedly asked for her hand. Emma had never told Felicity this, but she was sure that Benjamin probably had mentioned it at least a few dozen times. It certainly was no secret that Benjamin disliked Edward immensely.

At ten minutes to two, the doorbell rang. One of the servants answered it and entered the parlor to announce Edward Findley.

"Please show him in," said Emma. Both women stood and waited for Edward. He did not disappoint them. He entered moments later dressed in his very best, complete with a red coat.

"Edward, welcome to our new home," said Emma as she greeted him warmly. He came over and kissed her hand gently.

"Welcome to Williamsburg Emma. It is so pleasing to see you again."

"Edward, this is a dear friend of my family, Miss Dillingham. She is staying with us whilst her parents attend to some business. Felicity, this is Mr. Findley."

"Actually, it is Lieutenant Findley now."

"Lieutenant?" asked Emma.

"Yes, it is a long story, but it is certainly a pleasure Miss Dillingham."

"Lieutenant Findley," replied Felicity. Emma had to admit that Edward had not lost his charm; though she also knew that both Felicity and Edward only had eyes for one person in their lives. Felicity had Benjamin, and Edward was still enamored with Emma.

Just then William entered the room.

"William, how good to see you. How have you been?" asked Edward.

"Good I suppose. How are you?"

"I am well. How do you like Williamsburg so far?"

"It is all right. I haven't seen much. Yesterday we saw the plantation."

"You went out to Beacon Hall yesterday?"

"Yes, it was really nice. It was just like our house in England," said William.

"I know. I've been there. It just surprises me that you went out there without your father," said Edward.

"And why shouldn't we?" asked Emma.

"No reason, none at all. I was merely surprised you made it out there so quickly."

Emma knew that William was done with the visit and she could see that Felicity was looking for a hospitable and eloquent way to exit the parlor so Emma asked her, "Felicity, would you mind bringing William upstairs? He has some things he needs to attend to."

"Of course," replied Felicity. "Come along William. Let's go upstairs."

After they left, Emma asked Edward to sit down. They sat together on one of the sofas.

"Emma, I wanted to tell you that I was extremely sorry to hear about your mother. I am sure her loss has been tremendously difficult on you and your family. Your mother, Lady Huntington, was one of the most kind and eloquent ladies I have ever had the pleasure of knowing," he said as he took her hand.

"Thank you Edward. That is very kind of you. It has been difficult. In all honesty, that is why we went out to the plantation yesterday; I wanted to visit her grave," Emma replied shifting her weight slightly away from Edward.

"That is completely understandable. Emma, are you all right?"

Emma answered his question with silence. In all actuality, she was not all right.

"Emma, you know you can tell me. I would never tell anyone anything that you confide in me."

Emma took a deep breath as she stared at the floor. "Everything is just such a mess Edward."

"Such as?"

"I'm supposed to be in England. My mother is supposed to be alive and welcoming me with open arms. My father is supposed to be here waiting for us. Benjamin is taking it all very hard. He has not come from his room in two days. I know that William understands, but I question if he truly understands the finality of it all."

Edward embraced Emma and she allowed a single tear to fall upon his shoulder. Emma felt so safe in Edward's arms. It was as if, at that moment, he could fight the world and all her hurts away. It was times like this that Emma wondered if he might be right in his affection for her. She certainly did not love the man that now held her, but she felt as though she could live a very happy life with him and he would take such good care of her. She knew she certainly would never want for anything. But was that enough?

"It will all be all right Emma. I promise you. Everything is going to be all right. I know that nothing is as you expected, but you have made it safely to Williamsburg and that is something to be happy about."

"I only wish that we had made it here a month or two earlier Edward. Perhaps then my mother would still be alive and even if she wouldn't have survived, I would have at least seen her again."

"I know Emma. I can assure you, however, that your presence would not have saved her. She was very ill. I hope you take comfort that she is in a much better place now."

"Were you here then?" Emma asked pulling back from Edward mildly surprised by his previous statement.

"I was able to visit your mother a few times before her death. My company arrived in Williamsburg in late January."

Emma looked at Edward now with surprise and curiosity.

"Your company? Edward, surely you haven't done something silly and joined the army?"

"I have indeed. In fact, that is how I found out you had arrived. Some of the men in my company were amongst those who stopped your carriage when you first arrived in Williamsburg. I read the report and found Benjamin's name. I assumed you were with him and I came over almost immediately to see you.

However, you were out, I assume at the plantation, and so I left you my note."

"Yes, I received your note. When did you join the army?"

"Soon after you left your aunt and uncle's home. I didn't think they would ship me to Virginia, but here I am and what a coincidence it is," said Edward happily.

"They made you a lieutenant then?"

"Well, my father had a hand in that. I don't have my own company yet, but it won't be long I should think. I am second in command of my company now and have learned a fair lot from my commanding officer."

"I never thought you would join the army Edward," said Emma still surprised by all this news.

"To be honest, nor did I. However, I was growing tired of the home life. I began to yearn for a bit of adventure and my father suggested the army. After all, it couldn't be that much work and I would be able to travel a bit."

"Do you enjoy it then?"

"For now I do. I certainly can't complain about it. They treat me well and I am taken care of. But what of you? I want to hear all about your travels."

"Well," Emma began to relate the past seven months to Edward. When she reached Christmas, she decided they best have tea. "It is such a fine day, do you mind terribly if we have tea out in the yard?" asked Emma.

"Not at all. That is a fine idea," replied Edward.

Emma asked Francis to have tea set for them and they went out into the backyard.

"Please continue, after Christmas, what happened?"

"After Christmas my cousin, Helena Seager, was married."

"Really? To whom?"

"To a man named Frederick Alamonté."

"Alamonté? Surely he isn't English?"

"No, I believe his relations are from Austria. That is where they went on their holiday anyway."

"Was it a nice ceremony?"

"It was actually Edward. It made me feel as if…"

"As if you wanted to be married?"

"Edward, you know how I feel about this subject," said Emma now realizing the trap she had set up for herself.

"Emma, don't you see the hand that fate has dealt to us? You and I, both in Williamsburg together; what are the odds?"

"I'm sure that they weren't favorable, but Edward…"

"Emma, have you even given thought about what I said whilst we were still in England? About us being happy together?"

"Even though I do not feel any affection for you greater than friendship?"

"I have said before, and I still believe Emma, that were we married your affection for me would grow. Emma, you know that I could take care of you, give you anything," said Edward, now holding Emma's hand across the table.

"I know that Edward. I do not know if that is enough."

"I want to take care of you."

"Edward, now is just not a good time," replied Emma. Emma's real fear was that she might just say yes to Edward. He had such a good argument, and all she wanted at the moment was for someone to take care of her. She had grown so tired of taking care of herself and everyone else.

"I understand but please remember what I've said."

"I promise that I shall keep it in mind," said Emma gently.

The rest of Edward's visit was very nice for Emma. They spoke about England and the memories that they had had there. Emma continued to tell Edward about their travels to Williamsburg, and also about all of the people they had met. Emma left out the information about her family's connections to people, who were seen as less than reputable to the British, as well as the midnight meetings she had seen and the many conversations she had heard concerning the Colonies.

Edward told Emma about his joining the army and his experience so far. Emma listened politely, still surprised by what had sparked Edward's sudden interest in the army.

After tea, Edward took his leave, asking if he could return to visit.

"Edward, of course you may. You are welcome any time. It is good to see a friendly face again," said Emma genuinely.

Edward smiled and kissed Emma's hand as he bid her goodbye.

After he left her, Emma went into the house. It was nearly four o'clock by now. Dinner would be ready in a couple of hours and she still had not seen Benjamin come out from his room. Emma decided that it was time to pay him a visit.

She went upstairs and knocked on his door. She got no response. Emma put her ear to the door to see if she could tell if he was sleeping or not. She heard nothing.

"Benjamin, it's Emma. Please let me in," she said softly. She took a couple of steps back from the door, held her breath, and waited. She was just about to turn away when the door opened a crack. Emma took this as invitation to enter. She pushed open the door just enough to slide through and shut it again behind her. "Are you all right?"

Benjamin was sitting in his desk chair facing away from Emma and towards the window that overlooked the backyard.

"Was that Edward Findley I saw out there with you?" he said in a quiet and low voice.

"Yes, he is here in Williamsburg now."

"Why?"

"Apparently he has joined the British Army. He's a lieutenant." Emma sat down on the bed and took off her hat and bonnet.

"Such a strange coincidence, don't you think?"

"Yes, actually I do." Benjamin now turned and faced her. She could see his eyes were bloodshot; though she could not tell if it was from tears or from lack of sleep. Most likely it was from both. "Benjamin, have you slept at all?"

"A bit."

"Are you hungry? I can have something brought up if you don't want to come down yet."

"How is Felicity?"

"She's all right. She has been very worried about you though."

"Is she angry with me?"

"Why would she be angry?"

"Because I have been ignoring her when she has come up."

"No Benjamin; she understands. I promise she is not angry."

"How is William?"

"He's all right. I told him the other night, before you arrived home. He took it rather well, all things considered. He cried a bit until he fell asleep, but he has not mentioned it much since. I am not sure he understands the finality of it all though," said Emma as she breathed a heavy and heartfelt sigh.

"Probably not. Forever is a vague concept to a child. It can be such a long time and such a short time, depending on the circumstances. Forever is a vague concept to me."

Emma listened to her brother and watched him. He was doing better then she had originally imagined. It was true that Benjamin was strong and withstood most types of pain quite well, but when something did bother him, it was difficult for him to deal with and he would think about it for a long time. Death was among the worst for Benjamin. In most cases, he did well right away, after first hearing the news, but after a day or two, he would fall apart and isolate himself, just as he was doing now. However, after the day or two of isolation, he would reemerge with a renewed sense of strength, which had always amazed Emma.

"I went out to the plantation yesterday with William."

"And?"

"It's lovely. In fact, it is just like our house in England."

"Really?" Benjamin asked with little interest in his voice. Emma, having nothing better to talk about, continued on.

"Yes, Father imported much of the furniture from the old house, even our bedrooms look the same. Also, I stopped by to see Mother's grave." Emma hesitated to see how this information was taken. Benjamin looked up at his sister before he spoke. As he began to speak, tears fell from his face and Emma went over to him. She knelt down and he put his head upon her shoulder.

"Emma you have been so strong through this all. I don't know how you have done it. I'm so sorry. I should have been the strong one, but I couldn't be. I never expected this Emma. I can still scarcely believe it."

"I know Benjamin; you have nothing to be ashamed of. We all deal with things in our own way. I am glad that I was able to be strong for you and William."

"It shouldn't be this way," said Benjamin pulling away from his sister as she let him go.

"It shouldn't be any particular way. Benjamin, you have been there for me countless times before. In fact, you were there for me just a few days ago, after Mr. Ainsworth died, remember. I needed you then and you need me now. It is as simple as that. That is what families do for each other. We all need time to grieve Benjamin and it is all right to take that time. We hadn't seen Mother in about a year and a half and when we finally are close to her, we find we have missed the opportunity. Benjamin, that is tearing at my heartstrings, and I know it must be tearing at yours, but it is God's plan. We need to remember that."

"I know and I shall be all right now. The worst has passed."

Emma nodded as she spoke. "What you need now is a good meal and a good night's sleep. It really did wonders for me."

"I think that I will go out to the plantation tomorrow then

and see everything."

"Would you like me to go with you?"

"No thank you. I really think I would like to go alone."

"Of course. Now, why don't you freshen up just a bit and come down for some dinner," said Emma standing again and regaining her cheerful voice.

"Emma, before you go, may I ask you something?"

"Of course."

"What did Edward want of you?"

"He merely stopped by to visit."

"Did he ask you again?"

"In a way. Sort of," replied Emma turning her head to the floor.

"What does that mean?"

"Well, I sort of walked into it, and he asked if I had thought about what we last discussed."

"What did you say?"

"I told him now was not a good time to discuss it, but my answer was still the same."

"So you have not changed your mind then?"

Emma hesitated for the briefest of moments and then sighed. "Most days I still say no, which is why I will not tell him yes. However, even I must admit that there are some days when I want to say yes to him for the simple fact that he really does have a strong argument and I know that I would be well taken care of as well as all of my family and…"

"And?"

"Well, he does truly seem to love me."

Now it was time for Benjamin to sigh. "Emma, I have no right to tell you what to do but do not rush into it if you are not certain."

"You mustn't worry on that account. Now, come down to dinner." Emma was glad to change the subject so easily.

"I'll be down in a few minutes. I just want to clean up a bit," said Benjamin. As Emma left the room she heard Benjamin say almost under his breath, "Odd that he's here. I find it very odd indeed."

Emma knew the comment wasn't meant for a reply from her so she shut the door the rest of the way and went down to dinner. She was joined shortly after by William and Felicity and just a few, short minutes later, by Benjamin. Benjamin looked so much better in Emma's opinion and with the way Felicity's face lit up at the sight of him, she knew that Benjamin would be glad he came to dinner as well as Felicity's worries being laid aside.

Dinner turned out to be a fairly gay affair. Felicity was in excellent spirits at the sight of Benjamin, and Benjamin put on a very good show for her benefit. William was telling them all about his day and they all spoke merrily for quite some time. Emma was probably the quietest. She did not say much at all during dinner but not because something was wrong. Indeed no, for the first time in quite a while, everything seemed right. She sat amongst the people she loved and they were all very happy. Emma merely sat back and smiled at the whole affair. For the first time since she had arrived in the Colonies, Emma felt she was home.

Chapter 8
James's Dinner Party

April went out amidst beautiful weather and warm days. May bloomed with lovely flowers; many types Emma had never seen before. Things seemed to be looking up a little. At least the weather was an accomplice at attempting to pretend like things were getting better. It was hard to grieve or sulk when the weather was so nice.

On May tenth, the town of Williamsburg, and in fact the all of the Colonies, received notice that the Tea Act would be taking effect. That meant that there would be a three penny per pound import tax on tea bricks arriving in the Colonies. The tax itself was enough to infuriate Colonists, but the effects of the act enraged them even more so. The British East India Company had been near bankruptcy before the act was passed; afterwards, they were given a virtual monopoly on the market because they were able to sell directly to colonial agents; thereby bypassing any middleman and thus underselling all American merchants.

The talk in the town was filled with cries of outrage at the act. Emma had scarcely seen people so openly angry. Many people could no longer afford tea from the Colonies, but refused to buy tea from the British. The Huntington family continued to buy tea as needed. Emma saw no reason to stop drinking tea simply because it was British instead of American. In her opinion, British tea was probably better. After all, the King certainly must know what was best for his subjects.

On the fifteenth, they celebrated Benjamin's nineteenth birthday. It was a joyous occasion. They spent the day at the plantation. Emma was glad of the fair weather. At least it was a nice distraction from the world's events that seemed to put such a damper on everyone's moods.

Finally Emma decided that William needed to begin with a tutor again, much to the child's dismay. The tutor came to their house in Williamsburg for five hours every day during the week. Emma wasn't too sure about the man who came to tutor her younger brother, but Benjamin said he had come highly recommended and had no qualms with the man, so Emma said nothing more on the subject. However, she was slow to remove her ever watchful eyes from the man and his interactions with William.

All in all, life stayed pretty monotonous through May. Emma spent her days here and there whether in town or at the plantation. Edward came to visit her often. Most days, Emma was delighted to see him. She enjoyed his company so much as it reminded her of happier times. Benjamin, and especially William, on the other hand, did not enjoy Edward's frequent visits quite as much.

June came in with almost oppressive heat. Emma was used of humid summers in England, but they did not compare with the heat and humidity mixture of southern Virginia. It was all she could do some days to get out of bed. But then again, her bed was often soaked from sweat when she awoke each morning, which encouraged her get out of bed fairly quick.

By the middle of June, Emma, Benjamin, William, and Felicity had grown quite comfortable in Williamsburg. They had all established their own routines, but always had dinner together in the evening. All four had met much of the townspeople and had become quite popular, well liked, and even fairly well respected amongst them.

By mid-summer, Emma found she often spent her days out at the plantation. She enjoyed how comfortable she felt in the familiar house. In fact, Emma's practice was to visit the townspeople and do whatever needed to be done in town in the mornings, head out to the plantation in the afternoons, and spend each evening with William, Benjamin, and Felicity back in town. Sometimes Felicity or Benjamin joined her, but they often spent their afternoons together whether at the plantation or in town.

At least once or twice a week, Emma would have a visit from Edward. He had also established a routine, and usually stopped in on Tuesdays and Fridays to visit with Emma. On these days, she did not go to the plantation. Edward wisely did not bring up marriage again, at least not outright – though he did often try to hint at the subject. Other than this small annoyance, Emma continued to enjoy her visits with Edward, mainly because he brought her past with him.

Life in Williamsburg was turning out to be quite pleasant and enjoyable for Emma and her brothers. The only thing that continued to bother Emma was the lack of her father's presence, as well as an even greater worry that sprang from his lack of correspondence with his children. Emma had never gone so long without hearing from her father, and she grew more worried with each passing day.

On June twelfth, it was Felicity's turn to have her birthday. She was now eighteen. Her parents had sent her a parcel with a few gifts, but Felicity's favorite was a new dress. The dress was cream colored with little, delicate yellow flowers with bright green leaves embroidered on the material. It truly brought out Felicity's red hair and bright green eyes.

Summer wore on. July brought only more heat and humidity. Then, one day, late in July, Emma was sitting in the parlor. Edward had just left her and she was about to make sure all was ready for dinner, when a carriage Emma had never seen pulled into the drive. She stood and looked out the window to see who it was. Emma had to rub her eyes a little before she realized who was about to enter the house; it was her father.

Emma rushed to the front door and had it open before he had even stepped up to the walk. The servants were out collecting his belongings but he entered and Emma wrapped her arms around him.

"I can't believe it. You are finally home," said Emma and she felt the tears run down her face freely.

"Father?" came Benjamin's voice from the staircase. "William, Father's home!" and Benjamin too ran down to greet his father.

William came bounding down the stairs and ran at his father. James Huntington, a fairly tall man with light, smooth chestnut colored hair and eyes to match, held his weeping daughter in one arm and picked up his youngest son in the other.

"Has it been so long?" asked James. "You are all so big, especially you William."

"I'm almost six, Papa" said William.

"I know, Son. August second has been on my mind for a while. I knew I had to be home by then, and here I am. But what has happened to your arm William?"

"It's all right. I get to be done with it all in just a few more days."

"It is a long story, Father," said Benjamin. "But he is fine and yes, the doctor told him he could take it off on his birthday, but not a day before."

"Then that is what shall happen," said James. "Now, what on earth are you crying for, Emma?"

Emma didn't think she could answer him, she hardly knew

herself. It was just as though a wave of emotion had collided with her and her tears were the result. Emma finally did calm down though; her father hugged her and smiled at his three children.

As all three Huntington children led James into the parlor to sit down for a rest, Felicity entered from the backyard.

"Who has come? I thought I heard a carriage just a moment ago," began Felicity before she even looked up. "Oh! Mr. Huntington. How wonderful to see you!"

"Felicity, it is lovely to see you as well. I am glad that you have found your way back to Williamsburg with my children."

"I am pleased that they agreed to have me along."

There was definite warmness between the two and Emma felt as though her family were finally coming back together, although her heart still ached. She knew this was because her mother would never share in any more of their adventures, nor in any more of their moments.

"Well, I shall let Francis know to put out one more plate for dinner," said Felicity and politely excused herself so that the Huntington family could be alone.

James sat on the sofa with William on his lap and Emma at his side. Benjamin took the armchair next to the sofa.

"Father, where on Earth have you been? We have been worried sick about you," said Emma as she leaned into his side with his arm around her.

"We hadn't heard from you in quite some time Father," said Benjamin.

"I too have some long stories but for now, let us just say that the mail is not entirely safe at the moment, and I have my reasons for not wanting certain people to know my whereabouts."

"Like who?"

"Well, like the same people who stopped your carriage the night you arrived in Williamsburg," he said.

"How did you know about that Father?" asked Emma sitting up and looking at James.

"I have my ways. Besides, did you not notice just how many people I know here?"

"And everywhere else in the Colonies it seems," replied Benjamin laughing. Emma leaned back into her father's side and relaxed a bit.

"So it would seem," said James mysteriously. "Now, did I hear something about dinner being ready?"

"It should be by now; we usually eat around seven thirty, but it is already seven fifteen," said Emma.

"Well then, let us not tarry for I am famished. My journey was a long one today and I have not eaten all day."

"Well then, we best go have a fine dinner," said William, and the Huntington family laughed and went into the dining room with William leading; his father's hand in his just to keep him close.

Benjamin went to fetch Felicity and soon they were all seated around the table with James at the head, where he belonged. Conversation was light during dinner. It mainly revolved around the children telling their father about their own journey. Benjamin and Emma allowed William to do most of the talking; they knew they would have their own chance later that evening.

"And we went hunting, Papa," William told James.

"Where?" James asked with surprise.

"We went with the Moyers," Benjamin told his father.

"That's where I broke my arm, but not before I saw Benjamin fire a couple of shots. He's a very good shot you know."

"I'm sure he is."

Benjamin laughed.

"He's probably only second to your sister, William."

"Emma, you can shoot a gun?"

Emma blushed but said nothing. Benjamin affirmed what his father had said.

"Now, I want to hear more about this broken arm."

Benjamin told James he would explain the whole event of the broken arm later.

After dinner, the five members of the household went into the drawing room to relax and visit some more. Finally, ten o'clock rolled around and Emma had to pry William off his father and force him to go to bed. Felicity too said she was tired, but Emma knew she was merely being polite so that Emma and Benjamin could have some time alone with their father.

"So from what William has told me, you've had quite the adventure. What with being kidnapped from your Aunt and Uncle Bradbury's home, on a ship with pirates, and then all of your travels here; I can certainly see that he hasn't lost his imagination."

"No, he certainly hasn't," said Emma laughing a bit.

"Now how about the real story?" asked James.

"Well, it is all sort of a blur now. We haven't really thought much about it lately. I suppose it started last August when Benjamin decided on this crazy plan," said Emma.

"Now don't pin this all on me. You certainly agreed to the whole thing," teased Benjamin.

"Anyway, from there we got on a ship and two months later, we landed in Boston."

"Now you are leaving things out," said Benjamin.

"Would you care to tell the story?"

"As a matter of fact, yes. So, from deciding that we were going to leave, I got a friend of mine, Thomas, remember him?"

"I do; I keep correspondence with his father still," said James.

"Well, he helped us. He brought us to the docks and we set out that night. The trip on the ocean was nice enough. We were very lucky to have such good weather. William and I learned all about being sailors."

"I hope you don't go getting any ideas," said James jovially.

"Oh no. I could never be a sailor, neither could Emma, though not for the same reason as I," teased Benjamin. Emma gave him a cold but joking stare.

"I take it the sea did not agree with your stomach dearest?" asked James.

"It wasn't all that bad. It merely took a few days to become used of the constant rolling."

"It often does for many people."

"Anyway, after two long months, we finally arrived in Boston; unbeknownst to me, Emma had written to Uncle Alexandre and told him of our departure."

"And thankfully, our arrival as well," said Emma.

"It would have been all right had he not been there you know," said Benjamin.

"I'm sure it would have, Benjamin. In fact, I hear that the Boston Harbor is quite nice in the winter. It would have been a lovely spot to have our Christmas holiday."

All three people were now laughing again.

"All right, so you met up with Alexandre," said James.

"Well, we stayed with them through much of November. I was also able to go to the town meeting were Mr. Samuel Adams spoke."

"And how was that?"

"It was extremely interesting," said Benjamin.

"Good, and Emma?"

"Well, I didn't go but it is just as good I didn't. I didn't think too highly of the whole affair."

"Mmm," replied James.

"From Boston, we headed to Aunt Margaret's in Maryland. That trip took us a while, almost two weeks, but thankfully Uncle

Alexandre knows enough people that we were able to merely switch out horses instead of having to stop."

"Well, that must have made quite a difference in the time you were able to make."

"I'm sure it did," replied Benjamin. "Well, Aunt Margaret and Uncle Peter were quite excited to see us. Of course you know most of this."

"I did receive your letters, if that is what you mean," said James.

"Yes. Well, Christmas was nice. It was nice to spend it with family, though we certainly missed you here. After Christmas we waited until March and when the weather finally decided to cooperate a bit, we set out for Virginia."

"Now you are leaving things out. In January, Helena had her wedding."

"How was that? I feel terrible I was not able to make it."

"It was very nice. Benjamin and I were both in the wedding party. Helena took off for her holiday in Austria shortly afterwards. From there we spent most of our time meeting people and entertaining guests with Aunt Margaret and Uncle Peter. We met some of the nicest people Father, as well as some of the most interesting."

"I'm sure you did. Did you meet anyone I know?"

"We met lots of people who know you, including the Carrington family."

"You met Brent and Cordelia Carrington then?"

"Yes, and three of their sons. They are wonderful people, Father. I just loved the time I spent with Mrs. Carrington. Benjamin spent quite a bit of time with Mr. Carrington. He showed him much of Maryland."

"Yes, we went hunting for just a few days in late February. It wasn't a long trip by any means though. We were barely gone two days. Anyway, after all that, we set out for Virginia," Benjamin looked at his sister to make sure she wasn't going to interrupt him again. She nodded to him and so he continued. "When we reached Virginia, we stopped north of Fredericksburg and stayed with the Moyer family."

"That is where William broke his arm, Father," added Emma. "Mr. Moyer took Benjamin and William hunting with him and some other men."

"But unfortunately we ran into some Indians in the woods."

"Well, I hate to say it but northern Virginia, especially along the western border, is known for that."

"Well, while we tried to get out of there safely, William fell from the horse and ended up rolling down a hill. That's how he broke his arm," said Benjamin but then he hesitated. Emma knew he wasn't sure whether to talk about Mr. Ainsworth or Colonel Fones but James broke the silence.

"It is all right, I know about what happened in the woods. I just didn't know about William's arm. A friend of mine sent me word of their deaths."

"Well, from there we came to Williamsburg and have been here since," said Emma.

"And how do you like it all here?"

"It is nice enough. The plantation is lovely," said Emma.

"I thought you might like that. Your mother certainly did. She spent most of her time out there."

"Father, what happened to Mother?" asked Emma.

"Well, your mother was sick when I left her in December but she was not too terribly bad, and we both knew that it was imperative that I went. I told her I would stay and have someone else attend to my business but she insisted. She continued to write to me via a friend of ours, but did not tell me about her worsening health.

"I received word of her death and I mourned for her. From what I have been told, your mother was extremely ill but refused to call to any of us for fear that you would be traveling whilst it was not safe, and for fear that I would drop my business. God help me, I would have had I but known. Her letters were so full of joy and happiness that I never guessed she was getting worse," said James.

"It's all right Father," said Benjamin. "The news was shocking to us as well."

"How did William take it?"

"Fairly well. He was upset of course, but I was amazed at his resiliency," said Emma to her father.

"And what of you two?"

Emma looked at Benjamin but said nothing.

"It was a hard blow to bear. Emma was very strong though. She carried us all through the difficult time."

There was silence in the room again. Emma watched her brother and her father.

"Well, Benjamin, what do you think of Williamsburg?"

"I must admit that I liked Boston better, but Williamsburg is exciting enough I suppose. I like the people here at least."

"Good and just so you know, I think that Williamsburg is going to be much more exciting relatively soon," said James.

"Why do you say that, Father?"

"Just a hunch. My goodness, it has gotten late. I think I need to turn in for the night," James said as he stood up.

"Oh, Father," said Emma suddenly remembering a promise she had made, "Mr. Washington asked me to give this to you as soon as you arrived home. I'm sorry I forgot until just now." Emma took out the letter that she had continued to carry on her and handed it to her father.

"No matter, I have not been home long and it has been a while since that letter was placed in your care," replied James with a smile as he took the letter and looked at the address on the front. "I am glad that you were able to meet Mr. Washington. He is a very dear friend of mine and one whom I respect very much."

"He was extremely good to us while we were in northern Virginia. He sends his best wishes to you. Benjamin and I liked him very much," concluded Emma.

"Thank you for delivering this Emma," said James. "Now, if you two will excuse me, I truly need to get to sleep."

"Of course, it is late anyway. We should all probably head to bed," said Benjamin as he followed his father. Emma was right behind them both. Benjamin and Emma went up the stairs and James headed to the master bedroom, the only one on the main floor. James's bedroom was in its own wing of the house and away from everything else. Neither Emma nor Benjamin had entered it since they had arrived in Williamsburg.

Emma lay down in bed and breathed the biggest sigh of relief that she had since her parents had left her nearly two years before. Emma slept better than she had in that time as well.

The next day, Benjamin and Felicity decided to go out to the plantation and spend some time there, William was engaged with his tutor, and this left Emma with her father's full attention for a while.

"Did you sleep well, Father?"

"Very well. It was nice to be back in my own bed. I find that others' beds just aren't as comfortable as your own."

"Isn't that the truth?" asked Emma.

"I have some business in town today if you would care to come with me, Emma."

"I would indeed, Father." And so Emma put on her bonnet and hat and they set out for the day.

"So, do you really like Williamsburg, Emma?"

"Yes, it is very nice. I have grown quite fond of it actually. The town is very nice and I have met some very nice people."

"That's good. There are some very nice people who live here."

"Father, I have a question for you."

"Yes my dear?"

"How do you know so many people? I mean, not just here in Williamsburg, but all along the Colonies?"

"I have my connections," said James.

"So I have noticed."

"Emma, did Mr. Washington say anything to you when he gave you my letter?"

"He merely asked me to keep it secret and to carry it on my person until I hand delivered it to you. I didn't feel it was my place to ask what its contents were."

"Ah you are a good daughter, Emma."

"When did you meet Mr. Washington?"

"He was my commanding officer during the French and Indian War. We have remained in contact since. I had the pleasure of meeting up with him again almost as soon as we arrived in Virginia."

"What business does he have with you?" asked Emma. Her curiosity was overwhelming. She knew it wasn't proper to ask but she couldn't help herself. However, before her father could answer, they were interrupted by another.

"Mr. Huntington," said the Reverend.

"Reverend Quillet," replied James. "It is good to see you again," said James smiling as both men shook hands heartily.

"And you. When did you return?"

"Just yesterday."

"Well, it is truly a blessing to have you back here. We have enjoyed having your children in church on Sundays."

"I am glad that they have had the opportunity to hear your sermons."

"So will we be seeing you on Sunday this week?"

"Most assuredly Reverend. I shall be there with my children in my usual pew." The men finished the polite conversation and bid goodbye to each other.

"Father, why don't these people use your title?" Emma asked referring to James being a Lord.

"Perhaps because they do not know my title," James replied simply.

"How do they not know you are a Lord?"

"Most likely because I have not told them."

Emma and her father spent the rest of the morning walking through town. James had a few minor things to purchase but nothing out of the ordinary. At last, they entered the dry goods store and met with Mr. Withers.

"Paul, good to see you," said James.

"James! How are you? When did you get back?"

"I'm fine. I got in yesterday evening."

"And how are things up north?"

"Fine, fine. The weather is grand, and I was able to visit with some interesting people."

"Really?"

"Certainly. However, if you would like to stop over for dinner on Thursday evening, I would greatly enjoy the company. In fact, why don't we have the whole crew over to supper and then perhaps chat a while? It will be great fun to have dinner guests."

"Not everyone is currently in town, and I know that some are engaged elsewhere, but I can pass the word around if you like."

"I would be honored, Paul. We shall see you Thursday evening around seven then," said James as if the matter were decided.

"Seven it shall be James."

"Come Emma, we have much preparation to do for dinner then."

Emma and James bid goodbye to Mr. Withers and they headed back to the house.

Upon arriving, they quickly learned that William was outside working on his lessons and Benjamin and Felicity were still at the plantation. James sent a messenger out to them to inform them of their new dinner plans on Thursday and then set about trying to get things done. However, things didn't go so well at first. James ended up in an argument with Francis about dinner, and one with Curtis about the number of carriages that would be arriving. Emma later found her father in his study in quite a state of ill temper.

"Father?" asked Emma timidly. "May I come in?"

"Yes, come in. What is it?" asked James briskly.

"Are you all right?"

"Fine, fine," he said waving her away.

"Is there anything I can do to help? Would you like me to arrange dinner?"

Then something strange happened. James sat down in the high back armchair and placed his head in his hands, letting out a great sigh.

"What is it, Father?"

"It's your mother."

"Mother?" said Emma not quite comprehending her father's words.

"Yes, Elizabeth used to take care of this type of thing. I am afraid I am just no good at it," he said sitting up and giving a strange sort of chuckle at the apparent irony, which Emma did not see. "Your mother was such an eloquent hostess."

"She certainly was," replied Emma watching her step.

"I remember this one time. We were having about fifty people over to dinner and your mother had prepared for the whole affair for weeks. You were just about three years old then. Well, about two hours before everyone was to arrive, the cook informed Elizabeth that much of the food they had ordered still had not arrived.

"Well, your mother got in the carriage and went to the nearest market and she picked up the most wonderful foods; dates, almonds, a pheasant, and a variety of desserts. When she returned, she gave instruction on cooking the pheasant and set forth the other foods as hors d'oeuvres. Then she had people mingling about instead of seated and thinking about the dinner that wasn't cooked yet. The guests were delighted about it all and the pheasant was wonderful." James let out another great sigh. "No one but your mother could have pulled that off."

Emma smiled. She did not remember the story her father had just told her, but she liked hearing about her mother.

"It shall all be all right Father. You'll see. I will take care of it all. You just get ready to have a nice dinner."

"Thank you Emma."

"In the meantime, I think that you should apologize to Francis and Curtis."

"Mayhaps you are right my dear. I shall do just that and then leave the rest to you." James stood and kissed his daughter on the forehead. Emma smiled at him and then headed to the kitchens to find Francis.

Emma had become quite adept at controlling the household, and the servants liked and respected her. Emma spent only five minutes with Francis and everything was settled for the dinner. She then went to find Curtis and within ten minutes had solved the carriage problem.

Thursday came and the household was extremely busy. People were in and out delivering things all day. Benjamin and Felicity decided to go out to the plantation for the day so they were out of the way. William's tutor had been cancelled, and William was sent with Benjamin and Felicity.

Finally, the afternoon gave way to evening and Emma went to her room to dress for dinner. As she entered the hall, she bumped into Benjamin and Felicity. They had just returned from Beacon Hall.

"Emma, I have been meaning to ask you what is this dinner all about?" asked Benjamin.

"I'm not really sure. Father met with Mr. Withers, from the dry goods store, and invited him and some other guests to dinner. He told me he wanted you here tonight. Truly, that is all I know of it."

"Strange," replied Benjamin. "But, if that is what he wants."

"How was the plantation?" asked Emma.

"It was lovely, as always," said Felicity.

"And extremely warm," added Benjamin. "I'm not sure if it is warmer inside or outside to be honest."

"Inside," said William, as he was sent upstairs to change. He was going to have dinner by himself before the guests arrived.

"It is as if the heat is trapped in the house. However, strangely enough, there is a very cool room downstairs," added Felicity.

"It's that second drawing room that Mother insisted on having. The one with the blue flowers on the walls."

"Oh, the one that leads to the cellar," said Emma.

"There is no cellar door in that room," said Felicity. "It is outside and on the other side of the house."

"Well, the cellar door is outside, but you can get to the other cellar from the room," said Benjamin. "It is a strange thing and would take quite a while to explain to you. It is one of my father's strange quirks, but I cannot condemn him for it."

The three walked upstairs and into their respective rooms. Emma knew the dinner would be quite eloquent so she took out her favorite summer gown. The gown was made of teal colored satin and had pearl beading around the waist and stomacher as well as the collar. The stomacher was cream-colored satin ribbon that matched the cutaway part in the skirt. She then had her hair put up into an eloquent knot that sat squarely on the back of her head with ringlet curls that fell from it. The servant who was doing her hair took out little pearl beads and placed them delicately in Emma's golden hair. She finished the whole thing off with a single strand of pearls around her neck.

Emma left her room to head downstairs and make sure everything was going well. Francis informed her everything was perfect and dinner would be ready promptly at seven thirty giving the guests a bit of time to chat before dinner.

James came down next. Emma knew he had been ready for sometime but she did not know what had been occupying his time.

"Can it possibly be? Is that really and truly my very own daughter?"

"It really and truly is, Father," replied Emma.

"When did you become such a lady?"

"I think it happened sometime ago… but not too long ago," laughed Emma.

"And she is witty to boot. I cannot believe how long ago it was we left you children in England. You were but fifteen years old, still a child, and now look at you. You are as beautiful as your mother was."

Emma blushed but admittedly reveled in the compliment. She liked being compared with her mother. Emma felt her mother was probably the most beautiful, kindest, and most eloquent lady in the world and she unconsciously compared herself to Elizabeth frequently.

Benjamin and Felicity soon joined Emma and James. With Emma playing the hostess, she was escorted by her father and that left Benjamin to escort Felicity, which Emma was certain neither one minded.

At six fifty-two, the first guest arrived. Benjamin and Felicity headed into the ballroom where the guests would be until dinner was served.

Emma did her duties as hostess quite well. She was charming and eloquent. Finally, about seven thirty, James made the announcement that dinner was being served in the dining room.

All of the guests headed toward the dining room led by James and Emma. James took the seat at the head of the table and Emma sat to his left with Benjamin next to her. Felicity ended up across from Benjamin. There were many people at the dinner; Emma guessed about twenty; excluding herself, Felicity, Benjamin, and her father.

Some of the faces were familiar. Mr. Richard Henry Lee sat at her father's right side. Reverend Quillet was among the guests, as well as Mr. Rablin, Mr. Withers, and Mr. Welsing. However, though most of the guests were not familiar to Emma, all of the diners, with the exclusion of she and Felicity, were men. Emma found this strange but did not ask questions of her father; nor did she act in any abnormal way toward her father's guests.

Dinner was going extremely well. Emma noticed an open chair near the end of the table and this troubled her. From her spot next to her father, Emma was unable to read the card that sat in front of the empty spot.

The conversation at dinner was light to begin with. The men asked after each other's families and business affairs. Many of the men gave Emma high compliments as well as asking her many questions, which led Emma to speak with those around her about her travels, as well as her new life in Williamsburg compared with her old life in England. Despite the lack of the female gender, Emma found that she was quite enjoying herself. In fact, Emma felt that had the room been filled with women as well, dinner might not have been so enjoyable. At the very least, she did not have to contend with idle gossip.

After dinner, James invited his guests into the parlor for after dinner drinks. Emma did not follow. It was a general rule that women did not engage in the after dinner affairs of numerous men when they involved alcohol.

Thus, Emma and Felicity stayed in the dining room until all of the guests had exited and gone into the parlor.

"Well, that was quite the affair, Emma," said Felicity.

"It was. It is strange to see the familiar faces of people I met in Maryland and Massachusetts."

"I'm sure. However, they are all from around here. It is actually odder that you met them when and where you did."

"I suppose this is true." Emma and Felicity each stopped chatting and took a deep breath. It was nearly nine thirty by now. In the silence, Emma could hear the broken conversation of the guests from the parlor.

"Mr. Rablin, are you saying that you disagree with the whole idea?"

"I'm merely saying that I don't know if it is the best idea. Will it not enrage the English?"

"That is the idea Mr. Rablin. They have wronged us yet again and still, we talk instead of act. I ask you gentlemen, what will it take for someone to tell the English no?"

"Avery, calm yourself. We need to be in agreement and I feel it is imperative that we hear all sides."

"What was decided at your conference, James?"

Emma could not hear her father's reply. What conference were they talking about?

"Kendrick, what say you?"

"The tax is absolutely unfair. There really is no more to be said about the tax. I agree it is time to act."

"But Kendrick, don't you think you are being a bit harsh about the whole affair?"

"Mr. Lee, your thoughts?" Emma heard her father ask calmly.

"I think that the three-penny tax is absolutely ludicrous and I shall give my reasons so that none may rightly argue. The main reason the tax was passed was to help out the East India Company from going bankrupt; we all know this to be true. However, is it right to undersell every American merchant so that he can no longer make his living? I say nay! I believe that we do need some form of action, though I do not necessarily feel it needs to be so extremely drastic. If American merchants cannot sell tea because The East India Company is underselling them, then we simply shall not buy tea until there is fair trade."

"Not buy tea? But tea is part of everyday life."

"I can't afford it at the prices tea is going for anyway right now. I am not made of money gentlemen."

"Then it seems we have no other course of action."

The men seemed to agree with this idea for the most part. They may not like the idea of not buying tea, but the thirst for action was greater than their thirst for tea.

Emma's eyes had grown so that they were almost falling out of her head. She could not believe what she was hearing coming from her very own parlor. This was the same talk that had followed her from Massachusetts to Maryland and then to northern Virginia. Now, apparently, it had followed her to Williamsburg. But what shocked Emma the most was that it was being said in her house, with her father and her brother in the room, and in complete ability to stop the conversation.

But they did not stop the conversation. James was an active participant. Emma did not hear Benjamin say much more than a yes or no every once in awhile. Just then, the doorbell rang. Francis went to open the door, but Emma was curious who it was. Being she was the hostess, she felt it was only right for her to greet the new visitor.

When Emma entered the hall, Francis had already let the man in. Obviously Francis knew him from how she spoke to him. Emma's father had also come to the hall to see who the new guest was.

"Good evening," she began but when Emma looked up, she saw another familiar face, though this one was not of someone she had met up north. "You're..."

"Hello, I didn't think I would be bumping into you again," said the man.

"Emma, do you know Mr. Carrington?"

"Yes, I met him in Maryland," replied Emma not fully understanding why her father was asking her this now.

"No, no. You met Mr. Brent Carrington in Maryland. This is one of his sons, Mr. Cole Carrington."

"We've sort of met, Mr. Huntington," replied the man.

"What do you mean, sort of?"

"We sort of collided with each other a few months ago. You were visiting the Wren Building, I believe."

"I was." Emma's face was flush; she knew she was blushing which made her blush even more.

"Don't be embarrassed, please. In all honesty, I should be the one who is embarrassed. You see Mr. Huntington, your daughter was taking a tour of the Wren Building and I came running down the stairs, much too fast as I was quite late, and I ran right into her. Unfortunately, I did not have my manners about me that day, and I'm afraid that I ran off without truly expressing my apologies or introducing myself."

James laughed, as he now comprehended the whole situation and the circumstances of their first meeting.

"Well, you sure have a way of making an impression Cole. Come in, come in. We have been waiting for you. Well sort of. You missed dinner, but I am sure that I can have them fix you up a plate."

"No thank you Sir, I have already eaten. I do apologize for my tardiness however."

"Not at all Cole. You are just in time actually. But first of all, I think it is time you two properly met. Mr. Cole Carrington, this is my daughter Miss Emma Huntington."

"It is a pleasure to meet you Miss Huntington; I have heard many good things about you."

"And I have heard much of you as well, Mr. Carrington."

"Really? And who speaks so highly of me."

Emma had now found her voice and some of the color had begun to drain from her face. Now that she knew who the man that stood in front of her was, she felt a strange attachment to him as well as feeling as though she already knew him from hearing his parents speak of him.

"I did not say they spoke highly of you."

Both James and Cole laughed at Emma. She was glad they saw the humor.

"Well then, surely you have spoken to a sinner Miss Huntington because the person you heard from is most certainly a liar." Again Cole and James laughed. Emma found herself chuckle a little.

"Actually, Mr. Carrington, the people who know you and have spoken of you are none other than your parents."

"My parents? How did you come upon them?"

"I met them whilst I was staying in Maryland with my aunt and uncle."

"You did. I remember them now mentioning a charming and beautiful girl that they had met. You must be whom they were speaking of."

"I fear that they spoke too highly of me then," said Emma now blushing again.

"Well," said Cole as James was heading back into the parlor and motioning for Cole to follow, "I do not yet know about the charming, though I am sure it must be so, however I quite agree with the beautiful." With that, Cole entered the parlor.

Emma felt her face become quite red from embarrassment. She watched the men in the parlor, but did not stay long for fear of eavesdropping on them. Emma had gotten herself into enough trouble with eavesdropping over the past few months, so she decided to go upstairs and check on William. As she reached the top of the stairs, she met Felicity.

Felicity's face was completely aglow and she pulled Emma

into her guest bedroom, which was the nearest one. Felicity was almost in a fit of giggles by the time Emma sat down with her.

"Well he is certainly charming himself," said Felicity.

"He is pompous," replied Emma plainly.

"I thought you liked the Carrington family?"

"I do, very much. However, Mrs. Carrington failed to mention the audacity and arrogance of her third son."

"You shouldn't be so hard on Mr. Carrington. He is quite a good friend of your family, and he really is quite a nice person."

Emma did not feel like discussing the issue any further.

"I need to go and check on William," she said and left the bedroom and Felicity.

It was now after ten and William was fast asleep. Emma kissed her younger brother on the forehead and pulled up his covers a bit. She then went back downstairs. As the hostess, she really felt it her duty to say goodnight to everyone, but it did not sound as if the party was going to break any time soon, so Emma went into the drawing room and took out her copy of Benjamin Franklin's book on slavery. It was her fourth time in reading it and she enjoyed it more each time.

Around one thirty, Emma was awoken by Benjamin.

"Emma, the guests are probably going to be here quite a while longer, why don't you say your goodnights and head to bed?"

Emma could barely speak as she yawned. "Do you think that anyone would mind terribly?"

"No, and besides, you can't even keep your eyes open."

Emma agreed and entered the parlor with Benjamin. The men stopped talking at once and watched their beautiful hostess.

Emma was graceful to say the least, and she spoke eloquently while keeping her words short.

"Gentlemen, thank you all for coming tonight. It has certainly been a pleasure to see old friends and to meet so many new ones, but I do beg your forgiveness as I believe that I am going to head for bed."

Everyone in the room bid Emma goodnight and within about ten minutes, Emma was able to make her way back out of the parlor and up to her room to finally get to sleep.

Friday morning came early. Emma awoke to find the sun already up, not that this was unusual for a summer morning by any means. She got up and put on a fresh white dress that had a blue, green, and pink boarder that formed the waistline. She then headed downstairs to have breakfast.

She ate alone, the rest of the house still asleep except for William who was already in lessons for the day. Emma thought about the day ahead of her. Edward would be coming over that afternoon which meant another day without going to the plantation. Emma had truly grown to love Beacon Hall, and tried to spend as much time as possible out there. However, it would be good to see him.

Then Emma's thoughts began to fall back onto the party from the night before. Had she heard all that she remembered hearing? What was her father doing being part of that conversation? Emma had not heard all of the conversation, which she well knew. Perhaps her father was truly trying to be the mediator between the two vastly opposing opinions.

That must be it. He is trying to find a compromise that will benefit each party. Emma found herself lost in her own thoughts.

Satisfied with her newfound answer, she decided to go out on her morning errands and take a long walk around town plus she still had to get a birthday gift for William. His birthday would be in a few days and she had yet to decide on his gift.

Emma walked through the various shops and spoke with many of the townspeople. She went into the bookstore to see if there was anything there for William. The bookseller, Mr. Avery

Dillis, was happy to catch sight of Emma again. He had been among those in attendance the night before. Emma was quite familiar with Mr. Dillis though, as the bookstore was probably her favorite store in the entire town.

"Good morning, Miss Huntington," he said as he greeted her.

"Good morning Mr. Dillis. How are you this fine morning?"

"I must tell you Miss Huntington, I am actually quite fatigued from last night's events. It was quite late when we finally all dispersed. I really had no idea the hour was so late actually."

"Really? What time did everyone leave?"

"Well, I didn't leave until almost three o'clock. I am glad that I don't live far. However, there were quite a few men still there discussing. I had no choice but to leave you see, as I had to be here this morning. However, it was quite a lovely party."

"Thank you Mr. Dillis," said Emma kindly, "I am glad that you were able to be in attendance. How is Mrs. Dillis?"

"She is well. She is visiting her mother in North Carolina so she is not around."

"How long will she be gone?"

"It depends actually. Her mother is getting on in years and to be honest, we don't expect her to live much longer, so I think that Mrs. Dillis wants to be with her as much as possible."

"I suppose so. Is her mother ill?"

"Not to speak of. She is just really getting on in years."

"Hmm. Well, it is good fortune that Mrs. Dillis could visit her then."

"I agree. Now, what can I help you with this morning, Miss Huntington?"

"Well, my brother, William, is turning six in a few days and I am in need of a very special birthday gift for him. Do you have any suggestions?"

"I take it he is a reader then?"

"Sometimes. I suppose I really am the reader in the family, but I am trying to influence him."

"It is a good influence. Let me see what we have here," said Mr. Dillis with a little laugh as he set about looking through his store. Emma began to browse whilst he looked about for her.

Emma loved the bookstore and would gladly spend all her days there; many mornings she often did. She was thankful that Mr. Dillis was so kind to her as to allow her to browse and linger about. Books were so expensive that Emma certainly couldn't have afforded each one she wanted, but she felt that she had a fair collection of many of the classic works.

"Is your brother much to liking adventure stories?"

"I believe those are his favorites," replied Emma with a smile.

"Well this one might be interesting then. It is all about pirates and kidnapping and hidden treasures."

"That sounds perfect for him," replied Emma thinking back to their voyage to the Colonies and smiling to herself, "I shall take that one then."

"Very good. I'll just wrap it up for you, since it is a birthday gift."

"You can also add in some parchment and ink for me. I am running low."

"You just bought some recently, Miss Huntington. Do you keep that much correspondence?" asked Mr. Dillis. Emma felt herself blush but did not reply directly. "I apologize profusely. That is none of my concern. I should not have asked you."

"It is of no concern. I have merely met a fair number of people since my arrival in the Colonies, and I try to be good about keeping up with my family up north as well as those in England."

"Of course," replied Mr. Dillis. "Again, I apologize for my impoliteness."

"Apology is not needed Mr. Dillis."

Mr. Dillis gave Emma her total and handed her the packages she had purchased. She felt better about William's upcoming birthday and from there, she made her way through the town. Emma soon found herself walking away from Merchant's Square and toward the Governor's palace. She would often walk by and see the large residence. She had never been past the gates of the house, but she had been told there was a large garden maze in the backyard and she often longed to see it.

Finally, around noon, Emma returned to her house. She had seen many of the guests from the night before and spoke to each, politely thanking them for their attendance. They all complimented her on a wonderfully successful party.

When Emma entered the house, she removed her hat and went to find Francis. Francis gave her the list of where everyone was.

"William is out wid that man ya'll call a tutor," she began. Francis did not like William's tutor but would not discuss it, which only gave Emma more reason to mistrust him, though she still had no idea why. "Mr. Benjamin went wid yo' father. They left this mornin' 'round 'bout ten or so, and Miss Dillingham is 'round here somewhere."

"Thank you Francis. I was wondering if you could have lunch served on the back porch today? Perhaps in about ten minutes or so?"

"It is ready when you is, Miss Emma. An' you can eat anywhere yo' heart desires. It'll be there in five minutes."

"Thank you Francis."

"Welcome Miss Emma." Francis went to talk to the kitchen. Emma knew that Francis liked her. She was only this receptive of Emma's requests. Emma had witnessed James get into many arguments with the servant over silly things. Benjamin rarely asked for anything, but when he did, he was not too good about giving Francis much time to prepare. Also, Emma was sure that

Francis was grateful of Emma's routines being so regular for the most part. Emma almost always ate lunch around noon so she knew that it would be just about ready anyway.

Emma put her packages away upstairs. She returned to the ground floor and placed her hat back on and went out to the porch. She sat down at the table. She had grabbed some parchment and ink. Emma had been neglecting her letter writing and owed more than one person a lengthy letter. She was glad that she now had things to tell her correspondents, such as her father finally returning to Williamsburg.

Lunch was served within five minutes, as Francis promised. Emma dined alone, but she could see William and his tutor in the gardens. She vacillated between eating lunch, writing her letters, and watching her younger brother.

After she finished eating, she had the table cleared and continued to write. It was such a fine day and Emma hated to waste it by being inside, even if it was very warm and humid.

Finally, about ten to one, Francis returned to announce Edward's arrival. He followed the servant knowing full well Emma would receive him. Francis didn't seem to think this was right though; she made a sort of snorting noise after Emma agreed to see him, though he was directly behind Francis to which Emma had to laugh a little.

"Edward, please sit down," said Emma cordially. Edward took the seat across from Emma and thanked her. "How are you today?"

"I am well thank you. How are you?"

"Good. Very good even. It was a fine morning. I finally got William's birthday present which takes a load off of my mind."

"What did you end up getting him?"

"It is an adventure book he should like." At this time, Francis had the tea served to the two on the porch. Emma thanked her and Francis went back into the house.

"I'm sure he will like it very much."

There was a brief amount of silence.

"Edward, is there something troubling you?"

"Well, now that you ask, there is something mildly troubling me."

"What is it Edward?" asked Emma pushing aside all of her letter writing materials to give him her full attention.

"Emma, there was a party here last night."

"Yes, but how did you know that?"

"It is now my job to know these things."

"I see," Emma replied leaning back in her chair taking on a defensive tone in her voice.

"Do you know what the purpose of this gathering was?"

"I suppose it was to catch up. My father just arrived home a few days ago and he was anxious to see some of his old friends. What is meant by this line of questioning, Edward?"

"Is it possible there was another motive Emma?"

"I'm sure that I truly don't know Edward. I suppose it is possible, but I only dined with them. As we dined, the only purpose that I could see was to chat and enjoy each other's company. I still don't understand what this is all about."

"I'm not sure I entirely understand either, but it is certainly curious that there were people who did not leave this house until as late as five o'clock this morning."

"Five o'clock? My goodness, it was a late night. However, that is not a crime and besides, how do you know when everyone left my home?"

"Again Emma, it is my job to know."

Emma folded her arms across her chest. "And what job is this Edward? I do not think I like you watching over my house so closely."

"I cannot tell you Emma. I am unable to discuss the matter," replied Edward calmly. Emma was a bit put out with her childhood friend, but she tried to pass off the matter without concern.

"Tell me about your family Edward. How are they doing?"

"Well enough. My father was to visit with King George himself the other day. His Majesty often asks my father for advice on important matters."

Emma knew that Edward was grandiose in his renditions of family matters but she did not stop him.

"My mother is very well. She has been in Wales a bit lately visiting relatives there."

"It is good to hear they are so well Edward. You must send them my regards."

"Of course I certainly shall and I am certain they send theirs as well. They ask after you often. They would most certainly enjoy seeing you again."

"I would enjoy a nice visit with them as well. It is such a pity we are so far from England."

"That could be remedied you know Emma."

"Edward, I believe I have given you my answer."

"Emma, I do not wish to pressure you into anything you are unsure of, but I do not understand you."

"Edward, we have discussed this again and again."

"But Emma, I cannot understand how you can refuse my request when you have no other real alternative."

"I do not agree. Also, to be completely honest Edward, I do not feel that I am ready to marry anyone, it is not merely you," Emma replied sitting forward again on her chair dropping her full attention from Edward.

"You are already seventeen."

"I am only seventeen. I have many years ahead of me before I feel I must be married. I simply do not want to jump into anything that I may later regret simply because it was a good alternative at the time."

"So you believe you will regret me?"

"I didn't mean it that way Edward," replied Emma looking up at Edward's face.

"Emma, my affections for you are very real. Why can you not reciprocate them?"

"That is not an easily answered question Edward. I wish, for your sake, that I could but I have told you my position."

"And I still believe that your feelings would change if only you would allow them to. If we married, you would grow to return my affections, of this I am positive." Edward was leaning across the table and speaking in low tones. He might be anxious for Emma's hand, but he still retained composure and did not wish to be overheard.

"Edward, I do have much affection for you but it is the affection of a close friendship and nothing more. I cannot share your certainty that my affections would make such a shift merely because I wore a ring about my finger."

With the slight pause in the conversation, Felicity happened to come onto the porch and see Emma and Edward. Emma was glad to see her. She knew that Edward would desist if another person were present.

"Felicity, would you care to join us?" asked Emma.

"I do not wish to interrupt anything," said Felicity.

"It is truly no interruption, Miss Dillingham," said Edward, much to Emma's surprise. Edward returned to his comfortable position leaning back into chair.

"If you are certain…"

"Of course, please sit down," replied Edward standing to pull her chair out for her.

The rest of Edward's visit was spent reminiscing about England and chatting about Williamsburg and the surrounding area. Edward even gave the girls a brief history of Jamestown, which was not too far from Williamsburg.

Around four, Edward took his leave of the women and Emma and Felicity bid him goodbye. Edward said goodbye to Felicity and kissed Emma gently on the hand and left without another word.

After he was gone, Felicity was the first to speak.

"Well, he is certainly charming," said Felicity.

"You think everyone is charming," replied Emma. She was in a fairly sour mood.

"I do not. So, what is going on with you two?"

"Nothing," replied Emma curtly.

"That's too bad."

"Edward and I grew up together; we have been friends for a long time. It is just really nice to have someone around who remembers the same things I remember."

"And what about Benjamin?"

"What about him? We get along just fine."

"Can't you reminisce with him?"

"Honestly, Benjamin has never been one to reminisce."

"He does look to the future."

"Which is not entirely a bad thing," said Emma.

"Not at all."

"I just don't want to forget, that's all."

"I just don't want you to live in the past so long you forget to live in the present and to look toward your future as well."

"You sound like Benjamin. Speaking of…"

"There is no news to share."

"Felicity, this is an entirely inappropriate question and if you do not want to answer it, I will completely understand."

"Emma, you know you may ask anything of me."

"Do you enjoy my brother's company?"

Felicity put on a very serious face before she spoke.

"Well, in all honesty, I feel as though even though I do enjoy my time with him, I just don't share that much in common with William. I mean, he is only going to be six."

Emma laughed. "You know what I mean."

"I know," said Felicity laughing a little herself. "I haven't thought that much about it but it is a strange thing."

"What is?"

"I do enjoy my time with Benjamin, but it is almost as if I cannot remember any time before him. It is almost as if my life started when I met him and my life cannot continue without him."

"You are right, that is strange," said Emma teasingly.

"Oh you," replied Felicity.

"Miss Emma, Miss Felicity," said Francis, who had just entered the porch, "it is growin' quite cool out, sure sign of a storm if you ask me. Maybe you two should be comin' in now. Besides, it is almost time fo' dinner."

"All right," said Emma, "even though dinner isn't for another hour or so."

"Actually, yo' father sent me to you too. He is wantin' to see you."

"All right, I will go see him now," replied Emma.

Francis and Felicity followed Emma into the house but as Emma headed toward her father's study, Felicity went towards the parlor and Francis to the dining room. As Emma approached the study, she could hear three men talking. Two of the voices were familiar to her but the third was from a stranger.

Emma's father caught sight of her as she neared the study and he called her in.

"Emma, I want you to meet someone. This is Mr. Lindley. Mr. Lindley, this is my daughter, Emma Huntington."

"Miss Huntington, it is a pleasure to meet you. I have heard so much about you from your father. All good of course," he winked as he said this. Emma liked this man. He was an older gentleman, but he was very clean-cut and came off as quite proper. However, he had a strange accent that Emma had not yet encountered.

"Thank you Mr. Lindley. I am sure you are much to kind," replied Emma cordially.

"Nonsense."

"Mr. Lindley is from New York. He is visiting on his way down to Charles Town in South Carolina."

"How was your trip Mr. Lindley?"

"As well as can be I suppose. The trip seems to become longer each time I make it though. My old body isn't what it once was."

"Mr. Lindley," said Benjamin, "you seem to be as spry as ever, sir." At this, all three men laughed aloud. Emma found this comment odd, especially since Benjamin had never met this man before today as far as Emma knew.

"Well, at any rate, the roads were good, and I have made good time and met with good friends. I could not ask for anything better."

"Well, I am glad you have stopped here. It looks as though the rain is going to set in. The roads will be in no condition to travel on for a few days."

"You are probably right Mr. Huntington. I do thank you again for your accommodations and your hospitality."

"It is my pleasure. I wish that I could do more."

"From what I hear Mr. Huntington, you are doing more than your fair share."

"Anything to help out Mr. Lindley. Benjamin, I am sure that Mr. Lindley would like to rest before dinner. Why don't you have Curtis bring his things up to one of the guest rooms and show him where he will be staying?"

"Of course Father. Mr. Lindley, would you care to follow me?"

"Thank you; that is a fine suggestion. My things are in the carriage."

"I'll just fetch Curtis to take care of them and they will be brought up immediately."

With that, Mr. Lindley and Benjamin left the study leaving Emma alone with her father.

"Emma, please have a seat, I have some things that I wish to discuss with you."

"Of course Father," replied Emma obediently.

"First of all, I have not had the chance to thank you for taking such good care of William. His tutor seems to be working out well, and I am glad he is continuing his studies."

"I didn't think Mother would want him to fall further behind than he already is."

"I agree and you have done an excellent job." With this, her father began attending to putting away some books from his desk onto a bookshelf that sat behind him.

"It is not an act worthy of thanks, it was merely my duty."

"Secondly, how is Edward?"

Emma began to remember her discussion with her childhood friend. He had aggravated her during his visit with his elusive comments and his mentions of her father's business.

"He is well enough. Actually he has joined the British army."

"Oh?" asked James with interest as he turned back toward his daughter briefly pausing in putting his books away.

"Yes, he has been made a lieutenant."

"Isn't that lovely for him? I suppose his father is proud?" James returned to put the last three books away and sat down to begin straightening his desk up a bit.

"I suppose so. I think his father had some influence in the matter," said Emma.

"I'm certain he did. But, congratulations to Edward are in order. I am sure he will serve his post well."

"I'm sure he will. Father, Edward said something to me that was a little disconcerting," began Emma.

"Oh? What was that?"

"Well," said Emma but she stopped. For some reason she was

hesitant to tell her father that her childhood friend was involved in a watch on their home and that she had no idea why. However, Emma was not able to finish her sentence because William entered the study.

"Hello Father, Emma," he said. James sat down and motioned to William to join him, which William gladly did.

"Hello William," said James. "How were your lessons today?"

"They were all right but I am tired of them."

"Tired? You even had a day off this week. How on earth can you be tired of them already?"

"I just am. Why doesn't Emma or Benjamin have to do lessons?"

"Because they have done lessons beginning many years before you were born. When you are Emma's age, if you want to stop your lessons, you may do so without any objections from me." William seemed content with this answer. It must have merely not dawned on him that he would be in lessons for at least eleven more years under those conditions.

"How was your day, Father?"

"It was nice. We have a guest for dinner tonight. His name is Mr. Lindley. I want you to be very polite to him and behave yourself while he is here, all right?"

"All right."

"Now, I need to finish talking to Emma."

"I will go and get ready for dinner then. I sure am glad it is almost time for dinner," said William as he headed toward the door to the study.

"Why is that Son?" asked James.

"Because I am really hungry," said William matter-of-factly with a tone that implied his father should have certainly known that without asking. With his final comment, William left the study and pulled the door shut behind him.

"I can hardly believe how big he has gotten, and how much

he has grown in all ways. It seems as though he was born only a few months ago."

"He is a good child," said Emma.

"Emma, I have something else to tell you, which is the real reason I wanted to speak with you."

"What is it, Father?"

"I am going to be leaving Williamsburg again for a while."

"What? You just finally returned. Where are you going? How long will you be gone?"

"I am being called to Philadelphia; then most likely to Boston. I will probably be gone until the end of the year, hopefully returning for Christmas, though most likely not until after the New Year if I end up having business in Virginia."

"When are you to leave?"

"Depending on the rain, which has already started I see, as soon as the roads clear up well enough to travel. Otherwise, I will be leaving within a week."

"A week? What is so important that it again calls you from your family?"

"It is important, that I can assure you, but I cannot discuss the matter with you."

"Does this have anything to do with the letter I gave you from Mr. Washington?"

"In an indirect way. It is difficult to explain to you, well to anyone for that matter. Emma, do not be upset with me. It is for the best, you must trust me on the importance of this matter," said James as he put his arm around his daughter.

"If you say it is important, then I shall trust that it is. You need to do what you need to do and your family shall not object."

"There's my brave girl. Thank you. I have just told Benjamin as well, but William does not know as of yet; I do not wish to tell him until after his birthday."

"I suppose I have to agree with that."

"I must ask something of you again, Emma," said James returning to his seat behind the desk.

"What is it, Father?"

"I need you to look after your brothers, both of them."

"I will most certainly do this, although I believe Benjamin capable of looking after himself."

"I am afraid that Benjamin is going to make a rash decision he may regret."

"I'm sure I don't follow you, Father," replied Emma quite perplexed.

"I'm sure you don't but whatever Benjamin decides, you must force him to think about his decision. You shall understand if and when the time arrives."

Emma was not as certain as her father seemed to be but she nodded.

"I shall do my best."

"I can ask nothing more. Also, if anyone asks after me, tell them that I am headed to Maryland to visit your Aunt and Uncle Seager. I do not want you children mixed up with any of this. We shall tell William that is where I am going to be as well."

"Of course," replied Emma not knowing what her father was mixed up with, not to mention why on Earth she couldn't tell anyone he was going to Philadelphia. "Is there anything else you require of me?"

"I want you to take care of yourself, and I don't want you to make any rash decisions of your own either."

"What rash decisions would I make?"

"I hope none, however a time may come when you do not know where to turn, and you turn to the very place you have been avoiding for so long."

"I do not understand, Father."

"You shall, I fear. There will come a time when you shall remember these words I have spoken to you, and I hope that you heed my advice. Now, I suggest we go get ready for dinner. I am sure it is almost ready and you haven't even dressed yet."

Emma nodded, her father kissed her on the forehead, and she went up to her room to change for dinner.

Dinner was a quiet but pleasant event and Emma went to bed soon afterwards.

The rain that had begun ended up turning into quite a storm that night. The much-needed rain ended up being too much and the roads were reportedly in terrible condition. Thus, Mr. Lindley ended up staying with the Huntington's for a few days.

Mr. Lindley ended up being quite an absent guest, not that Emma minded much. He was gone most of the time during the days and was really only around for dinnertime. He spoke little during dinnertime, though he made polite conversation.

During many of their dinners lately the Huntington's had another frequent guest – Cole Carrington. He and Benjamin had grown to enjoy each other's company quite a bit and Emma's father had always liked him. Emma still found him arrogant and pretentious, but she had to begrudgingly admit that she had fun when he was around.

Each day of the following week moved far too fast. There was so much going on and Emma knew her father was leaving any day, which seemed to make the time race by.

Sunday came and the entire Huntington family and Felicity went to church, just as Mr. Huntington had promised the Reverend. Emma was glad to be going to church with her father. She was just beginning to get used of having him home again. The sermon was nice enough and afterwards, they drove out to Mr. Withers's home to have Sunday brunch with the Withers family.

Monday came and with it came William's birthday. Emma allowed him to take the day off of lessons, but made him promise to not be a nuisance whilst the party décor was being attended to.

Late that afternoon, guests began arriving. William's party wasn't a big affair but he seemed to have a wonderful time, and he told Emma that hers was the best gift of all.

Tuesday came and went without much commotion. Except a fairly brief visit from Edward and Mr. Lindley's departure there was little to speak of. Then finally, Wednesday arrived. Everyone in the family now knew of James's departure. William had taken the news fairly hard, but he was doing well enough now that the actual day had arrived. It was again time to say so long to their father. Emma wondered how long it would really be this time.

The Huntington children awoke early to say farewell to their father as his carriage was loaded. He kissed each of his children, said his goodbyes, and climbed in. By the time the sun had fully broken over the horizon, his carriage was at the end of Duke of Gloucester street and turning toward the road leading out of town. Emma questioned when her family would be able to be together again, permanently.

Chapter 9
A Tea Party in Boston

The rest of August passed by quietly and with oppressive heat and humidity. Emma heard from each of her correspondents again. Felicity's grandmother was getting on quite well in England. She was telling Emma about many of the people in England and much to Emma's surprise, she actually knew quite a few of them. In her most recent letter, Emma discovered that she had met Emma's Uncle Bradbury and was going to have her Aunt Sylvia over for tea very soon. Emma didn't know whether she pitied Sylvia or the elderly Mrs. Dillingham more.

Margaret had written a few times. It seemed as though all was well in the Seager home. Maria had had her seventh birthday and Joseph would turn nine in September. Helena had finally returned from her trip to Austria and she and Frederick were setting up house in Maryland very close to Margaret's home, though in town. Bianca asked after Emma, and Christopher was becoming impatient to be finished with schooling. Emma could hardly believe that Christopher was now sixteen. He had always seemed so much younger than her, but he was only a little more than a year younger than Emma, with his birthday being in April.

September came and went. With September came a bit of relief from the heat and humidity, but not much. Emma had received only one letter from her father thus far. She knew it was because he did not wish his whereabouts to be well known. He had arrived in Philadelphia and was meeting with some of the town councilmen there, though he did not say who or for what reason. Emma's father told her about seeing Philip Carrington. After this small bit of information, he sent his best wishes to the children and signed the letter.

September gave way to October and Emma was amazed at the fact that they had been in the Colonies for a year already. In some ways, it seemed as though they had been in the Colonies forever but in other ways, Emma felt like they had just arrived in Boston Harbor. She began to realize what a vague concept forever really was.

With October came a lovely season change and Emma was able to see her first fall in Williamsburg. The trees were lovely, and Beacon Hall had become even more beautiful. Yet nothing of notable interest happened until November twenty-ninth. Of course, Emma and the Huntington household did not receive word of any of this until a few days later when Edward came for one of his routine visits.

Emma had received Edward into the drawing room and tea was served. Edward seemed a little out of sorts, so to speak and Emma was not sure how to ask what was the matter, but she did not have to ask.

"Emma, have you had any news from up north?"

"None, to be completely honest. Why? What has happened?"

"Well, I don't know if you have heard how upset the Colonists are about this tax on tea. I think it is silly to be honest. A good company like the East India Company deserves a little bit of help. The company has been around for a long while and they are an established company with a good reputation."

"But what has happened?"

"Well, the Colonists have been throwing fits when it comes to this tax on tea and in October, Philadelphia decided to take actions that they will live to regret I'm afraid."

The mention of Philadelphia sparked Emma's interest, as that was the last place she knew her father to be.

"Well, a committee forced the British tea agents to resign their posts to oppose the tea tax and the advantage that has been established by the East India Company. Boston seemed to find this a good idea and tried to follow suit. Boston is a troublesome town. In fact, I don't know if Boston or Philadelphia is worse to be honest."

"So what is so wrong with trying to have a fair market?"

"If it is not what the King intended, then it is wrong. Anyway, they have recently decided to send the tea on a ship called the *Dartmouth*, back to England without paying for the import duties."

Edward paused for the effect, but Emma waited patiently for the rest of the story.

"Well, then, Thomas Hutchinson, the Governor of Massachusetts ordered that the harbor officials hold the ship in the harbor until the taxes have been paid in full. Good man, that Hutchinson. I am sure the King will smile upon his actions."

"I'm sure," replied Emma finding the whole thing a little ridiculous.

"So, Boston is in an uproar and my company may be sent up there to offer aid."

"What type of aid?"

"Controlling the populous and such."

"When will you be leaving?" asked Emma with genuine concern and interest.

"It won't be for at least another month. Boston is in no immediate distress and Christmas is coming soon."

"Where are you going to be for Christmas, Edward?"

"I'm not entirely sure to be honest. I hadn't really thought about it."

"Why don't you spend Christmas with us? I don't want you to be alone and we have plenty of room. You are more than welcome to stay with us out at Beacon Hall. You haven't been out to the plantation lately, have you?"

"No, I haven't had the pleasure."

"Oh Edward, it is so wonderful. It makes me remember England and our home there. I do miss it sometimes, but Beacon Hall is such a comforting place for me."

"It is a beautiful home and if it is not too much trouble, Christmas with your family would be wonderful."

"Then it is settled."

"Well, I must be taking my leave of you. I have much work to do, especially if we are really going to be setting off for Boston in another month or so, though I highly doubt it."

"Thank you for coming over. I have enjoyed your visit, as always."

"As have I; I am glad that we can spend these times together, Emma."

"So am I Edward. I shall see you in a few days then?"

"Yes, I am sure you shall see me soon enough."

Emma said goodbye to Edward as he left the house just off of Duke of Gloucester Street and mounted his waiting horse. Emma had to admit; he certainly looked handsome in his red uniform.

After dinner that night, William headed for bed and Emma sat in the parlor with Felicity and Benjamin. She suddenly remembered the conversation she had had earlier with Edward and relayed the information to Felicity and Benjamin.

"So they are boycotting the tea tax then?" asked Benjamin.

"It certainly seems that way."

"You know, there has been a cry to boycott buying tea here in Williamsburg, as well as around the Colonies, or so I hear," said Felicity.

"I have heard the same, and I think tea is going to be difficult to come across very soon," said Benjamin.

"Perhaps we should pick up some more then," suggested Emma.

"Honestly, I think we should boycott the tea as well," said Benjamin quietly.

Emma looked at her brother with strange curiosity.

"Are you serious Benjamin?" asked Emma.

"I am. I agree that it is not right to give the East India Company the corner on the market so that they can undersell American tea traders. Surely you must agree it is wrong Emma. People are losing a lot of money over this, not to mention their jobs."

"I'm not entirely sure what to think. I certainly don't think it is right for the American tea traders to not be able to make their living because of a silly tax, but I feel that this is a strange battle that the Colonists have chosen."

"It isn't entirely the tea Emma. It has to do with the unfair advantage the East India Company has been given simply because they are a British company rather than an American company."

"That just doesn't seem right," said Emma earnestly.

"It isn't, Emma," replied Benjamin very matter-of-factly. "It isn't."

Soon after this, Emma decided she was tired and ready for bed. When morning came, it would all make more sense to her. She left Benjamin with Felicity and headed to bed.

But morning came and nothing made any more sense than it had the night before. Emma was torn between her nationalism and her virtues, two things that had continually gone hand in hand up to this point in her life. She was also still replaying the conversation from the evening before with her brother. She saw his point, but she just couldn't bring herself to boycott tea and go against the King's wishes.

November was over and December had blown in with an icy fury. The wind had a strong chill in it, but there was no snow. Mr. Withers had told Emma that the southern portion of Virginia seldom received much snow during the year, and December, though it might bring icy cold rain, rarely brought snow either. Emma was glad to hear this; it might mean that her father would possibly be home for the Christmas holiday.

On the eighth of December, Emma received a letter from her Aunt Margaret. Emma read the letter twice through and then went to find Benjamin. She found him alone in the study reading over a few things of his own. When Emma entered the room, he looked up and smiled at her. However, as he did this he moved all of the papers he was reading aside so that Emma could not tell what they were.

"How are you Emma?"

"I'm fine. I received this letter from Aunt Margaret."

"And how is she?"

"She seems well. I want you to read this," said Emma hurriedly.

"Is everything all right?"

Emma did not answer her brother but simply handed him the letter. He scanned it quickly and then reread it more slowly.

"What do you think?" asked Emma.

"I assume you have the same suspicions as I do."

"What do you think, Benjamin?" she repeated.

"I think that father is no longer in Philadelphia."

"Where do you think he is?"

"I really don't know."

"From the sound of the letter it seems as though you do."

"I'm really not sure what Aunt Margaret is speaking about. I can only assume he is in Boston where he said he might go after Philadelphia."

"Benjamin, look at me and tell me the truth."

Benjamin looked up and Emma found a strange look of concern in her brother's face that did not often reside there.

"What is it?" asked Emma.

"I don't know. I just don't have a great feeling about this all. Margaret's letter seems to be dripping with a secret, but it is not really clear, even to you and me. However, from what she says, she does know where he is and he is not in Philadelphia. He told us he might go to Boston before he left, remember?"

"Yes, I do. Do you think that is where he might be now? Honestly?"

"Honestly, I truly do think he might be in Boston."

"How do you know?"

"It is just a feeling I have, nothing more. However, Margaret makes it quite clear we should not expect him for Christmas."

"I understood that too. That is too bad, William will be sorely disappointed."

"As will you and I."

"Yes, as will we. What are you doing Benjamin?"

"I was just going over some things, nothing serious. I have an idea, what would you think about heading out to Beacon Hall and staying there until after Christmas?"

"I suppose we could do that."

"You haven't really any business in town that is pressing us to stay here."

"No, I don't suppose I do. We can if you want to, Benjamin."

"I would really like to do that."

"Is everything all right?"

"Yes, I suppose I am just a little homesick."

"I have been that way lately as well. It all comes from not having much family around. By the way, that reminds me. I have invited Edward to have Christmas with us so he doesn't have to be alone."

"That's fine. I agree that no one should be alone on Christmas, which reminds me..."

"What?"

"I have invited someone to have Christmas with us as well."

"Who is that?"

"I think you might remember him, Cole Carrington? He has been here a few times. He came that night father had that big dinner."

"Yes, I remember him Benjamin." Emma said with some bitterness in her voice.

"He has no family here Emma. Besides, I just thought it would be nice for a few reasons. I agree no one should be alone on Christmas but furthermore, Mother and Father always had him for Christmas as well, and I thought it would be a nice gesture, in Mother's memory."

"Of course Benjamin. It really is nice of you to remember him. Do you see him much?"

"Not too much lately. I see him sometimes when I have business around town and he is also a pretty good friend of Mr. and Mrs. Dillis; so and when I dine with them, he is often present."

"What do you think of him?"

"Well, I don't suppose I know him that well. I only see him once or twice a month. I get the feeling you don't like him."

"I don't know him."

"But you think he is too sure of himself?"

"He certainly comes across that way."

"I get the feeling he isn't that bad of a fellow. He seems a decent man. He comes from a good family, and he is extremely intelligent. He is also very fair and seems quite honest. You shouldn't judge too harshly."

"That is a fair statement coming from you Benjamin Huntington," said Emma sarcastically.

"It is odd you judge him at all, to be honest."

"Why do you say that?"

"It is not like you to make judgments so quickly, especially when it comes to people. Is there something else about him?"

"No, you are right; I am being unfair."

"Well, give him another chance; he really is a good man." With that, Benjamin went back to his papers and Emma stood and left him to his work.

Emma had not wanted to tell her brother this, but there was something else about Cole Carrington that bothered her though she could really say what it was. However, whenever he was present, Emma felt herself grow nauseous.

Two days later, Emma and Benjamin had gotten everyone out to the plantation. Benjamin seemed happier, which Emma was glad for. She too felt a bit more contented than she had whilst in town. No more was said about their father except briefly in passing. Edward continued his visits, though now came out to Beacon Hall as well.

During Edward's first visit, Emma had shown him the house, though it hardly seemed necessary.

"It is as though you have never moved Emma, or perhaps as though England has followed you."

"Isn't it wonderful?"

"It certainly is. I am glad to see you so happy again."

"What do you mean?"

"You just seemed to be out of your element whist in town; you are much more relaxed and at home here."

"Well, I am at home here."

"This is true."

"Have you heard any more about going to Boston?"

"Not much, in fact, I really am of the belief that we are not going to be going to Boston at all."

"Really? Why is that?"

"I don't believe there is any purpose for us to go there. The harbor is blocked; the ships are not leaving until the tax is paid. Our men on land will do nothing of usefulness."

"It is always difficult to say."

"Well, I haven't asked you for a while, how is your family?"

"Well, William continues his studies. He is doing quite well. His tutor says that William is very advanced for his age. Benjamin too is doing well. He was a little homesick I think, but coming here has certainly aided in improving his demeanor."

"I can see why. But I am glad he is no longer melancholy."

"As am I," replied Emma.

"And your father?"

"He is well. I do not hear from him very much. His business keeps him from us at present but he is due to return soon; however not soon enough I am afraid."

"So he shall not be returning for Christmas I take it."

"It does not appear so."

"Where is your father again?"

"I am not sure to be honest."

"Not sure?"

"Well, he is in Maryland with my aunt and uncle, do you remember them?"

"Which ones are those?"

"The Seagers. My Aunt Margaret is my mother's sister."

"I see. I do not believe I ever had the pleasure of meeting them."

"They are quite a lovely family."

"That is where you stayed while in Maryland, correct?"

"Yes, we stayed there for quite a few months."

"I see."

Edward's visits were often longer now and he came earlier. Emma did not begrudge him this, as the trek was a bit longer than before. She also honestly was enjoying the company. Benjamin and Felicity spent much of their time together and it left Emma feeling a bit lonely. Edward helped fill that void she was feeling.

After Edward left that day, Emma decided she wanted to spend some time with her mother. She pulled out her cloak, put on a hat, and picked up a muff. She then went out to the stables and had a horse brought out for her. The walk to her mother's grave was fairly long and Emma knew it would be getting dark soon, not to mention the air was quite cold.

After a short ride, she dismounted the horse and tied his reins to a low tree branch. She then went and sat down on an obliging bench near her mother's grave.

Emma found herself doing this from time to time since they had arrived in Williamsburg. She did not speak and really tried to not even think very much. This was her spot to clear her head or to work on solving one problem at a time. The area was quiet and very peaceful. She always said hello to her mother when she arrived and said a little prayer before she left, asking God for the safety of her family members and thanking Him for His blessings.

***

Just before the Christmas holiday, the Huntington household received word of up north. On December sixteenth, about 8000 people from Boston had discovered that Governor Hutchinson had repeated his command to not allow the ships carrying the tea out of the harbor until the taxes owed were paid.

"Then, apparently that night a bunch of Colonists disguised themselves as Mohawk Indians," said Edward to Emma during his visit.

"Why Mohawk Indians?"

"It was a good disguise because no one got a real good look at the men."

"Then what happened?" asked Emma with rapt attention.

"Then the men boarded the ships carrying the tea and dumped all the containers of tea bricks into the harbor."

"It can't be," said Emma.

"But it is. It is costing the East India Company a fortune in the loss of tea."

"How much tea was lost?"

"Three hundred forty-two containers."

"It is just so difficult to believe that the Colonists were allowed to do this. How could the British merely allow this to happen?"

"They didn't let it just happen, Emma," replied Edward with a tinge of anger in his voice.

"I'm sorry Edward, I meant no offense."

"Forget it, there is none taken. However, King George himself has said it, 'the die is now cast; the Colonies must either submit or triumph'. He's right you know."

"I was wondering Edward, why don't you stay on for dinner tonight?"

"I would love to accept the invitation Emma but I am not able to."

"Why not?"

"That brings me to the real reason for my visit."

"Which is?"

"My company is being called to Boston to help straighten this whole matter out and to help keep the city under control."

"When will you be leaving?"

"Almost at once. My company is actually leaving late this afternoon. I did, however, want to come out and say goodbye."

"Is it that serious?"

"It is quite serious. This is a major event, Emma and the

people responsible for this shall be severely punished when they are caught."

"How long shall you be away?" asked Emma with concern in her voice.

"I am not sure. We shall stay until we are no longer needed there or until we are needed more somewhere else. I would assume we should return within a month or two though."

"A month or two? But that is quite a long time."

"And you make it all the more difficult to go Emma."

"Me? How do I make it more difficult?"

"Just remember that the memory of you will remain with me whilst I am away and I would like to add that when I return, I would like very much to make you my wife, Emma."

"Edward-" Emma began not really sure what to say.

"Do not answer me now, not even if the answer might be yes. I just want you to think about it while I am gone. Promise me that?"

Emma nodded but did not reply.

"Good. Well, I need to be off then. We are leaving within an hour and I need to see to a few more things before we go," said Edward.

Emma walked Edward to the door. He took her hand and gently kissed it goodbye.

"Until we meet again Emma," said Edward.

"May God allow that time to be swift," replied Emma with complete sincerity.

"I shall pray it is so."

"Be safe Edward and take care," said Emma.

"I will. I have a favor to ask of you, dear Emma."

"What is it Edward?"

"May I have your permission to write to you whilst I am away?"

"Of course you have my permission," replied Emma. She leaned forward and hugged him. She looked up into his eyes and smiled. Edward, with his arms around her leaned forward. She closed her eyes waiting for a kiss. Surprisingly, Edward kissed her forehead. It was a tender kiss, gentle.

"Then my journey shall be all the more bearable." With that, he left the doorway and mounted his horse to leave Beacon Hall. Emma reentered the house and closed the door behind her.

It was a long evening. Emma had told Benjamin and Felicity about the news Edward had brought to her. They reacted with little surprise to the news, which surprised Emma greatly.

"Do you not care?" asked Emma when they were alone in the parlor after dinner.

"Of course we care Emma," replied Benjamin.

"It is just not a surprise, that's all," added Felicity.

"I don't understand you, either of you. All that tea has been lost and it was wrong of the Colonists to do what they did."

"Emma, the Colonists are enraged about being forced to pay this tax. We have spoken about this before. Unfortunately, Governor Hutchinson does not understand what he has forced these men to do," stated Benjamin in a way that was irritatingly calm.

"This is an act of retribution and that should be heavily frowned upon," said Emma.

"This was an act of desperation," Benjamin responded.

"This was an act of treason," Emma spat.

"These men had no other alternative Emma," said Felicity.

"Of course there was another alternative; there is always an alternative to violence, Felicity."

"Normally, I would agree with you Emma, but the Sons of Liberty have tried other methods and they do not work."

"The Sons of Liberty?"

"They are a group of men, mostly from the north, who are building a resistance to the crown," explained Felicity.

"Then they are traitors and truly should not be dealt with at all, except to punish their desperate act, as you call it."

"Emma, I would not jump to sentencing so quickly if I were you. These are not merely nameless faces; these are people with families and lives that are not so unlike our own."

"Benjamin, how can you be so tolerant of such obvious treachery?"

"I am not tolerant of treachery; merely I do not believe that you should assume guilt before you know all of the facts."

"Emma, what Benjamin is trying to say-"

"I understand his words Felicity, I do not require you to translate my brother's statements to me," said Emma as she stood and left the room.

Emma was in quite a bad temper. Her family was acting so strangely. Emma went straight to her bedroom and slammed the door before she remembered that William was already asleep. She hoped her younger brother did not wake, but she was in such a bad temper she felt it would serve both Benjamin and Felicity right to have to deal with him waking.

That's not fair, thought Emma. *It has nothing to do with him.*

Emma sat down on her bed and placed her head in her hands. She felt a wave of exhaustion fall across her body. She was so tired. A moment later, there was a knock on her door. She did not feel like talking any more so she did not answer. Suddenly, Benjamin's voice came in the room through the door.

"Emma, I know you aren't asleep. I am coming in so you had best be decent." Benjamin opened her door and shut it behind him. Emma did not look up at him. "That was quite the ruckus you just made. Thankfully William didn't wake up. He has always been such a heavy sleeper." Benjamin sat down on Emma's bed with her.

Emma still did not look at her brother. She was quite irritated with the entire evening and did not want a lecture from Benjamin.

"Well, I am not going to beat around the bush Emma. I think you should apologize to Felicity."

"Apologize? For what? For stopping her from treating me as a child?" Emma asked sitting bolt upright as she felt the flush of anger creep back into her face.

"You are acting like a child, Emma. I think you are being too sensitive about this. We were merely trying to discuss this matter calmly and diplomatically. Why are you so upset?" Benjamin asked her without emotion which irritated Emma even further.

"I think you are irritating."

"Well, at least we are being honest with each other."

Emma flung herself back onto her pillows. "Benjamin, I don't wish to talk with you any more tonight. Will you please leave me?"

"No, we need to talk."

"Why?" asked Emma standing and taking a few steps toward her window. She still did not look at Benjamin; the world that lay beyond her window was much easier to watch.

"Because I want to and you are having some difficulty that I don't understand. What is going on with you Emma? You are taking everything so seriously, we can't even joke around with you anymore."

"Benjamin, I said I don't want to talk about this anymore."

"Surely this can't have anything to do with Edward leaving?" said Benjamin still sitting on the bed.

Emma was silent. She was thinking. *Did this have anything to do with Edward? Was she truly overreacting? Was she being too sensitive?*

"I asked you a question."

"I'm thinking about it."

"So it does have something to do with Edward."

"I don't know, honestly," Emma replied with a slight stutter and turning to her brother, but then deciding she still did not want to meet his gaze.

"What is going on between you? Is there, is there some sort of, understanding between you two?"

"Heavens no."

"Are you thinking about allowing Edward his wishes?"

"I merely am going to miss his company Benjamin," said Emma finally meeting his gaze.

"So you don't think you could marry him still?"

"No… I don't know."

"What do you mean you don't know?"

"Well, I don't love him, I don't think," Emma replied returning to her bed and sitting next to Benjamin.

"You don't think?"

"Benjamin, can I ask something of you?"

"You may."

"Are you in love with Felicity?"

"Well, we haven't discussed anything, but I certainly have a very strong affection for her. I suppose you could call it love."

"What does it feel like?"

"What do you mean?"

"I mean, for example, how does it feel when you see Felicity?"

Both Emma and Benjamin had calmed their tempers and Benjamin gazed about the room as he thought for a moment. "Well, when Felicity walks into a room, I feel my stomach turn a bit. It is a mixture of nerves and excitement. It happens each time I see her. It is as though my heart jumps and can scarcely contain itself, but it is a wonderful feeling."

"And what about when she leaves?"

"I've been lucky to not have to deal with her absence for more than a day or two at most. But, even when I am not with her for a few hours, I begin to miss her company." Benjamin sighed. "It is an odd thing Emma, but we can sit and not even speak for hours and be quite content. I am happy to merely be in the same room with her. Do you believe you feel these things about Edward?" Benjamin asked now looking at his sister again.

"No, I do not. It is just, sometimes I feel as though he loves me enough…"

"Enough for what Emma?"

"Enough for the both of us."

"Emma, that type of marriage will never be a happy one and you know it."

"It's just, I am so lonely sometimes Benjamin."

"I know, it is difficult. I would venture to say it has even been the most difficult for you. Now, I don't want you to be rushing into anything with Edward. You are not alone here Emma."

"I know. I shall apologize to Felicity."

"That's a good idea."

"I thought you might like it," said Emma with a small amount of teasing in her voice. Benjamin nudged her arm a little. Emma pushed him back and they began a bit of a friendly pushing match until Emma ended up pushing Benjamin onto the floor and both were laughing.

"It is good to see you laugh, it has been a while you know," said Benjamin to his sister. Emma smiled and silently agreed with him. It had been much too long since she had last laughed aloud. "I need to apologize to you Emma," said Benjamin.

"For what Benjamin?"

"For you having to grow up so fast. You were cheated out of the last few years of your childhood and have taken on the role of advisor, role model, and even that of Mother to William."

"That might be going a bit far Benjamin."

"I don't believe it is. However, I have never expected you to take on each new role with such eloquent dignity and grace."

Emma blushed at her brother's kind words.

"You do not owe any apology to me Benjamin; none of it is your fault."

"All the same, I am sorry for it happening."

"Well, what is done is done," sighed Emma.

"Yes, it is done." There was a brief pause before Benjamin spoke again. "Well, I am going to go to bed. It is getting late. Goodnight Emma."

"Goodnight Benjamin and thank you."

"For what?"

"For being such a wonderful brother."

Benjamin smiled and left the room.

Emma went to find Felicity. She was still sitting in the parlor. Emma guessed that Benjamin had asked her to wait there. She apologized to Felicity who in turn apologized to Emma. The girls both laughed at the awkward situation.

"Emma, you have become one of my dearest friends. I would never want to jeopardize that over something as silly as a political argument."

"I agree Felicity. You have grown very dear to me as well. Let's just put this all behind us; sound good to you?"

"It does."

The girls spoke for a little longer and then decided to go to bed.

***

A few days later, Christmas had arrived. Cole Carrington indeed did come out to the plantation bearing many gifts for the entire household. Though Emma had not spent much time with Cole, he had spent a fair amount of time at the Huntingtons' home. He and Benjamin got along perfectly and they spent quite a bit of time together. In fact, Cole was out to see them as often as two or three times a week now, though he spent little time with Emma. William had also grown quite fond of the young man. During the course of Cole's frequent visits, he had even taken William with him around town and to the college.

"Cole, Cole! Emma, Benjamin, Felicity, Cole's here," shouted the child before Cole had even gotten out of the carriage. William ran out to meet him before he reached the house. Emma ran out after William with a coat and Felicity and Benjamin joined them all to greet their Christmas guest.

"Cole, good to see you," said Benjamin.

"And you Benjamin. Thank you all for having me out. Christmases would be so lonely without being with the Huntington family."

"Well, no one should be alone on Christmas, Cole. I am glad you could come out," replied Benjamin as they entered the house.

"Well, Felicity, Miss Huntington, it is good to see you as well."

Emma and Cole, not spending much time together, were still very formal around each other. Though their families were quite well acquainted and Cole was such a frequent guest of Benjamin's and even before, they truly had spent very little time together and Emma still felt her stomach turn over each time she saw him. She assumed that this was in reaction to their first meeting as she still found him to be a bit on the arrogant side.

"Oh Cole, how was the trip out here?"

"Fine, fine," he said as they brought all of his packages into the parlor and set them under the tree.

"We'll see that your bags are brought up to your room," said Emma as she went to find Gracie.

"Gracie, have you seen to Mr. Carrington's room?"

"Yes'm, his room is ready fo' him. He should be quite comfortable up there. I also put some mo' blankets up there. I know this house has been gettin' cold at night."

"It has. Please have his things brought up there right away."

"Yes, Miss Emma."

"Thank you, Gracie."

"Yo' welcome, Miss Emma."

Emma then returned to the parlor to find Cole telling some story about his classes at William and Mary. He had Benjamin, Felicity, and William in fits of laughter. As Emma sat down, the story was being wrapped up.

"And then I told my professor that he had something in his wig," said Cole, laughing so hard himself that he could hardly breathe.

"Oh, Emma, you missed a good story," said William still laughing.

"What a pity," said Emma. She did not much mind she had missed the story, but she did not wish to be rude either.

"Miss Emma, I's sorry to bother you but this jus' arrived fo' you," said Gracie coming into the parlor with a letter.

"Thank you, Gracie. I appreciate it," replied Emma. "Please excuse me," said Emma to the four other members of the room. No one really noticed her leaving, as they were quite engrossed in yet another story of Cole's ingenious and witty yarns.

Emma went into the study to open the letter; it was from Edward.

Dearest Emma,

I hope that this arrives on Christmas because I first want to wish you good Christmas tidings. I have been thinking about you much and I must admit that I miss you a great deal. It has only been a few days since our last visit, but it already seems as though eons have passed by.

Secondly, I hope this letter finds you in good health and happiness. I am well, though my mission has been changed. Unfortunately, I shall be gone longer than first anticipated. We are not heading to Boston as originally planned. Instead we are heading first to Delaware. My mission there is a secret so I am unable to tell you the purpose of our sudden change in direction but I want you to know that I am well.

I will be continually in contact with you, but you will be unable to return my letters now that my mission has changed. I hope that you accept my letters with open arms and will continue to keep those arms open until I may return to you. Please keep yourself safe and well. I will sleep more soundly knowing that you are satisfactory, to say the least. Also, please give my best Christmas wishes to your family. Until I can see you again…

    Sincerely,

    Lieutenant Edward G. Findley

"I wonder what that is all about?" asked Emma to herself. The letter had put a smile on her face, but a question in her heart. "What is happening in Delaware?"

Emma put the letter in her pocket and returned to the parlor.

"Oh, Emma, what time is church tonight?" asked Benjamin.

"The service is at nine o'clock."

"Good, that gives us plenty of time then," said Felicity. Emma looked at the clock in the parlor, it was five forty.

"Dinner will be ready in a little less than two hours," said Emma. With that, Emma again excused herself to check on dinner and to begin to get herself ready. Felicity followed her and Emma heard a comment from the parlor as they reached the stairs.

"Women; they take so long to get ready. I cannot imagine what takes them more than an hour to dress for dinner." The comment came from Cole.

"He obviously has no idea what it takes to actually dress, does he?" Emma asked Felicity. Felicity's only reply was a small giggle.

Emma came down to dinner about seven fifteen. Benjamin,

William, and Cole were waiting for the girls in the hall.

As soon as Felicity joined them, all five people went into the dining room together. Benjamin pulled out a seat for Felicity and then took the seat at the head of the table. Cole politely pulled out Emma's chair and then took his seat next to her. William sat next to Felicity.

Dinner was a grand event. They had pheasant as well as a lot of other food. For dessert, Emma was looking forward to Indian pudding.

"So Cole, the hour was worth it, eh?" asked Benjamin teasingly. Emma saw Cole's face redden, and Benjamin gave a little chuckle at his own joke.

After dinner was finished, Emma made William go up and change for church. She marveled at how messy her younger brother was when he ate.

"Benjamin, why don't you have the carriage brought up for us," said Emma.

"Of course," replied Benjamin as he went to comply with his sister's request.

Emma went into the hall to put on her cloak and muff. William came down a moment later looking a little better off then when he had left them. Emma helped him put on his winter clothes as well and within a few minutes, they were all informed that the carriage was waiting for them outside.

The rest of the evening was spent in church and then, upon arriving home, they all went to bed.

Christmas Day was just as lovely. They exchanged gifts and had a grand feast again. Emma was glad that they had invited Cole. He had made their Christmas a little merrier. However, Emma still missed her mother and Christmas was the hardest time she had encountered thus far.

Benjamin invited Cole to stay until the end of the year, to which Cole happily and quite promptly agreed.

The next day, Benjamin took William into town to pick up a few things. Felicity had made lunch plans with the Hamblin's from the college, and so Emma and Cole were left alone in the house.

"Miss Huntington, would you care for some company?" asked Cole as he found Emma sitting in the drawing room at a table writing some letters.

"Of course, Mr. Carrington. Please come in. I was merely writing a few letters. I am behind on my correspondence yet again."

Cole took a seat not too far from where Emma sat.

"Do you often get behind?"

"Unfortunately; I have been quite busy and my correspondence does not always come first. However, to answer your question, no, I do not often get behind."

"I meant no disrespect, Miss Huntington."

"I did not think you had, Mr. Carrington."

A pause. Emma continued to write her letters.

"May I ask you something Miss Huntington?"

"Of course Mr. Carrington."

"How well do you know my parents? Benjamin says you became quite close with my mother."

"I had the pleasure of spending quite a bit of time with your mother. That reminds me Mr. Carrington, your mother asked me to give this to you a few months after our first meeting. She has included a note for you," said Emma handing Cole the small box that had been entrusted to her months earlier.

Cole took the box and opened it but Emma was not able to see what was inside. He took out the note and read it quickly, smiled, and then replaced the note putting the box in his pocket. Emma desperately wanted to ask what his mother had sent him, but she knew it was none of her business and it was quite improper for her to ask.

"So you get along well with my mother then?"

"Your mother is a wonderful lady. In fact, I enjoy the company of all your family."

"Except me, eh?" Emma looked up from her letter. "It's all right you know. The rest of my family is quite proper and quite likeable."

"I did not mean that at all Mr. Carrington. You are quite respectable and courteous as well."

Cole laughed at Emma. She knew her face was red now.

"Do not worry about it Miss Huntington. I know I am not to everyone's liking at all times. However, you and I have had a strange beginning to our knowing each other."

"What do you mean Mr. Carrington?"

"Simply that we knew too much about each other before we actually met to stand on all the pleasantries of new acquaintances."

"I suppose you are right," said Emma admitting to herself that this was probably true. Cole had never been rude to her in any way; he had merely acted as though he knew her better than he actually had, almost as though they were friends before they met. "I must admit that I feel I know more about you than I should for the time we have spent together."

"The same goes for me about you Miss Huntington. How much of my family have you met?"

"Your mother and father are quite good friends with my Aunt and Uncle Seager in Maryland, which is where I met them. Then, for my Cousin Helena's wedding, your brothers came and I had the pleasure of meeting them."

"So you've met the whole family then? What did you think?"

"I think that your family is respectable and amiable. I am not really sure what you mean?"

"What did you think of Kenton?"

"What does this have to do with anything?"

"He was married a little while ago."

"That is what your mother told me. He seems very happy though."

"I think he is. Did you even meet Philip?"

"Yes, he was home for Christmas from Philadelphia. It was funny; he is working for Benjamin Franklin, who happens to be a good friend of my father's. He has stayed with us in England on more than one occasion."

"He is a good man," said Cole.

"He is."

"Miss Huntington, I was thinking of taking a walk. Would you care to accompany me?"

"I suppose I could do that. Let me just clean this up and grab my cloak."

"Of course, I do not mind waiting."

Emma smiled and picked up her letters, parchment, ink, and quills and put them all in the drawer. She then went into the hall and Cole helped her put on her cloak and handed Emma her muff. Cole then put on his own coat.

As they entered the yard, Cole offered Emma his arm, which she gracefully accepted and they walked along together, arm in arm.

"So how do you find Williamsburg?"

"It is very nice. I am actually surprised that I have become so accustomed to being here, to be completely honest."

"So you are planning on staying for a while?"

"Well, as long as my father is here…"

"But your father is not here," replied Cole.

"Oh you," said Emma nudging her escort gently. "You know what I mean. What about you?"

"I love Virginia. After I finish with school I wish to stay here. My uncle has put me in his will to receive his plantation after he is gone, so I shall probably live with him after school is finished."

"So you want to be a plantation owner?"

"I do. I enjoy the quiet life."

"So you wish to own slaves?" asked Emma with a hint of warning in her voice.

"Well, not exactly. I have been learning how to give your workers fair wages and still make a profit. That is how your father runs his plantation. We decided to try it to see if it would work."

"It was your idea?"

"It was. Your father has been wonderful to me since my arrival here."

"He is a good man."

"Your mother was also always very wonderful to me."

Emma glanced down at the ground.

"I'm sorry; I did not mean to make you sad."

"It is not your fault. It is just difficult to think of her, especially during the holidays. I just miss her."

"I'm sure it was very difficult for you. I, myself, took it very hard and she wasn't even my mother. However, if it makes you feel any better, she went the way she wanted. Your mother passed away in her sleep, peacefully, and not being a burden on anyone."

"Yes, that certainly sounds like my mother."

"She missed you so much Emma."

"Then why didn't she call for us?" asked Emma suddenly. "I'm sorry. I didn't mean to ask you that. I'm sorry."

"Don't be. That is how you feel. I cannot speak for her for certain but my guess is that she wanted you to be happy, and did not want to tear you away from the only life you knew. Plus, I am sure she was worried for your safety to have you traveling during this highly chaotic time. She was most likely waiting for a safer time to call for you."

"I believe that as well. I just miss her."

"I'm sure. I'm sure it hasn't been easy."

There was a silence between them as this last statement sunk in. They continued to walk along in silence for some time before Emma broke the silence.

"How much longer are you going to be in school then?"

Cole switched the subject with Emma flawlessly and for this, Emma was glad.

"It depends."

"On what?"

"On the events up north actually."

"Why?"

"Well, I am almost done. In fact, I should finish by the end of the summer, but if things get much worse up north, I think I am going to have to travel home for a while to be with my parents."

"Of course. You know Mr. Carrington," began Emma, "your mother always speaks very highly of you."

"I did know that actually. She has always spoken highly of all of her children."

Emma laughed. "I suppose that is a parent's job."

Cole laughed as well. "I suppose it is, Miss Huntington."

"Why don't you call me Emma? After all, you are an old family friend. Not to mention I feel as though we were friends before we even knew each other," said Emma smiling coyly at Cole.

"All right Emma. You can call me Mr. Carrington." Cole laughed. "Just kidding. I would be honored if you would call me Cole."

"Cole it is then."

They continued to walk a little while, and then returned to the house for lunch.

The New Year came and went and there was still no word from Emma's father. She was beginning to worry he would be gone even longer than originally anticipated. She was right. By the time Emma's eighteenth birthday came on the twenty-sixth, there still had been no word from her father, but her Uncle Alexandre had written to Benjamin to inform him his father was safe and staying with them, but to not tell anyone. He also wrote that their father would not be returning to Williamsburg until the spring now. Emma was relieved her father was all right, but was confused about all of the secrecy involved.

Cole continued to visit frequently. In fact, he was often at the plantation almost each day now. He often spent his visits with Benjamin or William, but was also spending quite a bit of time with Emma. Emma had grown to enjoy his company immensely since their walk around the plantation grounds over the Christmas holiday. She even found that she even missed him while he was away.

Emma was anxiously waiting the spring now. She missed her father sorely and could not wait for his return.

March finally arrived, and with it came strong winds, though not the snow that had plagued the Huntington children's travels in March of the previous year. However, in March came more news. This time, the news came from England.

"The English Parliament has truly upset the Colonists now," said Cole one afternoon.

"Why?" asked Emma. She was sitting in the parlor with Cole and Benjamin.

"Have you not heard yet?"

"We don't get much news out here Cole," said Benjamin.

"When are you coming back into town then?" asked Cole.

"Probably at the end of this month actually," said Benjamin. "The planting has been started and that is the main event out here until the crops are harvested."

"But what has Parliament done, Cole?" asked Emma impatiently.

"They have passed more Acts. They call them the Coercive Acts, though the Colonists are calling them the Intolerable Acts, which truly seems the better name."

"Why have they passed more?"

"It is in response to the rebellion in Massachusetts last December."

"So what does it all mean?" asked Benjamin.

"It means a lot of things, but the first thing is that all commercial shipping in the Boston Harbor has been shut down until the taxes owed on the tea that was dumped into the Harbor is paid, not to mention Parliament feels that Massachusetts should reimburse the East India Company for the lost tea."

"That seems awfully rash," said Emma. "Doesn't that affect a lot of the business in the Colonies?"

"Yes, it does. There are a lot of commodities that come via the Boston Harbor," replied Benjamin. "I'm sure that there has been uproar about all of this."

"I'm sure there has been. I know that mail is not getting through very well now, so I haven't heard from my parents to know what is actually happening. I'm sure your father won't risk writing to you right now either," said Cole.

"I'm sure he won't, but he should be almost back to Williamsburg now," said Benjamin.

"Good, it will be good that he is in Williamsburg instead of up north."

"I agree," said Benjamin. Emma was confused but she agreed that her father would be better off in Williamsburg.

"Well, I best be off now. I have things to accomplish this afternoon before it gets much later."

"It was good to see you, Cole. We'll be back in town within the week but we'll let you know when we return," said Benjamin.

"I shall look forward to your being closer," said Cole. "Benjamin, Emma, good to see you, as always."

"Have a good day Cole," said Emma. "I'm sure we shall see you soon." Cole nodded and after putting on his hat, mounted his horse and took off.

By the end of the week, the Huntington family had returned to their home in Williamsburg. Though Emma enjoyed her time at Beacon Hall, she was glad to be back in town. Cole continued to visit frequently, and Emma found herself spending more time with him. She began to not only enjoy his visits but to look forward to them. His visits were certainly nowhere near as regimented as Edward's, but Emma found that she even anticipated Cole's visits more because of this.

Chapter 10
Two Revelations

At the end of March, James finally arrived back in Williamsburg. The Huntington children were immensely glad to see him. After a long dinner, William went to bed and Emma, Benjamin, and Felicity were left to speak more openly with James about his lengthy trip.

"Now that William is in bed, where have you really been Father?" asked Emma.

"Well, I'm not sure how much you know about what is happening up north."

"We have heard about the Boston Tea Party, if that is what you mean."

"That is part of it. Anyway, I did first go to Philadelphia, as I had planned."

"And how long were you there?" asked Emma.

"I left Philadelphia shortly after October ended. From there I headed to Boston to deal with similar business. I stayed in Boston until December eighteenth at which point I headed to Maryland and stayed with Peter and Margaret. I remained there almost until I returned home."

"Where did you go after staying in Maryland?" asked

Benjamin.

"I went to visit a friend of mine in Northern Virginia."

"Do we know them?" asked Emma.

"I believe you do. I stayed with Mr. and Mrs. Washington at Mount Vernon, their plantation."

"How are they doing?" asked Emma politely.

"They are quite well, but busy as ever."

"It is good to hear they are well," said Emma sincerely.

"But what were you doing for so long?" asked Benjamin.

"A variety of things," replied James elusively. Felicity laughed at James's evasive answer.

They continued to talk a while about their family that James had visited. It seemed everyone was doing well enough. Helena and Frederick had indeed returned and their house was lovely according to James. After a while longer, both Emma and Felicity decided that it was time to go to bed for the evening thus leaving Benjamin and James to talk a while longer.

It seemed odd to Emma that her father was so near all of the action that had recently taken place. She wondered what he had seen. She wondered why he'd been there. She wondered when things would finally settle down. She fell asleep that night continuing to ponder these questions. It would be a while before she had her answer.

The next few weeks were much of the same. The windy March weather was finally giving way a little as April came. It was still fairly cool however, which Emma was told by people in the town, was quite unusual for April in Williamsburg.

James spent most of his time out at Beacon Hall. He entertained many guests, most of which Emma had never met before. At one point, Mr. Lindley returned again. Even the Moyer family came down in late April. It was nice to see them again, but Emma did not spend much time at all at Beacon Hall. Most of her time was spent at their home in town.

Life remained pretty stable through April. Cole continued to visit four and five times a week. Edward continued to write to Emma at least once a week. Emma continued to look forward to each visit and each letter. It was nice to not feel so lonely. William was doing well in his studies, which pleased the entire family. Benjamin and Felicity grew even closer until one day, James asked Emma about it all.

"How close are we talking here?"

"Well, though neither one has really discussed it with me, I feel that there can be no denial that there is some affection between them."

"Do you feel that it is serious?"

"I-"

"I know you don't wish to betray your brother's trust but I swear the secret is safe with me. I won't let on. Besides, I already have my suspicions."

"I can't deny that they are most likely serious about each other, but nothing will happen until Felicity's parent return to North Carolina, I'm certain."

"You think so?"

"Well, from what Felicity tells me, she isn't sure when they are going to return. I can't imagine what is keeping them away so long."

"It is complicated, but I believe they shall be returning soon enough."

"Do you know something then?"

"No, just a hunch."

"It has been a long time since we have seen them."

"They have been much engaged. However, not that this is much of a comfort, but Felicity is used to such long absences."

"What do you mean?"

"Her parents are often gone for very long periods of time and even when they are home, they are extremely busy."

"That isn't too good."

"Well, it is the life that they have chosen, and though Felicity may suffer a little, many will profit from their exertions."

"But is that truly good enough? To sacrifice the few for the good of the many cannot always come at any cost."

"However, the needs of the few cannot outweigh the needs of many."

"They can, actually."

"In what way Emma?"

"Can you honestly tell me that if William were in grave peril you would let him suffer because strangers needed you?"

"I see your point. However, this is not a situation of grave peril. I would daresay Felicity is a bit more comfortable with us than all that."

"You would most likely be right," Emma laughed.

"I may even go as far as to say she is happier with us than with her own family."

"That might be a little harsh, Father."

"It might be."

April ended with a gust of wind and little relief from the cool temperatures. With April's passing also ended the calm routine that Emma had come to depend on. May came and with it came turmoil.

On May fifteenth, Benjamin celebrated his twentieth birthday. They kept the celebration small, at Benjamin's request, but everyone present enjoyed themselves.

At the end of May, the Huntington household received a letter from James's brother, Alexandre.

The letter came during lunch one day. It just so happened that Emma, Benjamin, and Felicity were dining with James that afternoon. After reading the letter once through, James asked Benjamin to close the dining room doors and he then read the letter aloud to the others.

Dear James and Family,

I am writing to let you know about recent events here. On May 12th, we had a meeting to call for a boycott of British imports. This is, of course, in response to the Boston Port Bill. Many Bostonians are quite angry about the whole affair, quite understandably. Governor Hutchinson still does not allow for the British ships to leave without compensation for the tea and the paying of the tax for the tea. The people of Boston have refused and this boycott is our means to accomplish this.

In response to our actions, however, General Thomas Gage, the commander of all the British military forces in the Colonies, arrived in Boston the very next day to replace Hutchinson as the Governor. This means that Massachusetts is now under military rule, which undermines the entire right of Massachusetts to be a self-governing colony. General Gage's arrival was followed by the arrival of four British regiments. Boston is under constant surveillance by these troops.

Beginning on May 17th, Colonists in Providence, New York and Philadelphia began to call for an inter-colonial congress to overcome these horrendous Intolerable Acts. They also wish to discuss a common course of action against the British. It now seems, dear Brother, that our worst fears are coming true with a complete certainty that even I could never have imagined. However, there is more.

On May 20th, Parliament enacted another series of Acts that include the Massachusetts Regulating Act and the Government Act, which virtually ends any self-rule by the Colonists in Massachusetts that may have remained after General Gage took over. Now, the English Crown and the Governor assume political power exclusively. Parliament has also enacted the Administration of Justice Act that protects royal officials in Massachusetts from being sued in colonial courts, not to mention the Quebec Act establishing a centralized government in Canada controlled solely by the Crown and Parliament. This act also extends the southern boundary of Canada into the territories claimed by Massachusetts, Connecticut, and even Virginia.

As you can see, we are in desperate times here and are again in need of your services, though in a much different capacity. I am sorry to call upon you, as I know you have just returned home, but I feel as though I have no other choice. I have come to believe that the only way to fight a common enemy is to join in a united bond. This means that we are in need of the support of all the Colonies. Their support must be rallied around a common goal. I am asking you to be a voice of reason now, as we have discussed. The time has come and we can no longer delay. Please keep me informed of your progress. I have reason to believe (from our dear friend Samuel Adams) that there will be a grand meeting coming; one where every colony is represented and we must come to this meeting with open minds that are ready to unite under our common goal. Please consider what I have said carefully. I shall anxiously await your answer.

Please give my best to the children. I know that this experience will put a strain on your family where there is already strain. I will be glad to hear from you and hopefully will have the pleasure of seeing you in a few months.

Sincerely,

Alexandre Huntington

After James finished the letter, a hush fell over the room. No one wanted to be the first to speak. Emma felt everything slowly sinking in, like a weight seeping into wet sand. Emma swallowed hard. She was fighting back an impulse, though she couldn't put her finger on what she was feeling.

"So you will have to be leaving again then?" asked Benjamin.

"Eventually. I have things I need to take care of here first. People I need to see."

Felicity did not speak. She looked from James to Benjamin to Emma, but barely managed to breathe. Emma too looked around the table. There was a surprised look on everyone's face but it was not the same look that Emma seemed to be feeling.

She could hear Benjamin and James talking, but she had one thought going through her mind. She did not even wait for a break in the conversation but merely interrupted whomever it was that was talking.

"What does Uncle Alexandre mean about your services? What common enemy are you supposed to be uniting against?"

Her father paused and then took a deep breath. "Emma, I have read this letter to you because I do not wish to lie to you. I believe it is going to be impossible to keep this from you any longer. I know about your feelings concerning the Colonists and their decisions, but now you need to know mine. I happen to think that the Colonists are right in what they are doing.

"I think that King George and Parliament have made outrageous demands upon the Colonies and have given no just compensation. You can hear from Alexandre's letter how many new regulations are being forced upon them. I feel as though the Colonies do need to band together and I fear, with near certainty now, that we are going to go to war with England.

"However, I still do not ask you to choose sides. I only repeat my warning about making rash decisions, and I remind you that we are a family, for better or worse."

"Did my mother know about this?" Emma asked as calmly as she could.

"She did. In fact, Elizabeth is the reason that I have been doing all that I am doing. I would never have gotten so heavily involved as I am now had it not been for her."

"And how heavily involved is that exactly?" Emma asked with a sharp tone.

"I am a member of the Sons of Liberty, a patriotic group concerned with the welfare of the Colonies despite the rule of the Crown. I believe that you have met many of the other members. Our founder is Mr. Samuel Adams."

"I see," said Emma remembering when she met Mr. Adams in Boston. "Is this what you have been involved in while you were away?"

"It is. I went to Philadelphia to serve on the committee that forced the British agents out of the city. From there, I went to Boston where I aided with the Boston Tea Party, both the organization and execution of it. I was unfortunately injured during the raid and spent two days unconscious in Boston. When I awoke again, I knew it was not safe for me to remain there so I went to visit your mother's sister, Margaret. I stayed there long enough to recuperate and make the journey toward home. Whilst on my way, I stayed with Mr. and Mrs. Washington, as I said. We spoke about the state of affairs in Virginia and I have been appointed to an advisory committee with Mr. Washington, among others."

"Do I know them as well?"

"You know some of the members at least. Mr. Lee and Mr. Thomas Jefferson are both serving on the committee. However, all of this must remain a secret Emma."

"How long?"

"How long must this remain a secret, or how long have I been involved in this?"

"The latter."

"Since before I arrived in the Colonies. That is truly the main purpose that your mother and I decided to come here."

"How could you not even tell me? Or Benjamin?"

"Actually Emma, I knew. I've known since we were in Boston."

"And you didn't tell me?"

"I didn't think you would agree, and I did not want to cause distress, especially while we were still traveling."

"And I suppose you are involved in all of this as well?"

"I joined the Sons of Liberty at that meeting I went to in Boston. I found myself agreeing with Mr. Adams and the others. Even you have agreed that it is not morally right Emma. To blindly follow the Crown simply because we have done so for centuries is no reason to inflict the suffering that is caused by its decisions."

"So you are both going to be part of this, this crusade?"

"We are not alone, Emma. Many of our friends and family are even more involved than we. It does not make them bad people."

"Such as?"

"Well, Peter and Margaret and their family, Alexandre and Isabelle and their family, the Withers, the Moyers, the Carringtons, including Cole and all of his brothers, Captain Tillig, Mr. and Mrs. Dillis, Mr. Lindley, among others. However, do not assume that all of our friends and family share our feelings. That is why this must all be kept so secretive."

"How do you feel about all this Felicity? Have you even bothered to ask her, Benjamin?"

"He has. My mother and father are in England now trying to form negotiations with key people in Parliament. That is why they have been absent so long. My parents are deeply involved as well, and I will be true to this cause until justice is done."

"So none of you feel what you are doing is wrong? You know you are not only placing yourselves at danger; think of William."

"I have thought of him and of you, Emma. I do not want my children, or their children to grow up under such oppressive conditions; that is why I remain tied to this effort. I am going to reply to Alexandre that I whole-heartedly agree with him and that I shall take on the task that he has asked of me."

"And the letter I delivered to you, the one from Mr. Washington?"

"Yes, it has to do with all this too. It was concerning this committee we have formed. It also explained to me about Benjamin and his feelings as well as his capabilities. That was how I found out about Benjamin's new beliefs."

"So I have been involved in this plot unwillingly? I have been placed in harm's way because of your new acquaintances?"

"You were never in harm's way. That is why Mr. Washington gave you the letter. Remember how Benjamin was taken from the carriage upon arriving in Williamsburg, but you were not even questioned? It is because I told Mr. Washington about your connection with a certain Lieutenant in the British Army. I knew he would not allow them to touch you in any manner."

"If you will excuse me, I am no longer hungry."

Emma stood from the table. James looked at his daughter and Emma saw the hurt in his face, but no one tried to stop her from leaving. Emma started to head up to her bedroom but decided against it.

"Curtis, will you have the carriage brought up for me?"

"Yes'm, is you all right Miss Emma?"

"Fine, please just bring the carriage around for me."

"Yes'm."

Emma entered the carriage and told the driver to head to Beacon Hall. She wanted to spend some time with only one person, her mother.

Upon arriving at Beacon Hall, Emma exited the carriage and found Grace waiting for her.

"Miss Emma, we didn't know you was comin' out today. Is everythin' all right?"

"It's fine. If any of my family comes to call, please tell them that I am here but do not wish to be disturbed."

"Yes'm," replied Gracie.

"Also, please send for some of my things to be brought out, I think I am going to stay for a few days."

"Ah course Miss Emma. I do that right away."

"Thank you." With that, Emma left Gracie and did not even bother to enter the house. She walked straight past it and made a direct line to her mother's grave. The lengthy walk would make her feel better.

Quite a long time passed; Emma wasn't sure how much. She looked up from her spot on the bench next to her mother's grave and saw it was very dark. She shivered slightly in the cold. The day had been nice enough that she had not grabbed a shawl but merely a hat. She now regretted this decision a little.

Emma said a small prayer to say goodbye to her mother. She then stood and began to walk back towards the house. Despite being cold, she walked slowly. When she finally did return to the house, she found James and Benjamin waiting for her, much as she had expected.

They stood the second she entered and brought her to the sofa in the parlor.

"Gracie, please get Miss Emma a nice hot cup of tea," said Benjamin as he got a blanket to wrap around her. "Emma, you are nearly frozen solid. Don't you know how cold it is out there?"

"I thought you were boycotting tea," said Emma with no emotion in her voice.

"You aren't. It will do you some good."

After Gracie brought in the tea, Benjamin had her shut the doors behind her. Emma sat in silence. She could barely look at two of the men she loved most in her life.

"Emma, say something," said Benjamin.

James merely sat quietly in the armchair waiting for his daughter to speak. After what seemed like ages, Emma finally found her voice.

"Why?"

"Emma, we didn't want to tell you because I knew it would upset you but there has been much going on of which you are unaware, and some of which you are. Your Uncle Peter told me about you discovering his meetings," replied James.

"I promised him I wouldn't tell anyone, and I have not," replied Emma still in her monotone and still refusing to look at either Benjamin or her father.

"And we all appreciate that."

"Father, do you not think this is treasonous?"

"To whom, Emma?" asked James with a curtness in his voice that Emma had never heard before.

"To the King?"

"What about to oneself?"

"You are an Englishman," said Emma finally looking at her father with cold fury. She held her tea in her hands but did not drink.

"You are my daughter."

"It does not mean that I will live your beliefs," replied Emma now taking a sip from her teacup and lowering her gaze.

"Which is why I did not tell you Emma."

"I'm sorry?"

"I did not tell you about any of this because I wanted you to make up your own mind. Benjamin has told me about your feelings and I do not wish to influence you into believing anything you don't want to believe simply because I believe in it."

"I don't understand."

"I know you don't, Dearest, but you will."

"I don't think so."

"Emma, I believe in my cause, but lives may soon be at stake for the beliefs of many men, on both sides, and I do not want your life, nor the lives of your brothers to be at stake because of it."

"Then Father, I beg of you to stop this madness," Emma pleaded looking at her father. She could feel tears welling up in her eyes but she was too angry to cry.

"I cannot do that Emma. The rights of men are being slowly stripped away and I will not stand idly by and watch the life I love deteriorate because of the King's feelings. Things have already been set in motion and the inertia of it will carry me onward."

Emma could stand no more. She almost upset her tea as she stood and began pacing while she could feel her voice steadily rising.

"And I do not think it is right that you join this cause without regard to your family. My God Father, how many of your family must die before you see what you are doing? You weren't even here for Mother when she died and it was all because of this business you just needed to take care of and for what? For the rights of men? For the rights of men who do not matter to us? We have a good life, why must you destroy that?"

"Is that what you think Emma?"

"All I know is that my mother has died and you weren't even here to comfort her. She was sick and you left her; you left her in the care of strangers," said Emma. She was now crying. Benjamin, now standing and following his sister's pacing, took her tea and set it on the table. He then tried to put his arm around her. Emma shrugged him off but continued to cry as she sank back onto the sofa.

Emma had not truly cried about her mother at any point since learning of her death. She had shed some tears the night she found out, and a tear or two had escaped on a few occasions, but there had been no real grieving period for Emma. Her emotions had merely all bottled up inside of her and now the truth was flowing out of her as easily as her tears. It was true; she blamed her father's absence for her mother's death. Now Emma could do nothing but cry and try to catch her breath. She felt Benjamin's arm around her again, but she lacked the will to push him away.

James took a deep breath, let it go, and then breathed in again. "There are a few things you need to know Emma. Your mother insisted that I leave her. She knew all about my convictions and she shared each one, possibly to a stronger degree. I did not want to leave her, but she knew I was needed. Once I had left, she did not tell me of her illness. If I could trade your mother's life for my own, I would, but He does not give us that choice Emma."

Emma did not want to hear what her father had to say. She tried to block out his words. She tried to erase the memories.

"However, I do believe in this cause and I shall fight for it if it means my life. I ask for the respect and duty of my daughter to adhere to my wishes and to keep my secrets and nothing more. I do not stand before you to ask your forgiveness because I am not apologizing, and I do not ask you to agree with me because that is unfair. I ask that perhaps you take a moment and think about others. However, I am tired and have much to accomplish tomorrow. I am going to bed."

James left his two eldest children sitting in the parlor, Emma crying and Benjamin trying to console her.

"Emma, you mustn't blame Father for anything."

"I am going to bed."

"Let me help you," said Benjamin kindly.

"I can manage on my own," said Emma icily. "Goodnight."

Benjamin nodded but did not reply. It didn't matter though; Emma doubted she would have heard him anyway.

Emma did not sleep that night, or the next. The days were long for her; she spent the majority of them alone either visiting her mother or wandering about in the fields and woods that surrounded the plantation. Emma did not eat much and preferred to be away from the house as much as possible.

James was no longer staying at Beacon Hall. As he had said, he had business to attend to, and that business kept him in town. Emma overheard Benjamin tell Felicity that James would be leaving Williamsburg by June fifth. She didn't make an effort to see him off.

Emma continued to spend her sleepless nights and warm days alone. She preferred the solitude. Benjamin had decided it would be best for William to stay in town; Emma had to admit she was glad about this. He would never understand Emma's isolation and she did not wish to explain to him why she was angry, not to mention that she did not wish for company of any sort.

Emma received a letter on the sixth from Edward. She had not heard from him in a while and she was beginning to worry. According to his letter, his regiment was one of those sent to Boston, so he was finally stationed where they had originally wanted to send him. Of course, in his letter, Edward gave another plea for Emma to marry him. For the first time in her life, Emma seriously considered marrying Edward.

She knew that Edward could take her away from all that she was facing right now. She knew he believed the same as she did. She knew that he loved her and that he would give everything to her. Her life would be simple and happy, something that had not occurred in over three years. Emma began to draft a reply to Edward. In her letter, she had finally consented to marrying Edward on the condition that they would return to England as soon as possible. When her letter was finished, she placed it in an envelope and sealed it. However, something stopped her from sending it yet. Her father's words returned to her.

"...a time may come when you do not know where to turn and you turn to the very place you have been avoiding for so long."

Suddenly, these words made sense to Emma. She tore up the

letter she had just written. If, when Edward returned, she still wanted to marry him, she could tell him then. That would give her time to think about it all and make sure that she really wanted to marry him, and not just because she was unhappy. However, Emma was extremely irritated that it was her father who had given her this advice.

Felicity's birthday came and went. Emma did not attend most of the celebrations. She greeted some of the guests and then gave excuses of not feeling well.

Emma continued to spend her days in isolation around Beacon Hall. She spent almost every waking moment outside and away from everyone else. She slept now and then, but more from pure exhaustion than anything else. Emma still had no appetite and only ate when others were around so as to avoid the lecture from them.

Along Emma's wanderings she began to grow quite comfortable with her surroundings, and was familiar with every path around the plantation. Emma would often walk to the edge of their land and look out over the adjacent plantations. Beacon Hall was vast in its acreage but there were two adjacent plantations that were quite large as well. Emma never saw anyone who lived on these lands however.

Finally, on June twenty-fourth, as Emma was sitting out by her mother's grave and watching the eastern sky, thinking about her life in England, a man rode up on a horse. Emma figured it was Benjamin and so she didn't even bother to look up at the rider. The rider didn't bother her; merely sat in a grassy spot about ten feet from where Emma was seated.

The day wore on but the rider did not leave. Finally Emma decided to tell Benjamin that she wanted to be alone but when she looked over, she did not see her brother. Before her was none other than Cole Carrington. Emma felt her stomach turn a little and her face become red. Cole smiled at her but did not move from his spot, nor did he attempt to speak to her.

Emma sat a little longer now refusing to look at Cole and hoping he would just leave her be. When the sun was at its highest for the day, she said her parting prayer to her mother and stood up. She walked over to where Cole was sitting. He patted the grass next to him but still did not speak.

Emma sat down next to him and leaned against the same tree Cole was leaning against. "What brings you out this way?" asked Emma not looking at Cole.

"You," replied Cole simply.

"Me? For what reason?"

"I hear you haven't been eating much or sleeping very well. I thought you might want to talk about it and if not, I also hear that you have been pretty isolated so I thought you might like some company and if not, then I came to sit by this tree and make sure it was holding up ok."

"That's kind of you but if my brother or my father brought you out here-"

"They didn't. I just haven't seen you in so long."

"And you just happened to know where to find me?"

"Actually, yes; I mean, I figured you were out at the plantation when you weren't at home. Not to mention that Francis spilled the beans a little. But I did figure out where you were once I got here all on my own. In fact, no one but you even knows I'm here."

"Really?" asked Emma coyly finally looking at Cole though he did not return her gaze.

"Well, all right, I think Oliver might have caught sight of me. I mean, he waved at me and I had to wave back so I wouldn't raise suspicions, but other than him it is a complete secret," Cole said crossing his heart with his fingers and attempting to be as earnest as possible.

Emma allowed a little laugh to escape.

"Well, you can't be that down if you can still laugh."

"So what has everyone told you?" asked Emma returning her sights to the eastern sky.

"Basically that you found out about their political convictions and you weren't very happy about it and have taken to starvation and sleep deprivation as means of revenge."

"They think this is revenge?"

"No. I just added that part. It sounded kind of good, eh?" He laughed at his own joke and Emma found herself smiling. "So, you want to tell me about it?"

"Not particularly."

"That's all right," said Cole as both stared at the same spot in the eastern sky and leaned against the weeping willow. "I didn't really want to know anyway. I just came all the way out to Beacon Hall to sit on the grass under this tree for three hours in the heat and humidity to watch you not look at me and not speak to me only to find out that it was all for nothing. Well, at least the tree was kept company. That really was my plan, I swear."

"All right. It's true, I found out about everything. I suppose I was stupid to not put it together myself."

"I wouldn't say that at all," said Cole with complete sincerity.

"Well, I feel as though I should have caught it but anyway.... My father and Benjamin told me about their affiliations as well as yours, Mr. Carrington."

"Uh-oh. No, no. My name is Cole, remember? You are Emma, and I am Cole. I don't want to regress here," Cole stated sitting up and looking Emma directly in the eye.

"All right, I found out about your affiliations as well, Cole." Emma did not move but her gaze met Cole's and then turned back towards the sky.

"Does it change anything, Emma?" Cole returned to his comfy position against the weeping willow.

"Of course it does. I can't be associated with people who share your beliefs."

"Why?"

"You wouldn't understand."

There was a silence between them for a few moments.

"Emma, what is your favorite color?"

"What?"

"Just humor me."

"All right – blue."

"Why?"

"Well, my eyes are blue and I love the ocean and the bright sky; why are you asking me this?"

"All right, I can take those reasons, but blue is not my favorite color at all."

Emma sighed. "I'll go for it. What is your favorite color?"

"Green."

"Why?"

"Because green is the color of growth and renewal. Green comes alive in the spring."

"Those seem to be pretty good reasons."

"But Emma, we disagree."

"So?"

"So we can't be associated with each other. I like green," Cole said as he crossed his arms over his chest and turned away from her, "and you are a blue-liker. We can no longer be friends."

"I see where you are going with this. This is about color, something inconsequential."

"But what I am trying to get at Emma is that we have listened to each other's reasons and we agree to disagree. We don't end our friendship over something because we don't see eye to eye completely."

"Again, this is over something more important than color."

Cole sighed and seemed to think for a moment.

"All right, I have a better one. You know Mr. Washington?"

"Yes."

"He's a pretty decent man, right?"

"Well, I thought so."

"All right, politics aside, he's a decent fellow."

"Yes. I can agree with that."

"And you enjoy his company and find him amiable?"

"Yes, I do."

"He owns slaves. I know how you feel about this one. Does that change your opinion of him?"

"I disagree with his ownership of slaves."

"But he is still a decent man whose company you enjoy, and you still find him amiable?"

"I suppose so."

"But you have two extremely different beliefs on this."

"But I cannot change how he feels."

"That is the same with your father, with Benjamin, with Felicity, and with myself. We have different beliefs than you, but we still enjoy your company; we still love you, Emma. We just don't agree on this issue."

"I don't know Cole."

"But you see my point?"

Emma sighed. "Yes, unfortunately I see your point."

"Now, I want you to think about things from that perspective."

"Thank you, Cole. You truly are a good friend to me," Emma replied now looking at Cole again.

Cole met her eyes and Emma saw herself in those bright green eyes again. "You're welcome. But, don't tell anyone, I don't want it to get around. Pretty soon everyone will be expecting good advice and true friendship from me and I just don't know if I could really handle that."

Emma laughed and Cole gave her a hug. Emma felt her body relax slightly. She felt so safe in his arms.

When they returned to the house, Benjamin called them into the study.

"Read this," he said handing them a newspaper clipping.

"*New Quartering Act enacted by Parliament,*" read Cole aloud. "*A new version of the 1765 Quartering Act has been enacted by the English Parliament. This new version requires that all of the American Colonies must provide housing for British soldiers in occupied houses and taverns as well as in unoccupied buildings. Any colonist refusing to house British troops will be subject to the highest punishment the law can allow.*"

"Wow," said Emma.

"What do you think, Cole?"

"I guess I am not surprised. Where did you get this?"

"Your brother Philip sent it."

"I see, the *Pennsylvania Gazette*. Ah, leave it to old Philip to cause a stir. I swear his biggest idols are Samuel Adams and John Hancock." Benjamin and Cole laughed but Emma did not see the humor.

June came to an end in the normal blaze of heat and humidity. Emma had begun to eat and sleep again, though Benjamin commented daily on her paleness. Felicity's main concern was how thin Emma had become. Emma heard Felicity and Benjamin discussing this one evening, but she did not wish to argue any further and so ignored their discussion.

Emma had truly taken Cole's words to heart and though she still did not agree with the Colonists' beliefs, she worked each day to remember to not begrudge them or judge them on their actions. She had to admit she found tolerance to be a more relaxing road.

As June ended, William's tutor came to Emma and Benjamin to discuss some ideas.

"I feel as though his education would be better served if he attended a school in South Carolina. They have excellent teachers there. It is just like a university, but for children from ages eight to seventeen."

"But William is only going to be seven this August."

"I have discussed it with the headmaster and he is willing to make an exception for William, especially since he has already surpassed the curriculum they use with the eleven-year-olds."

Emma asked William to come in and how he felt about it all. William was very excited about the prospect of it and upon seeing William so happy, neither Emma nor Benjamin could say no.

"I'm sure that Father will agree with us, so he has our blessing," said Benjamin.

William yelled and jumped with joy. Benjamin had him go outside again.

"There are a few minor details that need to be put in place, but he can leave as early as July fifteenth if everyone is all right with that. That way he can be there for the start of the fall term and I will, of course, be going with him so you needn't worry about that."

Emma left Benjamin to discuss the details. She set about beginning a letter to their father who was now supposed to be in northern Virginia.

***

At the beginning of July, Emma and Benjamin received a letter from their father. He was writing from Monticello, the home of Thomas Jefferson. He was writing to inform Benjamin and Emma as well as Felicity and Cole that all the Colonies were going to begin meeting to discuss uniting under a common goal in September. The event, born from Samuel Adams, would be called the Continental Congress. He went on to ask them if they would like to be his personal guests in Philadelphia during the proceedings. Benjamin and Cole immediately said they were going. Felicity agreed to go too. Emma, though not keen on the idea, did not wish to be alone in Williamsburg, and so agreed to go as well.

They decided to wait until after William left for school. So, on July eighteenth, 1774, Benjamin, Emma, Felicity, and Cole climbed into a carriage bound for Philadelphia and the history books.

They stopped in northern Virginia and stayed with the Moyers for a few days. The weather was extremely warm, but Emma was handling it much better this year than the year before. The Moyers seemed very happy to see Emma and the others.

After a few days, they set out again on the road. Conversation was kept light. It surprised Emma that the others weren't talking about the political meeting they would be attending in Philadelphia.

By the time they finally reached Philadelphia, it was already September third. They had stayed quite a while in Maryland with Margaret. Peter and Christopher had already gone on to Philadelphia. It amazed Emma that Christopher was seventeen. In her mind, he still seemed fifteen. It was an odd thing how time stopped for people in your mind when you weren't around those people much.

Philadelphia was a new city to Emma. She had only seen two other cities like it in the world: Boston and London. It was extremely busy and bustling with activity. The carriage stopped right in front of the shop for the Pennsylvania Gazette. To Emma's surprise, Philip Carrington was the first to come out and greet them.

"Hello there," said Philip happily. "How is everyone?" he asked, helping Felicity out of the carriage, followed by Emma.

"Good, good," replied Cole as he stepped down. "Glad to be done riding in this infernal carriage, I tell you though."

"I would suppose so," replied Philip laughing at his brother. Benjamin had now exited the carriage as well. "Mr. Franklin offers his house for your use while you are in Philadelphia. Your rooms have already been prepared and your father," he said gesturing to Emma and Benjamin, "will be along tonight. He is presently engaged in business elsewhere."

"That is very kind of Mr. Franklin," said Emma.

"Well, I wrote to him to tell him about the Continental Congress convening and mentioned that Mr. Huntington and his family were coming up. He replied that he owes you all many returns on your generosity, and would not hear of you staying anywhere but here."

"It is much appreciated," said Benjamin.

"And you are in a prime location," said Philip bringing everyone inside. "This is the center of town. The Congress will convene less than a few blocks from here. You are very lucky you will not have to walk so far."

As they entered the shop, Emma saw the printing press used for the Gazette. The extremely large machine was fascinating to her. She stared at it while the others continued to talk and she tried to figure out exactly how it worked. She had it almost completely figured out when Cole interrupted her train of thought.

"Emma, Philip and I were going to walk around the city, did you want to come?"

Emma had a strange feeling of excitement. The city was bustling and it was all completely new. Emma agreed to go with Philip and Cole. Felicity had decided she wanted to take a nap for a few hours, and Benjamin informed Emma that he was going to meet with their cousin Sebastian.

"Well, we'll take you to the pub whilst we are about," said Philip. Benjamin agreed. Felicity said goodbye to everyone as Emma returned from going upstairs to change her dress and put on a bonnet and hat to shield her face from the sun.

Philip offered Emma his arm and the four walked back out into the street. The sun was shining quite brightly above, but it was not nearly as hot as the weather in Virginia. Emma was a bit grateful for the relief from the heat.

"I suppose you are used to this heat," said Philip.

"It really isn't that warm here Philip," replied Cole.

"Well, for us this is extremely warm for this time of year. We are usually beginning to cool down now and the weather is turning into fall, but not this year."

They walked on a little more. Philip was pointing out the sites to Emma and Benjamin. Cole had been to Philadelphia before, but not for quite a few years he told Emma.

After a few blocks, Philip pointed out the pub where Benjamin was supposed to meet with Sebastian. Benjamin said goodbye to Emma and the Carrington brothers.

"Benjamin, bring Sebastian over tonight. I would really like to see him."

"I will ask him. He and Alexandre are both here. Perhaps we can all have dinner tonight together. Regardless, I will relay your regards."

"Thank you. I will see you tonight," said Emma.

With that, Benjamin went into the pub and Emma continued her walk with Philip and Cole.

Philadelphia was an interesting city. Emma just could not get over how much activity there was. Even when she would take trips to London, she did not see so many people about.

"Granted there are people about, but not like this," said Emma concluding her story to Philip and Cole.

"Well, people have much business right now. It is not usually this busy around here but with the Congress assembling, we have many more people than usual."

"That makes sense I suppose."

"Ah, Mr. Hancock, Mr. Adams," said Philip as they passed two men.

They replied warmly to Philip and stopped for a moment.

"You gentlemen remember my brother Cole? Miss

Huntington, this is Mr. John Hancock and-"

"Mr. Samuel Adams from Massachusetts," said Emma.

"You know each other then?" asked Philip.

"We met only for a brief time Mr. Carrington," replied Sam Adams, no longer wearing his tatty red suit that he had become well known for in Massachusetts. "We had the pleasure of meeting at Miss Huntington's uncle's home in Boston. That was quite a few months ago however. I would never have guessed I would meet you again, let alone here of all places."

"Fate seems to have a sense of humor after all, Mr. Adams."

"So it would seem," he replied and the four men laughed. "Tell me, is your family here?"

"Are you speaking of my Uncle Alexandre?"

"Well, yes him and your father."

"I believe my Uncle is in town, but my father is most definitely in town."

"I assumed as much. John you remember Mr. James Huntington?"

"Oh yes. He is from Virginia, is he not?"

"He is," replied Emma cordially.

"Well, I shall certainly look forward to meeting with him again," said Mr. Hancock.

"Is your father a representative Miss Huntington?"

Emma thought for a moment. She wasn't truly certain if he was or not. She glanced and Philip and then at Cole. Cole gently nodded his head.

"Yes, he is," said Emma in reply.

"Well, then we shall certainly be seeing a lot of him," said Mr. Adams. "And I am most certain we will be seeing more of you as well, Miss Huntington."

"Most likely. That is, if you do not object to this."

"Of course not. We could never object to such a lovely lady bestowing her presence upon us," said Mr. Hancock eloquently.

"I would be most honored to see you again, Miss Huntington. We must be going, but please give your father our best and your uncle too, if you see him. I do hope that fate continues to have… a sense of humor," said Mr. Adams with a smile on his face.

Emma couldn't help but smile as well. She was still blushing from the compliment from Mr. Hancock, and laughing inside about Mr. Adams's joke as she said goodbye to the men.

This time, Emma took Cole's arm and they continued to walk about. Philip seemed to know everyone. He introduced Emma and Cole to all of them. Emma was sure she would never remember everyone's name, but they all seemed to at least know of her father if not know him personally.

"Philip, how do you know all these men?" asked Emma with curiosity.

"Well, most of them have dined with Mr. Franklin at one time or another. Others have stayed at his home while he is in England. Then there are the ones that I have met because of my own parents. Of course, there's the paper too. It is funny how you just keep running into the same people when you all share the same beliefs."

Emma smiled at this statement but said nothing in reply. Cole gave her a quick smile as if to say he knew what she was thinking. Emma had to laugh at Cole though she did not do so outwardly. Cole had always been a bit outspoken around Emma but as soon as they had reached Philadelphia and met up with Philip, Cole had become quite quiet.

By the time they returned to Mr. Franklin's shop, Emma guessed that she had met at least thirty of the delegates to the Congress, as well as many other people who ran shops in town, or just simply knew her father.

When they returned, Felicity was up from her nap.

"Your father stopped by with this note, Emma. He wants us to all meet him for dinner at some local tavern."

"I know where it is," said Philip.

"Anyway, he wants us to meet him in about an hour. Some of your other family members will be joining us."

"All right, let me just go and change and then we can go," said Emma.

"Good idea," said Cole and they all left Felicity in the sitting room.

Emma had never been in a house quite like this one. The printing shop was downstairs and the house was upstairs. Mr. Franklin had his whole house on the second floor. Philip told her that he also kept another home that wasn't in Philadelphia, but he rarely used it. His wife lived there with their children.

Emma changed for dinner. It was hard to know what to put on; she had never eaten in a tavern in the Colonies before, and certainly not when she needed to look presentable. Emma called Felicity up to see what she was wearing. Emma then dressed accordingly. Her dress was fairly plain but, as always, she looked immaculate in it.

"Somehow all of your clothes seem to make you look prettier," said Felicity with a bit of a laugh.

Emma blushed. "Thank you."

"It's your eyes I think. They are so blue. I don't know anyone whose eyes are as blue as yours Emma."

"I'm sure you are exaggerating, Felicity," said Emma.

"No, not really. Anyway, let's get going. I really hate being late."

"Of course, besides, I am sure Cole and Philip must be ready by now."

Emma and Felicity went into the parlor and found Cole but not Philip.

"He is still getting ready. He has to look just so, you know," said Cole laughing.

Emma laughed too. Philip had always struck her as the type

who was ambitious and wanted to please. This merely confirmed her suspicions. She held no ill will toward him as he was very affable and polite and had a lovely sense of humor.

Finally, after about ten more minutes, Philip entered the parlor looking quite debonair and refined.

"Good evening ladies," he said with as much charm as he could muster.

"Good evening Philip," they replied.

"Dear little brother, good evening."

"Uh-huh. Let's go. I'm sure everyone is waiting for us, and they'll never believe me when I tell them it was you who kept us waiting."

Everyone laughed now and the four headed downstairs. They had decided to take the carriage. It wasn't too long of a walk, but Philip pointed out that the hour might grow quite late.

Cole helped Felicity in first and then Emma. Philip followed them and Cole got in last. Finally, Philip told the driver where to go and they set off. Within a few minutes, they were at their destination.

Philip jumped out first. Cole made fun of him from inside the carriage and Emma couldn't help but laugh a little; she was merely glad that Philip didn't hear them.

"He just wants everyone to see him bringing two beautiful women with him so he doesn't look like such a lonely person."

Philip helped Felicity out of the carriage first. Emma followed her and Cole came down next. Cole offered Emma his arm and they entered the tavern.

As they entered, they spotted James and Benjamin sitting with quite a few other people. They went over to them and the men stood for Felicity and Emma. James kissed his daughter on the forehead as Cole pulled out a chair for her in between James and himself. Felicity found a seat next to Benjamin and Philip took a seat near Emma's Uncle Alexandre. Across from her was none other than Mr. Samuel Adams.

"Emma, this is a dear friend of mine, Mr. Samuel Adams," said James.

"We've met before," said Emma.

"Twice," said Mr. Adams. "I think fate must be turning red from laughing so hard Miss Huntington."

"Probably," replied Emma politely, but much less enthusiastically.

"Where did you meet?" asked James.

"At Alexandre's house in Boston," said Mr. Adams.

"Oh, you never said anything, either of you."

"Well, then we met for our second time just this afternoon," said Mr. Adams.

From there, dinner was served. Emma mostly listened to the conversation. It mainly revolved around, what else, but the rights of the Colonies and the convening of the Continental Congress.

After dinner, Emma found she was extremely tired. Her long days in the carriage and the lengthy walk they had taken their toll; this added on to the food she had just eaten was making it very hard for her to keep her eyes open. The men around the table were deeply engrossed in their conversations and their debates. Emma did not really want to interrupt but she knew she would not make it much longer. She saw no other alternative so she leaned over to Cole and asked him to take her home.

"Of course. Do you want to take the carriage? I can call for it and then send it back after we get to Mr. Franklin's shop."

"No, we can walk. I hate to make the driver come back after he brings us home. It isn't a long walk."

Emma tried to catch her father's attention but was unsuccessful. As she was walking toward the door, her cousin caught up her. Cole had gone to fetch her shawl.

"Emma, hold up a second," said Sebastian.

"Sebastian, how are you?"

"I am well. Are you leaving?"

"I am. I am extremely tired. It has been such a long day. Actually, it has been a very long week I am afraid I must admit."

"Do you have plans for tomorrow?"

"Not that I am aware of. I haven't had much of a chance to speak to my father though."

Sebastian smiled as though he knew something that Emma didn't.

"Well, I can assure you that your father will be busy all day. Why don't we get together for lunch?"

"Of course. Why don't you come over? We are staying at Mr. Franklin's printing shop."

"Yes, I know where you are staying. I will call around twelve thirty if that is agreeable?"

"That's perfect." Cole brought Emma her shawl at this time. "Oh, Cole, this is my cousin Sebastian Huntington. Sebastian, this is Cole Carrington."

"It is nice to meet you," said Sebastian.

"A pleasure," replied Cole.

"I will see you tomorrow then, Emma," said Sebastian.

"Tomorrow, twelve thirty. Goodnight Sebastian."

"Goodnight Emma, Mr. Carrington."

Cole nodded to Sebastian and Emma took his arm. They exited the tavern and took in the cool night air.

"The night here is quite chilly considering the heat of the day," said Emma.

"Are you cold?"

"I'm all right. We don't have far to go."

"So that is your family then?"

"Some of them. Sebastian is my cousin."

"May I ask you something Emma?"

"Of course you may Cole."

"Do you not like Mr. Adams?"

"We shared an interesting encounter when we first met. I cannot honestly say I do not like him. He has a good sense of humor. To quote a friend's good advice, 'we simply have agreed to disagree.'"

Cole laughed at Emma. Emma too began to laugh a little. Emma caught Cole looking at her and then she found herself in his bright green eyes again.

"What is it? Do I have something on my face? Has it turned green?" she said jokingly. "If I have something on my face, and you didn't tell me while we were at the tavern-"

"Your face is lovely and there is nothing present except what should be there. Besides, what would you do to me?" Cole asked jokingly.

"I would have to do something terrible."

"Oh? Well that scares me."

"It does, does it?"

"Just a little," replied Cole teasingly.

"Well, that's better than nothing. This is sort of a secret so don't tell anyone but, I'm not really that scary normally."

"Don't worry," said Cole.

"You won't tell anyone then?" asked Emma playfully.

"No, I just don't think you are that scary either, so it really isn't much of a secret."

"Oh you," said Emma nudging Cole a little. "You aren't very much fun."

Suddenly, Emma felt Cole put his arm around her waist and pull her towards him. Then she felt his lips press upon hers and her body felt like it went limp in his arms. Emma had never been kissed like this before. Her first impulse was to pull away but then she realized how much she actually liked it.

When Cole pulled away from her, he had a strange look on his face.

"Emma, I am really sorry, I just don't know what came over me."

"I was wrong about you Cole," said Emma seriously.

"Emma, I am so sorry."

"You are kind of fun," and Emma allowed a grin to form on her face.

Cole too had a smile on his face now. Emma let her hand find Cole's and they continued to walk toward the printing shop. Neither one said another word; both seemed to enjoy the silence. Emma watched the moon as they walked on. It was a beautiful full moon.

As they reached the printing shop, they went in and up the stairs. They stopped right outside the room that Emma and Felicity were sharing.

"Well, goodnight Cole," said Emma.

"Goodnight, dear Emma. I shall see you tomorrow. Thank you for allowing me to walk you home."

"Well thank you for walking with me… and everything else," Emma said as she blushed.

Cole leaned over and kissed Emma's hand. Emma felt her face flush yet again and she went into her room feeling happier then she had in the past two years. Emma slept better that night than she had in quite a while too. Things definitely seemed to be looking up.

Chapter 11
An Unexpected Family Addition

The next morning, Emma was awoken very early by the printing press running downstairs. Mr. Franklin had another man who came in each morning to run the press and get the early edition out.

Emma got up and got herself dressed. It was already starting to get warm for the day and the sun was barely up. Emma pulled out a fresh dress. It was light blue with a faint floral print that was just a little bit darker blue than the dress fabric. Emma put on a bonnet and grabbed her straw hat with the blue ribbon that matched the flowers on her dress. She looked in the parlor to see if anyone else had been woken by the massive machine. She was a little dismayed to see she was the only one up. Yet, as she and Felicity were sharing a room, Emma was even more surprised that Felicity was still sound asleep.

Emma wrote a note on a spare piece of parchment to tell everyone she would be back before too long. She then walked down the stairs into the shop. She stopped for a minute to watch the printing press. The whole idea of printing fascinated Emma.

Emma put on her hat and walked out into the early morning sun. She did not want to stray very far for fear she would not find her way back to the shop so she followed the road straight down and planned to follow it straight back. Emma found that the fewer turns one made, the less likely one was to become lost.

She looked around and found that there was a bustle of activity even at this early hour. There were so many merchants selling a variety of items. However, there wasn't much of an open market on the part of the street where Emma was, but she could see the fruit and vegetable carts farther on and assumed that there were other merchants there too.

As Emma walked along she saw so many types of people. *Philadelphia must truly be an assorted city, a blended city.* As Emma was thinking about this she ran into Mr. Washington.

"Oh, Mr. Washington, what brings you out this early?"

"I am a farmer Miss Huntington; I am always up with the sun. I might ask you the same question however."

"Well, I am staying at Mr. Franklin's print shop and the printing press does not make for good, early morning company."

Mr. Washington laughed at Emma's comment. "No, I suppose it doesn't. Would you care to walk with me on this fine morning?" he asked her.

"I would be delighted."

"Good, I find that it can be helpful to walk with someone when you walk in a town such as Philadelphia. That way you have a harder time of getting lost."

"I must admit, my plan was to merely walk in a straight line down the street and then turn around and walk back. That way I wouldn't have a very great chance of getting lost."

"It is a good plan. I must admit, however, that I know Philadelphia better than the first impression I gave. I have been here before, so you needn't worry about getting lost; not much at least."

Emma laughed politely. "It is such an interesting city."

"It certainly is that."

"I was just thinking to myself about all the different types of people you see here."

"Philadelphia is one of those cities that encompass the values we are trying so hard to obtain for ourselves in the Colonies."

"So I am learning."

"Your father has spoken to me about your positions Emma."

"I see."

"I do have to admit it surprised me a bit."

"Oh? May I ask why that is?"

"I suppose it has much to do with-"

"My family?"

"Well that, and… you seem to be a person of great principle. I find it odd that your principles dictate your current beliefs."

"Is your wife along, Mr. Washington?"

"No, she is at Mount Vernon."

"Is she well?"

"Yes, very well, thank you. I had the pleasure of seeing not only your father yesterday, but meeting your two uncles as well. They are fine gentlemen."

"It pleases me you think so. I'm sure they felt the same about you Mr. Washington."

"Miss Huntington, may I ask you a personal question?"

"You most certainly have my permission Mr. Washington."

"Why have you come to Philadelphia?"

"My father asked me to come."

"Is that the only reason?"

Emma thought for a moment. She hadn't really pondered this before. "I suppose so. Isn't that a good enough reason?"

"Of course it is. If your father summoned you here then it was certainly your duty to come. It was merely a question I had for you; perhaps something to think on."

Emma and George Washington continued to walk on a little in silence until they had finally returned to the print shop.

"Well Miss Huntington, here is where I shall leave you. However, I am certain we will see each other tomorrow."

"Tomorrow?"

"I was assuming that you were attending the Congressional meeting tomorrow. Perhaps I was wrong."

"No, you were correct. I just hadn't thought about tomorrow yet. Well, thank you for the walk Mr. Washington, and thank you for returning me to the printing shop safely."

"It was my extreme pleasure. Please give my regards to your family."

"I shall. Until tomorrow then."

"Until tomorrow. Good day."

Emma watched Mr. Washington walk up the path a little bit and then she went into the printing shop. It was only about nine thirty; Emma had three hours before her lunch with Sebastian. As she entered the shop, she found Philip was downstairs working on something. She walked over to him.

"Good morning Philip."

"Oh, good morning Emma. I did not realize you were up. But it looks as though you've been up for quite a while."

"I hope it isn't too much of a problem, but the printing press woke me up early and I went for a walk."

"I hope you found your way easily enough."

"I did. I actually met up with Mr. Washington."

"George Washington?" asked Philip suddenly extremely interested.

"Yes, do you know him as well?"

"Only by reputation. He was one of the great military leaders in the French and Indian War, sorry, I think the British call it the Seven Years' War."

"Yes, we do."

"He is revered by many and renowned by more. He truly is a great man. I am amazed you were fortunate enough to make his acquaintance."

"I met him while we were staying in northern Virginia, near Fredericksburg. My father also knows him quite well. He stays with him often on his travels."

"I am truly amazed Emma."

"I am glad that my family's acquaintances amaze you."

"Anyway, how was early morning Philadelphia?"

"It was interesting. It is a lovely city."

"I'm sorry the press woke you up. I have gotten so used to it I forget how loud it actually can be."

"It surprises me no one else woke up."

"Well, unfortunately your room is directly over the shop. I am amazed Felicity did not wake up, though. She must be a sound sleeper."

"It would appear so. What is this you're working on?"

"A story, for tomorrow's paper."

"What about?"

"Ah, ah, a good reporter does not share his stories before they are in print."

"Of course," said Emma with a slight smile. "I'm just going to be heading upstairs."

"All right. I will be up shortly. If you ask Jessica, she will get you some breakfast."

"Thank you. I will go find her then."

Emma went upstairs. Mr. Franklin's servant, Jessica, found Emma almost immediately.

"Would you like some breakfast, Miss?"

"That would be lovely, thank you."

"It will be ready in just a few minutes if you want to wait in the dining room."

"I will be there in a moment."

"As you wish, Miss."

Emma took off her hat and put it in the foyer area.

Breakfast was good. She had worked up a bit of an appetite on her walk. While she was eating, Cole came into the dining room with Benjamin. Emma felt her face flush a little as she remembered the night before. She hoped he wouldn't say anything in front of Benjamin.

"Good morning Emma," said both men.

"Good morning," replied Emma.

"You are up early," said Benjamin. "Then again, I don't suppose that is so unusual. My sister never sleeps, Cole."

"Is that a fact?"

"I have much difficulty in sleeping. I do not fall asleep easily."

"I see. Well, it is good to see you bright-eyed this morning. May we sit down with you?" asked Cole in his usual joking manner.

"I don't know. I was quite enjoying breakfasting alone actually."

"Well I am sitting down," said Benjamin.

"Jessica, will you bring in some breakfast for us?" asked Cole taking a chair.

"Of course, Sir," she replied.

"So, what are your plans for today Emma?" asked Benjamin.

"I am going to have lunch with Sebastian, but that is all I have planned. What do you have going on?"

"I have some meetings to go to. I probably won't be back until quite late actually. Are you coming with us tomorrow?"

"To the Congressional meeting? Yes. I am very interested in going."

"Good. It should be quite interesting," said Cole.

As they finished their breakfast, James came in and left after saying good morning and Felicity came in, sat down, and began to eat.

"Good morning Felicity," everyone chanted.

"Morning," she replied brightly.

"Felicity, may I ask you a question?" asked Emma.

"Of course."

"How ever did you sleep through the racket of the printing press this morning?"

"Oh that," said Felicity laughing as she pulled something out of her pocket. "It is quite simple you see," she said showing the contents of her hand to Emma.

"Cotton?" asked Emma incredulously.

"Of course, it is an old trick known to just about every plantation family in the south."

"Does it truly work?"

"Well, it does for me. It probably helps that I am a bit of a sound sleeper. Once I get to sleep, it takes quite a bit to wake me you see," she said placing the cotton back in her pocket.

"I may have to try that," said Emma, still in disbelief. "Well, I am finished here. I think I am going to go into the parlor for a while."

Emma left the dining room and after only a few more moments, Cole came into the parlor and took a seat near Emma's.

"I thought they might like to be left alone," said Cole. They haven't really seen much of each other since we arrived."

"We only arrived yesterday Cole," replied Emma with a bit of amusement.

"Oh yeah. It seems much longer, doesn't it?"

"Not really. I suppose it will be busy in town today," said Emma trying to politely change the subject.

"I suppose so. So this Sebastian, he is your cousin?"

"Yes, he is. He is the eldest son of my Uncle Alexandre and Aunt Isabelle. Didn't I already tell you this?"

"Did you? I don't remember."

"I'm so glad that you listen when I speak."

Cole stood and began to gesture very melodramatically, "How

can I be so attentive to your speech when your beauty takes my very breath away? When the sweet sound of your voice makes every ounce of my body want to sing? When your-"

"That's enough Cole," said Emma jovially, but blushing all the same.

"But you didn't let me finish," he said with mock hurt.

"How can I be so attentive to your speech when the very sound of your voice makes every ounce of my body cringe with disgust?" asked Emma mockingly.

"Ouch, that one hurt Emma," Cole replied with even more mock hurt.

"Oh, what can I say to make it better?" asked Emma with teasing sweetness.

"Well, I can think of one thing..." said Cole moving closer to her.

"You can? What would that be?"

With that, Cole leaned over and kissed Emma. It was not a long kiss, but it was sweet and made Emma blush. She was afraid that Benjamin would walk in any moment.

"I'm better now," said Cole leaning back into the armchair where he sat.

Emma had to laugh. "I'm glad I could help."

"Well, I need to be going."

"Where are you going to?"

"I have an acquaintance here in Philadelphia that I promised I would call upon. Do not worry though, I shall return by dinner."

"All right. I will see you tonight then?"

"Of course. I have grown too used of your company at dinner; I do not know if I could eat without your presence."

"Oh you. Maybe I won't come tonight then," said Emma jokingly.

Cole looked at Emma and stuck out his lower lip.

"Oh all right, I shall see you tonight then." Cole flashed a smile. "Goodbye."

"Until later." With that, Cole went out the door.

Emma stood and walked about for a few minutes. Soon enough, she found the library. Emma walked in and looked around. She had only ever seen so many books in the bookseller's store. Emma pulled a book at random and sat down. She spent the next little while reading in the library. Around eleven forty, she decided that she had best get ready.

Soon enough, Sebastian came to call. Emma was surprised to find the entire house was now empty. She had become so engrossed in her reading that she had not noticed everyone leaving.

"Sebastian, how are you?" asked Emma giving her cousin a friendly hug.

"I am well. And how are you?"

"I certainly cannot complain. I am enjoying Philadelphia immensely."

"I am glad to hear of it. Are you ready to go?"

"Where are we going to?"

"There is a small tavern a little ways off, but it has very good food and they are very friendly."

"All right. That sounds good. Allow me to get my hat and I shall be ready."

"Of course. I will wait for you downstairs."

"I will be right there."

Sebastian went back down to the street and Emma went to the hall to get her hat. She walked down to the street whilst she put her hat on.

Emma entered the bright lovely day and Sebastian helped her into the carriage. He then entered the carriage and told the driver where to go. Within a moment, they were on their way to the tavern.

"So, tell me, how is your family, Sebastian?" asked Emma.

"They are very well, thank you. My mother is still in Boston but will be joining us soon. My father and I have been here for about a week or so. Of course, it is has been a very busy week but it will all be worth it, starting tomorrow."

"Sebastian, what are they hoping to accomplish here?"

"Honestly, the main thing they are trying to accomplish is a sense of unity among the Colonies. This fight cannot be won by a single colony. We need all the Colonies to hold together now."

"I thought everyone was pretty much on the same side."

"Alas no, the people of Massachusetts are outraged; that is certainly true."

"Why are they so angry?"

"Well Emma, this new port bill has bottled up our harbor. Ships are not allowed to come and go and for that, commerce is suffering not to mention the tempers of our community."

"To be completely honest, I think that had Boston just paid the tea tax in the first place, this would never have happened."

"The port bill might not have happened, but it would have been something else. The Boston Massacre was truly a severe act and it enraged many. This isn't to mention the Townshend Act and the Sugar Act, as well as the actions of Governor Hutchinson."

"Sebastian, may I ask you something else?"

"Certainly."

"When did you begin to decide that you felt, your beliefs...?"

"A few years ago. My father has been pretty active in politics since the French and Indian War. He fought in that you know."

"Actually I didn't know that."

"He did. He served under George Washington with your father. Anyway, with all the articulate and committed people coming around our home, I think it was only natural that my beliefs grew into what they are today."

"I still think it is wrong."

At that point, their carriage pulled up to the tavern and came to a halt. Sebastian stepped down and helped Emma out. They were led to a table and ordered their meals.

"Now, tell me about your brothers and sister."

"Well, Marianne is well. Nothing much is new with her. Edmund is eleven now. He is getting anxious about the impending events."

"Why ever for?"

"He really wants to join the army."

"Well, he is certainly too young for that, thankfully."

"Yes, he is. Father has forbid it until he is sixteen."

"Sixteen still seems so young."

"Anyway, and Jonathon will be turning seven in October."

"Seven? My goodness. I still think of him as being so much younger."

"So do I. It is certainly difficult to believe he has grown so much. He is going to be quite tall I think."

"Really?"

"Yes, he is already almost as tall as our neighbor's child and he's nine."

"Ah, I know. I can't believe how fast they grow. William just turned seven in August. I still think of him as three years old."

"Where is William?"

"Right now he is in South Carolina. There is a very good school down there that he is currently attending."

"Really? That's good to hear. How did Uncle James feel about that?"

"Well, he wasn't really home when we decided about it all but he says he doesn't object. I suppose he isn't home all that much anyway."

"Well, actually I think your father might believe him to be a bit safer there than in Williamsburg."

"Why do you say that?"

"No particular reason. It is just a hunch. I know Williamsburg is a fairly central place of activity in the south."

Emma mulled over this thought for a few moments before Sebastian spoke again.

"How is your family?"

"You've probably seen them more in the past couple of days than I have, especially my father."

"Well, Uncle James is well, if that makes you feel a little better."

Emma smiled. "Well Benjamin is well too. I think he has been growing bored in Williamsburg. Though it may well be a center of activity in the south, it is certainly no real center of activity and I think the dullness is driving him a little stir crazy."

"Well then Philadelphia will do him good."

"I hope so."

"How is Miss Dillingham?"

"She is doing well."

"What do you think of her?"

"Honestly, I had my doubts at first, but I have really grown to feel quite attached to her. She has certainly become quite the confidante for me. I do really enjoy her company."

"Well that's good. I am glad that you are not spending all of your time alone."

"Hardly. When I'm not with Benjamin, Felicity, or William I have had many visitors and we have had quite a number of guests as well."

"Really?"

"Yes, Cole is over at least four or five times a week, if not every day, and my friend Edward Findley used to visit twice a week. He is in Boston now I believe."

"For what?"

"He, er, he serves in the, in the army."

"What rank is he?"

"He is a lieutenant."

"He is. That's strange, I haven't ever heard of him or his family. Are they from anywhere around us?"

Emma hesitated. "Well no, he actually is from England. That's where we met. His family and mine have been long acquainted. We grew up together."

"When did his family move to the Colonies?"

"They're still in England," said Emma. She didn't know why but she really didn't want to admit that Edward was in the British Army to her cousin. She was extremely hesitant to answer Sebastian's questions with very much specificity.

"I see. I see," repeated Sebastian as if a light had dawned.

"See what?" asked Emma.

"He is a British Regular, isn't he?"

Emma looked down towards the floor.

"It's all right Emma. You have nothing to be ashamed of."

"I am not ashamed," said Emma a little too quickly.

"It really doesn't matter much."

"Well, I'm glad it doesn't matter because there is certainly no changing it."

"I didn't ask you to."

"I'm sorry. Lately I feel as though I have to defend almost everything I say."

"I know the feeling."

"You can't possibly understand."

"Well, I'm not exactly in the, uh, popular majority in my opinions you know."

"It seems like you are actually."

"You are spending time with a very select group of people. Wait until tomorrow. You will hear a lot more people who share your beliefs than mine."

"I don't believe that."

"It's true. The Colonies are divided. We are hoping that they can come to some sort of compromise."

Emma and Sebastian continued to talk for a while. Eventually they decided to head back to the printing shop. They climbed into the carriage and off they went.

As they reached the shop, Sebastian had a strange look upon his face. Emma couldn't quite read him very clearly.

"Emma, there is something I want to say to you."

"What's that Sebastian?" asked Emma with a little bit of concern.

"I feel as though I owe you an apology."

"For what Sebastian?"

"For when you stayed with us in Boston. I was, a bit rude to you. I felt as though you were coming in and looking down on us for our way of life and our beliefs, but you didn't understand what you were talking about."

"Is this an apology? If it is, you aren't very good at these," said Emma jokingly.

"I just shouldn't have made you feel as I did."

"You didn't really make me feel too badly, Sebastian."

"I hope I didn't. I just shouldn't have jumped to the conclusions I did. You didn't look down upon us, you just don't agree with us.... That's all."

"Well, thank you for your apology, but it was certainly not necessary."

"Thank you for coming to lunch with me, Emma. I am sure we will be seeing each other much over the next few weeks."

"Of course. Thank you for lunch."

"Of course. I will see you tomorrow, Emma."

"Goodbye Sebastian."

"Until tomorrow Emma."

Emma went inside the print shop and upstairs. She was

surprised to hear quite a commotion going on upstairs. She continued up the stairs and began to listen more closely to what was happening.

"Mr. Randolph, this is not even about independence," said a man whom Emma did not know by voice.

"Mr. Dickinson, it is about independence and the right to make decisions about our own interests, but before we can even broach that subject, we need to discuss these blasted Intolerable Acts."

"Here, here," said many of the men. Emma guessed there were probably eight or nine men in the study. She wasn't sure from the voices if she knew any of them.

Emma did not wish to interrupt the men in the study, so she went into the library again to look at Mr. Franklin's vast collection. As she was sitting down to read again, a man entered the library.

"Miss Huntington, is that you?"

Emma looked up to see Andrew Welsing standing before her. "It is. How are you Mr. Welsing?" she asked, putting her book down and giving him her attention along with a welcoming smile.

"I am well. I am surprised to see you here, however."

"Why is that?"

"No reason. I just didn't expect it. It is a welcomed surprise, however, Miss Huntington."

Emma blushed a little, but did not make reference to the compliment. "Well, please sit down. How have you been? Where have you been?"

"I have been well. I have been quite busy with my engagements. I was in Connecticut for a while and then New Jersey before coming to Philadelphia."

"You have traveled a lot since we last saw each other."

"It is not unusual for me."

"It must be exciting to visit so many places."

"It can be. However, to really never be in a stable home can be disheartening at times."

"I'm certain it is."

"How is life in Williamsburg?"

"It is good, very good actually, thank you."

"Is it still unbearably hot down there?"

"Not too bad. However, if you are used to this northern weather, you still may well find it not to your liking."

"I am finding Pennsylvania weather to be quite to my liking, I must admit."

"It is nice here. However, I am told that the nice weather may not hold out much longer here."

"Ah, probably not, but it is nice now, isn't that enough?"

"I suppose we should be thankful," said Emma.

"You know, it truly is so good to see you again Miss Huntington."

"Thank you. I am happy to see that you are doing so well. I must admit I had wondered what had become of you."

"Well, like the wind, I drift from field to field, trying to find my way home."

"It must be difficult to find one's way home when one has no permanent home."

Andrew laughed. "You have me there Miss Huntington. I was merely trying to be poetic."

"In that case, it was a nice attempt."

"Now you mock me," said Andrew playfully. Emma knew this game all too well.

"A little, but even you must admit that it is a little deserved."

"I suppose it is. Well, I should probably be getting back to the study. I will be missed. It really was nice to see you again Miss Huntington. I hope that fate brings us together again in the future."

"I'm sure I shall see you again whilst in Philadelphia."

"I will hope for it. Good day Miss Huntington."

"Goodbye Mr. Welsing."

Emma smiled to herself and again picked up her book.

The rest of the afternoon was quiet enough for Emma. She read most of the afternoon away. She had, for a while, wished to have tea, but she knew her father's guests would not happily look upon the idea, and Emma doubted whether there was any in the house anyway. Thus, Emma contented herself with her book in the cozy armchair in the library.

Finally, Cole came into the library.

"Reading again?"

"I enjoy reading."

"May I come in?"

"Of course," said Emma. She marked her place in the book and set it down. "Besides, it is not every day that I have access to such a large library of books that I can view at my leisure."

"This is true."

"How was your day?"

"Long. I think tomorrow is going to be longer."

"Really? What happened?"

"Nothing in particular, just a lot of debating and a lot of hot air."

"I caught that part."

"It has been going on all day, everywhere around town. I am sure it will only get worse as time goes on."

"You are probably correct, Cole."

"But, how was your day? How was lunch with Sebastian?"

"It was nice. It has been so long since I have seen him."

"I'm glad that you were able to see each other then. By the way, I am supposed to tell you that everyone is going to the tavern again for dinner. However, your father doesn't think that you should come."

"Why?"

"Actually, he doesn't want you or Felicity to come. He thinks that people are going to get out of hand tonight. He thinks you will be safer here."

"All right, I will have Jessica prepare dinner here then."

"It is already being taken care of."

"Well, have a good time then," said Emma sweetly. She was a little put out about not being able to go with everyone else, but she didn't want to appear that way.

"I'm sure I will have a good time."

"Rub it in a little then," said Emma with half a smile.

"Well, it isn't everyday that I get to spend dinnertime with such lovely company you know," replied Cole.

"I don't know if lovely is an adjective I would use to describe many of those men Cole. Perhaps you should try interesting, intriguing," Emma paused for effect, "vain?"

"I don't think I would call you and Felicity vain. Interesting and intriguing, perhaps, but not vain."

"You aren't staying here for dinner?"

"Of course I am. Do you believe I would let you dine alone?"

"I won't be alone."

"Well, actually, Felicity is going to be dining with some of her mother's friends. I don't really know who they are. Anyway, I didn't want you to have to dine alone, so I offered to stay back and dine with you."

Emma smiled genuinely. "That was very kind of you, Cole," she said.

"Ah, it was nothing special. However, I am hungry and dinner will be ready very soon, so let's head to the dining room."

Emma nodded and stood up.

Dinner was nice. It was quiet and for that, Emma was grateful. Even though she had wanted to go to the tavern, it was very nice to have such a quiet evening.

After dinner, Cole and Emma spent a little time in the library again. They talked about many things, Emma's favorite subject being the vast array of books. Then, before any of the others returned, Cole said he was going to bed.

"It is going to be a busy day tomorrow, and I don't want to be tired."

"Of course, goodnight Cole."

"Goodnight my dear Emma," said Cole kissing Emma's forehead and leaving her in the library alone.

Emma did not stay up much longer either. There was really no telling when everyone would return.

The next morning, Emma was awoken early again. She was glad she had not stayed up too late. She got ready quickly and they were off to observe the First Continental Congress.

When they reached the great hall, there were many people standing everywhere. James took his daughter's arm and led her inside. Cole and Benjamin followed with Felicity. However, inside the hall was not any less crowded than outside. It was difficult to find a seat, but finally James found the other representatives from Virginia and sat amongst them. Emma and the others weren't able to sit with James. They were, however, lucky to be able to all find seats together, even though they weren't right next to the Virginia delegates.

Within a short time, Mr. Patrick Randolph called attention in the hall and began the first meeting of the Continental Congress.

Emma listened attentively but within a short time everyone in the hall was up in arms. It was difficult to tell who was supposed to be speaking, or what everyone was speaking about.

After the first day, Emma didn't think that these men were ever going to accomplish anything together.

However, after a few more days, things started to calm a little. Emma went with her father every day, no matter what. Cole was as ardent as Emma about going to watch. Most days, Benjamin would come as well, but Felicity decided she wasn't going to go much anymore. When Emma asked her why, she had one thing to say about it all.

"It is much too chaotic. One cannot hear oneself think there."

Emma had to admit she was right but things were getting better. By the middle of September, the Congress had agreed to boycott all British goods. On September seventeenth, the Congress declared its official opposition to the Coercive Acts.

It was determined that these acts were "not to be obeyed," as one delegate put it. The Congress also decided to promote the formation of local militia, though not every colony agreed to do this actively.

On September twentieth, Emma had a great surprise.

"Emma, I want you to meet a very good friend of mine," said James that evening. Emma was sitting in the library, as usual.

"All right," said Emma politely. She had met so many people since her arrival in the Colonies and even more so in Philadelphia. All of the delegates looked for her daily. She spent much time listening to the members of the Congress speak about their beliefs even after the session had let out for the day. She could not imagine whom her father had left for her to meet.

Emma put her book down and stood politely. As she stood, a woman entered the library. Emma was quite surprised to see this woman. She didn't know her father was acquainted with any women.

"Emma, this is a dear friend of mine, Mrs. Collingwood. This is my daughter, Emma."

Mrs. Collingwood seemed to be maybe twice Emma's age, though Emma couldn't be certain about that. She had extremely dark hair and dark eyes. She had lovely olive colored skin. Emma had not met many people with the same complexion as the woman who now sat before her. Then again, Emma had never met anyone with skin as pale as her own, except her mother of course.

"It is a pleasure to meet you Mrs. Collingwood," said Emma with much eloquence.

"Likewise. I have just heard so much about you Emma," said Mrs. Collingwood. Emma did not like how she was referred to. After all, she had just met this woman. "Your father speaks about you all the time."

Emma, Mrs. Collingwood, and James all sat down. Emma was quite nonplussed about the whole situation.

"Mrs. Collingwood is going to be staying with us for a few days to break her trip to Williamsburg."

"Oh, you are on your way to Williamsburg then?" asked Emma.

"Well, yes. Of course I am," said Mrs. Collingwood as if everyone should know her present course of action.

"Of course," repeated Emma.

"Mr. Huntington," said Jessica as she entered the room. "Mr. Huntington, please forgive me sir, but there is a gentleman downstairs who wishes to see you, but he won't tell me his name. So I says to him that he can't come in here if he doesn't want to tell me who he is, and then he says that he will wait outside but I need to come up and fetch you. Then I says back-"

"I will go down Jessica, thank you," said James. Jessica left the library again. "Please excuse me ladies." James left the library leaving Emma and this new Mrs. Collingwood alone to chat.

"So how long have you known my father?"

"Well, we have known each other for quite a long time, but we have become more intimately acquainted within the past year."

"I see," replied Emma not really understanding at all.

"Your father is quite a charming man you know."

"No, I didn't know. You know Mrs. Collingwood, you said my father talks about me all the time?"

"Oh yes, just all the time. He must mention you and your brothers ten times a day at least. Probably more to be honest."

Emma smiled sweetly. "It's funny."

"Excuse me, what's funny?"

"Oh, I just think it's funny you say that because he's never mentioned you before."

Emma watched the look on this woman's face change in a moment. Emma had no idea who this woman was, but she didn't think she liked her very much. There was a long pause in the conversation. Emma relished in the silence, but Mrs. Collingwood did not seem to enjoy the stillness.

"Well, that's taken care of," said James as he returned. "Just a man with a letter. I don't know why Jessica is so particular about who comes in here, or for that matter why she didn't just take the letter. Anyway, where were we?"

"Emma was just telling me that you haven't mentioned me before," said Mrs. Collingwood as sweetly as possible.

"I haven't? Well, it isn't as if I have had much of a chance to be honest."

"It's true," said Emma, "I hardly ever see my father." It was James's turn to change his facial expression. James glared at his daughter though he said nothing. At that point, Benjamin came in.

"Jessica told me you wanted to see me, Father?"

"Yes, sit down Benjamin, sit down," said James. Benjamin took the seat next to Emma. "I have something I want to tell you both; I hope you will be glad to hear it."

"What is it Father?" asked Benjamin.

"Well first of all, where are my manners, Benjamin, this is Mrs. Rebecca Collingwood. Rebecca, this is my oldest son, Benjamin."

Benjamin and Mrs. Collingwood exchanged pleasantries.

"Anyway, I have news."

"What sort of news, Father?" asked Emma with complete

bewilderment and curiosity, but expecting it to have something to do with the letter he'd just received.

"Well, I'm not quite sure how to say this," said James.

"What your father is trying to say," said Mrs. Collingwood, "is that we are engaged to be married, and plan to be married by Christmas."

Emma was floored. Had she heard this right? Her father was going to be getting married? Her father was going to be getting married to the repulsive woman who sat before her? Certainly she did not hear correctly but when she looked up, Emma saw Benjamin shaking her father's hand and kissing Mrs. Collingwood gently on the cheek.

"Well that is good news," said Benjamin. "I must say that I am quite surprised though. We didn't really know about you after all," he concluded with a laugh.

"Well, it has all happened quite suddenly actually. We have been keeping correspondence for many months, but after Rebecca's husband passed away, we began to become closer and have finally decided that we wish to spend the rest of our lives together," said James. Emma could see he was positively glowing. She was tired and befuddled and did not wish to create a scene. James was looking for her to follow Benjamin's lead.

"Welcome to our family," said Emma. She stood and continued to speak. "If you will excuse me, I am not really feeling all that well. I'm sorry, please excuse me," she said and left the library in a great hurry.

From there, she went into the room she was staying in. Felicity was in there and Emma did not want to talk about anything.

"Felicity, I was wondering, I'm not really feeling well and I think I am going to lie down for a while. Would you mind...?"

"Of course, give me one second and I am gone, and you can be alone to rest."

"Thank you," said Emma with a relieved smile on her face.

"My pleasure. I was on my way out anyway. Benjamin and I were going to go out for a while tonight."

"Have fun," said Emma lying down in the bed.

"Oh, I will, feel better though," said Felicity with much concern in her voice.

"I'm sure it will pass. I just need to sleep a little while."

"Of course, I will leave word that no one should disturb you."

"Thank you Felicity."

Felicity left and pulled the door shut behind her. Emma looked up at the ceiling of her four-poster bed and let out a sigh in the still darkness.

Married? Why does he want to be married again? He already has a wife. All right, so he had a wife. Does that mean he needs another? Can't he be happy with his life the way it is?

Emma thought about these things for quite some time. At some point, Emma must have slipped off to sleep because when she awoke, Felicity was in the bedroom with her and fast asleep. Emma stood up and opened the bedroom door. The hall was silent. It appeared that everyone in the house was sleeping.

Emma walked out to get something to drink. As she got to the study, she saw Benjamin sitting there by himself in the dark. She lit the lantern with her candle and went in to sit down next to him.

"So what do you think?" asked Benjamin quite suddenly.

"About what?" asked Emma, knowing full well what he meant.

"About the future Mrs. Huntington; what do you think I am asking you about?"

"Well, you must have noticed my reaction."

"Getting sick at the mere sound of the word engagement?"

"That would be it."

"That aside, what do you think of her?"

Emma paused for a moment. She hadn't really thought about her. "She seems awfully young," Emma said finally.

"She is just over thirty."

"How do you know?"

"She told me."

"Really? That's a bit odd."

"There's more."

"What more could there be?"

"You know how she is a widow?"

"Yes, Father said so at least."

"Well, she has children."

"How many children?" asked Emma.

"Seven."

"Seven?" asked Emma feeling her breath catch in her throat.

"Mm-hmm. And, the oldest one is sixteen."

"How old is the youngest?"

"Two."

"That is pretty young."

"It is, but, in the middle is a set of twins."

"Twins?"

"Oh yes. Ethane and Erin, I believe. They are eleven, just."

"Seven is a lot of children."

"Seven is most certainly a lot of children."

"Where is Mrs. Collingwood from?"

"Originally she is from South Carolina. She met her first husband there. However, when he died, she came north to 'take some time and figure out what to do next'. At least, that is what she told me."

"Where in the north?"

"She told me she was staying with her sister in Rhode Island."

"I see. Where are her children?"

"Staying with their aunt – their father's sister – in South Carolina until she returns, but it would now seem that they are going to be heading to Williamsburg to live with us."

"Where?"

"In our home, Emma."

"I don't know if we have enough room for seven children, Benjamin."

"Of course we do. We may have to share a little but-"

"I'm not sharing my room; especially not with some ten-year-old and two-year-old girls. No."

"I don't believe anyone has asked you to do that Emma. I think the girls will be all right. We may have to have a couple of the boys in the same room though. Well, anyway, it is a good thing that Father built our home like our old home in England."

"Why do you say that?"

"Well, when Father lived there as a child, there were four children. Before that, our grandfather was one of twelve."

"That's true. They all lived in that house."

"And, to be honest, Beacon Hall is actually bigger than our home in England. Not to mention we have our home in town."

"I suppose you are right. But Benjamin, can you honestly tell me that you are happy about this whole idea?"

"I don't know Emma. I'm not saying I love the idea but, if it makes Father happy, I cannot tell him not to marry her."

"I disagree."

"Emma," said Benjamin suddenly quite sternly and with intense eye contact, "you will not say anything rude about this whole affair. Father is happy. It does not matter what we think."

"But when his decisions affect us, are we not to have any say?"

"Emma, I repeat: do not say anything. We are going to welcome her into our home as well as her children. You are right, we didn't ask for this. We didn't even want this to happen, but it has and Father is happy. There is nothing more to say on the matter."

"You're wrong Benjamin."

"And what are you going to do Emma? Go and tell Father that

he is making a mistake, and that you won't love him any longer if he marries her?"

"I was hoping I wouldn't have to get that extreme," said Emma mockingly.

"Emma, I'm serious."

"I was just having fun with you. Of course I would never tell Father that."

"Good because that is the last thing he needs to hear right now."

"Why are you so concerned for him?"

"It is a long story, but basically because he is lonely. He really has no one here. I mean, he has friends and acquaintances, but no real family to speak of."

"He could come home and be with his family."

"You know he can't."

"So, what, does that mean, she is going to stay with Father here?"

"I'm not really sure Emma. They didn't really discuss that with me."

They paused in their conversation.

"Do you like her?"

"What?"

"Do you like her?"

"I hardly know her, Emma."

"But what does your heart tell you?"

"She's all right. I really don't know her at all Emma."

"Well, I have a bad feeling about her."

Benjamin stood and became quite angry.

"You have been suspicious of everyone since we arrived in the Colonies and I, for one, am getting sick of it, Emma. People are not inherently bad. You need to stop judging everyone. You are not exactly in a position to judge others."

"I do not make judgments that are unfounded Benjamin."

"You never used to. I kind of miss that about you."

"What is that supposed to mean?"

"I mean what I said. When we were in England, you never made such snap decisions and judgments about others. You never lost your temper or your grace. Ever since we arrived here, I feel as though you are so quick to judge everyone and make these snap decisions based upon nothing but your false judgments."

"Give me an example."

"Cole?"

"What about him?"

"Do you remember how you loathed him at first?"

"I never loathed him."

"You did. I could see it in your face. You detested him for his manner and his beliefs when you hadn't even met him for more than five minutes and now look at you two. You are like two peas in a pod."

"So we have grown close. Do not tell me that you liked him as much as you do now, either."

Benjamin sat down and his voice began to plead with his sister though his manner was still enraged.

"Of course I didn't, but I gave him a chance. I didn't know him and I didn't make any rash assumptions about him. Besides, I rarely like people as well when I first meet them as when I have known them for quite some time."

"Well, I don't think Cole counts but, who else?"

"You need another example?"

"Yes."

"Mr. Adams?"

"What about him?"

"You didn't like him at all when you first met him, do not deny it."

"I don't deny it, you are right. I didn't like him."

"But now?"

"Well, he is affable and a gentleman, I suppose; though his mannerisms can often lack eloquence and his beliefs are not aligned with my own."

"So he isn't the abhorrent man you once thought him to be?"

Emma paused for a moment and thought about what Benjamin was saying.

"My goodness. You are right Benjamin. I have done these things, the things that I swore I would never do. I am so sorry." It had hit Emma like a brick. She was not the girl she once had been, and was certainly not becoming the woman she wanted to be. "Benjamin, I will not say another poor word one about Mrs. Collingwood until I know her. I am going to stop these rash assumptions and I am going to withhold judgment until I have all the evidence. I cannot believe who I have become."

"Emma, you have become no one but yourself," said Benjamin good-naturedly with a sincere smile. "You merely strayed from who you want to be. Now that you are aware of this drifting, you will be able to stay the course and follow your path."

"Thank you Benjamin. I will welcome the Collingwood family into our home with open arms."

"Thank you Emma, for our father's sake."

Emma went back to bed feeling as though a weight had been lifted from her chest.

The next morning, Emma got up and dressed and had breakfast with the entire household before returning to the Congressional Hall.

Over the next while, Emma tried to get to know Rebecca Collingwood, but with spending most of her days silently listening and watching the Continental Congress argue and debate their way through many issues, it was rather difficult to find time to speak with her. This, of course, was not to mention that they rarely saw each other by themselves let alone in a quiet spot to talk.

Finally, by the fourteenth of October, Congress had passed

a Declaration and Resolves to oppose the Coercive Acts, the Quebec Act, and the other measures enacted by the British to remove self-rule from the Colonies.

The Colonists decided that life, liberty, and property were the most important rights to mankind and they asserted this in the document written to King George and the British Parliament. Emma had to admit that the letter was well written and quite concise. Among the words of the letter was a passage that Emma committed to memory to make note of later.

To these grievous acts and measures, Americans cannot submit, but in hopes their fellow subjects in Great Britain will, on a revision of them, restore us to that state, in which both countries found happiness and prosperity.

Emma was amazed at the continued attempt to make both England and the Colonies happy. The Americans were outraged, but they were not rude. They were concise and made sure that their point was heard, but they did not wish ill tidings upon the King. Emma thought about this for a long time over the next few months and it would tear at her heart for much longer than that.

On October twentieth, the Congress adopted their own type of act. They decided to call this the Continental Association. Under this, the delegates agreed to boycott all English imports and prohibit exports to Britain, as well as discontinuing the slave trade. This final piece, the discontinuation of the slave trade, was what took the longest to settle. Emma felt it was the best decision they had made yet.

Finally, on October twenty-sixth, 1774, the Continental Congress ended its secret session so that all of the delegates were finally heading home. Emma was glad that the session was over. She was excited to return to Williamsburg. However, they had decided they were all going to stop in Maryland and stay with Margaret and Peter. On the twenty-eighth, the day they left Philadelphia, they celebrated James's birthday.

Emma had many thoughts about her time in Philadelphia. She had heard and seen much. A lot had happened to her family. Her father was to be married. Her family was going to triple in size with the addition of the seven Collingwood children. She figured it would only be a matter of time before Benjamin and Felicity came to their own understanding. But it was more than the changes to her family.

Emma had a deep feeling that life as she knew it was about to change forever. The men who had argued, debated, and discussed so much had come to resolution. They were realizing that their homeland was turning her back on them, and though they were still reaching out, their arms were no longer wide open. They were becoming angry. They wanted resolution. They wanted what they thought they deserved, which was fair trade, and a voice to be heard by the King.

In the middle of all of this change and turmoil, Emma found herself changing too. She felt herself growing closer to Cole. She had never felt this way about someone before. She missed him when he left, and she found she never wanted her time with him to end.

It had been only a couple of years since they had left England. Time had gone by quickly and yet, so much had happened that it hardly seemed possible such a short time had passed. The First Continental Congress had met and disbanded. It was now up to King George to make the next move and, unfortunately, his move would not bring peace. As he had said, *"the die is now cast; the Colonies must either submit or triumph."* For the sake of her family, Emma hoped for the best outcome, though she no longer knew what that was. For the time being, Emma and her family were content to make the return trip to their home in Williamsburg. The die was indeed cast. Time would now tell whether the American Colonies would submit or triumph.

About the Author

Selena Joy Layden was born in North Dakota spending the majority of her childhood in Minnesota. Selena always had an interest in history, influenced much by her father who was an avid "armchair historian." Selena moved to Williamsburg, Virginia in 2000 to attend the College of William & Mary and would eventually earn a Ph.D. from the College of William & Mary. Living in Williamsburg sparked a further interest for her in the Colonial American era and the American Revolution. This interest prompted her to begin writing about the area and the time period. Selena's travels in the United States and internationally have also inspired her writing. Selena continues to enjoy history and writing as well as traveling, reading, and spending time with her husband and two golden retrievers in their home in Virginia. You can learn more about Selena, read her blog, and contact her at her website: http://selenalayden.com and follow her on Facebook: http://facebook.com/sjlayden and Twitter: @slayden1776.

Selected Bibliography

As I'm sure can be imagined, writing this book, or any historical fiction novel, took a large amount of research. My goal was to tell a story of a young girl growing up during the American Revolution. I started writing the story while I was in college in the early 2000s. I'll readily admit the internet existed and I definitely used it to check facts, determine timelines, and understand many of the locations I was writing about, but there weren't as many resources online then as there are now. As a result, I still had to do a lot of research the old fashioned way: books. I read a lot of books. Some were extremely good and, quite honestly, some were just plain terrible.

In talking with friends, I realized that many of them had never really thought about most of the thoughts I was having about this topic, including women during the American Revolution, the English perspective, the events of the American Revolution, the short-term and long-term impacts of what occurred, and all the other many thought bubbles I was carrying around while writing. Not only were those I knew not thinking about these things, when I talked about the topics and the books I was reading, they weren't necessarily excited to read about these things either.

As I began more focused reading on this era, I realized quickly there are few biographies that are honestly enjoyable to the reader. Many of them review mundane details, include long paragraphs listing facts, and skip around a lot making them difficult to follow and dry to read. In my experience, few are good at telling the story of the person and the time. I found this particularly odd as the people and events of the American Revolution and those leading up to it are really ripe for the kind of storytelling we typically enjoy. After all, the many characters are flawed but vigilant, the plot is fraught with peril and failure, and the ending was definitely uncertain. It really is an epic time period in American history. I was fortunate to find, however, there are some writers that are really good at taking the facts and turning them into a story that is not only accurate, but enjoyable to read.

After reading a good number of nonfiction books about the era and finding a few who could really tell the story, I found a new genre to read: historical fiction. I realized how interesting history could really be on paper. For me, historical fiction feels more like a novel or even a guilty pleasure where you can focus on the characters and the plot more than the details of the facts while still learning a thing or two. They tend to be easier for me to read than a nonfiction book and I can plow through chapters before falling asleep at night rather than hoping to get through a few pages before I'm too tired to concentrate any longer. Perhaps the difficulty of being a historical fiction writer, however, is that a good historical fiction writer still envelopes the reader into a world where the history of the time period of the plot is as much a character as the protagonist.

History, in simple terms, is really the story of people and events. If that is the case, then as a writer of history, I believe we are responsible for telling the story. *Path of a Patriot: The Die is Now Cast*, tells the story of the American Revolution but provides a unique perspective on the events of the era. While every effort was made to ensure the details of the story are historically accurate, certain details may have been altered to help tell the story from this unique perspective and it is certainly possible that one or two errors may have inadvertently crept in. Included here is a list of books that were consulted and valued during the writing of this book. The hope is that those reading this book will want to continue to learn more about the Colonial Era and the American Revolution and can use the subsequent list to further their knowledge.

Should you have other resources that you value, I would love to hear from you. You are welcome to contact me through my website: selenalayden.com.

Happy Reading!

Barnes, Ian. *The Historical Atlas of the American Revolution*. New York: Routledge, 2000. Print.

Bowman, John S., ed. *The Founding Fathers: The Men Behind the Nation*. North Dighton, MA: World Publications Group, 2005. Print.

Commager, Henry S. and Morris, Richard B., eds. *The Spirit of Seventy-Six*. Edison, NJ: Castle Books, 2002. Print.

Cook, Don. *How England Lost the American Colonies, 1760-1785*. New York: Atlantic Monthly Press, 1995. Print.

Ellis, Joseph. *Founding Brothers: The Revolutionary Generation*. New York: Random House, 2000. Print.

---. *His Excellency: George Washington*. New York: Random House, 2004. Print.

Ferling, John. *A Leap in the Dark: The Struggle to Create the American Republic*. New York: Oxford University Press, 2003. Print.

---. *Setting the World Ablaze: Washington, Adams, Jefferson, and the American Revolution*. New York: Oxford University Press, 2000. Print.

Isaacson, Walter. *Benjamin Franklin: An American Life.* New York: Simon & Schuster, 2003. Print.

Middlekauff, Robert. *The Glorious Cause.* New York: Oxford University Press, 2005. Print.

"The Reluctant Revolutionaries." *Liberty! The American Revolution.* Writ. Ron Blumer. Dir. Ellen Hovde and Muffie Meyer. Public Broadcasting Services, 1997. DVD.

CPSIA information can be obtained at www.ICGtesting.com
Printed in the USA
LVOW08s1646131113

361170LV00003B/604/P